I AM

Abraham

OTHER BOOKS BY JEROME CHARYN

FICTION

Under the Eye of God
The Secret Life of Emily Dickinson
Johnny One-Eye: A Tale of the
  American Revolution
The Green Lantern
Hurricane Lady
Captain Kidd
Citizen Sidel
Death of a Tango King
El Bronx
Little Angel Street
Montezuma's Man
Back to Bataan (young adult)
Maria's Girls
Elsinore
The Good Policeman
Paradise Man
War Cries Over Avenue C

Pinocchio's Nose
Panna Maria
Darlin' Bill
The Catfish Man
The Seventh Babe
Secret Isaac
The Franklin Scare
The Education of Patrick Silver
Marilyn the Wild
Blue Eyes
The Tar Baby
Eisenhower, My Eisenhower
American Scrapbook
Going to Jerusalem
The Man Who Grew Younger
  & Other Stories
On the Darkening Green
Once Upon a Droshky

NONFICTION

Joe DiMaggio: The Long Vigil
Marilyn: The Last Goddess
Raised by Wolves: The Turbulent Art
  and Times of Quentin Tarantino
Savage Shorthand: The Life and
  Death of Isaac Babel
Gangsters & Gold Diggers: Old
  New York, the Jazz Age, and the
  Birth of Broadway

Bronx Boy
Sizzling Chops & Devilish Spins:
  Ping-Pong and the Art of Staying Alive
The Black Swan
The Dark Lady from Belorusse
Movieland: Hollywood and the Great
  American Dream Culture
Metropolis: New York as Myth,
  Marketplace and Magical Land

I AM

Abraham

{A Novel of Lincoln and the Civil War}

JEROME CHARYN

LIVERIGHT PUBLISHING CORPORATION

A Division of W. W. Norton & Company

New York · London

30644 3985

R

For information about permission to reproduce selections from this book,
write to Permissions, Liveright Publishing Corporation,
a division of W. W. Norton & Company, Inc.,
500 Fifth Avenue, New York, NY 10110

For information about special discounts for bulk purchases,
please contact W. W. Norton Special Sales at
specialsales@wwnorton.com or 800-233-4830

Manufacturing by Courier Westford
Book design by Ellen M. Cipriano
Production manager: Anna Oler

Library of Congress Cataloging-in-Publication Data
Charyn, Jerome.
I am Abraham : a novel of Lincoln and the Civil War / Jerome Charyn. —
First Edition.
pages cm
ISBN 978-0-87140-427-5 (hardcover)
1. Lincoln, Abraham, 1809–1865—Fiction. 2. United States—
History—1861–1865—Fiction. 3. Presidents—United States—Fiction. I. Title.
PS3553.H33I26 2014
813'.54—dc23
2013041287

Liveright Publishing Corporation
500 Fifth Avenue, New York, N.Y. 10110
www.wwnorton.com

W. W. Norton & Company Ltd.
Castle House, 75/76 Wells Street, London W1T 3QT

1 2 3 4 5 6 7 8 9 0

This book is for

my redhead

Lenore.

CONTENTS

Prologue: The Silver Sword of Appomattox • XIII

NEW SALEM: *1831–1835* • 1

SPRINGFIELD: *1837–1842* • 69

ILLINOIS & BEYOND: *1858–1860* • 115

THE DISTRICT: *1861* • 167

THE DISTRICT: *1862, Winter–Spring* • 235

SOLDIERS' HOME: *1862, Summer–Fall* • 273

THE DISTRICT & ENVIRONS: *1863 & Winter 1864* • 299

THE DISTRICT & ENVIRONS: *1864 & Winter 1865* • 357

DIXIE LAND: *1865, March & April* • 397

Author's Note • 451

I AM

Abraham

The Silver Sword of Appomattox

THEY COULD NATTER till their noses landed on the moon, and I still wouldn't sign any documents that morning. I wanted to hear what had happened to Lee's sword at Appomattox. There'd been wild rumors about the fate of that sword. One tell was that Grant had given it to a young captain on his staff who proceeded to gamble it away at a local bawdyhouse. I was *mortally* embarrassed, wondering if that young captain was Bob. So I was tickled to learn that Bob was on the premises, that he'd come to see his Pa.

I'd had rough patches with him, and our *accommodations* as father and son had been a series of truces and declarations of war. But I locked everyone out of my office, even my secretaries, to have breakfast with Bob. We had black tea and *et* an apple with our knives, as I tried to imagine what a breakfast in the field would have been like.

"Bobbie, are you gonna make your Pa beg? What happened to Lee's sword after he surrendered it to Grant?"

Bob rubbed his mustache a bit and said, "Poppycock—sheer poppycock," like the Harvard man he was. And while we had our little truce, he told me the real tell.

Lee had shown up first in his finest grays, with a dark red sash and a silver sword in a scabbard embroidered with gold. He was six feet tall, with a head of silver hair; and in walked Grant with his usual slouch, and nothing to show of his rank but a lieutenant general's straps. He was all dusty from the road. He'd spent half the night bathing his feet in hot water and mustard, while Lee had sat alone in an apple orchard, wondering if he should wage a guerrilla war against Grant; but it would have saddened him to watch his own boys become bushwhackers. So he arrived at Appomattox with a single adjutant, bearing a white flag.

Radical Republicans, raucous as ever, demanded that I deliver Lee in chains to Old Capitol Prison—but these Radicals didn't run the war last time I looked. Lee scratched his name on several documents. His troops were starving, he said, and had to survive on lumps of chalk and a scatter of parched corn; Grant told him that his boys could have all the corn they required from our own cars at Appomattox Station, and then Lee stood up, bowed, and strode out onto the porch, where his war horse was waiting. Bob had been stunned to see how emaciated Traveller was. That iron gray gelding was reduced to a bag of bones. His nostrils quivered as Lee mounted up. Then Grant moved out onto the porch and took off his hat. Lee tipped his own hat as Traveller trotted off with all the pomp of a battle pony, his flanks hurling sparks of light that near blinded Bob.

My generals must have poisoned my mind. "Bobbie," I said, "are ye certain about the sword? Grant could have claimed it as a war trophy. He was within his rights."

"Sir," Bob said, as if berating a child, "Mr. Grant wouldn't have bothered about one silver sword. He'd come to Lee with nothing but a toothbrush in his pocket."

"But my commanders swear that a Rebel patrol just about captured you and Grant on the way to Appomattox. All of us might have ended up surrendering to Lee."

"That's preposterous," Bob said, resting his boot heels on my map table and lighting up a seegar. "We had them outflanked on every side. All my General had to do was wave his glove once, and the whole damn Army of Northern Virginia would have crumpled—and that's a fact. Mr. Lee raced to Appomattox in his red sash out of dire necessity, sir."

Bob kissed his Pa impulsively on the forehead and strode out the room, his spurs jangling with the cadence of a captain who sat at Grant's table. It mattered to him not one fig that he could wander into the President's office without bothering to announce himself.

"Please don't tell Mother I'm here," he said. "I have to return to my General, and she'll hold me in her clutches for an hour. I just can't spare the time."

"You could say hello, Son—that wouldn't cost so much. And she'll crucify me if she finds out we had breakfast and you never . . ."

He rolled his eyes and saluted me like some martyr. But at least he'd dash in and out of Molly's boudoir, and talk a little *soljer* with Tad. He loved his little brother, and wouldn't have disappeared without offering Taddie some token from headquarters—a discarded pencil case, a broken bootstrap, or a Rebel bullet pouch Bob had picked up in the field.

I didn't have much peace after Bobbie's visit. The Radicals hounded me in the halls. They wanted me to dismantle Dixie, toss out every single Southern legislature, like Grant's discarded pencil cases. I wouldn't listen to their rabid cries. We're changing landlords, a little, I said, that's all. And they cursed me and Grant.

The papers announced that I would be at Ford's tonight with the General and his Julia—Ford's was serving up the same old farce, *Our American Cousin*, with Laura Keene, the the-*ay*-ter impresario. I was in the mood for *Richard III*, and the rumble of kings, but I ain't certain she had *Richard* in her repertoire. The seats were packed once Grant's name was announced and prices soared to $1.05 a ticket—it wasn't on account of *Our American Cousin*; everybody wanted to catch a glimpse of the reclusive General. But at the last minute Grant declined; Julia and my wife just couldn't get along. Mary had insulted her on our last trip to City Point; and I suspect Julia couldn't contemplate sitting in the Presidential box at Ford's for three solid hours with Mary Lincoln.

I, too, would have declined, but I didn't want to wreck Laura Keene and Ford's. Still, it weighed on me, having to wear a fancy collar and a hat with a silk top, without the clatter of tin swords on stage or the death of one solitary king. My rotund Secretary of War wouldn't go to the the-*ay*-ter with me in place of Grant. Stanton said it wasn't safe. Any Rebel fanatic could take a shot at the President, no matter how secluded I was in my box.

"Well, Stanton, then I might as well pass the time playing checkers with Tad, while *soljers* prance outside my door."

"Mr. President, that would be a more reasonable policy than going to Ford's five days after Appomattox."

I wouldn't listen to that taciturn man in the long brown-and-gray beard. Still, I had a hard time in the President's palace; it was filled with sutlers who could no longer follow Grant into battle with their supply wagons and wanted me to offer them up a parcel of the South as their own private territory. These vultures were prepared to pay any price. I'd have laid them out with a *parcel* of my own fury, but the vultures had been loyal to Grant. So I hemmed and hawed, said I'd have to consult with Grant, and waited for my wife.

Mary appeared in her victory dress—with silver flounces and a blood red bodice. She'd decorated herself for tonight, had bits of coal around her eyes, like Cleopatra. But not all the rouge and black paint in the world could mask Mother's melancholy; the *dyings* were etched into her forehead, like raw ribbons of pain; even as the church bells pealed and the illuminations went up to mark our victory and memorialize the dead, she was reminded of the boy *we* lost in the White House three years ago.

"Father," she said, without a lull in her sharpshooter's eyes, "what is that nonsense I read in the *Herald*, that you did not have the slightest wish of returning to Springfield after we vacate this old Mansion. Springfield is where we raised our boys."

And danced for the first time, and I had to keep from stomping on your slippers with my country boots.

That damn mascara did make her look like a damaged queen. And she wouldn't let up drilling me, as if all the vitriol squeezed out some of her sadness.

"You told the *Herald* that you were resurrected on a river. Now that's the baldest lie. What river *remade* you, Father? Your Pa wasn't a boatman. He was a one-eyed carpenter if I recollect. And where in blazes will we go after your second term is up?"

She'd never understand that I was an outlaw, like Jeff Davis, that the insurrection had ruined whatever comity I had.

"To California," I said. "I'd like to cross the Rocky Mountains on a mule and see the gold mines with Tad."

Mother squinted at me with the same sharpshooter's eye. "Will we prospect for gold? And after that?"

"*Jerusalem*," I blurted, and I couldn't say why. It must have been my Bible reading. I reckon I wanted to see where King David ruled. It was all mixed up in my mind. I kept imagining Bathsheba inside her bathhouse, and David spying on her from the roofs, and that first glimpse of the sweet roundness of her body, like a glowing moon of flesh—Molly was my Bathsheba. I wasn't much of a king, but like a king I had signed writs that sent boys into battle. I'd had four whole years of writs. It *quickened* a man, took its toll. I could never become a country lawyer again, sit in my old rocker and watch a spider climb the wall. I'd grown too wild.

We went down to the carriage, while the maids curtsied and kissed Molly's hand. "Bless you, Madame President. The war is done." We had our own bodyguard, Mr. John P. Parker, a detective from the Metropolitan Police, who had once lived for five weeks in a bawdy-house, where he kept firing his pistol at the windows. Yet he was Molly's favorite bodyguard. She must have admired his rascality. He sat up yonder with the coachman, two pistols under his belt.

Inside the coach were our guests, Miss Clara Harris and her fiancé, a young major who worked at the War Department—Henry Reed Rathbone; both of 'em were part of Mary's circle; she could reign around Miss Clara, flirt with Clara's fiancé, but would have been *displaced* in her own carriage by the presence of General Grant.

We rode past the stables, with illuminations everywhere, on almost every wall. People were dancing in front of the Willard; their capes floated in and out of the fog, and I worried they'd come crashing into us and entangle themselves in the horses' reins. It was only one more of the night air's many *disillusions*. Still, it troubled me, and I sat hidden behind the curtains of the carriage, but Mary waved her handkerchief, as if she could separate the dancers from that gray filigree of fog. I stared at the illumination of Grant that covered the entire front wall of the Metropolis Bank on Fifteenth Street, or part of the wall I could see: Grant's eyes were like fiery holes in that fickle gust of light.

Mr. Parker had to stand like a semaphore in the fog and wave a red flag from the edge of the coachman's box, or we might have collided with half a dozen horsecars.

Mary clutched my arm. "Father, wasn't it grand that our Robert was at Appomattox? Did he sign any articles of peace?"

"Mother, Bob couldn't sign anything. He's an adjutant. And there

NEW SALEM
1831–1835

1.

The Clary's Grove Boys & Mrs. Jack

DOWN INTO THAT whirlpool I went, plummeting to the very bottom, and seeing stuff no sane man could ever have imagined—a stag with goggle eyes and antlers tall as a tree, a coffin with silver barnacles stead of handles, a musket with a barrel shaped like a bell, and sundry other things. My lungs must have gone to gills, because I could still breathe in that dark water, then all the air swooshed out of me. I rose right into the rapids, riding under a current that was about as safe as a slingshot—branches whipped at me and near tore my eye. I must have blacked out and been washed ashore like a worthless piece of wood.

Red faces were all around when I woke, raw as a world without light.

"Who are ye, son?"

"Abraham Lincoln," I said, with water still in my lungs.

"Are ye a convict from downriver?"

"No, I'm a free white man."

It was part lie. I remember Pa beating me like a mule and lendin' me out as his particular slave. I can still feel the strop, hear its hiss, a leather snake that snapped against my cheek, left me with a scar a finger long.

"How old are ye, son?"

"Twenty-six," I said. It was another damn lie. But I didn't want these strangers to think light of me. I broke from Pa soon as I was twenty-one and hired myself out as a flatboatman. I carried cargo to Orleans, survived the worst storms in the wigwam of my boat, bought myself a pair of boots with silver spurs, tucked away fifty dollars, and dropped the whole caboodle in a faro den. And now I had weeds in my eyes and silver fish in my drawers. My fingers were glued together, and I lay there on the riverbank without my boots—six feet four in my socks. I must have looked like a monster with wet bark to these strangers.

They dragged me up the hill, and that's how I landed in New Salem, on a bluff over the Sangamon River in the dusty bowels of central Illinois. It was a bald spot at the edge of the world that not even a man who fell right out of the Sangamon would ever have bothered to notice. But that's what pulled me into its orbit. I'd arrived without baggage, a wanderer without a pinch of paper in his pockets, a man from nowhere who'd come to another *nowhere* called New Salem. It did have one rudimentary road, cut out of the forest, but that road seemed to vanish inside its own navel. And it did have a sawmill, with a flimsy little dam that could have been mistaken for a beaver's bridge. It did have a general store and a blacksmith's shed, and a few log cabins that housed a doctor and a justice of the peace, almost by accident, or twist of fate.

It was as if I'd sailed *into* New Salem, and had never even known what I was looking for. Men with dust in their eyes, like mechanics under a bridge, washed the mud off my bones, fed me, clothed me, without once asking where I had come from. I could have been born in one of those cabins.

I was promised the clerkship of a new general store owned by some little baron from Springfield named Denton Offutt. But there was no store, and I couldn't hunt up Offutt on my own. I had to stitch myself together and wait until Offutt arrived with nothing but pieces of timber and a parcel of land—that was his notion of a general store. I had to build the damn thing with my own axe and carpenter's awl.

Offutt was a meticulous man who wore kid gloves and patent-leather shoes on the frontier. But he wasn't unkind. Both of us slept in the back of the store, with our own buckskin shirts as a blanket. Offutt farted a lot for such a meticulous man. We sold seeds, saddles, sugar, and salt. And if he lent me out to split rails or build a coffin—Pa had taught me all the tricks of a carpenter—I kept whatever profit I received and didn't have to share it with that entrepreneur. But he would badger me about something else.

"Son, why do you have such a miserable mien? I have never met a longer face or a sadder face on a man."

I could not read my own sadness, not even in Offutt's straitened mirror.

"I'm deficient," I said, and he let out a boisterous laugh that was like the bark of a sea lion.

"A lad who can wield an axe the way you can is far from deficient."

"But I'll never understand the tricks of grammar, Mr. Offutt. I can treasure up words and all their sounds, but not their proper placement. Every sentence I uncover is like a bear trap."

He laughed, but it was more like a grunt than a loud guffaw.

"Best run to Justice Green. He'll grammar you into marvelous condition."

Now Bowling Green was a portly man—near three hundred pounds—and our justice of the peace, who presided over whatever court we had. Bowling Green took a shine to me, but he wasn't much of a grammarian. So he borrowed a grammar book from the circuit judge in Springfield, and we studied together, Bowling Green and I. And after a month he said, "You're the master, and I'm the pupil."

There wasn't much truth in what he said. He was just as mindful of all the snares.

"Squire, look at *bunglingly*. It's handsome as hell but hard to pronounce."

"And just as hard to use with the right persuasion," he said and winked with one eye. "*Bunglingly* the Clary's Grove Boys wandered into town and ripped up the streets."

The Clary's Grove Boys had become a sore point with Justice Green. He couldn't control them, for they were wild and without a touch of pity. They stole from men and women alike, and went around on painted ponies with black nostrils and yellow eyes as fierce as the Boys' own fiery nostrils and eyes. Bowling Green could have begged assistance from the sheriffs of other townships. And he might even have had one or two of the Boys sit in the dungeon at the capital in Vandalia. But that would have meant open warfare with Clary's Grove. The Boys could have charged through town on their Indian ponies, trampled every one of our dogs, torn the blacksmith's arm out of its socket, destroyed our livestock, ransacked both general stores, and left us in a ruination we'd never recover from. Some wizard must have fashioned them from the *fiercest* clay.

That's why Bowling Green looked upon them with all the wonder of the world. He might have been as lawless as they were in his own secret heart. He'd watched them rip a prize sow from ear to ear, steal an old man's wooden limb and whittle it into a lance. You could no sooner stop the Clary's Grove Boys than you could stop a storm.

So it amazed me that Denton Offutt would interfere with the Boys. He might have been drunk or mad with his own power because he challenged them in my name. Did he want a whirlwind from Clary's Grove to wreck his store? He let it be known to one and all that New flew off the balcony rail. The Presidential box was all papered in royal red. My boots sank into a carpet that was like soft, silken mud. I could have been out at sea somewhere. I wasn't thinking of portents and dreams. I couldn't get clear of Lee's silver sword—it was the very last *figment* of war, as I imagined sutlers creating a thousand tin replicas, selling 'em to souvenir seekers gullible enough to believe they could smell the musk of silver.

I leaned forward. The play went on with its own little eternity of rustling sounds. Then I could hear a rustle right behind me. I figured the Metropolitan detective had glided through the inner door of the box to peek at our tranquility. *Jerusalem.* I would make my own pilgrimage with Molly, Tad, and Bob. We would walk the ancient walls of the City of David. I wouldn't have to stare at shoulder straps and muskets. I wouldn't have to watch the metal coffins arrive at the Sixth Street wharves. And suddenly I felt a sting behind my left ear and a hollow drumming inside my head, as if some stupendous bee had attacked with a fireball. Faces floated in front of my eyes. My mouth clucked like a maddened fish. *I'm President of the United—*

were no articles of peace and no articles of war. All Lee did was surrender up his troops."

And it troubled me that Jeff Davis was still lurking somewhere
in Dixie, planning mischief with a phantom army, when there was
nothing left but fools and sentimental sweethearts with their stars
and bars. But I understood Mr. Jeff better than my generals. *Killing*
had become the only cause he had left, even if the guns were gone.
We'd hound him like a fugitive while war was riven in his skull—a
narrative that could never end . . .

We rode through the fog and arrived at Ford's, with a wooden
platform over the gutter that buckled in the wind. An usher led us into
the big red barn of a the-*ay*-ter on Tenth Street, with our Metropolitan detective scowling left and right. We had to squint our way across
the lobby until the lamplighter ran about and lit the lamps again. The
usher screamed at him, but he shrugged his shoulders with a look of
defiance. "No one warned me the Lincolns would be late."

I had a dizzy spell as we climbed the narrow stairs to the dress
circle, and entered a little labyrinth of hallways that led to the Presidential box, with its own inner and outer doors. A plush red rocker
was waiting for me near the white lace curtains over the balustrade.
The performance had already begun. People clapped when they
caught a glimpse of us, and the band played "Hail to the Chief."

The actors stood frozen, as if they were part of some mysterious
tapestry. We fell into a long silence, and then those dolls on stage
shoved about, and we were caught up again in their furious patter.
Molly sat with one hand on my knee, while I rubbed the lace of the
curtain, like some weaver of silk.

"Father," she whispered, "what will Miss Harris think of my hanging on to you so?"

"Missy and her major won't think anything about it."

I couldn't bother myself with *Our American Cousin*. The words

Salem now had a *prodigy*, Abraham Lincoln, who could outwrestle and outrun the living and the dead in Illinois. He must have lost his reason, or he wouldn't have wagered ten dollars on his own untested clerk.

Still, New Salem was my new home, and I wasn't about to run. So I attended to the store until that hurricane of Indian ponies arrived from Clary's Grove—and a hurricane it was, of wind and dust. There were ten Boys, with short jackets and calico shirts, pantaloons foxed with buckskin, and held up with one suspender rather than two, as was the style of Clary's Grove. Their eyes were painted black, their noses masked with bits of red cloth, making them look sinister as ghouls; they had spikes in their arms and straw hats with missing crowns and rough, rawhide boots; their single ornament was a neckerchief with yellow polka dots that flashed in the sun and could be observed a quarter mile away. That and the wind and dust were the only warning we ever had. You couldn't hear the noise their ponies made, because the river roared night and day on account of the dam. And then they were upon you, ripping wood and flesh with the spikes in their arms. The Boys had mutilated themselves, punctured their arms with metal that must have been filled with poison and pus. But they'd wrapped leather bands around the spikes to hold them in place, and they sucked at the poison and spat it out.

Their leader was Jack Armstrong, who had studs around his eyes like a Comanche and wore on his left hand the metal glove of some Spanish knight; each of the digits was speckled with dry blood. He leapt down from his pony in front of Offutt's store, his boots blistering in the hot dust. I was a head taller than this champion, but he didn't have my scrawny shoulders; his were wide as a country barn. He alone among the Boys didn't wear a crownless straw hat; he had no ornament but the bits of metal around his eyes and his regal glove, made of the finest mesh. I didn't bother to count the number of men he must have scarred with those nimble digits. I had noticed gloves like that in Orleans. The bodyguards of gamblers and brothel owners wore them on their left hands as the mark of some grand seniority, I suppose. But I never got near enough to the crib-houses on my wanderings as a flatboatman to assay the value of a metal glove. What I learned, I could only learn by littles.

Jack Armstrong didn't waste much time. He shouted into the store in a voice that rattled the window panes.

"Mr. Offutt, where in thunder is your clerk? I've come from the Grove to wrassle him and rip out his eyes."

Jack didn't wait for an answer. He spat in the dust and turned to his own war party. "Boys, how many champions have I blinded?"

"Six, Jack—maybe seven. We cain't rightly recollect."

A crowd had already swelled up—men and boys from townships within a thunder's throw of New Salem to bet whatever coins and tobacco tins they had on the might of Jack Armstrong and his metal glove. I heard their idle chatter. Jack had blinded a man from Indian Point, had even vanquished the champion of Vandalia, pummeling him to pieces. But the matchmaker himself cowered in the back of his store. Offutt was hoping to drum up a little trade, but he hadn't reckoned that Jack Armstrong would bother coming from Clary's Grove to wrassle with a clerk. I doubt he had ten dollars in his cashbox. There wasn't that much cash in all of New Salem, with its collection of cabins on a cliff. The town was money poor. We bartered saddles and salt for a farmer's eggs and a hunter's strips of fur. And Offutt had to ride into Springfield to cash out whatever commodities we collected.

I stepped out the store. The Clary's Grove Boys eyed me up and down.

"That's the ugliest man on earth," they hooted. "Jack, his cheeks are as sunken as a sow's ass."

Jack's mind was on other things.

"Are you Mr. Offutt's giant?" he asked with a great growl. "Odds are twenty to one I'll ditch you in five minutes or under."

"And after you win?"

Jack Armstrong guffawed and revealed all the gaps in his teeth. "Well, son, you can come to Clary's Grove and be my blind body servant."

"Then I can't afford to lose," I said. Damn if I would mourn my own demise as a reader of books. I'd come out from under my slavery to Pa—my servitude—and I didn't intend to be Jack Armstrong's blind little boy. I needed both my eyes, and I meant to save them, no matter what fix I was in. Squire Green had rushed over from his little court at the tavern; he moved into the wind with all the gravity of a three-hundred-pound cruiser. He was the most graceful man I had ever seen, but he didn't have the manpower to arrest Jack Armstrong, so he offered to serve as our referee. I understood Justice Green's maneuvers. He wanted to keep Jack Armstrong from killing me.

"Armstrong," he said, "you can't wear that gambler's glove—not in this match."

"And why's that, Your Judgeship?" Jack asked, favoring his own left hand.

"Lincoln's not the local champion—he's a clerk."

"Then Offutt shouldn't have offered him up as a champion. He'll have to suffer the consequences."

And Jack shoved that three-hundred-pound man to the side with one swipe of his hand. He relished the situation he was in, pulled on each metal digit to excite the crowd.

I wasn't sure *how* to wrassle Jack. My bondage to Pa had served its own stubborn will. I couldn't recall a time when I didn't have an axe. Even as a boy I could wield it with one hand. And I loved to split a rail in the light of the moon. I near broke my back building fences when Pa pawned me off, but I grew stronger with every bite of the axe. You didn't have much of a swing unless you planted your feet into the ground. And so I had to protect my eyes *and* fight Jack Armstrong like a man who was readying to wield an axe.

We stood toe to toe, with our heads cradled in each other's arm, and commenced to tug. He must have been startled as hell. Jack Armstrong couldn't move me an inch. Next he tried to lift me off the ground and hurl me across the road. I could hear him grunt and groan.

"Boys, this damn fool's gonna bust my balls. I ain't no Hercules."

"Jacky," the Boys muttered with consternation in their voices, "should we ditch the cock-sucker for you? He ain't fightin' fair." They brandished the spikes in their arms. "We could do him with our own damn picks."

"Hurt him," Jack said, "and you'll have hell to pay."

He continued to grunt, but he still couldn't lift me off the ground. I might have thrown Jack Armstrong after all his straining, but I didn't even try. His Boys would have burnt every building in New Salem while Jack sat in the dust, recovering from his ordeal. I could imagine the Indian ponies kicking at people in fear of that pitiless fire.

He tried to pull himself loose and rip at me with his metal glove, but I pinned both his arms until Jack shouted, "Justice Green, ain't you supposed to preside over this match?"

"Ladies and gents," the Squire sang out, "considering the powers vested in me, I pronounce this match a draw."

Jack did flop into the dust, and that's when his Boys shoved Squire Green out of the way and charged at me with their spikes. I wasn't going to rush back into the store and barricade myself. My arms were much longer than any of the Boys', and I used them to slap at their foreheads and hold off the spikes that were starting to nick my eyebrows and draw some blood. So I knocked one of the Boys right through Offutt's window and tossed another into the road, with blood flying like gobs of red spit. But there were nine of them, and they attacked front and rear, with the damn spikes. I fell to the ground, and they commenced to kick at me with their hobnailed boots.

The Justice tried to intervene. "Murder," he shouted, moving his enormous paunch between me and the Boys, but they knocked him down and returned to kicking me. The nails of their boots near took out my eyes. Then suddenly Jack himself rose up and shouted, "It ain't murder until I say so."

The Boys remained in a rebellious mood. And Jack had to plead with them.

"Boys, can't you tell? Abraham's as big a desperado as we are."

That calmed them, quieted them. And while Jack smoothed the mesh on his gambler's glove, they constructed a makeshift ambulance out of a few boards and carted me back to their *wild oasis*, Clary's Grove—a pathetic copse of trees—so I could convalesce among them.

NAME ME A BACKWOODS BOY who don't believe in witches and I'll give you all the valuables in my pantaloons. Hannah Armstrong was Jack's devoted wife. But she was also the double of my own Angel Mama, Nancy, who died of the *milk sick* when I was nine. Ma had puked out her guts for a week, her tongue all white, and before she fell into a deep swoon, she clutched my hand and said, "I'm going far from this place, Abraham, and I won't ever be back. You look after your Pa."

And here was Hannah Armstrong, with Mama's opal eyes, as if some sweet angel had delivered her to me after my battle with the Boys. I must have been a great curiosity at Clary's Grove—the first of Jack's victims who ever survived. Hannah took pity on the lone survivor and fed me milk and corn mush, repaired my rough clothes, and chatted with me while she did her chores. I carried the milk pail for her, and I wasn't lonesome for the first time since I'd come to New Salem. Still, Clary's Grove wasn't much more than a pig pen in a little clearing beside a creek. Hogs rooted everywhere. Every shack in Clary's Grove was forlorn—there wasn't one solid wall. The roofs kept caving in. Jack and his Boys couldn't carpenter anything but their own chaos. They went on scouting missions to grab whatever spoils they could. Predators and pirates, the Boys left their hogs, their babies, and their women all alone. Problem is there was only one woman in Clary's Grove—Hannah Armstrong—and these babies belonged to Jack. Every other Boy was a bachelor, who might bring an occasional squaw into camp, and frolic with her under an indigo sky, but these squaws didn't last. And if they happened to leave a baby behind, Hannah would welcome that baby into her own brood.

"I'm fond of orphans," she said. And I don't know why I opened up to Hannah, but I did.

"I'm a bit of a bastard myself," I muttered, startled at my own words. "My Mama was born out of wedlock. She never knew her own Pa, but I like to imagine he was a Virginia planter—a cavalier."

She glanced at me with a harsh little glint in her eyes.

"Is that what you would like to be, Abraham, a cavalier?"

I couldn't tell her how I had a burning hate against Pa. He was born with a rotten eye, and I reckon that's how come he was so ornery—he never learnt to read or write. I could have been as word-blind as Pa if I hadn't willed myself to read. I would scribble words in sand and snow, or on whatever *foolscap* I could find. My college was the bark of a dead tree.

I didn't want to be no cavalier, with all that finery and fluff. But it was my own cruel way of belittling Pa and poking fun at him.

"Ma'am, I'd like to learn from books and accomplish a little with that learning."

Pa had never been fond of the few books I had—the Bible, *Æsop's Fables*, and *A Thousand and One Nights*. He complained that reading near the fire kept me from my chores. His face would twist up with that rotten eye if he caught me with a book in my hand. Sometimes he'd shake me until I was silly, and knock me down. I wouldn't fight with Pa. But I didn't want to live all my life in the woods, pecking away at hardscrabble.

Hannah told me about her own hard life—I was dismayed to learn she was no more than twenty. She said the puckers near her mouth had come from her fondness for a clay pipe. She was enamored of Indian weed, but weed alone couldn't have put so many marks on her face.

Her Pa had worked her to the bone, trying to make poor Hannah his *second* wife, her Ma being an invalid and all. Sometimes she had to spend half the day fighting him off. It wasn't all that rare in the hinterland to find fathers marrying up with a favorite daughter. Still, it disheartened me to imagine Hannah's Pa wanting to poke her.

"I was the family mule and milk cow," she recalled. Hannah had to cook and sew and attend to her brothers and sisters. She'd had no more schooling than a jackass. "I never learnt to cipher, and I barely learnt my ABCs." But she knew enough to memorize the hymn book after the preacher recited the hymns for her. She was a shouter at church. And she would cry out a hymn while the preacher was reciting the service. Her throat warbled like a songbird as Hannah Armstrong sang me one of her hymns.

> *Lord Jesus is in my arms*
> *Sweet as honey, sweet as jam*
> *Strong and hard as country ham*

Jack had courted her on account of the hymns, she said. It mystified me that they had met in church.

"Is Jack a religious man?"

"No," she said with a smile that softened the pucker lines—and
suddenly I saw the pretty gal she must have been before her Pa had
worked her to the bone.

"Are you religious?" she asked.

"I don't believe in the divinity of Jesus," I said.

"Neither does Jack."

"Then what was he doing in church, ma'am?"

"Trying to kidnap me."

Jack was riding with his Boys, after bloodying up a little town and
feasting himself on a farmer's wife, when he heard Hannah's voice,
and couldn't recover from it. "It haunted him. That's what he said."

The Boys had never been hypnotized by lady shouters and their
cries to Jesus. But Jack walked right into the church—a cabin without
a window that my own Pa might have built. This cabin had to burn
candles on the sunniest day, she said.

"And did he drag you out of church, ma'am?"

She knew all about the Boys from Clary's Grove. Hannah had seen
Jack ride on his horse, proud as a border bandit as he went around
pillaging people. But she still wouldn't have gone with him, even if
her face was all on fire. The ruffian got down on his knees in front of
that congregation of farmers and their kin. Her Pa was mortified. He
couldn't conceive of losing his own little girl. He whisked her away
from church and locked her up in the cellar. She didn't have to tell
me what happened next. He forced himself upon Hannah while she
screamed, and her brothers and sisters heard all that commotion and
carnage. They wouldn't interfere with their own Pa, but none of them
had counted on Clary's Grove. When Jack couldn't find Hannah, he
followed her Pa home, bust into his cabin, ripped open the cellar's

trapdoor, went down into that pit of black clay, saw Hannah in the dark, sittin' there like a bruised animal. He swaddled her in his own shirt, leapt out of that clay pit with Hannah in his arms, while her Pa begged for his life. Jack had an inclination to murder the whole family, but he was clever enough not to harm Hannah's kin. She might have shivered at the horror of it all, and then blamed him. So he sat her down on his saddle, washed the blood and filth off Hannah's face, and delivered her to Clary's Grove.

It must have been like entering a new kind of paradise for Mrs. Jack, away from those predations of her Pa, but I didn't see much that was heavenly in that sinister cabin she called home. It didn't even have a proper dirt floor. You entered the cabin at your own risk. It was rife with little caverns and holes, and I worried about mud slides for the babies and piglets of Clary's Grove. Jack's own booty troubled me the most—rings that were still attached to some poor devil's blackened finger, a snuffbox brimming with ants, a few dented skulls, gold teeth with the remains of their bloody roots, sacks of shit that the Boys must have collected to fling at their enemies, I suppose. The stench could burn off a man's nostrils, and as much as I admired Hannah, I never got used to it.

I had to be neighborly so I sucked on Hannah's pipe. The tobacco was like a bomb in my head. But I couldn't sleep because we had visitors—three ragged men with soot on their faces and scars on their cheeks, and the darting yellow eyes of maniacs. They were pilferers and vagabonds who preyed on frontier women. And they must have been from some far country, or they wouldn't have come near Jack Armstrong's camp.

Their yellow eyes had a preternatural gleam. They were carrying long, rusty knives. They poked around in the mud and dust outside the door; Clary's Grove was either wet or dry, depending on where the creek happened to gush from under the ground.

"Mother Cunt," they said to Hannah, "are ye the whore of Babylon or another harlot?"

I hunkered up on my pallet to rush at these vagabonds, but Hannah whispered for me to stay put.

"I'm Hannah Armstrong," she answered in the voice of a church shouter, "mistress of Clary's Grove."

"Well, we are desperate characters. And if we don't have the run of your yard, you'll never see the light of day again."

She sang to the vagabonds. "Lord Jesus is in my arms." And she must have seen the Lord while she sang. Her face lit up, and the sweetness of her voice confused the vagabonds. Now I understood how Hannah had hypnotized Jack and the Boys. But I couldn't just sit there. So I stood up on my battered knees and faced these pirates.

"Be gone," I said. My mournful squeal broke the spell they were in. They commenced to roar and slap their sides, while their scars rippled.

"Brothers, the mistress of Clary's Grove is living in sin, with Lord Jesus. Have you even seen such a tall pilgrim in your whole life?"

These pirates shouldn't have taken their brutal yellow eyes off Hannah. She ran out the cabin with her long rifle, clutched the barrel with both hands, and struck the first and second pirate with the silvered edge of the stock. Their blood began to spew, and their skulls seeped a strange white fluid. I heard the crack of bone as they seized their heads and wandered about, half blind. But the third pirate rushed right past her and was about to attack one of the babies with his knife. I was roaring mad. I tripped the sucker, grabbed him by the seat of his pants, and hurled him out the cabin like a sack of shit. And for a moment I did think of becoming his finisher once and for all. These pirates preyed on women. Wolves had much more honor than they did, but I just didn't have the stomach to become a one-man execution party . . .

The Boys returned after a week with dust in their mouths. They were pilferers of another kind. They might have plucked all the feathers out of a full-fledged camp, and battled for the spoils of war, but they would never have harmed a lone woman. The Boys were widow makers, yet Jack would often give up half his treasure to whatever widow he and the Boys had made.

After all their rooting around, they returned with nothing but some potatoes and a bag of beans. Hannah didn't scold them. She knew they were hapless cavaliers. They'd destroy a town and then rebuild it in their own reckless fashion. They couldn't hold a hammer or plumb a straight line with a carpenter's awl. And the Boys were stupefied when they discovered that the crooked cabin they had built with their own hands now had a wooden floor. I'd also corrected the walls.

Jack Armstrong commenced to groan.

"Abraham," he said, "we brought you here to convalesce, not to prettify."

Hannah watched him with the shrewd eyes of a shouter. "Jack, that's small thanks. We have a creek right under the cabin you built without a floor. We might have lost a child in one of those secret wells. And he'd be floating down the Mississip before we ever found him."

"Mother," Jack said, "it's awful hard to acknowledge the deeds of a new friend."

And then the Boys took to admiring the new strictness of their walls. They saw me as a wizard and I let them think I was. Jack noticed the book I was carrying in my pocket—a penny edition of *Æsop's Fables* that had also served as my ABC. It was bitten and raw at the edges, where Pa had thrown my book of fables into the fire. I burnt my hands rescuing it. And Pa would have thrown it back into the fire if my Angel Mama, who wasn't yet an angel at that time, hadn't shielded me from Pa's blows. *It's his learnin' book*, she said. *Let him learn.* She had no butter. So she blew on my hands with her sweet breath and bathed them in her own spittle. And she sang to me about Jesus. Ma had been a shouter at church, just like Hannah. But she commenced to cry in the middle of her song. I wanted to catch Ma's tears in my red hands, and I couldn't. So I held on to *Æsop* with all my might, even when I near drowned in the Mississip, or when I had to fight off ruffians in Orleans. They could have my pantaloons and my coins, but not *Æsop's Fables.*

Jack asked me to read the fable I liked best, but I sang it like a shouter at church.

"Four Bulls slept in the same field, and the Lord of the Lions was desirous to have these Bulls become his dinner."

"What the hell was stopping him?" the Boys asked, unfamiliar with the rhapsodic charm of a fable.

"Dunderheads, the four Bulls would have ruined him with their horns," said Jack. And he begged me to continue.

"The Lion had to conquer by degrees, had to proceed with a program of whispers and malicious hints, to sow discord among the four Bulls, to foment jealousy and disunion, until each Bull was suspicious of the other and fed in different parts of the field. And then the Lion devoured the four Bulls one by one."

Jack commenced to crow. "Ain't that our motto, Boys? Never let a Lion into your house."

The Boys sucked on their clay pipes and drank from their own little jars of whiskey. Soon they were snoring and swallowing their own spit.

"That's not the motto at all," said Mrs. Jack. And I realized soon enough that she had all the sagacity of a frontier judge. "The four Bulls are the heroes . . . and the victims here. They fell prey to their own disorder and disunion. No man or Lion could have defeated them four at a time."

"Mother, be quiet," Jack said, fingering his gambler's glove with the five metal digits. And he meant to crown her with his jar of whiskey—that's how mean he looked. I couldn't have abided that, even if Jack had succored me in his home. And it wounded me to watch Hannah. She wouldn't pull away from the madness in her husband's eye. As he strode up to her with his wild glare and his menacing glove, I plucked the jar out of Jack's hand. The Boys were astonished, and Jack was struck dumb with indignity. No one had ever interfered with him in his own house.

The Boys weren't worried about *my* welfare.

"Jacky, if you break her bones, who will feed us, who will mend our clothes? We can't get along without Mrs. Jack."

Jack didn't have to listen to his own Boys; the whiskey had unmanned him. He sank to his knees and commenced to snore. The Boys couldn't even hold on to their whiskey jars. They flopped beside Jack. The piglets squealed and the babies wailed on my new floor. Hannah was trembling, and I trembled too. We hadn't conspired against Jack, but it felt as if we'd traveled the globe together—and I could have been her father, brother, son.

But I feared for my own life in a cabin filled with desperados who wore armor imbedded in their bodies and grunted in their sleep like backwoods cavaliers. I wanted to light out of there, to be rid of the Clary's Grove Boys—rid of myself, rid of Mrs. Jack and return to the maelstrom that had sucked me under. I ought to have drowned, and did, a dead man who suddenly bolted out of the bottom, full of barnacles and stink weeds and fish in my pantaloons, and landed on the shore like a helpless sea monster, rescued by pioneers who'd carved a little clearing on a bluff, hidden from nature and mankind, and where a vagabond like me might collect himself and find his own future.

2.

A Feckless Candidate

THEY WERE STUNNED when they saw me, assumed I was an apparition, since no one had ever come back alive from that desperados' den. They pawed at me, pinched my arm. The town had abandoned all hope for their Abraham, hadn't even bothered to raise up a rescue mission. But I couldn't cash in on my own good luck. My venture with Offutt soon petered out. His store was still standing, though Offutt himself had disappeared with all the saddles and bags of salt. I lived in that deserted store with nothing but dust and dried beans, and a few field mice to keep me company around the bare walls and barren front room. Offutt stole the glass from our window, stole the counter, stole the chairs. That lonesome store rocked in the wind like a prairie schooner and moved an inch or so every time we had a sandstorm. I'd hug my knees in the corner and pray that those howling pellets of sand wouldn't eat into my eyes.

Justice Green and the schoolmaster, Mentor Graham, begged me not to wander. New Salem couldn't afford to shed another citizen. So I mucked about, doing odd jobs. I mended pickets after a storm, built coffins for the next plague year, swabbed the sores on the town's workhorse, and shoveled shit. And when I had to shut the store, I removed to Rutledge's tavern. It was the centerpiece of New Salem, even if it sat in the dust like every other building, and didn't have a reliable roof. It did have a window, covered with grime and a trail of dead beetles, and its speckled light fell with a pernicious randomness that had nothing to do with the time of day. The tavern's rear wall swirled like a gigantic kaleidoscope, with its own feast of colors that suddenly went black—we lived with a lot of candles at Rutledge's. It's where the luminaries of the village would congregate over a dram of whiskey and talk of their own prospects. Unless there was a river-run between New Salem and Springfield, the village would peter out, like Offutt's store. That's why New Salem had been built on a bluff over the Sangamon—to encourage river traffic, but the river was as unreliable as their roofs. It could overflow one season, become a puddle the next. And since I was a flatboatman who had come pitching out of the Sangamon's waters, I was looked upon as the pilot who would initiate the Springfield–New Salem run. But the Legislature at Vandalia wouldn't risk such an enterprise—it was filled with drunken louts who didn't care a whit about New Salem. And that's why the luminaries wanted *their* vagabond, Abe Lincoln, to battle for a seat in the lower house. They'd heard me pontificate around the cracker barrel at Offutt's before it was defunct. They nodded and shut their eyes when I said that women ought to have the right to vote.

"They're not cattle, are they? A woman can sign her name and ponder over a deed as well as a man."

They kept nodding, because they wanted their own man in Vandalia who would plead for the village's navigation rights. Meantime they surveyed Rutledge's daughter like pig-eyed men begging for a glimpse of her breasts. That's how secretive and salacious they were. They'd follow her right into the bathhouse if Rutledge gave them half a chance. I heard them talk about her berry bush when Rutledge wasn't around. But they were the luminaries of New Salem, and I was their candidate, who couldn't even defend the most voluptuous gal in the county.

Ann Rutledge had red hair and a face that was a marvel, with sultry silver-blue eyes, full lips, and nostrils that were shaped like perfect little bells. It stopped you in your tracks to watch her breathe in and out. She was deliciously plump. Annie attended to the tavern, but she'd been a pupil in Mentor Graham's class when I first drifted into New Salem as Mr. Offutt's prospective clerk. Now Ann was nineteen, as nubile as a fine young she-cat, who hoped to continue her education one day at the female academy in Jacksonville.

Every bachelor in New Salem who didn't have one foot in the grave—and even those who did—courted Ann. Her bodice heaved while she stood still, and her flesh seemed to shiver like some kind of forbidden fruit. But she was no temptress. Ann had made her pick. She decided on one of the luminaries—John McNeil. He owned a farm with grazing land and was a partner in New Salem's most successful store, McNeil & Hill. Sam Hill was another of her suitors, but Hill didn't have his lithe look. McNeil was a heart smasher, with whiskers that were barbered every day, shoes that a porter at the tavern blacked and polished with his own spit, and shirts ordered from St. Louis. He was older than the village vagabond by eight or nine years, and I couldn't have encroached upon his territories.

I wasn't wounded by his wealth, his silk shirts, or his proximity to Ann. His grammar hurt me most, and his diction. McNeil hailed from New York. And he had that pith of speech I envied in a man. I bathed in my own bile when I imagined the letters he must have written to Ann while he was on some sojourn to Springfield or St. Louis, wearing ruffled shirts and the finest cologne. He also corrected my first campaign address after I decided to run for the Legislature, though he never put on airs or tried to show off his learning at my expense.

"Lincoln, a speech should be like the crack of a whip, but tinged with honey. You have to trap every vote like a hunter. And what kind of speech will lure the voter in?"

"One that's short and sweet."

"But not too sweet." And he cut into my paragraphs with a heartless precision. I didn't even have to deliver my own address. It was printed up as a handbill with McNeil's help and distributed to the people of Sangamon County. There was some of McNeil's pith in it, but the modesty of the music was mine.

I mentioned how river navigation was much more practical than a railroad that would never be built, though the Sangamon was an ornery river that could flood an entire plateau, fling trout above the shoreline like a plague of locusts, or dry up in August and leave cracks in a riverbed as wide as a pregnant sow. I talked about the significance of education for every single man, how a lack of it would doom us and make us deaf to our own history, so that we would run around like blind beggars who couldn't even tell where we were from. I talked of my own peculiar ambition, how I wanted the esteem of my fellow men. I had no wealthy relations to recommend me, having been born in the most humble circumstances, with a Pa who was half blind.

The first reaction I had to my handbill was from Ann Rutledge. Her lip was palpitating, and there was consternation in her silver eyes.

"Why, Mr. Lincoln, you're mighty fine about education for men, but not for women. I couldn't find one word in your writ about the right of women to vote. Does that mean you think women should not read at all?"

I was the worst sort of scoundrel, ruled by political whim. I believed that women ought to vote. But it was Ann's fiancé who discouraged me from mentioning women's rights in my first address. Men would rather die than share the vote with women, he said. So I heeded Mack, as we called McNeil.

"Mistress, it's my maiden voyage. A man has to be careful of the shoals."

She pulled down her bonnet over one eye and said, "Would that you were a little less careful, Mr. Lincoln, and a little more candid."

I walked out the tavern with my tail tucked between my legs. And when I navigated the wooden planks that were laid across the sodden road, there was Hannah Armstrong in her own best bonnet. I was delighted to see her, even if she had the most wizened face I'd ever encountered on a twenty-year-old. She clutched my handbill, and it seemed like a malignant sign.

"You have the poetry, Abraham," she declared in her shouter's voice. "But you're feckless. You didn't mention womenfolk once in your handbill. Ain't we half the populace?"

"More than half, I'd imagine. But you've caught me at a disadvantage. I have to appeal to voters."

"Lincoln," she said, growing formal, "would my husband or his Boys ever vote without consulting me? Women vote in ways that were never assigned to us. And men ain't clever enough to grasp it by the handle. But I expected more from you."

Hannah confessed that she hadn't been able to decipher my handbill on her own. It was her preacher who had read the handbill aloud. And then Hannah had chanted it like a hymn.

I escorted her to McNeil & Hill, seized her hand once when she couldn't navigate a plank. It was the unschooled, like Hannah and me, who had such a hunger for words. We were like pariahs with a strange music inside our heads, a music we only half understood.

I meant to play checkers with Justice Green, but I wasn't in the mood.

A sudden excitement had come to New Salem. The luminaries raced round, looking for the swords and muskets they had buried somewhere before I was ever born, when they were captains of their own militia, involved in some blood feud they no longer remembered. Now the panic was everywhere. Women wouldn't even venture into their own gardens. Children couldn't play near the road. In fact, I couldn't find one child. The goats were tethered; cows moved right into the cabins. I heard whispers of an Indian uprising. Not a word had come down from the governor, but there were rumors that a farmer's wife in the next county had been ravaged and left to wander with nary a stitch of clothes. We kept hearing her screams, even without the governor's writ, and wondered when she would show up in New Salem, with mud under her eyes and marked with a savage's white paint across her back.

3.

The Black Hawk War

COVERED IN COW dung, Black Hawk had decided to declare war on Illinois. The chief of the Sauk and Fox tribes left his roost in Iowa, a patch of territory he'd never wanted, and crossed into northern Illinois with his warriors, his women, and his children in April of '32, ten months after I had landed in New Salem. He wanted to fight soldiers, not farmers and old men, but he'd had to kill the half-crazed farmers who shot at him. And he knew the soldiers would murder his children, so he traveled in his own war cloud, where only the wisest tracker would ever see him. Black Hawk was looking for his old hunting grounds near Rock Island, and was willing to destroy soldiers and land agents who had lied to him. He scalped the agents and nailed their carcasses to pickets the agents had built to wall him in, and smeared himself in their blood. He'd promised to remain west of the Mississippi, but there was nothing in Iowa for Black Hawk— Iowa was a pigpen.

The land agents had huckstered him, the generals and the governor of Illinois had sold him a bill of goods. Black Hawk was sixty-seven years old, and before he died he wanted to see and *feel* the ancestral lands where he had picked gooseberries and plums as a child and fished along the rapids. Iowa had no gooseberries and no plums; he wanted Rock Island back. It was now the site of Fort Armstrong, with a garrison of soldiers that wasn't grand enough or sufficient to subdue an army of the Sauk and Fox that could still move by stealth and hide in the shadows like apparitions in war paint.

I understood the attachment Black Hawk had to his native village, but my pity for him and his own lost nation was mingled with the remembrance that he was an Injun like any Injun, no matter how grandiose he happened to be. Yet I couldn't help admiring him, even in his cloak of excrement.

The governor of Illinois hoped to raise up a militia fifteen hundred strong to put down the insurrection and was offering a reward for every Indian hide. He promised Sangamon County its own contingent of a hundred men. I knew it was a killing party, but I had no choice. I would have been drummed out of New Salem and tossed back into the river. So I joined our little company and was elected its captain. I was given a sword and free grub that kept body and soul together. But I didn't relish chasing after a war cloud of women and children.

I had no trouble finding recruits. The whole of Clary's Grove joined the company, and I made Jack Armstrong my trusted first sergeant. He kept the other ruffians in line, poking at them with the digits of his gambler's glove. He near blinded one or two, but I couldn't get him to relinquish that damn glove. Few of my men could read or write, and they weren't much used to marching in formation. They stumbled into one another with each order I gave, and several recruits shouted in my ear, "Fuck Black Hawk, sir."

We passed through a shrunken forest, crossed a stream that smelled of piss, and marched to Beardstown in a reasonable time— it was fat with gamblers and whores who hoped to pounce on raw recruits. But the gamblers had a hard time of it, and the harlots left after one day. We were locked inside a horse corral that had become a temporary camp for sixteen hundred men, crowded together like hogs. We barely had enough room for a shithouse—none of the officers slept inside the corral. The regular soldiers despised us. They pretended we were insects, outside their own concern.

It seemed an imbecilic way to fight a war, but I was only a captain, with a contract for a month. The Clary's Grove Boys couldn't abide a *prison* camp. They prowled that corral like marauders, broke into the supply sergeant's tent, and swiped five buckets of whiskey and wine. I could hear bodies sway and shout, and I was convinced that Black Hawk and his braves had come to camp in my sleep. At dawn, as the companies moved out of camp, Jack serenaded me with one eye shut, while his Boys shat in the middle of the road and marched into trees.

The Provost Marshal rode up to us in a great fury, his eyes goggling out of his head. I had to return to the Provost's tent while my company wandered across the plains without marching orders. I went before a military board of captains and colonels—told 'em how I had my sights on becoming a lawyer. One of the colonels frowned and said that lawyers were the biggest wastrels and liars in the land. I was sentenced to wearing a wooden sword.

I had to strap it on in front of the Provost Marshal. I returned to our company like some mediocre player strutting around in a soldier's suit. The boys did their best not to laugh. We'd lost contact with our own regiment while I was under arrest. And we had to strike out into the wilderness on our own. Lincoln's company of louts.

We marched through woods and swamp that twisted under us like a hundred snakes until our ankles were caught in the muck; the first of us who broke free had to pull at the others, and we didn't arrive at the mouth of the Rock River until the ninth of May. We still hadn't seen one sign of Black Hawk and his men, not even the women and children he could hide in the wind. The U.S. Army regulars chased this phantom on his phantom river. They paddled upstream in their barques while we militiamen slogged around in the muck of the riverbank. Horses vanished into the mud; wagons kept sinking. Soldiers disappeared without a trace, and then we'd find a boot with a feather in it, and we wondered who would be Black Hawk's next victim. We slept standing on our feet and arrived in Prophetstown like a little band of petrified stragglers. Order and discipline had broken down. Some of the other companies fled back to their own farms.

A solitary Indian wandered into camp. He was wearing a torn military tunic with moccasins and a wampum belt. His fingers were gnarled and his face was a little nest of crags. This old man startled us, because he was the first Injun we'd seen on this endless march, except for a couple of scouts. He wasn't like that mysterious feather in a missing soldier's boot. He hadn't come to taunt us in this battle between white men and Indian braves who couldn't be found. He was a victim, a scavenger looking for scraps of food, but men from another company grabbed hold of him and swore he was a spy for Black Hawk. They'd had their own little summary court-martial and wanted to nail him to a tree. I whacked at them with my wooden sword.

"Be gone from here," I said. These ruffians might have nailed me to the next tree if my own ruffians hadn't come along. They weren't that eager to battle with Jack Armstrong and his Boys. I could read the ferocious hunger in the old man's eyes—the fear that he wouldn't be able to scavenge and that his next meal might be his last. I watched him tear into our stock of beans and could conjure up the time I lay like a sick animal in my flatboat, wondering if I'd starve to death.

Soon as he was fed, the Injun told us his fate. He'd been cast out of Black Hawk's tribe on account of his daughter, who became the concubine of a colonel. The old man wandered from army post to army post, lived among white men, and like his daughter, scavenged and stole. We stared at this Injun who once rode with Black Hawk, stared at him with a new kind of respect—and pitied him too. But we didn't have the means to hire him as a scout. He gave his wampum belt to Jack, and let us have his last lick of tobacco. I had to send him off to scavenge somewhere else, or he might have stayed with us forever as our company mascot. It was unsettling. That old man was the nearest we'd ever been to a warrior.

The boys were silent after that. Then they looked at me and scratched their heads.

"Captain, what was it like, being a tall bachelor and a tomcat in Orleans?"

"Sweet as honey pie," I said.

I'd regaled them time and again with ribald stories of how I'd kept my own pretty lady in the back streets of Orleans when I wouldn't have known what to do with a lady—a captain with a wooden sword who liked to talk of poontail when all the while I was frightened of the whores in their crib-houses, of their damp aromas and the depths of their eyes . . .

We were chasing a phantom on his own former hunting grounds, where he could shift from warrior to wolf and back to warrior again. Our spies kept finding scalps, but it didn't look like Injun work, and we wondered if there was some insane butcher among our own people, or if that wolf-warrior was practicing to become a white man. So we were on the lookout for anything that was sinister or strange. And one afternoon, as we slogged upstream, we fell upon a traveling juggler who sought to entertain us as we marched. He seemed quite suspicious for a skinny man without much of a chest, and he tossed little canisters into the trees and captured them behind his back, while standing right above the rapids.

"Juggler, what the hell are you doing here in this lone country?"

And for a second I thought he was Black Hawk himself, assuming the form of an imbecile who juggled for soldiers without a penny in their pockets.

"Fellow pilgrims," he said, "I can hear the dead whisper. And I can smell a scalping party. I'll stay with you awhile."

"Then you'll have to join the militia. . . . Sergeant Jack Armstrong, will you swear him in?"

The juggler bolted into the woods, but crazy as he was, he proved to be a prophet. We marched inland and stumbled upon a settlement that had mostly been burnt to the ground. It didn't have the look of a real fort with barricades—but a pigpen on the prairie, with a roofless barn and a ramshackle fence that Black Hawk's braves must have torn to pieces with their tomahawks. The whole settlement had that sickening, sweet smell of seared flesh. We found a doll in the rubble and a torn bonnet. Two of the settlers had been scalped; there was a rough red mark on what remained of their heads, as if some madman had been sawing at them; most of their fingers were missing; one settler had a raw cavern where his nose had been; another had a leaky hole for an ear. Even Jack was unmanned for a little while. He and the Boys commenced to shiver while they stood and gaped. I didn't have that luxury. I had to write a report in my captain's book. I had to walk through the rubble and count the dead—six men and a woman, who had a skeleton's face. The fire had sucked up all the flesh.

"The thing that hath been, it *is that* which shall be; and that which is done *is* that which shall be done: and *there* is no new *thing* under the sun," I recited from Ecclesiastes while we buried the dead.

Suddenly we were no longer militiamen on maneuvers, picnicking in the prairie grass. We were thrust into a war where the enemy was a wisp of smoke, where madmen reigned with rude hatchets. We clung to each other in the rain. My marching orders were never clear. We heard coyotes howl. Half my men had the chills.

We wandered into a ghost town on the plains, an abandoned fort near Dixon's Ferry, where the wind whistled through the walls. I couldn't ascertain if the Sauk and the Fox had driven Army regulars out of the fort, or if it had been deserted long before Black Hawk's rebellion. There wasn't much sign of life, not even a kettle with the blackened dregs of some bitter soup, or a regimental flag on the flag-pole. And in the middle of this wasted land was a fifteen-year-old girl, all dressed in calico, as if she were waiting for us to deliver some apple pie. There was something peculiar about this girl. She had lost the power of speech.

We fed her a stale biscuit and a morsel of cheese. The biscuit broke in her hand, that's how hard it shook. Finally I had to feed her with my own hands. She couldn't have had a morsel of food in days, I imagine; her mouth moved like a frantic engine. I'm not sure why, but I stroked her hair. That seemed to calm her. She clutched at my arm with a preternatural strength—seems I was the last lifeline she had on the plains. It tore at me to look at her in that calico dress.

"Captain," said one of my ruffians, "maybe she belongs to that jug-gler we met near the Rock River. Jugglers like to travel with dummy girls."

Why would that juggler, mad as he was, have left her alone in a fort that was rampant with wild grass? But I solved some of the mystery. She was wearing a bracelet around her ankle with Indian feathers and beads, and that ankle was filthy with blood, and had scratches running to her calf. Her left nostril was also ringed with blood. Black Hawk's braves must have grabbed her off that burnt settlement where the two settlers had been scalped. Had they tagged her with a bracelet like a prize chicken, presented her to their women and children as a trophy to scratch at and shove around, and then tired of her? They hadn't torn her calicos; her bonnet still sat on her head with its strings. After she finished cracking the biscuit with her teeth, she commenced to lick my hand.

"Stop that," I said, pulling my hand away. She rocked her shoulders, and I wondered if her misadventures among the Indians had indeed made her into a dummy girl.

"Missy, what's your name?"

She wouldn't answer. She clutched at the pleats of her dress and started to dance in the wilderness of that empty fort—I could hear an orchestra in my brain, the thump of piano keys, the scratch-scratch of violins. She whipped her head back and forth, back and forth.

"My name is Emma," she said in a perfectly natural voice. She was the last living soul of that luckless settlement, and she told me a singular tale. Black Hawk's men hadn't caused that massacre. It was a band of renegade Sioux. They did all the burning and scalping. She remembered the black paint they wore, and how their hatchets swept through the air and split a child's back. They would have finished her, too, if Black Hawk hadn't heard their war cries and frightened them off.

"You saw the chief?" I asked, a little astounded. "What did he do, Miss Emma?"

"He wept."

Black Hawk wanted his homeland, she said, not this desolation.

"How do you know this? Did he have interpreters?"

"His English was a versed as mine, Mr. Lincoln. And he had the gentlest eyes. He sang poetry to me."

Suddenly I was suspicious of her tale. "What sort of poetry?"

Her eyes were caught in some strange rapture as she spun about in her calicos and chirped to a band of desperate soldiers.

With spiders I had friendship made,
And watch'd them in their sullen trade . . .

My boys were baffled. "What's she blathering, Captain?"

I could scarce believe it, an Injun quoting Lord Byron and *The Prisoner of Chillon.* How could I explain to my boys that Black Hawk had a philosophical bent, and understood that his whole life, with and without all the skirmishes, was a kind of captivity? And I didn't even have to ask why he deposited her at a dead fort. That philosopher was saving her for us. Black Hawk was a much better general than the generals we had. He had to fight the Regular Army, a worthless militia, and renegade tribes, when all he wanted was to pick gooseberries in his own garden.

A sadness and a cynical wind invaded my thoughts. I released my men of all obligations after their enlistment of thirty days was up. "Boys, be gone," I said. "Go on back to your farms and your wives."

Jack and the Clary's Grove Boys were loyal to their captain. They didn't want to leave me alone in hostile territory. I had to insist.

"Jack, your Hannah is ten times more valuable than this war."

I was mustered out after another month and joined up again, this time with Captain Jacob Early, who had his own independent band of scouts and spies. We were supposed to move with the stealth of Black Hawk, but we couldn't even capture the wind, and we always happened upon a battle after it was fought. We were buriers rather than hunters. Our company was disbanded on the tenth of July, and I was mustered out again.

I returned to New Salem, quiet as a dead fort. I couldn't seem to shake free of the Black Hawk War. I relived all the little campaigns. I kept seeing a brutal red sun in my eyes as I wandered among the ravaged people, whole families splayed out in the wild grass in some forlorn symmetry, husbands and wives trying to reach one another just as the hatchet fell, their fingers like blackened claws—it was something a militia captain couldn't forget. I was the veteran of a war where soldiers rushed around with their muskets, making a lot of noise, while civilians were split open and lay in the sun with half their heads.

4

Justice at the General Store

I HAD A ROUGH patch, clawing my way back into civil life, where I had to think of cash receipts, when all I could recollect was tomahawks. I went into business with William Berry, who'd been a corporal with me in the militia. We started up a general store that soon had a license to sell whiskey at 12½ cents a glass. But McNeil & Hill had a much bigger and better store. We couldn't compete with their prices, so my partner raided our own whiskey barrels. Berry had witnessed the same hatchetings as I did, endured the same bad dreams. He'd wander through the village in midwinter, and I had to track him down. I'd find him weeping in the snow with whiskey on his breath, caught in his own puddle of piss. I had to warm his feet near the stove while he muttered about all the women and children he had buried in north Illinois. I couldn't talk him out of drinking up our entire stock. Berry & Lincoln winked out, and I went into debt.

The luminaries elected me postmaster at the next general meeting in Rutledge's tavern. There wasn't a single *nay*, since no one else vied for the job. The pay was pitiful. The luminaries feasted on Annie Rutledge's bodice with their little pink eyes and welcomed

the new postmaster, his post office a tiny counter at McNeil & Hill.
The mail piled up in pyramids at the general store, and I had to
deliver letters out of my hat, stomping around until my feet were
sore. But I couldn't survive on a postmaster's pay. I was appointed
assistant land surveyor, even if I knew nothing of a surveyor's art. I
learned as best I could and bought myself a compass and surveyor's
chain. I had to wade through swamps and briar bushes to set up the
simplest measurements. And soon I was surveying roads and farms
and settling boundary disputes—I charged 37½ cents to survey a
small town lot, but I also built fences and an occasional barn. I wrote
up deeds and served on juries. I wanted to become a lawyer in the
worst way, but I didn't have the wherewithal. Whatever I did I did
alone.

I sat in on Justice Green's court. Sometimes I acted as bailiff, or
I pleaded for the plaintiff if that plaintiff had no one else to plead for
him. I crept into the legal profession through the back door—that is,
Justice Green's own bench at McNeil & Hill. That's where our court
was located whenever Justice Green decided to be in session, which
was as often as his mood and the weather struck him right. On rare
occasions I sat in for Justice Green himself. I had no legal status. I
didn't wear any robes. I just sat in his chair.

One of the cases on my *docket* was a family feud, a farmer versus
his son. I could have been witnessing my own Pa and *his* son as a
slightly younger man. This boy wasn't a rawboned giant, but he could
have been Abe Lincoln. His Pa had hired him to build a barn; they'd
settled on a price. Efram the boy was called. He slaved like a dog,
working beside his Pa, morning, afternoon, and night. He beveled
every single board. He scratched and scraped and put up the roof, but
after he was finished, his Pa said he didn't owe him a cent, since Efram
was underage. Efram broke his father's jaw, and now the farmer was
suing his son for damages.

They stood before me on the second Tuesday in October of 1833. The farmer's name was Obadiah. He was a man in his fifties, like Tom Lincoln, my Pa. He had Pa's surliness, even the same rotten eye. His broken jaw must have healed up, because there wasn't any sign of the break except for a certain blueness. It was Efram who hadn't healed, Efram who had all the bruises. He wasn't nearly as tall as his Pa. He shifted around in the sawdust, his shoulders slumped, like some half-wild creature who wanted to burst out of his clothes.

"And how much in damages are you asking, Mr. Obadiah Young?"

The farmer kept staring around the store. We had an audience of onlookers, since Justice Green's sessions were often the best entertainment in town, much more amusing than a monster show. I noticed Annie Rutledge slouching in a chair beside John McNeil. He was combing his whiskers and staring into her eyes.

"Five dollars," the farmer said, holding up the fingers of one hand. "Or fifteen days of solid work."

He seemed satisfied with his own summation, more than satisfied. His features were positively glowing, as if caught in the blaze of a fire.

"Efram Young, did you strike your father on the fifth day of September last?"

The boy was as sad a specimen as I'd ever seen. He had none of his father's glow. And he had great trouble finding his own speech. His eyes were etched in darkness, even in the light of McNeil & Hill's lamps. He pondered with a finger near his mouth, and finally he spoke in a voice pitched as high as my own. It was like a squeal.

"I did, Mr. Justice Lincoln."

I had an inclination to hold the boy's hand. "I'm not a regular justice of the peace, Efram. I'm only sitting in for the law."

"Then what ought I to call you, sir?"

"Abraham, or Mr. Lincoln. . . . And why did you strike your own father on that fore-mentioned day?"

Again the boy withdrew into himself to find his words. It rubbed at my heart, but I dared not reveal my own sympathy.

"Because he t-t-t-tricked me out of my wages. A promise is a promise."

And now the farmer rose up like a rooster and glared out his good eye. "I can promise him until an army of angels nest in my hair. It ain't a binding contract. I *own* that boy, Mr. Lincoln—until Efram comes of age."

But I could see that something else was troubling the boy; his eyes shrank deeper into his skull, and his shoulders shook, as if the *molding* of his body helped him shape his words, and he was a rifle about to spring.

"Pa beat me black and blue when I was a child," he blurted out. "I ain't never healed, Mr. Abraham. I'm *deef* in one ear."

And now Obadiah snarled. "That ain't relevant—not in this case. I can beat my son if he wants beating."

My mouth commenced to twitch. I wanted to lash out at Obadiah, pummel him as I would have pummeled Pa, but I had to uphold the law. I'd listened to the judgments and readings of Justice Green. I'd watched him suffer under the rudeness of laws he had to defend.

"Lincoln," he'd mutter over a game of checkers, "everything is open to interpretation."

So I pondered for ten minutes, with a pulse beating near my eye like a hammer under my skin. "Efram Young," I said, "you had no cause to strike your father. The court cannot condone it. But I will grant your father no damages. A contract is a contract, even if you are legally bound to him. . . . Obadiah, you will pay your son what you promised, and he will also work two weeks without profit. Illinois has spoken."

That's how Justice Green would finish his sessions. *Illinois has spoken.* I'm not sure I gave much satisfaction to Efram or his Pa, who searched around for a congenial eye. His son simply marched out of McNeil & Hill, like there was no substance to him at all, and he was a feather caught in the wind.

A substitute judge wasn't allowed to celebrate the decisions of his court. But the spectators hurrahed and stamped their feet and poured punch into my mouth. Nothing excited them as much as a court case, where they could smell victory and defeat. I didn't see Ann rejoice. She still slouched in her own brooding contemplation, as if she had been summoned to court as the first lady judge. Her beauty was reflected in the fireplace—the light broke against the walls, and her red hair seemed to blaze, as her bodice shifted in the shadows, grew larger and larger until it swallowed half the store. I wanted to leap into that reflection, lose myself in it. Ann was spoken for, but my nearness to her in the glow of the fire was like the deep whisper of a magical harp—that harp of a thousand strings.

Ann finally rose out of her chair and pecked at my arm with one finger; she had a tiny twitch between her eyes that she couldn't control. "Why, Mr. Lincoln, that dear boy does appeal to me. But you cannot reward him for striking his father."

McNeil was still combing his whiskers.

"Mack," I asked, "do you agree with your intended?"

"Lincoln, I would have flayed that old skinflint alive, law or no law. What kind of a father would cheat his own boy?"

Mack's announcement made me singularly sad. I'd dreamt of striking Tom Lincoln, not for any wages lost, but for my own birthright as a reader, for the hours I had to give up to drudgery, for the words I might have won over, for the scholar I might have become rather than a shipwreck caught in strings of language that would forever remain a mystery.

Then I recalled that Pa couldn't read the Scriptures or a line of Shakespeare. He was the doomed ship, wandering in a sea without words. I pitied him for the first time in my life, or was that some frontier Satan mocking the pity I had for myself? I didn't believe in Satan.

5.

Miss Ann

MACK WAS A heart smasher with his own dancing walk in wine-colored shoes. He was the only one of us who carried Lord Byron in his saddlebags. That's how he must have wooed Annie Rutledge. We all heard him recite from *Childe Harold's Pilgrimage.*

> *And now Childe Harold was sore sick at heart*
> *And from his fellow bacchanals did flee . . .*

But Mack had another name—McNamur. I'd first discovered it on a deed. And then I'd found it in letters addressed from New York. I didn't spy on him as postmaster of New Salem, but I had to deliver John McNamur's letters to John McNeil, the nabob of Illinois. Finally he confessed to Ann. His Pa had fallen into ruin near Albany, and Mack had come out west to make his own fortune. He'd changed his name to McNeil, he said, to keep his father's ruin from falling on him. And now he was returning to Albany to rescue his father and mother and bring them out to his farm seven miles from New Salem, where he intended to make a home with his future bride.

Mack pleaded with me. "Will you look after her, Lincoln, for the love of Christ?"

There was talk that our Childe Harold was a gambler and a rake who would run out on his creditors every two or three years and *rekindle* himself. I didn't believe it. He was our pilgrim, Lord Byron of the prairies, who'd abandoned "concubines and carnal companie" to be with Ann. The heart smasher rode off with tears in his eyes. Ann's former suitors didn't give Mack a moment of reprieve. They wanted Ann to break her vows. I heard them whisper about the sweetness of her berry bush. I won't lie. I also dreamt of Ann's dark aromas when I should have been protecting her from that vile brood of cock-suckers.

I kept away as much as I could, but Ann accosted me while I was carrying letters in my hat. "Lincoln, why haven't you come courting?"

"Mack's my friend."

"Well," she said, "that hasn't stopped half the tomcats of New Salem. Didn't you promise Mack to look after me while he was gone?"

I was a lustful, lying hypocrite, and my tongue got all twisted in my mouth. I yearned to see her naked, to touch all her parts, to feel her nipples and the fur between her legs. Her other suitors had tomcatted in every town, and all I ever did see was the outside of a crib-house in Orleans. But my tongue untwisted, and I rolled out another lie.

"I was mighty reluctant, Miss Ann. I didn't want you to think I was readying to hop into Mack's shoes."

"Lincoln," she said, commencing to laugh while I suffered, since her bodice was breathing like the Devil's own engine. "You couldn't walk within a mile of Mack's boots. They come from a shoemaker in St. Louis who doesn't even have to advertise his wares—Senators stand in line."

And so I *courted* the town's one and only sweetheart, but it was a courtship without a handle. We never kissed. We never went riding in the woods. I wasn't much of a heart smasher. I delivered Mack's letters and could see the excitement flare up on her face. She blushed at the very glimpse of the prize I plucked out of my hat. Then she'd go off to some hidden spot and read that letter. I knew she had memorized the words. She wouldn't recite them to a cavalier in a ragged hat stuffed with letters, but I imagine they were as potent as Lord Byron's lines.

Maidens, like moths, are ever caught by glare . . .

She'd stroll right past me, muttering Mack's words to herself. It was like an affliction. It lasted for a week. Then she would post *her* letter to Mack and look for Abe Lincoln, but I was a busy man, laying out new roads as land surveyor. I went at it with my marking pins, following the illusive line of the Sangamon River, like some Columbus with a sixty-six-foot surveyor's chain. And if I couldn't become a heart smasher, I wanted to be something else. I'd run for the Legislature right after I returned from the Black Hawk War. I didn't know much about canvassing, and I was trounced—came in next to last. I could feel my own damn mortality, so I decided to make another run. I wasn't for that dictator, Andrew Jackson, who squeezed the piss out of Congress and ruled over us as "King Andrew." That heartless son of a bitch annihilated more Injuns than any other man in America and herded all the rest into the Territories—they were no more than cattle to King Andrew. So were his horde of *little people*—the Democrats—who helped him win. He beckoned them into the White House in their buckskin drawers.

I was a Whig, like the luminaries of the town. We despised anything to do with the dictator, yet I still had a strange affinity with him. He was a heart smasher who went about in the finest silk shirts and could draw crowds like a magnet in an electrical storm. And I knew I couldn't win without that magnetism. So I campaigned in a silk shirt, like Andy Jackson—and Lord Byron. Jack Armstrong and his Clary's Grove Boys were Democrats, but they decided to back their old captain. I ran across the county rubbing shoulders and shaking hands, with the Boys as my welcoming committee. Justice Green was my manager.

"Lincoln," he said, "whatever stand you take, there'll always be someone to take the opposite side. Best be neutral. That's politics."

"But it's a coward's way," I said.

"Lincoln, it's called electioneering. You can palaver all you want once you're in the Statehouse. But until you get to Vandalia, you electioneer."

So I marched around in the briar patches and was introduced as Captain Lincoln of the late Black Hawk War in Byron's silk shirt with an open collar. I didn't talk about voting privileges for the female population of Sangamon County. I didn't mention those despots and dictators, the Democrats. I didn't utter a word about education. I told tall tales, and the farmers liked them filled with smut. They couldn't get enough of Marie Antoinette's chamber pot or George Washington's privy. And I borrowed some barnyard fables from Æsop, but instead of the Lion and the four Bulls, I had a Queen Lion.

"Boys," I said, "the four Bulls had their designs on this Queen. They meant to poke her until she was silly."

The farmers guffawed and slapped their thighs. But one of the farmers was a bit more perspicacious than the others.

"Captain Lincoln, a Lioness is still a Lion."

"Sir," I said, "the four Bulls couldn't have subdued her singly. Their plan of battle was to steal upon the Lioness, and one would mount her while the others watched. But they'd never met a Lioness with a bread basket between her legs. She swallowed the four Bulls inside her royal quim."

That's how I proceeded until I didn't have enough spittle to recite another tall tale. But I won a seat in the Legislature, with the second-highest score in Sangamon County. We had a torch-light parade. Justice Green led the parade with a cutlass that he tossed into the air like a baton. Children flew kites in my honor and wore devil masks; the kites glowed in the dark and swirled over the treetops like gigantic bats. The blacksmith's wife danced with me. Rutledge near burned my scalp with his torch. "Hooray for Lincoln, hooray!" The luminaries slapped my back while they assessed my worth in the Legislature. Fizzle-sticks skated over my eyes. I was feeling as blue as a posthumous child. Seems like every soul in the county was there save one. And then she marched out of her father's tavern. Her eyes had a terrible flicker in that flare of light. Some dark dream had invaded Annie Rutledge. For a moment I thought she had run off the track. But that darkness fled. And she was gentle Ann, who had nursed me through many an illness while I boarded at her father's tavern.

I should have been ashamed, because I had lewd thoughts about Ann when I was slugging for votes—I'd endowed the Lioness in my fables with Ann's own bodice and quim. I wasn't ashamed at all. It was dreaming of her quim that drove me from campfire to campfire and made me feel *palpable* in my pantaloons.

"Did you miss me, Abraham?"

"*Yes*," I howled like a tomcat. I wanted to squeeze her nipples and touch her down below. I wanted to break her teeth with my own sucking mouth. Æsop wasn't in the barnyard. It was Abraham Lincoln, the teller of tall tales who had never been near enough a woman to break her teeth or breathe in the aromas of her berry bush.

I snuck off with Miss Ann right at the tail end of the parade, kidnapped her on my pony. I'd never been as bold in all my life, not even when I was a river pilot set upon by a small band of slaves that had been woken into thievery by their master. It was on the

Mississip, outside New Orleans. I flew at them with both arms while their white master watched from the shore. "Slug him, Jefferson," he said, "slug him, John." My heart was thumping like a crazy man as I pitched them into the water. But it thumped much faster now.

"Where are we going, Abraham?"

"Let the postman's horse decide," I said in a kind of raucous growl that seemed almost supernatural to my own ear, since I was a man with such a thin reed of a voice.

Miss Ann sat cradled in my lap, both her arms around me, her face next to mine. Our noses touched and then we kissed. And it's peculiar how imaginings can overshoot their mark. I didn't know the first thing about the taste of a woman's mouth—it was like that honey the shouters cry about in their hymns; Ann had honey and spice on her lips. But with all the learning of a land surveyor, it was still hard to kiss on a horse.

I'd inherited an Indian pony from my constituents, the Clary's Grove Boys, and this little horse had a mind of his own. He stopped in the dead of a tiny clearing, about a mile north of New Salem. And I let Ann slide down off my lap, and then I dismounted.

"Mr. Lincoln," she said, with a quiver in her cheeks, "did you bargain for more than a kiss?"

Her eyes had flecks of crazy silver in them.

I'd never bargained with a woman before. Oh, I'd visited a whores' camp while I was surveying near Petersburg. I didn't do a damn thing. The whores were as worn as I was. And the cash I paid them was a kind of charity. But I wasn't quick enough with Ann.

Her mood changed, and the quivering was gone. "There's nothing worse than an old maid with a betrothal hanging around her neck like a noose."

"Miss Ann," I said, "you're far, far from twenty-one."

I tried to kiss her, but she pulled away. The light in the clearing burnt a deep red in her hair. My whole damn body was like a wounded pulse. And Miss Ann seemed to take a little pleasure in my pain.

"We're back to bargaining," she said. "Well, Mr. Lincoln, what would you like?"

"To see under your bodice," I said.

The words could have flown from the beak of some bizarre parrot. That's how wildish they were. But she didn't blush to hear them. And she didn't look down as she removed her bodice and her chemise. Her silver eyes were fixed on Abe Lincoln. My knees buckled out for a moment. Even my pony stared at her bosoms. They were higher and firmer than I had ever imagined, the nipples pink in the sunlight, each breast with tiny islands of blue veins.

I didn't howl in the warm wind that came off the little trees. I reached over and touched her nipples with my rough hands. Then I surveyed her breasts with the same hands. In all my dreams I couldn't have created another such delight. The pony snorted.

Ann had freckles on her shoulders. We stood like that, my hands trying to remember the contours of her flesh. I can't even say how long we were in the clearing . . . until she broke the spell in a voice that was half a whisper.

"Abraham, that's more than Mack has ever seen."

She was shivering now. She put her chemise back on, and I hoisted her into the saddle; we rode in silence, with Annie near the horn.

6.

Vandalia

THE STATE CAPITAL was a town of eight hundred citizens, with its own peculiar civilization—you could find a passel of squaws, hucksters in velvet hats, women in the finest skirts, cardsharpers in candle-lit coffeehouses, and Legislators who had to live in one of Vandalia's clapboard inns—I chose the Sign of the Green Tree, which might have also been a haven for gamblers and whores. I had two other bed companions at the Green Tree; one slept with a pocket pistol under his pillow, and the other slept with a knife.

The long carriage ride must have weakened my fortitude, because I doubted whether I would survive Vandalia's own vandals and varmints who might steal your wallet and slit your throat while bathing in French perfume. That was called frontier justice. But I was tall enough and mean enough to navigate on my own. The harlots in petticoats and dainty boots followed me along patches of winter grass that masqueraded as sidewalks in Vandalia. They had hideous smears of lipstick on their mouths and as much war paint as one of Black Hawk's braves. Their eyes looked like bits of burning charcoal.

"Mr. Long Man," they cooed, "would you like to take a trip to paradise?"

And while they cooed and grabbed at my arms, a dwarf would come out of nowhere, creep under my coattails, and commence a digging expedition in my pockets. I had to hurl him into the frozen streets by his outsized head, or suffer the fate of a pauper.

Soon the harlots and their dwarf accomplices tired of me and moved on to another Legislator. There was an endless flow of human traffic; I saw bodies, alive and dead, curled up in some dank corner. Vandalia had a hurdy-gurdy man, who cranked up his mechanical banjo and croaked Christian hymns with all the raucous holler of a bullfrog. It mortified me to listen. He could have been stealing from Annie's own hymnal.

Vain man, thy fond pursuits forbear . . .
Reflect, thou hast a soul to save.

I'd swear he was a spotter for pickpockets and thieves. I avoided him and all the other likely birds of prey. But I was still in mortal danger at the Legislature. The Statehouse, which had collapsed in a firestorm, was rebuilt with shoddy material. This ramshackle pile of brick faced the town square like a tottering, two-story mountain. There must have been leakage throughout the building, since the walls bulged in peculiar places, and we all had to worry about plaster missiles falling upon us. I never entered the building without my hat.

The Senate convened right over our heads, while we *lower* members of the Elite occupied a less grand salon on the ground floor. We could hear the Senators tramp around in the midst of their sessions; the ceiling swayed, the dust flew, and we soldiered on, with cracks appearing in the walls. On several occasions we had to run for our lives.

Members of the lower house sat three to a table in chairs that could be moved about. We had cork inkstands and quill pens, and a gigantic sandbox served as a spittoon. For refreshment we had a pail of water and a quota of tin cans that hung from a wall. And our evening sessions were lit by candles in great brass holders, leaving shadows on the wall that looked like a constant camel train.

I was the youngest member of the lower Elite—that's what I had been told. And I kept to Justice Green's credo, remaining as silent as I could. Surrounded by lawyers far richer than Abe Lincoln, I resolved to listen. And while more practiced Legislators championed their own pet bills, I joined a committee or two, shook hands in the halls, and discovered as much as I could about border passions and frontier politics. Others speechified about incorporating banks, bridges, and female academies, but I couldn't have done much to widen or deepen the Sangamon River, even if I had politicked day and night. We didn't incorporate too many female academies, but we did appropriate funds for the killing and maiming of wolves and wild cats. I can't recall how I voted on that measure.

I sat with pen and paper at the Sign of the Green Tree half a dozen times, but I couldn't seem to accomplish a letter to Ann. It wasn't Mack, or the ghost of him, who got in the way. Mack wasn't such a heart smasher, more like an invisible man. I jerked my own jelly night after night, with spiders and ants as my lone companions in the privy, while I rose above the stink and dreamt about her aromas and red bush. I kept imagining Ann under a wedding veil, and it frightened the tar out of me—I wanted to rip that veil and run like a prairie hog. But I heard her Bible songs in my ear.

What are thy hopes beyond the grave?
How stands that dark account!

Vandalians were making a rumpus in the next room. The lantern shook. I shivered in my nightshirt. And like a fool with his own dark account, I never writ that letter to Ann.

❦

A CELEBRITY HAD COME to the capital. The generals had used some of Black Hawk's own stealth to wear him down and capture that old warrior, and now the country had put him on display. He wasn't shackled. He met with that dictator, Andy Jackson, at the White House. He stood with Jackson in the East Room—general to general, king to king—while an artist sketched them together and Jackson palavered about peace treaties with Black Hawk's band, when he was nothing but an Indian killer with a chief on his hands too famous to kill. And then Black Hawk was hustled off to a fortress inside Virginia. He remained there less than three weeks. He'd become a national sensation, like a monster in his own monster show. He even wrote his autobiography—*The Book of Black Hawk*. It was the first account of an Indian chief that ever appeared in the press. He went on a speaking tour—the crowds lined up for him in Philadelphia and Baltimore, entranced by an Injun in a blanket who could vanish with all his warriors into the wind. People wanted him to vanish right there—he wouldn't. They were still eager to hear about his late rebellion against Illinois.

But the Vandalians didn't consider him much of a warrior. He was no different from a caged animal. They built a straw dummy of Black Hawk and set fire to it. He had a hard time lecturing at the town hall. A dozen soldiers stood near Black Hawk to guard him from any threats to life and limb. He was wearing a silk hat over his Indian bonnet—and a frock coat, like some medicine salesman. People wanted to know why he had murdered women and children.

They were mystified when he answered without the help of an army interpreter. His English was far more melodious than theirs. They were struck dumb by the sound of it, yet I grabbed at every word. It near ripped my throat to listen—and watch a man with such skill and pluck treated *worse* than a zoo animal in the capital of Sangamon County.

"I did not murder," he said, like some tragedian at a playhouse. "Children died. That is true. But I took no delight in this. I fought to save my homeland. I had to set houses on fire, or the white generals would not listen. They were deaf to all my pleas. 'Go away, Black Hawk,' they said. 'Go away. You are a nuisance.' And so I made them listen."

The audience was silent for a moment. Folks hadn't expected to meet an Injun with a logic as fine as any white man's. Then they grew angry. And they wanted to attack the stage.

"Liar, liar," they shouted, "you and your devil tongue."

A small army of them strode onto the platform and were ready to tear into Black Hawk, even with a dozen soldiers at his side. These were Andy Jackson's scalp hunters in another guise. So I leapt onto the stage and hurled them one by one into the laps of their neighbors as gently I could.

"Who is that giant?" the audience screeched. "Is he an Indian agent who's gone sour?"

"No, no," someone shouted from amidst their fold. "That's Long Lincoln, the Legislature man from New Salem."

"Well, he'd best account for himself before we hang him with the Injun."

I stood in front of Black Hawk, who hadn't twitched once, while his bodyguards hugged each other and moved away from him.

"I'll account for nothing," I said in my reedy voice.

Folks guffawed in their seats. "Friends, he's as fine as any soprano."

I didn't have to ask the gods for help—the reediness went away. And my voice could have shot out of a barrel.

—*I'll account for nothing.*

I commenced to pace that platform like a panther in a tall hat.

"I fought against this man," I said. "I would have followed his tracks, but there weren't any. He saved a young girl from getting scalped, and to calm her down he read Lord Byron to her."

"Who's Lordy Byron?" someone rasped with mischievous delight.

"Shut your trap!" said another from the opposite end of the hall. "That's Captain Lincoln. I rode with him in the Sangamon brigade."

"Then why don't he talk like a soljer."

"Because," said this unnamed recruit of mine, "that's the way a real soljer talks."

I watched that orneriness grow as I paced the platform—the beady yellow eyes that jumped out of the semidarkness. Vandalia wasn't a town that believed in too many lanterns inside its town hall.

I may have won a seat in the Legislature, but I didn't have much purchase here; I could calm this mob for a minute, distract it, but little more than that—these Vandalians belonged in a circus, not Black Hawk.

I whispered in a soldier's ear, and we marched with Black Hawk behind a public curtain, while the audience hectored us and stamped their feet.

"Kill Black Hawk and the Injun lover!"

The soldiers clamped on their bayonets with jittery hands as we went out the rear door and climbed into a military ambulance. Vandalians hissed and hurled mud cakes at us all, but Black Hawk never wavered in the carriage. He had a lot more dignity with mud all over him than most suckers with mud on their coats. I wasn't as gallant as Black Hawk—I ducked those mud pies. I accompanied him and the soldiers to the edge of Vandalia and climbed down from the carriage.

He spoke to me for the first time.

"You have courage, Captain Lincoln."

"Majesty," I said, "I *jest* climbed on a platform and yodeled a bit."

He shook his head. "Not that. It takes courage to return to such loud people."

And I found myself in a predicament, having to defend white folks to a king.

"You must have had some troublemakers in your tribe."

He laughed with his yellow teeth. He had real juice in his eyes. "Yes, but they do not talk constantly and make an ugly face that could frighten a squirrel . . . and you must not praise me so much, Captain. I remember you and your riders. My own riders were fascinated by the size of your head. We are not as civil as you have made us. My riders would have liked to have your head as a trophy."

"Then why didn't you give it to 'em?" I asked like a substitute judge at Justice Green's court.

"I nearly did."

And he rode off in that ambulance, a king in an alien land.

7.

Snow Bride

I DIDN'T EXPECT A bunch of dwarfs to clap at me with their cymbals, and white horses to dance in the snow with silver ribbons on their legs. Still, I did expect some kind of a homecoming. I had none at all. I landed in New Salem in the middle of a storm—the flakes were sharp as crystal and scratched my cheeks. I couldn't even return to my old room at Rutledge's tavern. Rutledge had winked out while I was in Vandalia. He removed to Mack's old farm, seven miles from New Salem, but I did find Ann wandering about near the tavern, with snow on her eyebrows. She must have been collecting things for her Pa. But she shied away from me and cringed, as if I'd come to deliver a blow. And she sang from the Book, like a woman trying to break some deep spell.

There is none holy as the LORD: for *there is* none beside Thee: neither is *there* any rock like our God.

She was summoning up her own strength. "Abraham," she cried, "I'm worse than Jezebel. I lured you into the wild and stripped down like a harlot."

My knees were knocking. I would have clung to Ann, kissed her eyes, her ears, and cheeks almost as hollow as mine, if only she had let me cling.

"Miss Ann, I'll treasure that moment in the woods all my life."

She tittered like someone half crazy as she peered from beneath her winter shawl.

"You could be Satan come to taunt a troubled girl," she said.

"Satan wouldn't have such big hands and feet. He'd mask himself as a much prettier man."

"Abraham, why didn't you write from Vandalia, or send me a crushed flower in the mail?"

I didn't know what to say. I was like a circus dummy in the snow. The trees had gone as bald as convicts, but I was bold enough to grip her hand in the dark.

"We could run away," I said.

I could have been a leper with a leprous hand. That's how quick she broke free. "And become your whore, I suppose—your pretty lady. And live without the benefit of the Book?"

With Ann around I didn't feel a failure washed ashore like river trash. "But I could marry you."

"It would still be a sin," she said. "I'm pledged to another man. I'd have to writ him a letter and ask for my release . . ."

"I'll write Mack," I said.

Now her silver eyes wandered in different directions. "Don't you dare—I'd have to move into the wilderness, or else marry that sinner Sam Hill. He offered to buy me from Pa. I'll become his harlot with a bridal veil. I'd rather run *nek-kid* in front of a thousand men."

"I wouldn't let ye."

And she laughed. "Abraham, we're just too poor to marry."

We *were* too poor. I didn't even own my saddle. That was the crusher. But she fell into my arms, as if she were my bride. We kissed until our mouths were flecked with blood, and she rubbed into me—I prayed my jelly wouldn't spill. We ran inside the gutted bones of the tavern until the storm broke. I was reckless with my bride, carrying her onto a pony I borrowed from Justice Green's barn. Ann slept in my saddle, my little horse with rags around his hooves to keep us steady in the snow. But the snowdrifts were too deep. And I had to pilot my pony from the ground, clucking at him and pulling at the reins. I near lost my way in a narrow patch of woods.

Ann must have woken from a dream. The woods were dark, even with that eerie white blanket. There wasn't much of a moon, and the wind was howling.

"Abraham," she asked, "where are you, honey?"

"With you and the horse."

"I have a solution," she said. "We'll get rich and pay off what my Pa owes Sam Hill and Mack. We'll go someplace fine—after we've been to the preacher and you promise not to stray from the Book."

"Promise," I said. But I'd already strayed. I was *deef* to God, like King Saul. I couldn't hear His voice—only Ann's. I'd read the Book, how Saul tried to kill that ruddy boy, David, God's anointed one. I wasn't anointed. I was closer to Saul, that unholy king who was higher than any of the Hebrews from his shoulders up. We were both cut loose from other men.

We'd arrived at the gate of the farmhouse. I carried her down from the saddle, would have carried her to the farmhouse door, but she knocked away my tall hat and tugged at my scalp.

"I'd best go in alone."

A fork appeared in her forehead, like some thunderbolt under the skin. Her eyes were wandering again. The warmth was gone. She could have been a witch, passing over into the other world, not my Ann, but a shouter who had shoved me away.

The Lord killeth and maketh alive; he bringeth down to the grave, and bringeth up ...

She was like a gunslinger with the Book, could spit from the Bible with both barrels. She ran into the snow—I thought it would bury her alive, but she waded deeper until she got to the door.

I stood there with my pony, a sinner in the dark. Our tracks were gone. We could have been stuck in a wall of white cake. The silence in the woods was unnatural. The wind had died, or fled to another county. And that's when I saw him, a great big black bear prowling in all that whiteness, his eyes red as a silk garter strap, but raw red, with a crazy dance. He must have been starving. I clutched my pony's ear, kept him from kicking and shying, yet I couldn't look away from the bear's red eyes. The Lord might have sent him searching for sinners. He rose up on his hind legs, swiped at the air with his claws, and raced into the wilderness like a furry black furnace breathing yellow fire.

8.

Unholies

G OD WAS ABSENT from Illinois that summer of 1835. The rain pounded relentless and wouldn't let up until the wells overflowed and washed cabins over the cliff, and New Salem was like some ark on the Sangamon River, but with an outbreak of *brain fever.* It was the hottest summer in history—apples fell from branches like dry little bombs; flowers closed tight as fists—and the fever struck like lightning. Sam Hill wandered in the streets, with his galluses near his ankles, his eyes ablaze, his cheeks flooded with a green fluid. The blacksmith's wife ran into a wall and split her head so deep, we feared she wouldn't survive. Our doctor's little girl went raving mad; she bit her own Pa and ripped at whoever came near her with her long fingernails. Coffins had to be built, and I became the coffin builder.

One of Annie's younger brothers sought me out while I was building a coffin in the blacksmith's shop. He couldn't stand still, that's how nervous he was. He kept pawing at my shirt.

"Are you Senator Lincoln, sir? I don't mean to bother ye none, but can I speak with you, Senator?"

I tried to calm him down. "I'm not a Senator, son. What's wrong?"

"Sister's sick," he said, his eyes bulging with sadness and a hint of fever. "She's begging for you, Senator."

He'd run seven miles, all the way from Sand Ridge, his Johnny suit covered in mud thick as molasses. We couldn't slosh around in all that muck on my little horse—he would have failed us in the middle of the journey, fallen down. I'd have had to lash that pony until he bled. I didn't have the stomach for it, and no amount of lashes would have gotten us a minute closer to Ann.

I carried the boy on my back, because he was ill with the fever and worn out, and we navigated through the mud until we came to Sand Ridge. The Rutledges should have been against me, caught as they were in McNeil's grip, but they worried over Ann, and their faces were raw with the signs of that worry. For the first time they felt like kin.

Jim Rutledge clasped my hand with his own red paw. I could see the veins on his nose. He must have had too many drams.

"Is that you, Lincoln?"

I nodded yes. He couldn't have mistaken a man who was as high in the shoulder as King Saul. But he kept scrutinizing me.

"Is the dyin' bad in Salem?"

I didn't want to scarify him. We lost Preacher Martin's wife this morning—found her stiff as a board, and bathed in green bile. "Where's Miss Ann?"

"You won't let her cross to the other side, will you, Abraham?"

"I'll cling to her best I can, Mr. Jim."

Ann lay behind a closed door in the Rutledges' sickroom—a kind of storage closet. I knocked gently as I could and entered the room. Her sick bed loomed like a gigantic cradle. Her beautiful red hair was all knotted out, and as bumpy as a copper mine. Her sered mouth was like a blister, and her silver eyes were sunk deep inside her head, as if Satan's own assistant had been gouging at her with a stick. But she smiled so, so wanly when she saw me and held out a quivering hand. All her ripeness was gone. She was a rattle of bones.

"I was hoping you'd come, Abraham. I've been adding trinkets to my trousseau. Pa says you'll have to pick the preacher."

Her hand was spittin' hot. I trembled at the touch.

She shut her eyes. "Postman," she rasped like a river pilot, "are you looking for a concubine or a bride?"

I wouldn't cry in front of Miss Ann.

"Abraham, you sure know how to deliver a letter, but you never delivered me none of your own."

"I *jest* couldn't. I let Mack come between us like a ghost."

"I love *you*, Abraham," she said in a kind of stutter, soft as silk, "not the ghost that got away. I don't have the breath for it, honey, but if I tell you the words, will you sing my favorite hymn?"

I didn't want to sing about death and destruction, but I did.

> *Vain man . . .*
> *Thy flesh, perhaps thy greatest care,*
> *Shall into dust consume;*
> *But, ah! destruction stops not there;*
> *Sin kills beyond the tomb.*

The lines seemed to soothe her, but I couldn't hold on to the heat in her hand—it went cold as a bird caught in an ice storm.

"You never danced with me, Abraham. Ain't you my beau?"

"Annie, my legs are too long. I'd ruin it if we ever did the reel."

She tried to laugh, but the sound rattled ominously in her chest, and turned into a terrible cough—her eyes seemed to dance right out her skull.

"Silly," she said, "we wouldn't have to do the reel. You could trot without moving your legs at all."

She tapped out a tune on the sideboard of that cradle bed with the last bit of vigor she had left.

"Tra-la-la-tra-la-la-la."

She shut her eyes in the middle of her tapping, the tra-la-las tapering off. Her head swayed to one side like a magician's harp, and fell upon my shoulder. I sat with her close to an hour. And for the first time since I could recall, I prayed to God. *Keep her with us, keep her with us.* No one else in that farmhouse seemed to have the fortitude to keep her from crossing. Her sisters and brothers sat in the gloom, while her Ma and Pa slunk back and forth, carrying water from the well. There wasn't an ounce of healing music among them. They lived in their own shattered silence, waiting for Ann to cross.

I visited her every morning, wiped her forehead, sang bits and pieces of her hymn. I washed her hands and feet, praying I could cover her bones with some of my own flesh. I kissed her arms, ladled broth into her mouth with a long wooden spoon. I willed her to stay awake and look at me.

"We'll have our own farm, with a hundred roosters that can lay eggs."

"Oh, Abraham," she muttered, "there's never been a rooster what can lay an egg."

"Ours will, ours can."

Her eyes were clear as well water. I fondled the blisters on her mouth with my finger as she fell into a long sleep. I couldn't revive Ann, no one could—it was like watching Ma sink of the *milk sick* right in front of my eyes, only worse, much worse, because I wasn't a child, with a child's meager stash of tricks. I had all the cunning and strength of a grown man, but much as I tried, I still couldn't hold on to Ann, save her from her own fiery wind and the Lord's fierce pull.

It didn't matter that I groveled near the ground like an earth creature, bereft of the Book. I built the coffin with my own hands, sanded it down so it looked like that cradle of hers. When I saw her in the box, with her brittle hair and the silver sheen gone out of her eyes, I just about broke to pieces. I should have consoled her brothers and little sisters, but they were the ones who consoled me.

"Abraham, you kept her here long you could. It's the Lord's will. He took her from us."

I wasn't much of a believer in the Lord's will. Some satanic angel had been dealing out dice with Ann's soul. I hadn't shaved in weeks, or had a genuine meal. My old, worn raiments were rotting on my back. I looked like a vagabond out of the river when we buried her in the graveyard at Concord—Annie's vagabond.

⁂

LIGHTNING AND THUNDER mocked my grief. It wouldn't stop raining after Annie went into the ground. I rescued a family of hogs from our flooded road. We had to put all our chickens in the attic, keep our horses on a hill. I was at the blacksmith's shop building a coffin when I suffered such a black spell I wasn't sure to survive. I couldn't bear the thought of rain or sleet falling on Annie's grave. I'd heard about the hypochondriasis that had attacked other men, a kind of permanent melancholia. Julius Caesar may have suffered from it. He had the *hypo*—that look of misery—before most battles. It wouldn't wear off until he dipped his armor in enemy blood. And from the reports I'd heard, Black Hawk suffered from the same sunken spirit. No wonder I liked that gloomy warrior. Witnesses swear he carried the *hypo* with him wherever he went, that he cried in front of his own braves, and they didn't think the less of him. They knew his melancholia couldn't prevent Black Hawk from riding with the wind, or from wrapping women, children, and old men in some strange cloak that white men couldn't wear. He himself had become an old man. He no longer had the breath to swim in the Mississippi. And after the generals finally captured him, Black Hawk wept for his people and for the gooseberries he would never pick again.

The generals couldn't unman him, but I had unmanned myself—didn't even have the strength to wield an axe. Our schoolmaster, Mentor Graham, who barely had a child left to teach, had to lock up all my razors. There were mornings when I couldn't even manage to remember my name.

Mentor brought me to Justice Green's house on a secluded hill a mile south of New Salem. The Squire and his kin were quite kind to me, but I had to wear a bell if I strayed too far from his abode. The Squire tucked me in at night and strapped me to my bed in case I had the habits of a sleepwalker. While I dreamt, Annie wouldn't lie still. She rose out of her coffin like a paraclete in a shroud and decided to run away with her Abraham. It was some kind of elopement *after* death. We traveled on my pony, her fierce tra-la-las rending the night air, but the horse must have gone blind overnight, because no matter what direction he took, we always ended up in the same spot—the graveyard in Concord.

The Squire heard me scream and said that a game of checkers might be a good palliative—my checkers hopped over his like Black Hawk's braves. But his court wasn't in session while I was his guest—his prisoner—his compatriot.

"Squire, I'll move into the woods."

"You will not," he insisted, and he had near three hundred pounds of him to hold me in check.

I lived like that for two weeks, tied to a bell. The *hypo* grew worse and worse in rotten weather. An ashen sky added to my delirium. I kept having a notion to carpenter my own box right next to Ann's. The Justice and his wife had to strap me to a chair when the winds were fierce. And suddenly the Squire's isolated hill crackled with a strange sound—it was the hum of ponies. You could feel their breath before we sighted a single one. We were besieged with guests—the Boys from Clary's Grove.

Jack stood on his pony like some trick rider and yelled with his hands cupped against his mouth. He'd come to kidnap Captain Lincoln, he said, and would wait there until the Apocalypse. Jack did a handstand on his saddle to prove how determined he was.

"The wife has heard about his *hypo*, and she intends to feed him some of her own sunshine. She's a shouter—she works miracles."

I didn't believe in Mrs. Jack's biblical sunshine, but I still believed in Mrs. Jack. So I hugged the Squire, got rid of the bell, and rode to Clary's Grove on the rump of Jack's saddle.

I felt much more at home in the dishabille of Clary's Grove—its squealing babies and piglets, its pissy clay floor, and all its ruffians, with their farts and groans. Mrs. Jack ruled this chaotic kingdom without ever having to unseat Jack. Hannah Armstrong must have been twenty-four by now, her teeth with varying shades of ebon, some pure black.

"Abraham, it must hurt like a hundred devils, losing Ann. I'd perish in a minute if I lost my Jack. Some would consider it ain't manly to grieve, but I'm not of that persuasion. If I had to cross over, and Jack and the Boys didn't grieve for five whole years, I'd rip at them from the grave."

She really must have been a witch, or some mistress of the weather, because this dark cabin became lit with a preternatural light minutes after I arrived at Clary's Grove—or perhaps it was the combination of Hannah and the sunlight. Because the *hypo* commenced to lift—and the black ink inside my soul receded a little. Hannah put some baking powder on my cheeks to lighten my somber look. And she lent me one of Jack's razors.

"Know this, Mr. Lincoln, if you slit your throat, Jack will certainly slit mine."

I listened to myself roar—the sound of my laughter startled me—
that's how long I hadn't heard it. But the *hypo* had a wicked will. I was
sad as Moses a minute later, with a tear on my cheek that formed a
riverlet in the baking powder.

"It's the blue unholies," she said. "It comes and goes."

She grasped it much better than Mentor Graham or Squire
Green—the *blue unholies* that could arrive with a certain kind of wind,
like a sirocco, or a winter pull. I didn't have to wear a bell at Clary's
Grove. Hannah had her trust in me.

We slept near the fire, and amidst the cacophony of farts that
protected these Clary's Grove Boys, Black Hawk arrived like some
apparition—or devil—with the ink in my mind. I could have rubbed
his forehead with my hand. That's how close he was. He was wearing
his tribal bonnet and his war paint. I had summoned him from the
spirit world, but Black Hawk had certain oddities. He almost seemed
like a white man under his war paint. He had Pa's weak eyes and the
shoulders of a carpenter, not the suppleness of a chief who could hide
women in the wind. I didn't know how to address this personage. I
tried to take the cuss off my own curious situation.

"Pa," I said, "it's your only living son, Abraham."

He leaned over, and one of his feather tips scraped against my
scalp.

"Lincoln, you shouldn't have left me in the ground."

I near shivered out of my pants, because this devil now had a girl's
voice; not the resounding music of a church crier—this crier couldn't
have shattered glass. I was listening to the soft, honeyed tones of Miss
Ann. And it was hard to deal with when she also had the looks and
manner of a white man in war paint.

"Abraham," *she* said, "will you ride with me to heaven, sit with me
in the Lord's own saddle, and forsake the brittle bread of this world?"

I squeezed my eyes shut and rode through the roof of a cabin filled with all the familiar stinks of Clary's Grove. I was giddy in that first gush of air. I was never sure who I clutched—Black Hawk, or Miss Ann.

"Annie girl," I shouted into the wind, "couldn't I see your face?"

We traveled over battlefields, where Injuns and settlers lay, with clumps of clothing scattered about—a bonnet, a boot, a mirror that blazed in my eye, and then we wheeled over New Salem, with its sawmill on a cliff, and its cabins and road looking like irregular ruts on a merciless bald plain, but I couldn't hold on forever. I fell out of the sky, like some plummeting human bird, and landed in the Sangamon, while the Bible crept into my skull. I thought of Saul, the king who was, and David, the king who was to be, and how David *scalped* the Philistines, cut off their foreskins and delivered them in full tale to the king.

Then I tumbled *outside* the Book, woke like an orphan, without kings or Injuns or Miss Ann. I couldn't abide this dark world. And I had no harbor. I was still caught in the currents, bobbing up and down in the river, without a creature in sight. And then the Lord mocked my five years in New Salem. Its citizens had rescued the drowning man-child, turned me into a land surveyor, lent me an abode. It was the bitterest sort of lesson with Annie in the ground. I took Jack's razor out of my pantaloons, having decided to end it all with a single cut, but someone snatched that razor from my hand—wasn't another inflammation in my mind. "Ma," I said, "Ma." It was an angel with blackened teeth and a burst of sunlight in her hair. She rocked me in her arms, singing tra-la-la, and cradled me into the deepest slumber I had ever had. I could still *feel* the sludge of that river, as if I hadn't crept out of the Sangamon, never studied land surveying and the law, and had arrived at another empty cliff, where strangers groomed me into a crocodile without grammar and the sad gift of words, so I wouldn't have to mourn Miss Ann. A crocodile could covet, I suppose, but it couldn't have contemplated the color of her eyes and the richness of red hair.

SPRINGFIELD

1837–1842

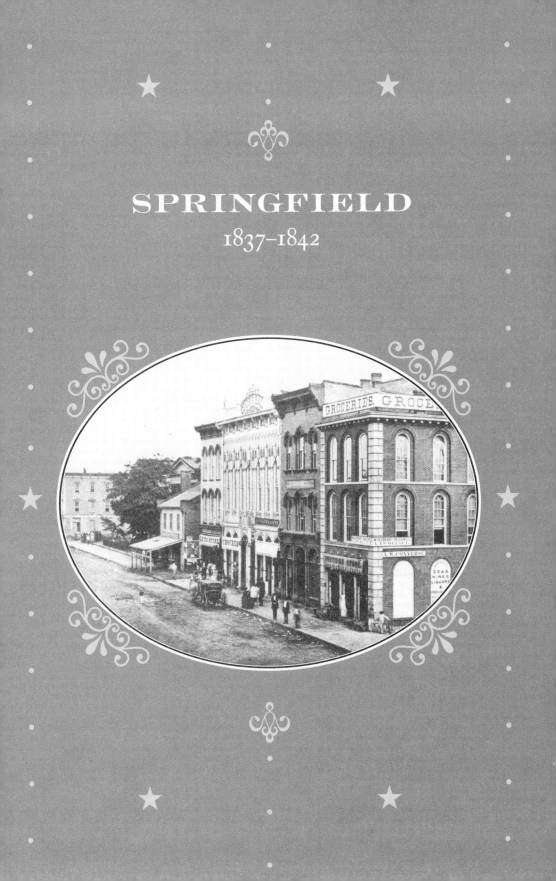

9.

Embrigglements

A COUPLE OF MILES out of Salem I saw a ragged girl at the side of the road. She couldn't have been more than thirteen—she stood like a scarecrow, pummeled by the wind. She had astonishing red hair and a silver sheen in both her eyes, and she was one of the skinniest girls I had ever met. She wore paper shoes. Her hands and face were filthy. There'd been beggars on this road before, but not a beggar like this.

I didn't have much nourishment in my saddlebags—some raisins and dried apricots—but I offered to share whatever I had. She wasn't interested in apricots.

"Mister," she said in a monotonous voice, "would you like to see my titties? Only cost ten cents."

She could have been rehearsing that little speech half her life. I had pity for this child—and a terrible anger at whoever had put her up to this task. I climbed down from my horse. I was swamped by a pair of scrapping boys who crept out from behind a tree in farmers' overalls; they had rusty, makeshift hatchets in their hands, but they didn't try to molest me.

"Sir," they said, "you could marry up with my little sister for half an hour. We can provide the wedding veil."

My dander was up, but I couldn't have helped that sad girl by ditching her two older brothers. Someone else was in charge of this enterprise. So I played along with their scheme.

"That's mighty fine, but where will the wedding take place?"

"At our mansion," they said. And clutching the reins of my horse, I followed them along a crooked path to a single, isolated cabin that would have made Hannah Armstrong's shack at Clary's Grove look like a sultan's palace—this *mansion* had no real roof and its one window was covered with rotting oilcloth. I entered the cabin with the ragged little redhead and her two brothers; she insisted on holding my hand.

"Husband," she asked, in her singsong voice, "what's your name?"

She had no light in her eyes—nothing at all. And I was worried that the engineer of this enterprise had drugged her with a drop of opium.

"I'm Abraham," I told her.

"And I'm Becky Sue . . . and it would tickle me, sir, to become your bride."

A voice shot out of the dark. "Not so fast. We haven't arranged the particulars."

I squinted hard and saw a man sitting at a table that tilted to one side. He fired up a lantern, and that's when I noticed he had the same astonishing red hair as the ragged girl.

"Are you her Pa?" I asked.

"And suppose I am? Are you prepared to pay?"

I didn't see a single cot or pallet in that God-awful hole. They must have slept in the forest and used this cabin as a marriage bower.

"What I'm prepared to do is break your head."

I'd startled him. He had the hysterical laugh of a hyena. "Son, there are four of us—with Becca. And one of you."

"I'm an officer of the courts," I bellowed.

He kept up that hyena laugh.

"In those pants? I'd say you were a water boy at the circus."

He must have signaled his sons, for they shook their shoulders like a couple of lunatics and licked the rusty edges of their hatchets. I wasn't amused by them, and it didn't take much of an effort to seize the hatchets out of their hands.

"Are you a magician?" their father asked.

I wanted to take the girl with me to Springfield and deliver her over to the sheriff; but I could tell how frightened she was, and how frightened she would have been riding into a strange town. She was a little touched in the head, even without the laudanum. And she might have been more comfortable with these critters than at some asylum. I had to decide—lightning quick.

"Father, I travel this road all the time, and so do my associates. And if they ever find your little girl selling herself to strangers, I won't bother with the sheriff. I'll come back and kill you—and kill your sons."

It was damn awful to say, but it had to be said. I wouldn't have harmed those two half-mad boys. But I loped across the cabin in the somber lantern light, plucked that man out from behind his table, and commenced to strangle him. His two sons sat in the corner and whipped their heads while that ragged girl begged me not to harm her Pa. I took half the wind out of him before I let go. I had to scarify her Pa, play the monster and *scarify* them all. I couldn't even say goodbye to the little redhead, my quondam bride. It would have softened me in their eyes. And they had to fear me worse than the Devil.

I started out the cabin, but I couldn't leave her—it would have been like selling that little girl's loins into eternity. I knew they'd have her out on the road again an hour after I was gone, that some *pride* of raucous men and boys would dip their peckers into her, one by one, and poke her until a permanent silliness settled over her eyes. And that miserable man must have read into my mind. He grabbed my shinbones.

"Don't kill me, Captain Lincoln."

I was even more suspicious.

"I served with you," he said. "In the Black Hawk War. I was under your command with the Sangamon boys."

I didn't remember him at all. I wouldn't have forgotten that heap of red hair.

"Who was the sergeant of our company?"

"Jack Armstrong," he said.

I didn't care if he got drunk with Jack and the Boys a hundred times over, or if he served with me on the plains. He was no different from those scavengers who scalped little girls and torched entire settlements. So I grabbed his windpipe again. He didn't plead or cry. His eyes went all white, like a wounded animal. I just couldn't do it. I didn't want to be haunted by the rattle in his throat for the rest of my life.

I wasn't some prairie rat who murdered strangers. I was a member of the Long Nine, Legislators from Sangamon County who hovered over Illinois like a pack of hungry lions. The nine of us had brokered a deal to remove the State capital from Vandalia to Springfield, seat of Sangamon County. I'd rattled the other Legislators, bullied them, and sweet-talked them too.

I tried not to think of that little girl and her rapacious Pa as I rode into Springfield, a town that didn't have as many dwarfs and whores as Vandalia. It had its own sense of civilization, with a courthouse in a square dotted with general stores, millinery shops, several hotels, and a barbershop. Still, I was troubled as I arrived on Justice Green's horse. Hogs and roosters seemed to crowd horses and their riders right off the streets, and I felt forsaken, since I had nowhere to live.

I entered the largest general store on the square and encountered one of the clerks. He was a young feller of twenty-two or so, and it amused me, because he wore a ruffled shirt. He had blue eyes that could startle if you looked long enough, and both his ears were covered with a lick of dark hair. His name, I soon discovered, was Joshua Speed, and he was a full partner in the store. I was carrying a saddlebag on each shoulder, the Kentucky cavalier who was twenty-eight years old and had never really had a legal residence.

Joshua knew I was a member of the Long Nine, and had heard me speak in the halls of Springfield and Vandalia. I peered through endless rows of merchandise that could have been the fixtures of some fanciful bazaar. And Joshua caught me looking. *He* was the cavalier. His Pa owned a plantation outside Louisville. Speed had gone to a real academy, not a blab school, to learn his ABCs, and he belonged to the Louisville elite. He could have stayed put, married some heiress, and managed his Pa's affairs, but he ran from all the aristocrats and wanted to make his own rough life on the frontier. I suppose that's why he was drawn to a country lawyer like me. And I liked his Louisville manner. I hadn't met much chivalry on the plains.

The mattress and other stuff I wanted tallied up to seventeen dollars. I couldn't even strike a bargain with the cavalier. I had no cash in my pocket, but I told him that if he credited me till Christmas, I might be able to pay him then. And it was odd, because he wasn't even interested in my seventeen dollars. Joshua must have seen the anguish on my face. He had a large room with a large double bed, and I was welcome to share it without cost. It smelled of charity, but I realized soon enough that Speed, with all his fine airs, was just another stray dog without a permanent home.

He pointed to a stairway that was part of the store. I climbed up the stairs with my saddlebags, located Speed's bedroom, which was more like a barrack. I figured Speed's clerks also slept in the same prison. I plunked my saddlebags on the creaky floor and went back downstairs.

"Well, Speed, I'm moved."

Trouble is Joshua wasn't such a sound entrepreneur. He would disappear for a week and return with his clothes all ruffled, and then ask me out of the blue if I'd ever been engaged. No, I said, I'd never had any kind of *embrigglement*. I couldn't talk about Miss Ann, or I would have had the *unholies* all over again. Meantime, he absented himself from the store again like some truant and returned with a torn lip and welts on his face.

He did have an *embrigglement*, it seems—a gal he kept in storage at a brothel near the edge of town. Her name was Sybil Weg. He could visit her whenever he liked, *sport* with Sybil, stay with her for weeks at a time. But it wasn't enough to have a pretty lady at his command. Joshua wanted to marry Sybil Weg. He wouldn't have been the first cavalier to marry a whore, but this damn sporting house refused to release her.

Sybil shared his passion for books, he said. "You can talk Shakespeare or politics with her—she'll listen." And when he tried to steal her from the brothel, her manager, known as Niles, thrashed him in front of Sybil's other clients, a list that included the mayor and all his men.

I tried to reason with Joshua. "Speed, you're in Illinois now. You can *live* with her at the brothel."

"That's not good enough," he said.

Sometimes he'd howl in his sleep, wake up all the clerks, kick me in the middle of a dream, scratching my shins with his toenails till they scarred up, and I reckoned I'd have to do something about Sybil Weg if I wanted to maintain the peace in our little paradise above the store.

❦

IT WAS A MANSION next to the cornfields, on a street that didn't even bear a name. I knew I was risking my future in Illinois, but I couldn't watch Speed suffer like that. I had to take up the alarm in a town where the sheriff and the mayor were both on the other side. This sporting house had seen a load of lawyers and Legislators. I knocked three times and announced myself twice. A maid in narrow skirts led me into the parlor, where I stood under a cluster of chandeliers; none of the candles had been lit yet, and I had to squint just to catch a little light. There were meat pies on the table, but folks had gnawed into them, and as the maid lit the candles with a long fire pole, I could puzzle out the teeth marks in the pies.

I asked to see Mr. Fred Niles.

He came down into the parlor wearing a cummerbund and a silk cravat. I was startled some. I'd expected to see a former prize fighter, like the ruffians in Orleans who watched over the crib-houses and could knock a man senseless with a single blow. But Niles was a mulatto man with the exquisite bones of an aristocrat. There wasn't a mark on his face. His eyes seemed much too soft for a brothel keeper.

"You've come here to see about the Louisville boy," he said in a Kentucky drawl.

"Sir, Joshua Speed's not a boy. He owns the biggest general store in town."

"He's still a boy," intoned the mulatto man. "His people would never tolerate Sybil. He could bring her to Kentucky as his concubine, and I offered to sell her as such. But she'd only come back here in six months. It would break her heart, having a whole damn society snub her."

I didn't know how to answer Niles. I considered sending for the Clary's Grove Boys and having them stir up a tiny tornado at the mansion, but Jack and his Boys had gone over to the Democrats, and I was loath to ask a favor of them. Besides, that wouldn't solve a thing. Niles could move his sporting club out of the mansion and settle someplace else. I had to defeat him with pure sagacity.

"Mr. Niles, couldn't he purchase Miss Sybil from you and have some sort of trial marriage? You could keep his cash on deposit, and if the marriage don't work, well . . ."

I could see the ripples in his cummerbund as he guffawed.

"Mind you, Counselor, we don't have rental brides at this establishment. I groom every gal, teach them manners, and marry 'em off at a whopping profit. Sybil is a rare breed. I'm saving her for a general from Ohio."

I had to sabotage that sale, yet I didn't have much insight into Niles, who seemed to own Illinois from a mansion near the cornfields.

"Sir, Joshua is twice as rich as your general. You'd have a better sale with him."

I had offended this sporting-club man, and I could feel the anger well up inside. He clapped his hands and a blonde angel appeared in petticoats, clutching a parasol. Her hair was piled into a beehive, like Marie Antoinette and some of those other royal ladies. She had no blush on her cheeks. Her eyes weren't painted. She bowed to Niles and permitted me to kiss the white glove on her hand. She couldn't have been more than seventeen, but I could tell that something was going on between our local Marie Antoinette and her fancy feller in the silk cravat.

Niles introduced us. "Sybil, meet Joshua's man. I suspect he's come to kill me, and he's shy about it. He sits up in the Legislature, with other nabobs—the Honorable Abraham Lincoln."

Sybil twirled her parasol, as if a body told her it might rain under the chandeliers.

"Joshua has talked about you," she said, in a voice that was savage and cultivated at the same time. I wondered if Niles had found her in some lonely corral. He purred at Sybil, but I saw the menace in him now, the wild twitch under his cheek that was a touch away from murder. He must have had a pike in his cummerbund.

"Honey, tell Mr. Lincoln why you could never marry Joshua Speed."

Suddenly all that polish and high tone were gone, and she was a seventeen-year-old child who had no more education than I ever did. Niles hadn't groomed Sybil—he'd just about manufactured her.

"Mr. Lincoln, Louisville would swallow me raw. I'm not cultivated like Mr. Josh and his people. Why, his family is from the finest linen."

That son of a bitch had rehearsed every syllable for her.

"But Joshua loves you," I said.

She twirled her parasol again, blinked, as if she'd half forgotten her lines, and then she pulled out of that slumber Niles had put her in.

"We've never left this establishment, not once. We've never had a proper dinner, just wine he pays for by the glass. Mr. Lincoln, I have ten marriage proposals a month."

"But do you love him?" I had to insist.

Her eyelids trembled. She searched Niles' face for some artifact or clue. He wouldn't help.

"*Yes*—while I'm with Mr. Josh. And then the maids come in and wipe his jelly off my legs. And they wash my ass too and perfume me for the next customer. I'm a high-card whore, Mr. Lincoln, and I could never be a storekeeper's wife."

She tossed her parasol at Niles and ran out the parlor. The parasol struck him on the chest like a blunted spear. He laughed and pretended to lick at his wounds.

"Young Joshua is always welcome with his pocket money, but if he tries to *elope* with her again, even his Mama won't recognize him."

I never told Joshua I'd visited the mansion, or that I'd seen Sybil. And a few months later she *did* marry that Ohio general, just as Niles had predicted. There was a short notice of it in the *Sangamo Journal,* where Niles called Sybil his niece and never mentioned the general by name, for there was no Ohio general. She'd been banished to another bordello in the hinterland, where Joshua would never find her.

I was riding the circuit with ten other lawyers and the district judge when we all stopped at a tavern a hundred miles north of Springfield—there was a ruckus going on behind the tavern. I figured the barn had been rented out to a Bible camp. I didn't find a bundle of preachers and church criers—I met lawyers and judges who must have been on another circuit ride, but I couldn't fathom why we had all descended upon the same patch of land.

That barn was no Bible camp—it was a traveling bordello. And Sybil was the star attraction. Now I understood that devil of a sporting-house man. He wasn't banishing Sybil—no, he was punishing her for the sin of falling in love with a Louisville aristocrat. Joshua's courtship had shaken the mansion loose from its pegs and shoved a mulatto brothel keeper into the public eye. Sybil would float from barn to barn until she was used up, and then Niles might marry her off to some butcher in Beardstown.

I had to deliver three dollars to the dwarf who served as her bodyguard and wait in line for an hour to see Sybil. She didn't recognize me at first. She was wearing war paint and a flimsy silk garment—I could see her nipples and her honey pot underneath. But she was too tired and forlorn to intoxicate a man.

"Pilgrim," she growled, "it will cost you an extra dollar if you want my bum."

I didn't see a parasol in this barn, just a filthy pallet and a shallow tub where she must have washed a customer's balls. Her eyes couldn't seem to focus under a whore's mud. Her shoulders were shivering—Niles was more sinister than I had imagined. The only bridal veil she'd ever wear was inside a box.

I startled her once she heard my voice, and she recognized my singular size.

"I could take you out of here, Miss Sybil. Joshua will look after you."

She clucked at me like a crazed chicken. "Josh can't even look after himself. Niles would slit his throat."

"Niles ain't the law," I said. "We could run to the sheriff."

The clucking stopped. "Lincoln, you're one fine imbecile. The sheriff also owns a piece of my tail. You'd best be gone. That dwarf is vicious. He'll tattle on me. And don't you tell a word to Josh. I wouldn't want him to see me in such a circumstance, you hear? *Promise*, else I'll blind ye with a stick."

She didn't have a stick, and I wasn't afraid of Niles and his dwarf. It was another matter. She was so pathetic in her porous silk blouse, I had to promise . . .

Niles didn't last very long, even with the sheriff and half the town behind him. A rich slaver, who'd come from Missouri to look for whores who could perform the filthiest tricks while swinging from a chandelier, didn't cotton to a colored sporting-club man and broke his neck in a drunken brawl. He never even sat in jail. He bribed the coroner and sailed back to Missouri.

And we *sailed* Illinois, Joshua and I, rode through every patch and cornfield, where we might find a whore's barn, and found none. That traveling bordello must have disappeared with the sporting-club man's demise. When we returned to Springfield, Sybil was waiting there for us with her parasol and her petticoats. The whore's mud was gone, with the flimsy blouses and skirts. She wouldn't accompany Joshua to Louisville as his concubine or his bride. Sybil had me prepare a lawyer's letter. She was adamant about it. Joshua would lend her a fixed sum—five hundred dollars—to start her own establishment, and she would go back to being his pretty lady, and reimburse him out of the proceeds.

He mulled over the proposition, because he still wanted to marry her. I had to pull on his ears with all my might to convince him that Sybil had more sense.

"Speed, that girl is volunteering to love you the only way she can. You'll shrivel into dust without her."

I knew he would outgrow his love of the West, would pack up and return to Louisville in a couple of years, and he wouldn't pine for his pretty lady. If there was any heartbreak, it would belong to Sybil.

10.

McIntosh

EVERY TIME I touch the Ohio, I still dream of slaves aboard
some flatboat, shackled together, their lips parched, their eyes
inflamed, as they are being shipped to the markets of Orleans like forgotten freight. I never saw a white child offer a piece of peppermint to
a black child on that boat. I didn't have the gumption to do it myself;
besides, I couldn't have afforded my own stick of peppermint as a boy.

I feared the Abolitionists just as much. They'd ride in from New
England with fire and brimstone in their hearts and rattle a town—
they always wore black hats and black coats, like hangmen or under-
takers. They arrived in Springfield with a bitter wind, in the autumn
of 1837, their torches lighting up their pink little eyes, and rented a
hall near the capitol. I rambled over, paid my 2½ cents for a ticket, and
wandered into the hall. The place was packed with female sympathiz-
ers in winter bonnets and black shawls, with lawyers and Legislators
like myself, and with half the colored folks in the county—tenant
farmers, fancy men, stevedores in brown coveralls, and the slaves we
still had left.

The Abolitionists were in high dudgeon. They had nothing to

lose in Illinois. They would have been happy to turn our villages into arsenals, drown Legislators in the Sangamon River, march on the capitol, and torch it into the ground. "Friends, neighbors, Illinois is a rotten sink that doesn't deserve to survive." But they didn't help themselves or the blacks in that hall.

A mob hammered its way in with pipes and cudgels and bargemen's poles. There was a preacher among these ruffians with the same brimstone as the Abolitionists and the same black hat. "Ye godless men and all your Jezebels," he spat, "you've beshit yourselves. You walk among the black devils and give them succor. Shame on you."

He jabbed one Abolitionist after the other in the chest with his bargeman's pole, while his ruffians attacked the rest of us with their cudgels. They were out to blind every black man in the hall and smash his skull. The sheriff arrived with a brace of pepper-pot pistols under his belt—each one with multiple blue barrels and a golden trigger—but he just stood there and wouldn't involve himself in a farrago that was turning into a slaughterhouse. Women clutched their bonnets and shrieked as I watched a poor soul with his own bloody eyeball in his hand, staring at it like a crazed jeweler. Another colored man had a hole in his head fat as a fist. And the sheriff looked on like some little Napoleon of the West.

"Lincoln, I'm not paid to protect niggers and Abolitionists."

I grabbed a pepper-pot from under his belt, pulled that golden trigger, and shot a chandelier—the fracas ended in an instant. People stood frozen under the shower of glass and a socking sound that was like a thunderclap. Shards spilled through the air; and it amazed me, more than a little, to watch the patterns of spinning glass, as if I had created a new world in under a minute. And then there was a musical noise, like the hiss of a harp, as the glass spun and spun.

We all stood under that shower, the best and the worst of us. I aimed my pepper-pot at the renegade preacher and cocked the hammer again. He and his ruffians disappeared, and the New Englanders clapped their hands and danced a jig in their Abolitionist boots.

"Brothers and sisters," I said, "go on out of here whilst you still can, and the next time you talk about firing up a building, make sure you're not in it."

Much as I tried, I couldn't stop the burning and the bloodshed, since Illinois was a State with a Southern soul. Abolitionists often found themselves stuck inside a coat of tar and feathers. There had been little uprisings and insurrections in Illinois and in Missouri, across the Mississip; most of the uprisings had been spurred on by the Abolitionists or a mob of slavers, with colored men and women caught in the middle.

In St. Louis, last year, a mulatto cook named McIntosh—a freeman—who worked on a steamboat, tried to rescue a couple of black crew members; these boatmen had been apprehended for fighting near the docks; and when he interfered in their arrest, McIntosh was arrested, too. One of the deputy sheriffs mocked McIntosh and told him he would have to sit in jail for five years. McIntosh pulled out a knife and stabbed him to death. The report of this stabbing spread like wildfire that April. An angry mob plucked McIntosh right out of jail and dragged him across town. The mob chained McIntosh to a chestnut tree, set him on fire, and watched him burn. The next morning his charred body was still chained to the tree. His skull had become a plaything for the children of St. Louis. They shot peas and tossed rocks at the holes where his eyes had once been. And there weren't a lot of folks who were really astonished.

I couldn't bring McIntosh back with words scratched on a page, but at least I could remember him. And when the Young Men's Lyceum, that society of social lions, asked me to deliver a speech, I decided to talk about McIntosh and the mob rule that had descended upon the United States in the spring of '36. I didn't hobnob with most of the lions, though I might have, since Joshua Speed was part of their company when he wasn't gallivanting with Sybil Weg. But I wouldn't have been comfortable in a ruffled shirt, and I lacked the funds to buy one. So I appeared in my usual garb of dusty gabardine at the Second Presbyterian Church one Saturday night in January, nine or ten months after I'd removed to Springfield—the wind was howling fierce.

I stood up at the pulpit in front of these fine men, several of whom served with me in the Legislature—others were bankers and shopkeepers—and delivered a talk entitled "The Perpetuation of Our Political Institutions." I'd labored long and hard on that address. The written hand wasn't natural to me. I had to polish and re-polish the speech, deliver it in front of a mirror in Joshua's bedroom, with a few of the store's clerks as my audience. Joshua might have helped the novice lecturer, but I wouldn't ruin it for him. I wanted him to hear the *shock* of my delivery for the first time at the Young Men's Lyceum.

I'd babbled in front of the Legislature, I'd electioneered, but I wasn't a fire-breather like the Abolitionists—I couldn't electrify an audience, have women swoon at my feet. There were no ladies at the Lyceum. And many of these social lions weren't used to the timbre of my voice, that sudden squeak.

I warned the lions. "Shall we expect some transatlantic military giant to step the ocean and crush us at a blow? Never! All the armies of Europe, Asia, and Africa combined, with all the treasure of the earth (our own excepted) in their military chest, with a Bonaparte for a commander, could not by force take a drink from the Ohio or make a track on the Blue Ridge in a trial of a thousand years. . . . If destruction be our lot we must ourselves be its author and finisher. As a nation of freemen we must live through all time, or die by suicide."

I talked about a certain madness—the madness of mob rule—that threatened a land where negroes and whites supposed to be leagued with them were chased into every corner, "till dead men were seen literally dangling from the boughs of trees upon every roadside, and in numbers almost sufficient to rival the native Spanish moss of the country as a drapery of the forest."

I mentioned McIntosh, how he had suffered an inglorious death, "all within a single hour from the time he had been a freeman attending to his own business and at peace with the world." I didn't condone the stabbing he did—the death of that deputy. But no justice was served by chaining McIntosh to a tree. The mob of tomorrow will burn and hang the innocent and the guilty at will, and make a jubilee of it, I said. The spit was flying. The screech in my voice was gone. Suddenly I was a baritone, in full force.

Thus I spoke to the Lyceum. My lips were dry. My throat was parched. My voice had fled into the roof. I didn't belong with these young lions. I could have been the monster at a monster show I'd seen as a child. There were two or three tents. The monster might have been a bearded lady or a man with a shark's skin. I never had much faith in these unnatural beings, assuming with a boy's cunning and bewilderment that both the beard and the fish skin had been painted on. But still I looked and looked. I couldn't take my eyes off the monster. And I must have haunted these young men the way the bearded lady had haunted me, as someone only half authentic. The bearded lady couldn't sing out her lament. She had no voice beyond her deformity, real or unreal. And I, Abraham Lincoln, with my wild hair and look of a gigantic scarecrow, must have amused them, even *frightened* them a little with my harangue about mobs and political institutions.

I talked of the Founding Fathers and their wild experiment that folks might make their own destiny without a tyrant to guide or govern them. "If they succeeded, they were to be immortalized; their names were to be transferred to counties, and cities, and rivers, and mountains; and to be revered and sung, toasted through all time. If they failed, they were to be called knaves, and fools, and fanatics for a fleeting hour; then to sink and be forgotten. They succeeded."

The Revolution had created a living history, with scars and wounds. But the histories found in every family were now gone. "They can be read no more forever. They were a fortress of strength; but what invading foeman could never do, the silent artillery of time has done—the leveling of its walls." And we had to fight against that silent quarry with sober reason. "Passion has helped us, but can do so no more. It will in future be our enemy. Reason—cold, calculating, unimpassioned reason—must furnish all the materials for our future support and defense. . . ."

I had been wrong about these social lions, including Ninian Edwards and other members of the Long Nine. They clapped and clapped in their silk and satin for the monster on the pulpit. And then I thought of McIntosh, his skull and bones clinging to a tree.

11

King Richard & the Lexington Lioness

UNTIL MY SPEECH at the Lyceum, Ninian and his wife, Elizabeth, had never invited me to their house on the Hill. Elizabeth Edwards was a busybody and the biggest matchmaker in town. She had a long nose, like a bird of prey, and piercing silver eyes. She took it upon herself to summon up suitable brides for Springfield's most eligible bachelors. And since it was hard to find belles of good breeding, she had to import them from Louisville or Lexington, where she had grown up. She herself was a Todd, one of Kentucky's *superior* families.

When I showed up at Elizabeth's Saturday-night soirees, wearing white gloves, she was polite enough, but she never glanced at me with her eagle eyes. Elizabeth wasn't going to waste her time on a no-account like Abe Lincoln. She could chatter on and on about my exquisite lecture at the Lyceum—it had been published in the *Sangamo Journal.* But she didn't believe for a minute that I belonged on Quality Hill.

I kind of felt the same way. I couldn't dance up a storm even with some of the second-rate belles who were allotted to me. I shuffled around, with the skirts of my coat flaring up like a rooster's crippled wings. I didn't know any of the latest steps. I'd never been to dancing college. So the boundaries were crisp and clean. I was at war with Elizabeth Todd Edwards, but it was a war of whispers. She was always whispering when I was around, as if I were a tall skeleton in white gloves, and it wasn't worth her while to match me up with one of her belles.

I drank her punch, I politicked, and avoided her cotillions as much I could. Still, I was included in the Coterie, that inner circle of lions and young lionesses around Mr. and Mrs. Edwards, who must have calculated some, since I was a lawyer and Legislator to be reckoned with. The social lions might have had their fancy cuffs, but their tongues failed them in front of a jury, whereas I could clown and be the jackanapes. I could move a jury of farmers by telling a barnyard tale. Lawyer Lincoln was soon sought after in the near and far counties of Illinois.

I was a bit startled when Mrs. Elizabeth called me into one of her husband's closets on Quality Hill. She'd never spoken to me in private before. She poured coffee from a silver pot. We had little cream cakes. This was serious business. I was wondering when she would skin me alive.

"Lincoln," she said with a lilt in her voice, "you're not getting any younger, you know." And I figured I was in mortal danger, or she wouldn't have squandered all that music on me.

"You must be forty!"

I wasn't a day older than thirty, but I wouldn't contradict Mrs. Elizabeth when she was in one of her moods. She must have caught the deep blush on my leather face. I'd never had a pretty lady, and I wouldn't have known what to do with one.

"It's time you were married," she said. "You won't get far without a good wife."

"I'm not sure I'm the marrying kind."

"Nonsense," she said. "Mr. Edwards and I have picked a bride for you."

I had to keep my mouth from twitching. That's how mortified I was. But I wouldn't turn my back on Mrs. Elizabeth and climb down Quality Hill.

"Dear Lincoln," she said, "I do believe our Miss Angelina Snell is a perfect matrimonial fit for you."

Angelina Snell was one of the family's poor Lexington relations. And Mrs. Elizabeth had appropriated her as a glorified servant and secretary. Miss Angelina took part in the cotillions, but then she disappeared and had to supervise the other servants in the back rooms of the mansion. She was a walleyed maiden of twenty-nine or so and had the flattest chest in Illinois. I wouldn't have married her if Mrs. Elizabeth had given me all the gold her husband had and offered me my own mansion on Quality Hill.

"I appreciate your concern, ma'am, but I reckon I'll remain a bachelor for the time being."

I didn't realize the cunning behind that proposal until another few months passed. Mrs. Elizabeth's own sister, Mary Todd, arrived from Lexington to stay with her and Ninian. Miss Todd I discovered was escaping her stepmother, who had her own brood of children now—nine or ten, I believe—and didn't need such a constant reminder of her husband's first marriage. Elizabeth had also fled the same household and married Ninian when she was sixteen. And Mary Todd, already twenty-one, was considered just about *ripe* for a Kentucky gal. She wasn't walleyed, like Miss Angelina, nor was she a mouse. She had a whopping temper and liked to talk politics. I saw her throw a book at one of the maids and cuss a man out for uttering an unkind remark about her hero, Henry Clay. She flirted with every young lion, and with some of the older ones. She had six or seven marriage proposals a month after she arrived in Springfield, some folks said. All these swains began to tire her, and soon she had an altogether different crop. She tired of them, too. She wasn't very tall—she stood a touch under five feet—and had handsome shoulders, light brown hair, and blue eyes that seemed to have an oceanic pull.

I wouldn't have called her beautiful; she had a tiny, turned-up nose, a broad forehead, and wide jaws, but she liked to wear gowns with a low neckline that revealed the startling curve of her bodice. And her intelligence was as fierce as any lion on the Hill, though she had all the wiles and flirtatious charm of a Lexington lioness.

Now it was perfectly clear why Mrs. Elizabeth was so eager to capture a bride for me. A matchmaker of her stripe couldn't afford a major catastrophe—a Todd like Miss Mary, who had studied French at the finest schools and had had her own body servant, had to be kept away from a rough boy who had never outgrown the forest and a dirt floor.

It's diabolical how Elizabeth's own disregard dragged me toward her sister—Little Miss Todd. I kept dreaming of what lay under all that fine silk, and couldn't get her fat little tail out of my mind, even while I was addressing a jury. I ought to have been locked up, an officer of the court who was so damn lascivious. I'd imagine her dancing without a stitch, and pull on my root half the night. Still, I was the shiest of suitors, and if Mrs. Elizabeth hadn't been so spiteful with her tricks, I might have waited a while before I approached Mary Todd. But at the very first cotillion, I edged in front of all her other suitors, and said, "Miss Todd, I want to dance with you in the worst way."

She didn't decline my invitation. She scrutinized me with her own fierce eyes that shimmered a lot and were flecked with gold. I was the tall one—that giant out of New Salem—and she was the Lexington mite. Had to stoop and stoop again to hold on to Mary. And with her little pink hands caught in the cage of my white gloves, we whirled about the polished floor to the rhythm of a Viennese waltz, while I prayed that my prick wouldn't brush against her gown. I couldn't help myself and my own horse's pole inside my pantaloons. Mary wasn't embarrassed none. She was wearing velvet ballroom slippers that seemed to glide along. And I had to knock about in my boots, careful not to lunge too far and become the spectacle of Quality Hill. Mrs. Elizabeth would have harrumphed like hell if I had landed on my ass. But I went right to the end of that Viennese, while Mary put one of her little hands behind my ear and caressed the flap with a tenderness that touched me to the quick and ate into my own raw hide. Here I had been dreaming of cocks and hair pie, drowning in my own jelly, when she showed me a kindness I didn't deserve. I was enraptured by that little Lexington lady, caught in the spell of her Parisian perfume, as I climbed down Quality Hill.

WE WERE NEVER ALONE. There were horse rides into the woods, garden parties, cotillions, lectures at the Second Presbyterian Church, but I couldn't fondle her, even hold her hand. There was always Mrs. Elizabeth looking down my shirt, and sending Mary off on some picnic with one of her other beaux. Even if our lovemaking was mostly chatter, we still discovered things in common, like Henry Clay. Mary had known him ever since she was a child, had visited his manor house in Lexington, had even gone for rides on the great man's pony.

She called him Uncle Henry, and I felt a kind of ravenous rage. I envied nothing but the time she'd spent with Clay of Kentucky.

"Why, Mr. Lincoln," she said in that lovely voice of Lexington's gentle class, "I might as well have been his niece—I was at Ashland *all* the time."

And once, Mary said with just a little bit of swagger, she had happened upon the Senator during a dinner party, and she was invited to join the table. "If I'm ever elected President," he said, "I'll be damned if Miss Mary Todd isn't my first guest."

She answered him like some actress in a minstrel show. "Senator, I would *adore* living at the White House." And she couldn't have been more than thirteen at the time.

She'd turn quiet while twisting a flower into her hair—she liked to decorate herself with flowers. And then she'd grow volatile, as if a wild wind had visited her. "Mr. Lincoln, don't you hate *your* stepmama!"

I didn't hate Sarah Bush Johnston, who was a genuine mother to me after Ma died. Pa had brought her to our cabin with her quilts, her spinning wheel, and her own three children. But she never once favored them. And she shielded me from Pa and his blind wrath. Sometimes I'd read to her at night—about Sinbad the Sailor or one of Æsop's dishonest foxes. She loved tales of villainy.

Mary Todd was also fond of villains. She couldn't have survived without Shakespeare's villains, she said. Richard III had comforted her while she *boarded* with her Pa and his new family.

"Lord alive, what I wouldn't have given to lock them in a tower!"

She was like a quake of raw energy and some kind of sun goddess, and I was *quickened* whenever I was in her orbit. Sometimes I'd hold her hand, and I could feel an electric spurt. Mary herself said that the two of us had "lover's eyes." I still felt ungainly around her, like some gigantic frog with warts on his face.

I was called into the parlor again by that provost marshal, Mrs. Elizabeth, with her eagle's gaze. She would have ruined me forever if she had a hatchet in her hand. I never saw so much hate and bile in a body.

"Lincoln," she said, "this will not do. I forbid it. My sister has come from Lexington to find a *husband*, not to mingle with some tramp without a penny in his pocket."

I was in her husband's house, and it would have been ungracious if I went and whipped his wife. So I had to crucify my feelings in front of Mrs. Elizabeth.

"The two of you have *nothing* in common. She speaks much better French than a Parisian. Why, she has read Washington Irving and Fenimore Cooper, even Victor Hugo, and one day she'll probably dine in the White House. Lincoln, you will not come here again—or go riding with my sister."

"Ma'am, are you banning me from Quality Hill?"

"A gentleman would know when he's not welcome." She was twitching now, and it was hard for me to stare down all that hate. "Sister is keeping company with Mr. Douglas. I expect to announce their engagement in a week or so."

I saw him climb Quality Hill, Douglas with his dancing step and deep baritone voice. He wasn't a vagabond like me. Stephen Douglas had the finest cut of clothes and was a mite taller than Mary Todd. I noticed Mary flirt with him, how her eyes flared in his presence, how he'd capture her hands in his.

So I avoided Quality Hill. I rode out on the circuit with a gaggle of lawyers and the district judge. The circuit court was like a sideshow. There was always a hullabaloo when our little court arrived in some hamlet or tiny town. Often a menagerie accompanied us for most of the circuit, with their own minstrels in black paint. I laughed at the buffoonery, but it grew wearisome after a while—the same exaggerated gestures and wild eyes.

I couldn't stop thinking of that Lexington lioness up on her Hill, the aroma of red hair, the dampness of her body through all that silk. I avoided the Quality people. I still had holes in my pockets, with pantaloons that couldn't even cover up my winter underwear, but I was the only lawyer in town who could fill the gallery. I still had the taste of tin in my mouth. So I wandered up to Quality Hill for the last soiree of the year, in my white gloves and coattails with some maverick thread hanging down to my heels. I discovered Mary Todd with a new crop of swains that clung to every word, though I didn't see Douglas in his perfumed cuffs, like a Mississippi gambler.

I wouldn't scribble my name all over Mary's dance card. I sat in Mrs. Elizabeth's ballroom, under the magnificent candlelight that left swirling shadows on the far wall. It was Mary who glided over to my chair in her slippers and ruffled gown.

"Mr. Lincoln," she said with a quiver over one eye, "you are the rudest man in Springfield. You've ignored me for two solid months."

It wasn't the words alone that cut me. The melody was gone from her voice.

"I meant ye no harm, Miss Todd."

She hissed at me like a plump snake. "My friends call me Molly. And you have earned that privilege."

"But where's Mr. Douglas?"

That ripe attack had gone out of Mary Todd. I must have startled her.

"And what on earth does Mr. Douglas have to do with me?"

"Your guardian told me that you intended to marry him. And if I dared pursue you, I wasn't welcome in this house."

She lost her voluptuous look. The flesh had gone out of her, and she could have been some eerie creature from the wild. She rocked on her heels like someone caught in a macabre dance.

"What guardian?" she asked. "I have none."

"But Mrs. Elizabeth said . . ."

And that's when I saw her explode for the first time. The gown tilted on her shoulders at a crazy angle. Her luscious arms flailed about. She ripped up her dance card in front of my eyes and raced over to Mrs. Elizabeth with her all fury. The two sisters flew from the ballroom together. And when they returned, Mary Todd was composed as a cat, but her married sister was shaking.

Mrs. Elizabeth walked over to me like someone in a trance; all the color had fled her face. She could have wandered out of her own coffin.

"You must forgive me, Mr. Lincoln. I had no right to speak for my sister. Molly has never, never been my ward."

I had small pleasure wounding her. She was protecting her little sister from a vagabond with a lawyer's license.

I stooped and kissed her hand. Her eyes floated in her head as she feigned civility. She would have liked to pluck my eyes out, I reckon, but she couldn't do that with her little sister around. Yet the signals were all there—the brutal pull of her upper lip, the crooked smile, the crazed look. She wanted me to know that Molly could kiss me into tomorrow, and I'd never be welcome on Quality Hill.

I wanted Molly, and I wasn't gonna let her witch of a sister win. So I tucked in my coattails and poured on my own civility, but Mrs. Elizabeth could see that hard little horn between my eyes.

"I'm delighted, ma'am. I'll cherish the day when I can call you *Sister.*"

She was white as a ghost, whiter even. She was used to getting her own way, to plucking bachelors out of her own favorite pile, and rolling all the others right down the Hill. And she hadn't expected me to make war like a Comanche among her own little coven of aristocrats. But I should have been more careful. She was a Comanche, too.

She stared at the horn between my eyes and said, "I'll leave you to your own devices, Brother Lincoln." And she went back to sit with all the other matchmakers, while I watched her little sister like a bird dog. Mary was *almost* voluptuous again, but she didn't have the same silver glow under the chandeliers.

"Now, Mr. Lincoln," she said with a slight lisp, "do you think you might start pursuing me again?"

And there wasn't the least hint of a smile at the corner of her mouth.

THE WEATHER TURNED. I could sniff the snows that would soon pile up on the prairie. I could *feel* the flakes covering the woods and the fallow fields. I had a dream just before winter solstice, the darkest night of the year. I was climbing Quality Hill, but it had no mansions on this night. It was a graveyard, and the falling snows had a dizzying effect. I lurched across the yard. That singular snow didn't cover any graves with its own fierce powder—it *uncovered* the tombs, wiped away stone and rotten wood. I didn't see raw bones and funeral clothes devoured by worms. I saw my mother's face—not a skeleton—but cheeks and lips alive with color, a mouth as moist as mine. And I had such a longing for Nancy Lincoln. I'd forgotten how bereft I was with her in the ground.

When I woke up, I was still caught in that dream. I had to struggle out of it. Joshua was lying there in his nightshirt, chewing on the collar in his sleep. And I realized that I'd always be an orphan around Quality people. I'd always see the contempt in Mrs. Elizabeth's eyes. I'd always have to do my own version of the Viennese around the Todds—Long Lincoln tripping over his feet like a big buffoon.

I commenced to scribble a letter to Mary Todd. I composed it like a brief, outlining to Molly why I couldn't marry her. We weren't compatible, as her sister knew all along. I was a lawyer who lived in his shirtsleeves, and Molly was an aristocrat who'd had her own personal slave in Lexington. She couldn't have abided my chaos and colossal mess. And I declared point by point why I didn't love her and never could.

I showed the letter to Joshua. I could tell how disconcerted he was.

"Will you deliver it for me, Speed?"

But he was the lawyerly one right now.

"Burn that letter, Lincoln. Go see Mary, and if you don't love her, tell the girl. Be careful not to say too much. Give your goodbye and for land sakes, don't linger."

I buttoned my coat, walked through wind and snow, and hiked up Quality Hill.

Ninian and his wife were either at some soiree in the middle of a snowstorm, or else they were hiding from me. Molly and one of the servants came to the front door. This girl must have been from the Islands, because Molly spoke to her in French. I loved to listen to the patter of her *Parlez-vous*. There was a touch of hysteria in her voice tonight, as if she were crying out a lament. I'd forgotten how late it was. Molly was wearing her nightgown and a shawl. She clutched a lantern, and it wavered in her right hand. I must have looked like a snowman from Mongolia. Molly was frightened of monsters, but the worry marks disappeared, and finally she laughed.

"You might have given me a little notice, Mr. Lincoln. I would have worn a much fancier gown—in your honor."

Then she saw my worry marks. She and the Island girl wiped the snow from my head with their handkerchiefs.

"Matilda," she sang to the girl in Lexington English for my own benefit—the lilt had come back into her voice. "You'll make a toddy for Mr. Lincoln, hear? He must be half frozen to death."

The Island girl ran into the kitchen, and Molly led me through the darkened halls with her lantern. She trembled now. She must have seen the little doom that was coming.

"Mr. Lincoln, you wouldn't have risked this weather for a lantern party. Something must be on your mind."

We went into Ninian's library. Molly lit the gas lamps, and the light sparked up and bloomed until the library looked like it was half on fire. We sat together on one of the love seats. I hadn't been alone with Molly like this in a long time.

She held my hand with her tiny fist—my own fist was like a red claw.

I could feel the heat of her hand.

"Mr. Lincoln, what is wrong?"

She had already caught the blizzard in my eye. She held my hand even tighter.

"Puss," I said—that was my pet name for her. I liked to imagine her as a kitten with many colors. "I *jest* can't marry you—I don't love you. Perhaps I never did."

She commenced to sob. Her head whipped back and forth, back and forth. "It's my just reward for leading on so many suitors. Some Illinois devil is punishing me right now—Satan himself!"

She let go of my red claw and commenced to wring her hands. I was *paralyzed*. But I seized her up and sat her on my knee for a second. Then I walked out the door—just as that Island girl had come along with my toddy. I didn't think it polite to drink it *after* I'd broken my engagement to Puss.

Perhaps I was the snowman of Mongolia—or worse—who'd come to the plains of Illinois to ravage whole populations, or break the hearts of Kentucky belles.

I plunged through the snow drifts in a dream.

Next morning that Island girl, Matilda, brought me a letter from Molly sealed with the Todd family's own special wax. I hadn't been wrong. Molly released me from my obligation to her, but said she would hold our engagement in reserve as an open question—or *wound*, I thought, an open wound. She herself hadn't changed her mind, and felt as she always did, with great affection.

Lincoln, you are free. I will not wrap you up in a cloak of words.
Promises do not bind. I will marry for love, and nothing short of that.
                                    Your Puss forever, Mary Todd

I should have been relieved but I wasn't. I felt like riding the snows back up to Quality Hill and carrying Puss off to the nearest preacher. I could not. I'd broken off the engagement and I'd have to let it lie there like a sick skunk. That sick skunk was Abraham Lincoln. I had a spell of the *blue unholies* I hadn't had since Salem. And I couldn't even count on the comfort of Josh's camaraderie—his Pa had died. Joshua was selling his own share of the general store and moving back to Farmington, his Pa's plantation outside Lexington. The cavalier was returning to his Kentucky roost.

Josh read that twisted look in my eyes. He hid all my razors from me. And he had his own bit of mourning to do. He'd promised not to kidnap his pretty lady—Sybil Weg—and hightail back to Farmington with her in the same saddle.

"I hate to leave her, Lincoln. But I'd like to bestow a little trust fund upon Sybil. Will you attend to the details?"

I couldn't even handle the details of my own life. I ran off the track. Pa had once told me that if you entered into a bad bargain, you had to hug it all the harder. Well, *I* was the bad bargain. I avoided all the Quality people on Quality Hill. Ninian Edwards commenced to advertise that Abraham Lincoln was now crazy as a Loon—talked to himself, wore the same filthy shirt, and shunned his own clients. I wasn't crazy. I was as wild and desperate as a hunted bear—bereft of humankind. I belonged to nobody. Should have stayed with Pa, and earned my keep with a hatchet.

I took to bed that January, while the Legislature was still in session. I couldn't bear to watch the dark descend upon Springfield. I lay near a lamp and never wandered, not even when Joshua brought me a bowl of soup.

It was the weather that helped me by littles. It rained less, and the dark storms subsided near the end of January.

Took my seat in the Legislature in the same rumpled shirt, with black rings under my eyes, and when Joshua left for Kentucky, I did feel like a Loon. I kept hearing about Molly and the cat fits she threw at her brother-in-law's mansion. She slapped one of the servants, tore up the vegetable garden. She even slapped one of her suitors. She visited her own people in Lexington and returned a little *riper* for it. She slapped a woman in Mrs. Elizabeth's sewing club in an argument over Henry Clay. Town gossips commenced calling her "that violent little Lexington Whig." I imagined Molly disguising herself as a man and become a duelist. Dueling had been outlawed in Illinois, but Molly could have crossed over to one of the Missouri islands with a pepper-pot in her cummerbund.

And to escape these phantasms and my own recurrent blue spells, I decided to visit Josh at his plantation. I had to voyage by steamer and stage, and a locomotive that left you with a mask of soot on your face, like a minstrel man. It was worth the displeasure. Farmington was like no plantation I had ever seen—it was ten times larger than New Salem, and ten times as rich. It brimmed over with all the hard sweat and labor of a working farm, where hemp was planted and twisted into rope and rags. As I landed at this farm for the first time, I rode down a long drive lined with locust trees—at the end of the road was a brick mansion that bristled in the sun, and a labyrinth of outbuildings and barns surrounded by fields and gardens. It could have been the mirage of some perfect village that fell out of a fairy tale.

Still, Farmington wasn't a fairy tale—it was a village of flesh and blood . . . and a small army of slaves. And once I settled in, I was startled to discover that I had my own colored servant. He'd been schooled and churched at Farmington, and was a better Christian than Abraham Lincoln.

I wanted to establish a degree of respect with this servant I had suddenly acquired. So I asked him his name.

"Abraham," he said.

This Abraham was wearing Josh's hand-me-downs. He was like a Southern gentleman in slightly cracked boots and a shirt with one missing ruffle. He knew his Shakespeare. Joshua must have teased my favorite plays into him.

"Lions make leopards tame," he said, mouthing Richard II. And I probed him like some lord of the catechism.

"And what does it mean, Abraham?"

"That lions rule and leopards don't," said my scholar-slave. And I could feel the sand in my craw, since Molly and me had both been fond of that foolish king—Richard II—who could speak in verse but didn't know how to rule. I hadn't come all the way to Louisville to have my deepest memories scratched. And I'm not so sure what happened next, but I tumbled into a black dream. I could feel my soul crack into a hundred shivers, like Richard's looking glass. I drifted as only a dead boy could drift. And when I returned from that void there was a pillow under my head. Abraham, my colored valet, was patting my chops with a piece of hemp and reciting one of Richard's soliloquies.

> *For God's sake, let us sit upon the ground*
> *And tell sad stories about the death of kings . . .*

"Boy," I said unkindly, because I was wounded by his equilibrium and his pluck, "who taught you to recite from King Richard?"

"Mr. Josh. He says he missed talking Shakespeare with you."

I'd never been humbled by such a scholar. He could hunt and fish and ride a horse, and soon I rarely took a step without him. All the Speeds considered him a prodigy. He often sat near us, at a small table he himself had carved, though I'm sure he preferred to be with his own people at dinner time. Joshua was grooming him to run the plantation.

Mrs. Speed wasn't overbearing, like other Kentucky matrons. And she told me that reading the Bible at regular intervals might be the best *tonic* for the blues.

"Mr. Lincoln, I intend to fatten you with peaches and cream and a little of Jonah's whale. Hurts my heart to see such a melancholy man."

We had another guest—a local gal with pearl-black eyes, Miss Fanny, Joshua's fiancée. It made me lonesome looking at her. And it just killed my soul to think of my lost fiancée. But something was wrong at the next table. Abraham didn't touch his peaches and cream. He left us in the middle of the meal, with his thumbs in his pockets.

"That boy has an awful lot of sassafras," said Miss Fanny, rising up in her chair like a swan with black eyes.

"Pay him no mind," Joshua said. "We had to lease out his wife for a little while. There's a sick child at the next plantation and Captain Jones could use another hand."

"But he has no call to sit there and smart—and leave without excusing himself."

"He's worried about his wife," Joshua said. "That little girl might have the measles, and . . . he's kind of moody. Pay him no mind."

I found a note in my boot next morning; Abraham had scribbled it with a little polish.

I wasted time, and now doth time waste me.

That scholar was quoting from Richard again, Richard in the dungeon, all alone, cropped of his crown. It wasn't so cryptical, even in the crookedness of black polish. Our Richard had run away. Joshua knew about it long before I read the note. And I was startled to find Miss Fanny in a hunter's hat with two silk tails—it wasn't her first hunt for runaways. The hounds had been collected from their kennels. Their skin was sleek, and their backs rippled with anticipation; they barked, and the lead dog leapt up and licked her hand.

"Now, Thunder, you be still," she said.

I'd never seen such a specimen. That dog's whole body pointed toward someone else's destruction. Thunder's eyes were yellow; his paws gripped the earth like talons.

He didn't take much notice until Joshua included me in the hunting party; then he bumped me with his skull; it was a kind of initiation rite, I reckon. I had to hold on to a musket with a barrel longer than my leg—it was used to hunt deer, large birds, and runaways. I didn't know what to do with this *deer gun*. I carried a bullet pouch and a bandolier, but I wouldn't have shot a buzzard or a runaway, even if my life depended on it. Yet there I was, in the middle of a hunt.

Joshua let that pack of hounds have a good whiff of Abraham's work clothes—a woolen sock, a slouch hat with sweat marks, a worn pair of pantaloons. Thunder's nose quivered with the raw delight of Abraham's sweat.

"Speed," I whispered, "you ain't gonna shoot that boy, are ye? You taught him Shakespeare, for God's sake!"

"I might not have a choice," he said. "We've had a rash of runaways."

And so we went on into the woods with five plantation boys— one was part Injun and meant to be Thunder's pilot, but Thunder piloted him; the dogs leapt about in their own twisted, crazy arc; they seemed to crash right through trees. The forest was an enigma to us, with beaver dams, holes and traps, and hidden bear dens, but a battery of pleasures to the dogs; they trampled snakes and ran down a doe, with Thunder breaking her legs in one long stride and leaving her with a gash in her neck, while he was still tracking Abraham.

Soon the hounds returned to us, whimpering like babies; they'd lost Abraham's scent; their yellow eyes commenced to cloud. Thunder was bewildered and yelped louder than the rest; he'd never suffered such a defeat. He still had the doe's blood in his mouth; but his ears flopped and his coat twitched, as if infected with flea bites.

Miss Fanny raged under her silk ribbons. "Joshua, are we hunting that boy, or chaperoning a bunch of worthless, lazy dogs?"

The whimpering stopped as some naked god stepped out of the woods with a stride as perfect and muscular as the dogs. The different pieces of him glowed in the forest's bewildering light—it was a black man who'd bathed himself in lime to mask his own scent. *Abraham.* He was translucent where he stood.

Miss Fanny cupped a hand over her eyes. "Joshua, punish him, you hear? I will not be obliged to look at that boy's testicles."

I would have hit her until her teeth clattered in her mouth, but she wasn't my fiancée.

"Mr. Josh," the boy sang in that Shakespearian tongue of his, "I went to visit my wife."

Joshua seemed chagrined, as if that coat of lime the boy wore had chastened him.

"You could have asked my permission, Abraham. I wouldn't have denied it."

"Then I will ask your permission, sir—after the visit."

"How is your Kate?"

"I did not get to see her. Captain Jones' hounds were barking up a storm, and I might have been shot as an intruder. I did not want my Kate to mourn while she was looking after that little girl with the measles."

And he marched right past us in that suit of lime. I could have sworn he signaled to me with one eye. But the forest light was no better than a mirage. And that image stays with me still. Joshua was obliged to whip him, of course. But he didn't have his heart in it, though Miss Fanny incited him, her tongue twisted in her mouth, like some reptile with a horn in the middle of her head.

"One more stroke, *dearest*. Another! Another! Teach that boy a lesson. He has no business attending to his wife while Captain Jones has an illness in the family."

Josh had to cage Thunder, who was delirious over the smell of Abraham's blood and took to whimpering and whining and banging against the bars of his kennel with such force that the damn contraption spilled and spun around like an iron boulder; the dog made such a racket that Joshua had to hurl an old boot at him.

"*Thunder*, be still, or I'll sell your hide to the glue man."

And that hound sat like a sergeant in his ruined kennel without whimpering once.

Josh returned to the whipping post, which was nothing more than a legless chair strapped to a rail. Abraham sat on this *throne* with his arms tied to the rail, leaving his back exposed to Josh's lashes and the raw wind. Josh used a fresh-cut switch. Abraham kept his eyes open and winced not once. He didn't look at man or beast, as the lashes bit into his back, while every soul at the plantation—colored and white—stood around the throne, as if they were at some raree show. Neighbors were there, too, from plantations near and far. The children had long strings of candy. They looked drunk with a kind of pernicious joy.

Miss Fanny was in a frenzied state. "Joshua, salt up his wounds and feed him gall."

And then a little colored boy arrived from one of the cook houses with some kind of snuffbox, as if he were carrying a silver chalice.

Josh removed a yellow salve from the box and traced every wound with a bit of balm. Then he untied Abraham, slid him out of the chair, covered him with a cloth, and the little colored boy accompanied him to a cook house.

Abraham never appeared at our dinner table again. Mrs. Speed pretended he didn't exist. Miss Fanny talked about her latest shopping bonanza in Louisville, how she was gathering up her trousseau like some avaricious spider with pearl-black eyes. I doubt Joshua listened to a word she said. I wondered if he was thinking about the plains, about all the prairie dust and the hogs roiling in the rain. He'd marry his black-eyed Fanny, remain the manor lord of Farmington, but that punishment of Abraham must have cost him plenty, like some public auction of the soul.

I ain't sure why, but my melancholia had wrapped itself around that whipping post, as if Josh was a magical man who could drive out *unholies* with a sharpened stick, while I drank up all that blood on Abraham like a backwoods demon. I was no demon. I was a solitary man who breathed in a parcel of that boy's pain, shrank from Josh's fiancée, and lit out of there as fast I could.

12.

Puss in the Parlor

I RODE ACROSS THE prairie for months at a time in that curious pilgrimage of a circuit court. We were entertainers—I was as adroit as any juggler who had to juggle between judge and jury. The judge, in his ermine robes, was king of our little court. And you couldn't mock him in front of the jury. You had to maneuver around him if you wanted to win your case. But if our king was dead against your client, you had to let him go. It was known as the *morbidity rate* of frontier justice.

That summer I was invited to a soiree at the home of Simeon Francis, editor of the *Sangamo Journal.* I wondered why his Missus kept insisting—I went to the soiree. There were the usual nabobs and the latest crop of belles. I didn't take a shine to any of them. Their necks were too long, their talk a little too shrill. I tired of 'em after twenty minutes. I thanked Mrs. Francis and muttered goodbye when I picked up Molly's scent, the sweet nectar that sat between her bosoms. So I wasn't startled when she walked in, but I was shivering like a holy man, and had to clutch a wall.

Her hair wasn't half as red as I had remembered. Her eyes still had that oceanic pull. I wanted her to shrivel without me, to look as sad and forlorn as a Widder Lady. I kept staring at her bodice like some creature at the monster show who hadn't been near a woman in a hundred years and was made mad by her scent.

It didn't embarrass her, not at all. She had a gorgeous swelling under her throat.

"Molly," I said, but I was frozen in my pantaloons—and lost, like King Richard, in one of his melancholy fits. It was Molly who loved to chide me the moment I had a fit.

"When will my poor *Richard* be himself again?"

She didn't chide me now. She marched right past with the least little nod and entered Simeon's parlor. I wanted to run howling to the wolves with the skirts of my coat in my hands. I stayed there and watched her chat with all those Quality people. Still, I couldn't stop staring. She drank some cider, hiccupped once or twice, and pounded on her chest with her fat little fist. Then she turned and glanced at me with a beehive of contradictions. That glance was as mercurial as her own nature, as if she could devour Illinois in a hurricane of hate and then have that hurricane melt away.

I marched over to her without a word, squeezed her hand in front of Mrs. Francis and all the other matrons. Molly's eyes darted for a moment—like a pinprick of fear—and then her face settled into a pale smile.

"Molly, Richard will never be himself again—but he's trying."

And she roared in the middle of that soiree. It was a reckless sound, a deep-throated laugh that flew up from her bodice.

WE MET BEHIND closed doors, in Mrs. Francis' salon, far from Quality Hill. I hated the intrigue. It was against my nature to steal looks at Molly like a liar and a thief. We were never alone. "Puss," I said, "couldn't we scurry somewhere, or drive through town in a rented carriage?"

But Puss was much more of a lawyer than I ever was.

"Lincoln," she said, "I do not trust the women and men of Springfield—they're uncertain and slippery. It's best to keep the business of our courtship from all eyes and ears."

So I had Puss in the parlor, clutching her hand, and listening to her breathe and trying to imagine the bump of her heart.

"Lincoln, I will not have another long engagement and watch it melt into nothing."

And so I played out my hand, like my old allies, Jack Armstrong and the Clary's Grove Boys, who love to bluff and could never win at liar's poker.

"Puss," I said, "we'll marry up this year."

"Come out of the wilderness, Mr. Lincoln. We're not children. I'll be fifty before you make up your mind."

"November," I whispered.

"That's not exact enough," she said like a circuit judge. "We'd slip into December if we aren't careful."

"The fourth," I said. "The fourth of November."'

And my Molly smiled. The little creases had gone out of her eyes—what some people called an old maid's web. But then that little fork appeared in her forehead, like the Devil's own mark, and much, much bluer than the little fork Ann Rutledge had.

"You must not tell a soul. Not my sister and my brother-in-law. I don't want their meddling."

"We'll need a minister . . . and I'll need a best man."

"Then you'll walk through enemy lines, Mr. Lincoln, and be as stingy as you can."

I made my maneuvers, went to that Episcopal man, the Rev.

Charles Dresser, and asked him to perform the service in his own parlor, on the night of November the fourth, 1842, but he was not to breathe a word. I went to Chatterton's jewelry shop on the west side of the square and ordered up a gold wedding band with the inscription, *Love Is Eternal.* Was it Molly's own devil mocking me? Did I inherit that fork of hers in my forehead? Fool that I was, I realized that the fourth of November was a Friday. And Fridays had never been lucky for the Lincolns. My own sister had given up the ghost on a Friday, with her dead infant in her arms. And Friday was when it first began to snow on poor Annie's grave, but I couldn't go to Mrs. Francis' parlor and ask Puss to postpone our marriage. It would have been like a curse.

I went to the Globe Tavern, on the north side of Adams Street, and rented out a room for matrimonial purposes—we'd have our bed and board. I'd dream of undressing Molly, of solving the little cords and bows of her bodice, reaching under her crinoline, cracking every little wire until the whole contraption dropped to the floor like a shattered bell, and then pulling her underskirts over her head, while I breathed in her aromas with both nostrils, and ran my rough hands through every sweet curve of her flesh. What if I failed Molly and couldn't perform my matrimonials? And my jelly spilled before I ever had a chance? I was mighty discouraged. That room wasn't much bigger than a coffin with a couple of pillows . . .

Mrs. Elizabeth came to visit my law office on the eve of the marriage. I hadn't seen her in over a year. The strings of her bonnet were all entangled. She'd been crying, and she had a handkerchief knotted in her fist. At first I thought her Pa was coming with his own Kentucky rangers to ride me out of Springfield. It had nothing to do with her Pa.

"You cannot wed Molly in a minister's office. I will not abide it."

I had all the ammunition now. "But it's Molly's wish," I said.

"Then you must dissuade her, Mr. Lincoln. I am her sister, her flesh and blood."

It was like going on a skunk hunt for aristocrats, but that skunk was Molly's kin. So I went to Puss and pleaded with her, and she flared up. Her face was on fire.

"She's a hypocrite. She said all the Todds would cut me dead if I married a Lincoln. And now she's faced with a fait accompli. And she doesn't want to be left out."

"Molly, you've been staying with her and Ninian for over two years."

"Yes, as my father's little ambassador. But how long will she welcome me once my father cuts us?"

"Aw, Puss," I said, "you'll have to include her."

And we did. I walked into a howling rain in my wedding suit and went up to that mansion on Quality Hill. The minister was there. A fire had been lit. Puss came down the stairs in a white muslin dress skirt without a bride's veil or flowers in her hair. And her sister trolled out of the kitchen with trembling hands and panic in her eyes—the wedding cake had fallen flat.

Puss wouldn't even console her.

"Gingerbread is good enough for Mr. Lincoln . . . and his wife."

And so we were married in that parlor. I slipped the ring onto Mary's finger and intoned the Episcopal vows. "With this ring I thee endow with all my goods and chattels, lands and tenements."

I didn't remember much after that, except that I had no goods and chattels—nothing but a whimsical law practice and a bridal suite at the Globe Tavern. We rode there, under the beating rain, in Ninian's carriage. Puss didn't complain, though that barren little room must have felt like a slap in the face. I dried her hair while she played with the ring. We were both in some kind of torment and nervous state. We undressed in the dark. I approached that coffin-bed in my nightshirt. She wasn't wearing a nightgown. I could see the swoop of her shoulders in the little light coming off the rain. The rest of her was woven into the dark.

"Mr. Lincoln," she sang in that cultured voice of hers. "I'd be much obliged if you took off that damn shirt. I want to feel your manliness."

I closed the curtains and we lay down together like wolf cubs wild with wonder, and I was maddened by my own paucity of knowledge—about ardor and its acrobatics, and all the fine little *ravelments* of love. First thing I felt was the soft bump of her belly, and then her fat little fingers on my cock. I wasn't prepared for the *wisdom* of Molly's touch. I leapt up like a man with St. Vitas, and I could have spilled all my jelly right on the spot if I hadn't asked the Lord to lead me out of this affliction. It was the delicate *burn* of Molly's eyes in the dark that calmed me down, not my prayers to the Lord. I licked the sweetness of her bosoms, reveled in the perfumery between her legs. Molly moaned like a little girl at a nun's palace. And that soft, almost painful purr deepened into a croak as I crept into Molly, and it was as if I had lived forever inside her wet well.

ILLINOIS & BEYOND
1858–1860

13.

Duff & the Shadow in the Glass

IT WAS SIXTEEN years—a flat sixteen—since our *honeymoon* at the Globe, with the constant rattle of the Springfield stage right outside our window to remind us of our narrow circumstances, with other guests at the tavern barking day and night, and I wondered when Mary would abandon the Globe, abandon me, and race back up Quality Hill. But she never complained, never winced once. She was Mrs. Abraham Lincoln, the wife of a country lawyer who *et* his vittles with a knife. And our habitation together was like a clothesline that leapt across the high plains during an Illinois *ripper* and still hooked itself to something—our own lives.

I was the culprit, a circuit rider always on the road, and Molly felt stranded in Springfield. It was the beginning of the *deluge*—that invisible cloth between us, the silence of wear and tear, the moodiness, the uncertainty, the anger deep under the skin. The childish *dimple* had gone out of her eyes. Marriage had become a broken bower where she had to boil my shirts and watch me stride into the kitchen, almost like a stranger, covered in dust. Yet she often smiled at that puzzling picture of my rawness and took some pleasure in scrubbing the dust off my bones, with her little hand as a washrag, circling over my skin with all the artistry of a harem girl.

That was our moment of delight. There'd been births and desolation and a terrible dying, and we still survived. Molly did have some solace, a little boy who smashed her heart from the moment he was born.

Bob was Mother's *first*. She had suckled Bob like some Arabian prince—the boy was unknowable, always would be, and could have been a fallen angel who landed in our lap. He commenced to run away from home before he was six, would hide in some root cellar or wander to the edge of town. What was he looking for? Where was he trying to alight? Lord knows. Molly had devoted half her life to Bob. When she had her blinding headaches, Bob would comfort her—he was the only one who could.

Her *blinders* were more frequent after our second boy was born— Eddie had a weak lung and coughed so hard he couldn't stand. I prayed we could keep Eddie with us if we didn't let any sinister angels into the house. Mother tried with all her might, fed him honey from her own mouth, while his lungs filled with black blood, until some angel grabbed him up when he was a few months shy of four. That was eight years ago now. Mother still couldn't stop grieving— and we didn't have much matrimonial bliss. Molly grew more and more mercurial, like that big sister of hers, Mrs. Elizabeth; she'd have boxing matches with the maid, hurl a book at my head. Bob soothed her some; he could spend an entire afternoon holding her hand.

Molly sent him to a highfalutin academy to soak up whatever learning he could. She dressed him up like a lord, in a velvet coat and kid gloves, and I wouldn't be startled if that boy was a little ashamed of his Pa. He didn't have a trace of my Kentucky drawl.

I had to content myself with Willie and Tad, my two wild boys.

They were born after Eddie passed, but they couldn't replace him—
no one could, not in her affections. So they ran wild. They tore up
our little garden, and other gardens in the neighborhood. Tad wasn't
more than a couple of years out of the cradle. He never learned to talk
proper. He had kind of a lisp. Willie and I were the only ones in the
world who could understand his chatter. Tad remained a mystery to
his own mother and our Irish maid, who would fuss over him, because
Tad couldn't solve the *impediment* of buttons and belts. Mary had to tie
him into his clothes, but she couldn't decipher a word he said.

"Mr. Lincoln, you're as bad as your own boys. But I'm wild to see
Bob. A woman can have a normal conversation with him."

Bob had his sights set on Harvard, and that was Mary's doing.
Harvard was closer to Lexington, Kentucky, with all its airs, than it
was to a town in Illinois.

I'd walk to the office with Tad on my shoulders and Willie clutching my waistcoat. I had a premonition that morning, as if something
strange and original might happen. I didn't dare look into the mirror,
because I would have seen a shadow that wasn't supposed to be in
the glass. And I worried that harm might come to my boys. So I spat
three times in the sand and held on to Tad as tight I could, but I could
still feel some presence—like a lick of air with its own perfume—
following me and the boys.

My law partner, Billy Herndon, wasn't that anxious to see them.
He knew how destructive the boys could be, and he was preoccupied
with my political career, even if I hadn't been elected to *anything* in
nine years. Billy was rather petit for a man, but he liked to wear kid
gloves and patent-leather shoes and douse himself in toilet water. He
was in his drams a lot, and Molly couldn't bear the sight of him. He'd
rubbed her wrong a while back when she was the prettiest belle in
town. Billy was rather blunt. He admired her dancing and meant to
compliment her—told Molly she moved with all the suppleness of

a snake. She cursed Billy for that remark and wouldn't invite him into the house, even after Billy and I sealed our partnership with a handshake.

What some folks in Springfield didn't know was that Billy was always hiding runaways. I could come into the office at noon and find a colored boy gnawing on a potato under my desk. Another boy might be in the closet. I'd play checkers with that boy until Billy found the means to sneak him past the slave catchers in a beer barrel. I had to bite my lip and keep quiet. Those catchers had the law of the land on their side.

Billy was always getting into scrapes. He'd crash his head through a window in a brawl, and I had to pay for the damages before the sheriff got to Billy and sent him off to jail. And so he was obliged to forgive me for my own little boys.

He'd stifle a groan whenever he saw Willie and Tad. And he'd sit like a martyr while they climbed up into the bookshelves and tossed our books like bombs. They spilled the ink out of their wells and scattered all the briefs written in my own hand, since Billy didn't have the faintest idea how to write a brief.

And while all this *merriment* was going on, there was a knock on our door. The curtain was down, and I could see a figure in the glass, like some strange shadow. At first I thought it was a runaway slave hoping for some succor. But it wasn't a runaway. Billy and the boys heard me gasp. I was trembling, because that figure looked like a ghost out of my past.

"May I come in?" the ghost asked in the rich voice of a shouter at church.

"Please," I squealed in that damned high pitch of mine.

She was wearing a shawl and a winter bonnet. I hadn't seen her in a century. She was a widow now—her husband had died back in '54, and I hadn't even sent Hannah as much as a note. Clary's Grove had winked out together with New Salem—settlements that never had much of a chance. She had the same wrinkles she'd had when I first met her as a twenty-year-old matriarch. Lord alive, she looked younger now than she did then, as if the wrinkles had reversed themselves. Still, I could see the trouble lines on her forehead. And I knew she hadn't come to Lincoln & Herndon on a social call. I was still trembling when I asked, "How are you, Mrs. Jack?" And while Hannah revealed the tribulations of her son, William "Duff" Armstrong, she still had a crackle in her eye for my own mischief makers.

"They're fine boys, Abraham."

She told me about Duff's *incident* with a certain James Metzker. They'd been attending a two-week revival meeting at Virgin's Grove near the old abandoned site of New Salem. And at a makeshift bar near the revival camp, Duff and a friend of his got into a drunken brawl with Metzker. Hannah's boy was twenty-four—he whacked James Metzker in the eye with his slung shot, the favorite weapon of the Clary's Grove Boys. The slung shot was *peculiar* to Clary's Grove; it was an eggshell filled with melted zinc, covered over with calfskin, and tied to Duff's wrist with a piece of powerful string. Metzker didn't survive that blow. Duff might not have been indicted, but a house painter who was also at the meeting—Charles Allen of Petersburg—swore to a coroner's jury that he had seen Duff strike Metzker in the full light of the moon and hurl that bloody slung shot into the grass; Allen himself had collected it.

"My boy will rot in jail," Hannah said, clutching her shawl. "He was caught in the moonlight by another man."

"Means nothing," Billy said. "We have the best cross-examiner in the county."

"Now don't you give her false hopes," I muttered, pretending to scold my junior partner. "But every witness has a weak point, and I'll find it if I can."

THE TRIAL WAS HELD in Beardstown a month or so later, at the Cass County court. The prosecutor there thought he had a pretty case. Duff was a wild boy like his own dead Pa. He even wore that polka-dot bandanna of Clary's Grove—a sure sign of his guilt. But the prosecutor, who was called Big Hank and had a way of breathing fire at a jury, hadn't bothered to uncover my own brotherhood with Clary's Grove.

He moved among the jurors with all his grandeur and built up his case against Duff *and* Duff's dead Pa. I didn't much care for how he dirtied Jack's name. But Beardstown was his bailiwick, and a lawyer like me had to bite his own lip.

Big Hank produced the house painter, and that man swore up and down that he had seen Duff strike Metzker.

"How can you be so certain?" Big Hank asked with a growl, pretending to attack his own witness. It was an old trick, and it always worked on a jury.

"The moon was in my eye," said the house painter.

Big Hank turned on his heels and said, "Your witness, Congressman Lincoln."

He was clever as a snake, since *everybody* in the courthouse knew how lamentable I'd been as a Congressman. But Big Hank couldn't rile me. I kept that house painter in the chair. And I walked among the jurors—I was familiar with most of their kin. I took out my knife and examined the slung shot that the house painter swore he had found after Duff delivered that fatal blow—it couldn't have stunned a rabbit. It was a mockery of a slung shot, sewn with pathetic string.

I asked the house painter to twirl that weapon for me. He did, and it fell apart in his own fist.

"Mr. Charles Allen," I asked the witness in his chair, "is this Duff Armstrong's slung shot, or is it your own?"

"Duff's," he said, with a squint in his eye. "Swear to *Gawd*."

Then I asked the court attendant to bring me an almanac. I flipped through it and stopped at the day Metzker died.

"Mr. Charles Allen, will you repeat the time you *supposedly* saw the accused strike Mr. Metzker in the eye?"

"*Gawd*, it was on the near side of midnight by at least an hour."

"And the moon was still on the rise?"

"It was like staring at a big fat cat in the sky," the house painter drawled.

I let him *poison* himself with his own words. And then I pounced.

"That's awful peculiar, sir, since the almanac remarks that the moon had set long before the fracas at Virgin's Grove—that big fat cat of yours had dropped right out of the sky. You couldn't have seen Duff Armstrong or anybody else in the light of the moon."

The jurors themselves started to gasp. I dismissed the house painter, but I wasn't really done with him and the prosecutor. And so, during the summary, I looked into the jurors' eyes and said, "The prosecutor likes to call me Congressman, but I was once dirt poor, and without a home. Duff's Pa took me in, fed me, sheltered me, and fixed me up with clothes." And my own knees started to buckle at the mention of Jack—and Mrs. Jack. I'd stunned myself, and I started to cry in front of jury and judge.

"I first met the accused when he was a babe—I rocked him in my arms, sang him to sleep. His Pa was the prince of fellows. Jack Armstrong may have caroused a little, but he helped the poor. And there wasn't a widow in the county who lost her home while Jack Armstrong was around."

It didn't matter what Big Hank did or said after that. The jurors were sobbing as hard as I was. They didn't have to deliberate more than half an hour. The charge of manslaughter—and every other charge—was dropped against my client. I hugged Mrs. Jack, smiled at Duff in his polka-dot bandanna, and lit out of there. I couldn't run fast enough from the residue of Clary's Grove and New Salem. However far I went, or where I landed, seems I was always a second away from drowning in the Sangamon River. I didn't have that raw power to settle in. I was like a man with a price on his head. No one has to chase you hard when you're so busy at chasing yourself.

14.

Long Lincoln & the Senatorial Ball

I T WAS MARY'S fault. She kept muttering to herself like a musical refrain, "President Lincoln, President Lincoln." It was at such moments that she stopped talking about Eddie, our little Angel Boy, and planned to revive my defunct career like some master carpenter with a plumb line and an awl. She swept away all the sad accumulations of dust on my clothes. "Mr. Lincoln, you are the most *unparlorable* man I have ever met. But I will teach you manners, sir. You will require some at the White House. And don't you spoil my chances, hear? Or I might not feed you again."

It was good to see her laugh, to catch Molly's old crinkles. She was a pure strategist. My path to the White House, she surmised, was through her old suitor, Senator Douglas. Dug was a wreck of a man after his first wife died; he went across the capital in tattered cuffs, drunk as a despot, stumbled around the Senate chambers, moved to the shoddiest boardinghouse. And then that slumbering shadow met and married Adèle Cutts, the grandniece of Dolley Madison. Adèle was half Dug's age. Some people called her a divine beauty, but her neck was overlong in my estimation. Yet I wasn't allowed to criticize her. Dolley Madison was the one woman in all of Washington who was kind to Mrs. Lincoln when I was a Congressman. Her first husband had been a Todd, and belonged to Mary's own kin.

Even so, I did have a legitimate gripe against Dug, who had changed his politics *overnight*, in 1854. He pushed the Kansas-Nebraska Act through Congress, shoved it down the throats of Northern Whigs. He offered the miracle of *popular sovereignty*, which wasn't much more than a smoke cloud. It was the Little Giant's way of extending slavery into the Territories—Kansans could vote on slavery and bleed to death over it. The Whigs couldn't fight Senator Douglas. So I *unwhigged* myself and joined the Abolitionists—and their new Republican Party.

Dug was up for reelection in '58, and Molly insisted I grab his Senate seat. "Win or lose, you have *aspirations*. You'll ride Dug's coattails right to the District."

That damn District! It had one cobbled street—Pennsylvania Avenue, with the glow of some eerie stars, because no other street in the capital was lit up by oil lamps, and the lamps sputtered and stayed dead whenever Congress wasn't in session. I didn't want to live at a boardinghouse on East Fourth Street again, where the slave catchers would descend upon us in the middle of a meal and shackle some negro waiter in front of my eyes. The biggest slave market in the land was five or six blocks from the White House. But Molly said I had a certain *prominence* now as a Republican. That's because all the nabobs were either from the East or in the Democratic Party. I gave speeches up and down Illinois for every other candidate—except myself. I'd stand with my back slumped against a wall, give myself a good long scratch, and then slowly rise up and stare into the audience's eyes. A woman fainted once, in Alton. They had to carry her out in an ambulance. Other folks pawed at me, said I could tantalize a whole population.

So I tossed my hat in as a challenger to Dug, even though Republicans *outside* Illinois favored his reelection, figurin' he couldn't be beat. Meantime, I geared up for our State Convention in Springfield that June. I worked for a month on my convention speech. I delivered it in my parlor again and again, while Mary clung to every word. She'd shut her eyes and say, "I want that speech to end in a perfect rapture."

The evening before the convention, I gathered *all* my generals—barely a dozen—and read my speech aloud. Most of my generals weren't pleased. My speech was too far in advance, they said, and would ruin Republicans in Illinois. But these were ruinous times. That vile skunk and piss-pot, Chief Justice Taney, had *dynamited* us all with the Dred Scott Decision—negroes weren't included in the Constitution, he declared. Scott couldn't fight for his freedom in federal court. It didn't matter if he talked like a duke and read the Bible better than white folks. He wasn't a human being. I couldn't pirouette around Dred Scott and palaver about the virtues of the Republican Party. I couldn't pussyfoot. Or we'd all be pissing in the wind. I had to declare war on Douglas and the Democrats. And declare war I did.

Delegates stared at me with a kind of timid wonder in their eyes. I was the savior of the Republican Party. Seems we had no other candidate to run against Dug. The Chicago delegation carried a banner, held aloft by fifteen men. *Cook County is for Abraham Lincoln.* Yet I heard an undertow of fear that the Little Giant would crush us all and prance away from Illinois with my own head on a plate.

And that evening I delivered my speech in front of all the Republican delegates. Long Lincoln stood there on the platform—all alone. My knees were knocking behind the lectern, but luckily, no one saw. I hadn't come to rally us—I'd come to warn.

"We shall lie down pleasantly dreaming that the people of Missouri are on the verge of making their State free, and we shall awake to the reality instead that the Supreme Court has made Illinois a slave state."

I talked of Dug and how the nation had breathed hot air on him and puffed him up into a tremendous man, while the rest of us were small. But Dug couldn't lead us now, not during this strife.

I quoted from the Book. "*A house divided against itself cannot stand.*

"I believe this government cannot endure, permanently half *slave* and half *free.*

"I do not expect the Union to be *dissolved*—I do not expect the house to *fall*—but I do expect it will cease to be divided.

"It will become *all* one thing, or *all* the other."

There was silence for a second—stone silence. And I figured I had made a failure. Then the whooping started up. Hats were tossed into the air. Delegates stamped their feet. The Cook County boys paraded their banner across the hall. And I was *apostrophized* like some damn little god—or lunatic—who would run against the Little Giant . . .

Mother sold a piece of land her father had given her, and she raised up our house on Eighth and Jackson a notch or two. She hired workmen to rip into our attic and add another storey to the rear of the house. "Mr. Lincoln," she said, "I just enlarged our *borders* a little." Our humble cottage now had a Greek Revival look, like her Pa's old Kentucky mansion on Small Street. The outer walls were painted a light brown, and we had dark green shutters to match the brown. There was a whole *infection* of bedrooms with false fireplaces and Franklin stoves. You were swept right into the mansion through a wide stair hall. I had my own library. And Mary's front parlor and family room could have accommodated a hundred generals, at least. It was in here, with its floral carpeting and refined furniture, that Mary meant to have her Senatorial ball—it wasn't a proper ball, with musicians and dancing partners, but a *victory* soiree with all the Republican grandees my wife could round up. I hadn't even run against Dug yet, but I was still Senator Lincoln in her eyes. I couldn't stop Mary's mania, her deep desire that welled through her like some black tornado that could knock down fences and kill a cow. And we had a singular celebration, since half the politicians in Illinois were suspicious of my nomination speech. But that would never have perturbed Mrs. Lincoln.

"I'm blind with pleasure," Mary sang, as the guests arrived. She wore a taffeta gown with a plunging neckline; she had three flowers in her hair, just like Lola Montez, the *danseuse* who'd come from London to give a lecture on the latest women's Fashion. My wife sipped champagne with every kingmaker she could find. She never mentioned Dug or the Abolitionists. It was as if my little victory was outside the *murmur* of politics.

She hired an extra Irish maid for the shindig. Our big table was heaped with condiments and wild strawberries, prairie chicken and quail, piled with peaches and cream. Mary flirted with all the rascals, even with me. And now, with the roar of voices around us, she put her arm in mine, and said with an exaggerated sigh, "Mr. Lincoln, I'm determined that my *next* husband shall be rich. You know how much I long to go to Europe. But poverty is our portion."

"And it will be," I said, "if we have to send Bob to Harvard."

All the flair went out of Mary's eyes. And she began to sob at her own soiree.

"Mother," I whispered, "control yourself."

"I cannot," she said. "I will not. Bob promised to come to the party. He swore on his life he would come."

I pleaded with her. "Bob wouldn't forget. He's still at school, studying for his entrance exams. Not every candidate's son can get into Harvard so easy."

I couldn't console her. She was having one of her fits. She tossed her fan at a general of mine who failed to tip his hat. I could feel the anger course through her, like a bundle of worms. A body might have thought she was possessed with demons—Mother did have a demon in her eye. She shouted at the Irish maids, snarled at her own sister. We all had to wait until her brush fire burned out. Billy called it the queen's *seizures*. But that was unkind. She was without a husband half the year. She bore it much better while Bob was around—he was her anchor after Eddie died.

And finally, after ten minutes or so, while she picked at errant strawberries, that demon in her eye disappeared.

"Bob would have come if he could," she muttered and recommenced to flirt—like Lola Montez.

One of my other generals asked Mary about her discarded beaux, including Dug.

"Oh, it was only the littlest flirtation, but we did have a *penchant* that way," she said with a touch of mystery. She couldn't invite him here, she told the general, because Dug would never stand in the same room with *her* Tall Kentuckian. People gathered around once that wild wind of hers flew in another direction. She had seized hold of the soiree again, lived at the center of it, and I felt more and more alone. Dug was Mary's age, a Senator in his prime. He ruled the District with his eloquence, had a much deeper voice than mine, and would inherit the White House one day soon. And I would inherit nothing. Champagne and wild strawberries wouldn't change that.

I was glad Mary was flitting about—the storm inside her hadn't completely gone away. The champagne shivered in her hand. And then the doorbell rang. I could see her neck curl up like a captured swan—as Bob entered the parlor wearing kid gloves and a swallow-tail coat, like the Prince of Wales. He was fifteen years old, and he had much more swagger and natural handsomeness than his Pa.

I sort of liked having a rival. I wanted him to go to Harvard as much as Mary did, and I would have used every trick I knew to help him get in. I thought of my own Pa, and how he had held me down, burning my books in the fire. I prayed I wouldn't repeat that.

Mary rushed over to Bob. The back of her neck was on fire. He hugged her, and then my oldest boy came over to me. There was a silver pin in his cravat, placed perfectly, but he had a look of alarm. He'd never been around such a rush of grandees, men who wanted a *piece* of his Pa. His lazy eye was acting up. It drifted around in his head. He'd inherited that eye from my own Pa and me. It was the Lincoln curse.

"Gracious," Mary said. She pounced between father and son and rescued Bob like some village sorcerer. She cupped a hand over his errant eye and held it there until the dizziness was gone. Then she grabbed our arms and propelled us into a crush of people. She was Lola Montez in the middle of a soiree.

"Mr. Martindale," she sang in that Lexington lilt of hers, "have you met the Senator's son? Our Bob has joined us to speed along his father's victory."

"Mother," I whispered, "I can't lick the Little Giant. No one can."

She was purring now, at her own party. Standing close to her and Bob, I could almost feel her heart beat under that taffeta gown like a solitary engine that would smash whatever was in her way— Republicans, Democrats, and the Little Giant.

15.

Dogging Dug

EVEN I HAD to admire that damn flibbertigibbet on wheels. It was fiery red, with a silver caboose, and raucous railroad boys rode shotgun on the roof. Somebody would have thought they were guarding a sultan rather than a Senator. Dug had his very own *line,* supplied by the Illinois Central, with a sleeping coach, a cannon, a butler, and a brass band. His greatest ornament wasn't that caboose or the cannon, but Adèle, who accompanied him. He wouldn't spend a minute without *that* ornament. Mary had assembled her own little treasure of hoop skirts and gowns, but I had no private car. I had to campaign as the country lawyer with a red handkerchief and a rumpled shirt. Dug had already *condemned* my wife as a Southern aristocrat, so her silky bearing would have rubbed my image as a backwoods lawyer raw.

I had to leave her behind. I traveled with no one. I had a single seat in the cars, without the littlest reward from the Illinois Central. My only lodgment was a stovepipe hat. Mary raged against her own fate as a female general who was banished from the field.

"I'm nothing but a worthless cow."

"Fiddlesticks. Ain't a belle in Springfield who's worth the flowers in your hair."

She was silent for a moment. I couldn't tell if she was building up a tornado, or figuring out an answer to my strategy. My talk of flowers had confused her. She didn't sulk. She simply realigned whatever troops she had and pretended to laugh.

"Gracious, you're a wicked man, Mr. Lincoln. Tomfooling with your wife, while you intend to gallivant across Illinois like Sir Galahad."

"Galahad? With prairie dust in my pocket?"

She perused me up and down, my own Puss, the warrior cat I had to leave behind.

"Mr. Lincoln, that's not a proper handkerchief—flaming red. What will all the voters think?"

"That I'm devilin' Dug."

She perused me again; there wasn't an ounce of self-pity in my Puss. "That might not be enough," she said. "Dug's a fighter, always was. And you're a pestilential fly abuzz in his ear. He's running for President from his own stage in Illinois. He can't anger the cotton men or the mechanics in New England. So he has to walk a tightrope. And you have to pluck him off that rope and let him crash to the ground."

"How?"

She smiled like some angel of mercy with raucous red-brown hair. And then her eyes tightened a bit. "Why, you have to contradict his contradictions and give him a very hard push."

I had to find him first. If he was in Cairo, with its ragged crop of farmers and merchants and rivermen, I landed there a few hours after he did. Dug was hoping to tar and feather me as a friend of the negro and to scarify every voter in the nation, *and* in Illinois. "Mr. Lincoln and his Black Republicans want to vote, eat, and sleep, and marry with negroes." He said that if we allowed such a *colored invasion*, the prairies would turn black as coal at noon. Illinois would suffer an eternal midnight. That's how he milked the crowd and mortified them.

And after Dug went off with that fancy wife of his, I would catch the tail end of the crowd, and say, "Oh, the Senator is much too fine to debate with a sucker like me."

Country folk liked that and they listened. "All the powers on earth seem rapidly combining against the colored man. They have him in his prison house; they have searched his person, and they have him bolted in with a lock of a hundred keys."

I challenged Dug to a series of debates—fifty of them. The Democrats mocked my little proposal, said I ought to latch onto a circus or menagerie if I wanted to find my own audience. Still, Dug was much shrewder than the Democratic Party. Half the nation knew Dug would be the next President, but if he protested too much, folks might fear he was afraid of the man from Springfield. So he decided to carry me along right on that tightrope of his, turn me into his accomplice, whom he could whip whenever he wanted and mollify with a pat on the head. But he whittled me down to seven debates—that's all the time a Senator like him could spare. Some of my generals wanted to bargain with Dug. But Mary said, "Don't you bargain. Seven is more than enough."

❀

HE HAD A DARK pompadour over one of his blue eyes, and a fine blue suit with silver buttons. Half of Ottawa wanted to shake his hand. It was a town of nine or ten thousand souls, eighty miles southwest of Chicago, and the site of our first debate. There wasn't a bed to be had in all of Ottawa—folks who arrived a day early slept on cots in some parlor or on the pews of a nearby church. And the line of those who arrived on foot or by wagon train stretched for miles—children, farmers, mechanics, old men, and women with babes in their arms. The town was deluged with dust; it clung to your mouth like sand or sea salt, but with a much more bitter taste, and a dust cloud sat right over the platform where Dug and I were meant to have our *mix* that twenty-first of August.

There wasn't a single chair or bench. Everybody in this little nation had to stand. The crowd must have swelled to twelve thousand or so. Dug had the advantage of speaking first—and last. He could refute whatever it was I had to say in the final half hour of the debate. It was like a jury trial, where the Senator was his own judge and jury box, and I was the plaintiff who appeared at his own lynching party.

His advocates in the audience kept shouting, "Hit him again, Dug, hit him hard."

I could sense how excited he was, rearing to rip at me, though I could hardly catch his eyes or his blue velvet coat in all that dust. He would come out of that dust storm just in time to pull Democrats right into his speech. He was building up the lather until all the faces around him were red with hate. He strutted on that platform, and said that my remarks about the colored man were like whispers that would fan a dark and endless fire.

He held the audience in the flat of his hand—he was like the shrewdest minstrel without the bother of black paint. Dug left me enough room to hang myself and not an inch more. I tried to tell folks that when Dug invited *anyone* willing to have slavery—he was blowing out the moral lights around us. But no one listened. I couldn't even hear my own knees knock in front of those red faces. Dug had demolished me in that first debate.

And six days later, at Freeport, while his cannon roared, a curious memory stuck in my head. We were just south of the Wisconsin line, where I had once chased Black Hawk and his phantom braves, a quarter century ago. I recollected all the little settlements on fire, the charred faces of white women, and all the ripped calico and shattered crockery, like celestial signs in the dead grass. And the Little Giant was slippery as Black Hawk—he'd whistle into the wind whenever you tried to pin him down. This canvass was just an excuse to hone him up for his cavalcade to the White House. He tested all his skills against the Tall Sucker, as the journalists commenced to call me. Freeport had swelled to fifteen thousand under a gray sky. There wasn't much place to stand or sit. I saw fathers with a child on each shoulder, like *saltimbanques* at a circus.

Dug attacked from the moment he climbed onto the platform with a flower in his lapel, peering at this crowd of Abolitionists in *Lincoln* country. He kept snarling and calling them *Black Republicans*. And they snarled back and serenaded Dug with a song of their own.

—*White Republicans, white, white, white.*

He strode across the platform and knocked on the boards with the nails of his boots. It was his own silent thunder, since you couldn't hear a sound in that hullabaloo—except that same chorus.

—*White, white, white.*

I saw one of his eyes twitch. He wasn't used to all that mudslinging. He'd never been vilified in his home State. He rose up like a rooster and said, "I have seen your mobs before, and defy your wrath."

There were stenographers in the crowd, hunching over and trying to copy our words; I was startled by their tight little fists that moved like squirrels across the page; they couldn't capture every word, but it didn't seem to matter. The Democrats picked up whatever they wanted to hear. They barked at us in their papers, called our canvass a conspiracy arranged by Lincoln and his rude band of "nigger lovers." Republicans barked back. But it was all part of the same circus. We'd become a monster show, a perennial match between the Tall Sucker and the Little Giant. And if you disagreed with Dug, he'd call you an *ulta* and crucify you. It hurt like hell, because Dug was always civil whenever we'd meet away from the battlefield.

⁂

DUG AND ADÈLE were the royal couple here at Jonesboro, the southernmost portion of Illinois, and the site of our third debate. "Little Egypt" was a Democratic arsenal, with dirt-poor farmers who despised all blacks. And Dug was hoping to skin me alive in this narrow neck of land that was further south than Richmond on the map. He wouldn't have to snarl at Jonesboro, where no Abolitionist had ever reared his head. The farmers cackled behind my back, called my little band of constituents "the Springfield Freaks."

But Mrs. Dug wouldn't subscribe to all their cackling. "Mr. Lincoln," Adèle said, sipping her afternoon tea like some Londoner. "We'll pay no mind to this pestilence. It's beneath us. And I'm just *tortured* your wife couldn't come. We'd have gladly given Mrs. Lincoln a berth on our train. I so enjoy her company. Are Tad and Willie still wild Indians?"

"Yes'm," I muttered, just like Pa. That's how he would have addressed a woman of such high Quality. And for a moment I kind of wished I had brought Molly along. I'd misjudged Adèle. She was as fine a general as the Little Giant. She talked to the wives of every farmer and merchant at the Union House, had a little tea party while she sold them on Dug. And then I imagined what Molly would have done in Little Egypt—she'd have fought the farmers with her fists, and the stenographers would have scribbled about the massacre at Jonesboro . . .

I sat with Dug and Adèle and gobbled some cranberry cakes. We laughed and reminisced for over an hour, but that didn't stop him from crucifying me in Little Egypt, and that damn town conspired with him. There were posters all over the place that said niggers and their allies weren't welcome. I found an effigy hanging from my doorknob at the hotel—a paper doll in a stovepipe hat, with both hands gone and half his neck missing. I didn't complain; the manager himself might have made that doll. So I went downstairs and climbed onto a speakers' platform that could have been a trapdoor. I had no friends in Jonesboro; the farmers had ripped up our Republican banners and took our tubas away. Dug figured he could *et* me alive. He performed for these farmers like some fanciful player, stroking his cravat, and shouting as if I were a phantasm on *his* private stage. He never once looked at me, acknowledged who I was or what right I had to be there. Dug danced to the edge of the platform, grabbed at the farmers' filthy paws, and kept harping on the Declaration of Independence, said that its signers did not mention negroes once "when they declared all men to be created equal."

There was no point contradicting him, not in that sea of red faces, where I was a notch lower than a dog—but I did try. "Douglas has set about seriously trying to make the impression that when we meet at different places I am literally in his clutches—that I am a poor, helpless, decrepit mouse, and that I can do nothing at all."

"But you are a mouse," someone roared.

Another farmer interrupted him. "That's a hog up there on the platform," and he commenced to snuffle and snort.

I had to scream above that storm. "I don't want to quarrel with Douglas—to call him a liar—but when I come square up to him I don't know what else to call him, if I must tell the truth out."

There wasn't much truth to be had, not in Jonesboro, where folks hunkered around the platform with mischief in their tiny, blinking eyes. I was lucky to slink out of Little Egypt with the skin on my back.

I WAS DISHEARTENED as I sat in my seat, with prairie dust on the windows and a sinister sun burning right through the glass, as if the canvass had become my own little Sahara, and I was riding the cars from one crucifixion to the next. It was like *wrassling* with a mirage. I couldn't seem to get my engine running at Charleston, which was Abraham Lincoln Country and the site of our fourth debate. Dug was the same ol' rooster. He attacked and attacked while I hemmed and hawed like a man in front of a gigantic spittoon. He had a smoothness I'd never have, a fiendish sulfur, with his broad forehead, his deep baritone, and the liquid moves of an impresario courting his public on a platform that was his private dance floor. He had what Billy called a kind of *magnetism*. I couldn't dazzle the way he could, with gold on his cuffs, the finest toilet water, and I was like a scarecrow with rust all over, and flakes falling out of my hair. But I wouldn't let him have his own sway. *I won't surrender,* I said, won't let Dug and his cohorts plant slavery over all the Union, regard it as a common matter of property, *and speak of negroes as we do of our horses and cattle.*

I didn't gain much ground on Dug. His partisans could smell the kill—I was ripe for it. He arrived with his company of tubas for the fifth debate, at Galesburg, near the Iowa border, swaggered on the platform, but he stalled in the middle of his attack. "Where is *this* Abraham Lincoln? Where . . ." His eyes seemed to startle inside his own head. His tongue thickened. He kept coughing into a silk handkerchief. The Little Giant had commenced to lose his voice. That black pompadour of his didn't have the same assurance. The canvass was wearying him and his wife. They wanted the fine cutlery of a private railroad car, and not the heat and dust and bonfires of a campaign, as Billy liked to say.

But I thrived in the heat and dust—wind and rain had always

been my companions on the circuit. I could live out of saddlebags. Dug could not. The Little Giant had come to a halt. Dug had desecrated the Founding Fathers, I said, trying to impose the footprint of slavery wherever he could and denying that all men were created equal—this was the electric cord that linked us together. I wiped my brow with my flaming red silk handkerchief, my one bit of pomp. I watched Dug. His voice was too hoarse to reveal very much. For the first time I had Dug and Adèle on the run.

I thought he would give up the *juggle*, collect his brass band, and ride away in his private railroad car with Adèle, who looked almost as pale as he did, as if the prairie had melted her down a little, removed all her shellac. I felt sorry for that royal couple, with their ruffles and silk parasols and velvet hats, and I wondered if I would have to climb onto the platform with Dug's ghost.

I should have realized that the Little Giant had too much at stake. He couldn't disappear from this rumpus just like that. He'd have lost his standing in the nation, so he rallied a little, came to Quincy, a river town right on the Mississip, with all his regalia—a brass band that filled up a railroad car, sentinels and marchers, and a float of sixteen maidens in the buckskin garb of prairie huntresses. This regalia made so much noise it covered up the arrival of Dug and Adèle at the meeting hall. Dug wore a winter cloak in October and a scarf around his neck that couldn't mask his viscous, yellow eyes. A pair of his own marshals had to escort him to the platform, for our sixth debate, else he would have toppled into the crowd. He swayed while he was up there, like a man caught in a dizzy spell. But I wasn't watching him or his wife. I was watching *our* live raccoon that crouched on top of a pole—the raccoon was a symbol of the old Whig Party, and we were hoping for a *resurrection* in Quincy, that all the "raccoons" in the audience would remain alive and vote Republican. But the Democrats had brought their own raccoon, a dead one, with its tail bound with strips of wire to a boatman's oar, so that the dead coon swung like a pendulum with pointy ears and prickly gray fur with a lone streak of red.

While Dug stumbled across the platform, our live raccoon kept staring at that streak of red fur. Dug had a pendulum of his own, as he kept saying over and over again that our Republic could exist *forever* divided into free and slave States. He saw a path to the Presidency and he took it—never mind that it was also a formula for a broken Union, an invitation to civil strife. Oh, he would cure *every* ill once he rode to the White House in the President's barouche.

I didn't even have the time to answer Dug. That live raccoon let out an electric wail that *pierced* the hall—it was somewhere between a growl and a long, relentless hiss—and he leapt off his perch on the pole, sailed over our heads like a furry ball with magnetic teeth and decapitated the dead raccoon with one rip of his jaws.

Several ladies in the Republican part of the arena swooned. Dug himself wandered in a daze, as if he'd been driven off a battlefield. And I wasn't immune to that wild leap. I shivered some, and wondered how a single raccoon could overwhelm our rumpus . . .

We stayed in Quincy overnight, but I couldn't sleep. It wasn't Dug's *palliations—and lullabies*—all the untruths he told—that kept me awake. I expected that, and even more, from him. I remembered Dug from the old days in Springfield, that essential swagger he had along with his fine linen, how he discovered the latest dance steps and scrutinized all the belles on Quality Hill, and considered every other *beau* in the room unworthy of him. His arrogance and self-aggrandizement had boosted his fortune and near crippled him blind. And it didn't seem to matter much that the nation would plunge into the ether, like that maddened raccoon on the pole.

We boarded the *City of Louisiana*, Dug, Adèle, and I, and sailed down the Mississip a hundred and fifteen miles to Alton, presiding over a panorama of cliffs. Not a word passed between us. Dug had to guard whatever little was left of his voice, but Adèle did invite me to dinner. We sat in the captain's cabin. The river had a yellow gleam. We hadn't come near Alton, and it felt as if we'd stumbled upon a landless universe—I squinted hard, but I couldn't uncover the shoreline. I was lonely all of a sudden. I missed my wife. Mother had *remade* me, even if I still had a hard time manipulating a proper knife and fork. Adèle pretended not to notice, while Dug pulled me right out of my reverie.

"Lincoln, we are moving toward an abyss. And the negro will not help us climb out. But I'd disappoint Illinois if I canceled the seventh debate."

Dug, you're the abyss. That's what I wanted to say. But I juggled with him.

"Well, if you're too ill, Senator. I wouldn't want to chase you."

He coughed, and poor Adèle had to wipe the spittle from his chin.

"This canvass has turned into a pugilistic contest," he suddenly said, gulping on all that spittle. And he left the captain's table, muttering to himself. I sat there with his wife. We ate in silence. She wouldn't utter a sound until she finished her compote. And then Adèle said how much her husband admired me—*admired me with a knife in his hand.* He was mortally tired, she said. "Every gesture he makes, every move, is *a little run* for the Presidency."

We'd have another Buchanan, a President who *compromised* with every spoon he took into his mouth . . .

And Adèle, too, left the table, with the bustle of her gown wandering like a deep ripple in the water. I sat there a spell, watching the implacable pull of the Mississip.

THE SUN SAT in my eyes when we arrived at the piers—could have been a half-blind beggar coming from the holy wars. And then there was the dazzle of Molly's own blue eyes, as if I'd come out of the deep, and had never once sighted land or sky and a red-brown crop of hair. I'd been bound up with other men's needs too long, and had shut in my own desires.

Molly wore a cape like some marine; I still had a rainbow in my eyes. I didn't give a hoot that Bob was with her on the pier, in the blue coat and white pants of a Springfield cadet. I picked her up in my arms and whirled her over the edge of the water until her dress flared out and her crinoline seemed to crash in the wind like soft glass.

"Mr. Lincoln," she said with a breathy growl, "I'm not a sailboat—I'm only your wife." But she laughed as I waltzed her across the pier. I forgot the canvass. I forgot Illinois.

She didn't gloat at Dug when he came down the gangplank with Adèle, a huge handkerchief wrapped around his throat. She curtsied to the Senator and took Adèle's hand—the wives of the two warriors. Adèle couldn't linger. She had to get Dug away from all the wind off the river. He looked saturnine at the beginning of the debate. His silver buttons weren't so clean. In a voice that trembled and could hardly be heard a few feet away, he went on the attack. "I hold that the signers of the Declaration of Independence had no reference to negroes at all when they declared all men to be created equal. They did not mean negro, nor the savage Indians, nor the Fejee Islanders, nor any other barbarous race."

His legions had arrived with their banners and floats, but Alton didn't belong to Dug—the Sangamon–Alton railroad had brought Molly and Bob at a special half-price *Republican* fare. Even with all our own bustle, I still had a bitter taste in my mouth. The crowds had dwindled; most of the stenographers were gone; this match couldn't have been much news in Manhattan—or London—or Philadelphia. A world-renowned Senator waging war against a local man for the privilege of his own seat, a seat I'd never win. But I couldn't let Dug go on lying—and lying—and lying, even if my words went into the wind.

We were at the courthouse square right on the river. Dug did his usual prowling, preened in pure silk.

And so I dueled with him for the seventh time. All the dust of the canvass had come to an end, with the fizzle-gigs and fireworks. Still, I wasn't finished, wasn't finished at all. It wasn't about Lincoln vs. Douglas—it was Lincoln vs. himself, the storming in my own heart. I had to unravel his lies, for my own sake, a stitch at a time. And the greatest lie of all was that the colored man was not included in the Declaration of Independence.

I told that audience of diehards and stragglers, the last remnants of our debate, that I had to combat this damn lie. "I combat it as having a tendency to dehumanize the negro—to take away from him the right of ever striving to be a man. I combat it as being one of the thousand things constantly done in these days to prepare the public mind to make property, and nothing but property, of the negro in all the States of the Union."

There were only two stripes, I said. "The one is the common right of humanity, and the other the divine right of kings. . . . It is the same spirit that says, 'You toil and work and earn bread, and I'll eat it.' No matter in what shape it comes, whether from the mouth of a king who seeks to bestride the people of his own nation and live by the fruit of their labor, or from one race of men as an apology for enslaving another race, it is the same tyrannical principle. . . ."

My throat was dry. I was all done. The bands had stopped playing, the crowds dispersed, and I could hear the river roil. I hadn't helped a soul. Black men would remain in their prison house—that house of a hundred keys—separated from their own kin. And the Republic was perilously close to some cliff.

I watched Dug step into his silver carriage with Adèle, that handkerchief still around his throat. His partisans grabbed the horses' gear and wouldn't let the carriage move until Dug smiled at them. It was a sinister smile—Dug looked deranged, as if the canvass had killed some essential part of him, had unmasked the horror of his own lies. But it wouldn't hurt him none. The Democrats controlled the Legislature—and the Statehouse would pick the next Senator from Illinois.

I stood around as the workmen commenced to tear up the platform and pile the planks of wood into wheelbarrows; they wore leather mittens and cotton masks to guard them from the dust and debris. They were reckless with the wheelbarrows, bumping into stanchions like wanton angels with their own mad abandon. They left deep tracks on the courthouse lawn. But they had their own miraculous rhythm; the platform vanished in front of my eyes, with all the banners and balloons. And in less than an hour there wasn't a single sign that Dug and I had ever come down the Mississippi to have a debate in Alton—except for those rifts in the grass from all the wheelbarrows.

16.

The Giant Killer

THE RAIN POUNDED our roof on Election Day, like pellets from Satan's own scattergun. Our cellar flooded, and if Mother and I hadn't found her bailing pails, we would have had our own Mississippi under Jackson Street. The fence tore right down in the wind and left a deep curl of wood. My captains had been correct—we took the popular vote, but the Democrats held on to their precincts, and the new Legislature, like the old one, would belong to Dug; come January, that Legislature would vote him in for another term as United States Senator. I told my captains, and told my wife, "I expect everyone to desert me except Billy."

I was out on the road half the time, trying to outrun death and destruction while I paid off some of our debts. Folks would stare at me, whisper to their wives, and I couldn't tell if I was a pariah or some little god who'd come off the plains. I was fifty years old, with layers of dust in my wild black hair and only one odd shirt in my carpetbag. The waitresses along the route were dustier than I; they wouldn't let me alone until I signed my autograph. The inns often ran out of bread and meat, but folks kept staring, even while they were famished. "That's Lincoln," they said. "That's him—Sir, can we *tech* your hand?" And I would ride off into the dust again, month after month.

Mary was chagrined that I wouldn't come home. She'd flail me in her letters. "The boys miss their father. They cannot recollect his face. They wonder now if Mr. Lincoln is tall or short. Or maybe there are two Lincolns—first the husband and then the Far Rider, who spreads himself across the counties. We all wish the Far Rider would come home."

The Far Rider was forlorn. Canvassing had nearly cost me my home and my practice. Lincoln & Herndon might have petered out if I hadn't ridden through dust storms like a desert creature in search of new clients. And when I did get back to Springfield, we had another blow. Bob failed his entrance exams to Harvard—he couldn't solve the enigma of geometry, or rhetoric, or natural history. Mary locked herself away in her room—no one could draw her out, neither Willie nor Tad.

I was stunned when Bob arrived at my office. He had never been fond of visiting Billy and me in our unruly quarters. His linen was so fine, and he had that silver pin in his cravat—a gift from his mother, an heirloom her own father had once worn. His lower lip was trembling.

"Father," he said, "I've come to work."

"I don't understand you, Son."

"I decided to apprentice myself to you and Billy."

I was as suspicious as an old fox about to raid a barnyard. "Is that what you want to do—tie yourself to Lincoln & Herndon?"

"No," he said. "But I'm a failure, and failures don't have much choice."

"Billy," I said, "lock the door." And we barred every other client from the premises. Then I sat Bob down in my own rocking chair.

"You're no failure," I said, in Bob's own schoolboy English. "It's your highfalutin academy that failed you. It didn't learn you a thing, and I paid that tuition with my blood. Now tell your Pa straight out what it is you want."

"To go to Harvard, sir."

"Then Harvard it will be."

It was Mary who had given him those Eastern airs—my wife believed in all the privileges Harvard could bestow upon a boy from the West. Springfield was a dusty barn she had to tolerate on my account. If she'd had her druthers, she'd have gone up to Harvard with Bob as its first female scholar . . .

Billy caught me shivering, and it was the worst case of trembles he had ever seen. I wasn't much of a magic maker. I neither had the money nor the prestige to get my boy into Harvard. And while we pondered, there was a knock on the door. Billy had pulled the curtain down and we couldn't see through the glass. And then I heard that delicious hauteur of Mary's voice.

"Mr. Lincoln, I don't want to repeat myself. Open that damnable door."

Billy opened up, and Mother came marching in. She had a cape covering her nightdress. And she'd ventured downtown in her slippers. But Mother didn't storm at Billy and me. She smiled like a half-crazed mountain cat.

"Mr. Lincoln, did you really promise to get your son into Harvard?"

Before we could utter a word, Mother informed us that we had to send Bob to Phillips Exeter Academy to polish up for his entrance exams. And then she was gone. That damn academy was where all the little Eastern dukes went once they had their hearts and minds set on Harvard . . .

Billy went off to run an errand, and I sat alone in the dark. Suddenly there was a noise coming from the street—like the whisper of a huge animal. I peeked through the blinds. A bunch of citizens had collected outside to serenade me. I was *Long Lincoln, the Giant Killer.*

Strangers continued to come by and gawk at the house. Dug had returned to the Senate, but *I* was the Giant Killer. Who could have imagined that seven debates—in wind and rain—had become a slice of Illinois? It didn't seem to matter who had won. I had to ride the rails; folks wanted me to relive my particular *calvary* with Senator Douglas—the clatter in the cars, the dust storms, the effigies, the bonfires that blazed in my eyes, the dead squirrel that near ruined our sixth debate.

Then a letter arrived at my office. I had to stare twice at the envelope. It was from Henry Ward Beecher's Plymouth Church in Brooklyn—that Church was practically a shrine. Senators and governors communed there with Ward Beecher, and now the Church was inviting the Hon. A. Lincoln to speak there on any topic and was willing to pay two hundred dollars—I was stupefied. How could I hope to palaver in Mr. Beecher's pulpit? I'd heard about his wild hair and even wilder Abolition ways. Women swooned in the aisles after one of his sermons.

I waved the letter in front of Billy. "I can't lecture there. They'll laugh at such a yokel. I don't have Beecher's gifts."

"Mr. Lincoln, you've been offered two hundred dollars. That's more than most mechanics make in a year."

Plymouth Church wanted me in November—but I decided on next February. Meantime, Molly scoffed at my campaign clothes.

"Father, you can't walk into Plymouth Church with prairie dust. It's the pinnacle of culture. We'll have to find a tailor for you."

I couldn't argue once Mary looked at me with her sharpshooter's eyes. I went to Woods & Heckle, the tailor on the square. It took Mr. Woods ten days to measure me up for a suit. I groaned at the bill. Suddenly Plymouth Church might become a losing proposition. I'd come back with ten more bills to pay.

I had the trembles for three whole months. I was frightened of

Ward Beecher and his Church—scarified of that man with the wild hair who had sent rifles to John Brown and wrote sermons about him and his bloody border raids. Brown was a lunatic with a long beard, and Beecher had called him a prophet in the wilderness. He startled the whole congregation at Plymouth Church when he produced the very chains that had bound the *prophet* at Harper's Ferry, and he stomped on them like a rattlesnake. I kept having nightmares, and in all of them I was waylaid by strangers in clerical collars and couldn't find the right road to Plymouth Church. Mary found me in the parlor, pale as a ghost in my nightshirt. She must have heard my nocturnal screams. We had our own bedrooms with a door in the middle after Mary had the house remodeled in one of her mad schemes. It was the latest fashion—the lord and mistress of the manor with connecting rooms, only I wasn't much of a lord, and we didn't live in a manor. Yet I'd crawl into her room in the middle of the night, and at other times I'd wake with Mary in my arms, scented flowers in her hair or between her bosoms, like Lola Montez.

But I could have sworn I'd been seared by lightning. I hopped like a wild Injun—had to clear my head—and strode outside in my slippers. And that's when I saw them under a dark moon, men and boys doffed in apparel as ill fitting as my own. None of them had been measured by Woods & Heckle, I'd imagine. Their shins poked freely from their pantaloons, and their ragged cuffs didn't reach much past their elbows; they outgrew whatever they wore, the way I had done. They'd walked fifty miles from Beardstown, with nothing but sips of well water and a few crusts that some farmer must have left for the crows.

"Are you Abe the Giant Killer?" their spokesman asked, a boy with a baritone as deep as Dug's.

"I'm Abraham Lincoln," I said, reveling in the aroma of rich earth on the boy's shoes.

"Well, we couldn't visit with ye in Alton or Jonesboro, sir. But none of us care for Douglas. He's with the railroad. And they stole property from Pa, threw us off our own land. We hear the conductors on the Illinois Central wouldn't even unlock their empty saloon cars, so you could have a little rest during the canvass—that's how much the railroad line was for Douglas."

That boy wasn't wrong. Billy had tried to negotiate with the railroad, but the damn conductors were all Douglas men, and wouldn't give me a lick of water, let alone a private berth in one of their cars.

Mother appeared out of the shadows, not in her nightdress, but in the same taffeta gown she'd put on at the Senatorial ball, with the plunging neckline and all—and those Beardstown boys were *galvanized*. Their eyes didn't stray very far from that swelling under her throat. They were like children clutching a kite string that held them in its sway.

"Mr. Lincoln," she said with that Southern lilt of hers, "are you going to entertain our guests in the light of the moon?"

She must have pitied the grime on their faces, pitied their long pilgrimage, and perhaps she saw them—man and boy—as potential voters. Motives don't matter much. What matters is she accompanied them all into the house, fed them from her pantry—marmalade and butter, water and milk and wedges of Jack cheese, and country bread as rich and fine as a silver lode. She sat with the boys, didn't say a word about politics to the men, didn't denigrate Douglas; and as that melody of Molly's floated through the house, all the phantom creatures flew out of my head, and I sat there, with the fire crackling, and watched these men and boys from Beardstown with their mustaches of milk and honey, and I didn't mourn the end of my political career.

17.

Manhattan Melancholia

I STEPPED OFF THE train at Jersey City with enough dust on my clothes to fill a prairie schooner. I had to wend my way through a crush of people to the pier at Exchange Street, where the men wore pugnacious little hats and the women had hair piled up like coiling snakes. I strode onto the Paulus Street ferry with my trunk and umbrella—and was stunned as we rocked across the Hudson River that February of 1860. It was like being pulled into a mirage of the Manhattan shore with every splash of wind on our faces; the buildings near the dock looked like a panorama of raw red teeth. And the buildings behind the dock could have been a labyrinth of even redder teeth. There seemed no end to it; the metropolis could have stretched to some eternity of its own. But all that luster was gone as we drew close to the ferry slip; I saw a rotting warehouse, where men with crooked backs toiled in the sun, *tinkered* in ragged undershirts, hammering heaps of snarled metal into more and more macabre shapes . . .

I was delivered to a palace, six stories high and loaded with pale granite squares that covered up the corners of a city block. The glass rotunda at Astor House climbed to a height that dizzied the mind—it was like standing under the cast-iron roof of the world with an end-less vertigo.

My apartment was as grandiose as a church vault, with gas lamps that glowed from within recesses in every wall. The windows had enormous swaths of glass that looked down upon a square as broad as a battlefield, where pedestrians dodged a deluge of horse-cars. The golden spigots near my bed pumped fresh water—hot and cold—and the hand towels were heated. But I wasn't allowed to rest. The Young Republicans seized hold of me. I wouldn't be delivering my talk at Plymouth Church; they had calculated that such a temple couldn't seat enough Quality folks. The venue had been changed to the Great Hall at Manhattan's Cooper Institute, which could hold a little army of grandees and their wives, and that only made me more and more blue.

Meanwhile I was ferried out to Brooklyn on Sunday morning to hear Henry Ward Beecher at Plymouth Church, a big brown barn on a quiet street. I couldn't imagine what all the fuss was about until I stepped inside the chapel, with its circular benches and a pulpit that floated above us like the cupola of a balloon held in place by pillars that resembled silver strings; my head swam at the sight of that contraption, and I was fearful that the pulpit would fall flat out. But it didn't fall. And Ward Beecher landed in the pulpit with his searing blue eyes, a melodious voice, and crop of thick blond hair that fell to his shoulders. I was glad my own squeals wouldn't have to compete with his *soft* timbre. The ladies all flocked to him, no matter what the subject of his sermon was. He stared at us from his cupola and talked of John Brown. He was shrewd as a backwoodsman, praising Brown and damning him in the same breath. "I disapprove of his mad and feeble schemes. ... His soul was noble; his work miserable. But a cord and a gibbet would redeem all that." He hesitated for a second, gripped the rails of his cupola, and sang to us in a deep whisper:

"Brown went to his death as men go to a banquet, and as he was led forth to the sacrifice he kissed a little child."

The blue eyes rolled about in his head like someone in a trance; it was a trick that medicine men used at a monster show. But none of them had Beecher's flair for drama, none of them had Beecher's passion. And slowly, he reconstructed John Brown.

"An old man, kind at heart, industrious, peaceful, went forth, with a large family of children, to seek a new home in Kansas. . . . He saw his first son seized like a felon, chained, driven across the country, crazed by suffering and heat, beaten like a dog by the officer in charge, and long lying at death's door! Another noble boy, without warning, without offence, unarmed, in open day, in the midst of the city, was shot dead."

I could hear men and women weep; I watched them clutch and flail their handkerchiefs, dab their eyes, as they sat on those circular seats, enthralled, fixing on Beecher's words, mimicking his sounds with little movements of their bodies. And then that gentle whisper was gone.

"The shot that struck the child's heart crazed the father's brain," Beecher said with a *Shakespearean* wave of his arms and a stamping of his foot that sounded like a thunderbolt coming from his cupola. "He goes to the heart of a Slave State. One man; and with sixteen followers!" Beecher ogled his eyes like a monster to make his point and tell us how such a *phantom* and his followers captured the arsenal at Harper's Ferry. That demented old man, he said, "is the most remarkable figure in this whole drama. The governor, the officers of the State, and all the attorneys are pygmies compared to him."

That snarling look of his grew into an angel's smile as he turned John Brown into a martyr. The whole congregation fell silent with the wonder of his tale. They would have resurrected Brown, if they could have, and carried him up to the cupola. And for a moment I did have a vision of John Brown standing with Beecher in the pulpit, his face all scratched and blood on his beard.

❦

THE MINUTE I ARRIVED at Astor House I realized that Woods & Heckle weren't the right tailors for Manhattan, and I wasn't much better off at Plymouth Church—I didn't have Mr. Beecher's soft satin look. So I wasn't sorrowful when a snowstorm was predicted for the evening of my lecture. I hoped to God that the snow would keep all the Quality folks away. I was filled with such melancholia I didn't know where to turn, whether to slink back across the ferry and ride the rails to Illinois, or lose myself somewhere in this wilderness of people. I'd been to Manhattan with Mary, three years before, when we visited half the emporiums and dry goods bazaars on Broadway; I watched that wonderment in her eyes, that pinch of gluttony, as if she meant to try on every sable coat and silver fox muff in Manhattan, while the floor managers stared at my country duds with suspicion and disdain . . .

The Young Republicans snatched me from the foolscap pages of my lecture and acted as my bodyguards on a stroll up Broadway. My *unholies* must have unhinged me a little, because I'd never seen such hullabaloo, like waves of people spilling out of a python's belly and shouting their own mad songs. Old men assaulted you, selling the finest silk umbrellas. Merchants came roaring out of their shops to entertain you and lure you inside with their feast of goods—fur coats and boots the color of blood, footstools and firearms, &c., &c.

The real encounter wasn't on the sidewalks. The road itself was a great shopping bazaar, with the interruption of coaches and other vehicles. There were tents in the middle of the road, hucksters who sold their wares out of a leather shelf that reminded me of the bits and pieces of an accordion; there were pickpockets and acrobats—they were all polite; and every single one had a sense of politics and a point of view. I could have spent hours engaging them in long discussions. The women and men were all skitterish around me. They recognized my stovepipe hat and long, lean look from some sketch of my debates with Dug. It's kind of odd but I felt comfortable near these hucksters and acrobats, as if they were vagabonds and circuit riders of their own, and their frenzied gestures could mimic the finest sandpaper— and rub off a bit of my melancholy.

I resisted the Young Republicans' pleas to sit down with their kinsmen, who would have mortified me with their Manhattan airs, and I labored over my lecture until dark. I kept thinking of John Brown and Beecher in his floating pulpit. I could sniff the storm from my window. I watched the swirl of snow until it was time to leave for the Cooper Institute.

The Great Hall was a huge rectangle about as long as a city block. The suckers had to pay twenty-five cents to get in and hear the wild man of the West. But the snow had kept a good portion of people away—still, there was a crowd of over fifteen hundred crackers in their Quality clothes. The women seemed as tall and aristocratic as Adèle Douglas; their diamond necklaces gleamed under the gas lamps. I hadn't lost my wits, even with all my sadness. I employed my own *spy*, asking an old acquaintance from Springfield to stand as far back as he could in the hall and signal with his cane if I couldn't be heard.

I stumbled over the first few sentences as I tried to lower the pitch of my voice. I didn't stamp my foot like Mr. Beecher or wave my hands like a windmill. I stood correct. I had to squint, because I wouldn't wear my spectacles in front of all the grandees, who might have thought a little less of me in my specs. And I lit into them like a duke.

Mary had worked with me for two whole months—had me shed *most* of my drawl. I would read the Bible with her in a sonorous tone, practice my vowels in front of the mirror until I spoke with the voice of a metropolitan saint.

I shoved the Founding Fathers into my speech. "This is all Republicans ask—all Republicans desire—in relation to slavery. As those Fathers marked it, so let it again be marked, as an *evil* not to be extended. . . ."

I told the audience that I wanted to address a few words to the Southern people. "When you speak of us Republicans, you do so only to denounce us as reptiles, or, at the best, as no better than outlaws. You will grant a hearing to pirates or murderers, but nothing like it to *Black Republicans.*"

I couldn't avoid the debacle at Harper's Ferry—it was like a bullet in the brain that would echo through eternity unless I stopped it right here and now.

"You charge that we stir up insurrections among your slaves. We deny it; and what is your proof? Harper's Ferry! John Brown! John Brown was no Republican; and you have failed to implicate a single Republican in his Harper's Ferry enterprise"—if an enterprise it was. A ticket to madness, I'd say.

"John Brown's effort was peculiar. It was not a slave insurrection. It was an attempt by white men to get up a revolt among slaves, in which the slaves refused to participate."

Then I stared down from the lectern; there wasn't a sound in that hall except the sizzle of gas. Men clutched their own arms, women hid under their veils, as if my words had corrupted them a little, like a snakebite. They were fearful—and eager to listen.

"You will rule or ruin in all events," I said of the Southerners.

"You will not abide the election of a Republican President! In that supposed event, you say, you will destroy the Union; and then, you say, the great crime of having destroyed it will be upon us! That is cool. A highwayman holds a pistol to my ear, and mutters through his teeth, 'Stand and deliver, or I shall kill you, and then you will be a murderer!' "

I appealed to all the men and women in the audience, that we should not be frightened away by menaces of destruction to the government, *nor of dungeons to ourselves.* "Let us have faith that right makes might, and in that faith let us to the end dare to do our duty as we understand it."

The silence was suddenly broken. The audience rose up from its seats—menfolk stamped their feet and tossed their hats into the air while their wives waved handkerchiefs. A few of them even whistled in an unladylike manner. My throat was as parched as a turkey caller after the hunt; the bones in my hands were as stiff as the dead. And then all these folks came rushing up to the podium, like I was some wonder who'd come to disturb their tranquility. They grabbed at my elbow to see if I was genuine or not. I was fearful now. What sort of devilment had I unleashed? Was I *another* John Brown, sent to rile the "countryside" of Manhattan, with my talk of highwaymen? I'd come into their lion's den with my own Republican thunder, and none of them were fit enough to steal it from me.

Yet I knew I wasn't made for these city folks, with their silk scarves and lorgnettes and opera glasses that a general might have used to espy a battlefield a couple of hills away. Bedecked in their silver fox coats, they had such a look of *acquisition* on their faces, it was as if they could own me with a simple clasp of the hand. I understood how Black Hawk must have felt when he was first trundled from town to town like a peacock in war paint, and folks were startled to hear him palaver in their own tongue and reason as well as they could. So I lit out of there after the very last handclasp with a prominent Manhattan prince.

18.

Prairies on Fire

I ARRIVED UNDER A witch's sky, black as blood, without the stationmaster to greet me or clutch my gripsack; every stall was locked in the middle of the night, but the miasma had commenced to seep out of me in the cars, the closer we got to Illinois. I wanted to wipe out the memory of that Manhattan hall, but I couldn't find much rest in Springfield. I had crossed some invisible line, and I couldn't go back to my regular route.

First they would come one at a time, stand outside the storm-riddled gate of our home on Franklin Street, with their hats in their hands, peek wild-eyed at my window and disappear, and then they arrived in droves, with their children, too. Some had traveled two hundred miles in a covered wagon; others had arrived on foot, and when Mary offered them a cracker or a crust of bread, they fiddled with their hats and muttered, "We *jest* came to have a look at Mr. Lincoln." And then they were gone, replaced by yet another crop of pilgrims, until I figured I'd never have a moment of peace.

Next my generals arrived with their whiskers and stern chins and all their tally sheets and declared flat out that my little hobnob in

Manhattan had propelled me right into the Presidential race. My talk at the Cooper Institute had spread like wildfire as a Republican credo. That still couldn't explain the pilgrims outside—most of them were as unlettered as I had once been. My generals told me I'd have to hurry up and present a line of attack if I wanted to be a candidate. The taste was in my mouth, a little. But first I had to meet with some of those pilgrims.

Not one of them had heard about that shindig in the Great Hall or had seen any handbills summarizing the speech. Then why had they come on a pilgrimage to Springfield? They shrugged their shoulders and covered their eyes with their hats. One of the pilgrim women was carting a tattered picture of Adèle. I thought she had witnessed my debates with Dug, and that had fired her up.

"Ain't that Dolley Madison?" she asked.

The other women tittered at her. "Dolley's *daid.*"

No, it had nothing to do with handbills or debates. These farmers had heard a fly buzz, and my name had been passed from farm to farm like an incessant melody, and a son or a neighbor or some vagabond who had eaten their corn told them about a lean man who had come out of the dust to represent a cousin of theirs in the circuit court, and they fell in love with tales of his Kentucky drawl, and so a whisper flew from farm to farm, and they had to see this Abraham for themselves, squat outside his house like some half-mad pilgrim and move on. They weren't thinking of canvasses; most of these men had never voted. Andy Jackson could still have been President for all they cared; and Dolley Madison could have been his mistress in the White House.

My communion with these pilgrims lent me a kind of raw courage, and I told my generals they could scratch my name on their tally cards. I was the Party's dark horse, with all the pale markings of a palomino—a maverick without much chance. Seward of Manhattan was the lead horse and Governor Chase of Ohio was hanging hard on to his tail. Chase men and Seward men got into brawls. We heard about these epic battles that could spill out onto the streets of a town until lamps shattered and Seward men lay moaning at the side of a ripped-up road. My generals worried that Seward men got bolder with each melee, and would *whup* us when it came our turn to fight. But they were mad dogs that loved the smell of each other's feculence. And while their generals battled among themselves over the convention site, our generals convinced the National Committee that the convention ought to be held in Chicago, where Republicans could find their Western whoop, and where we could pack the house with our own mad dogs. We stole the lightning bolts right out from under Seward and Chase.

They didn't build that monstrosity—the *Wigwam*—we did! It was a huge wooden barn at the corner of Lake and Market meant to look like an Indian lodge. It was put there to keep all the delegates far apart. New York had to navigate the entire floor to get near Pennsylvania. And those two were our biggest rivals.

I was still a failed Congressman with bony kneecaps. Photographers arrived from everywhere to make me over with a new kind of dazzle—they went at me like voracious warriors. They plucked the hairs from my nostrils, covered my moles with facial powder, but I was the same sad sort in the mirror. Mary sent the photographers flying with her broom, called them mountebanks. I still had no dazzle. So reporters on the Republican payroll plunged into my past, and while I told a couple of whoppers about chasing a bear with an axe, they invented a tall tale of their own. Suddenly I was *reborn* as the Rail Splitter, Old Honest Abe. It hypnotized my own generals as they pictured me in a coonskin cap. I wouldn't pose with an axe in my hand, but my generals prevailed. Our Republican journals screamed that the prairies were all on fire for the Rail Splitter. And it sure felt that way, as pilgrims rose out of some dusty high-plains fire and descended upon Springfield like a horde that was here to stay.

I couldn't even ride to the convention site in Chicago on my own tail; my generals didn't want me near the Wigwam. *Keep cool,* they wired. So I played *fives*—Canadian handball—in a vacant lot behind the *Illinois State Journal,* which had a wondrous rear wall. There was meanness in me, a kind of malice—that fury on the plains was inside my skull. My damn future was beyond my control, like a brushfire that crackled in the dry heat and went out into the wind. I destroyed my opponents with the help of that dry wind, won every point, slapping at the leather ball until my hand was raw, while Mary ran to the telegraph office and returned with chits of paper that could have been written in Chinese. And then she returned without the chits and a smile on her face, and we didn't need another word from the Wigwam that eighteenth of May. We'd grabbed the Republican nomination right out of Seward's fist *after* the second ballot.

"Father, we've won the nomination."

It didn't *taste* like victory—without all the sweat and stink of the Wigwam—though our little cannon boomed from behind the courthouse in Springfield, and the fire bombs shot into the sky with a whistle that havocked my ears for half a day.

No one but Billy understood my mood. I was bored—*badly* bored. A Presidential candidate had about as much bustle and wit as a totem pole. I couldn't criticize the President and his pusillanimous overtures to the South—he was walking into a maelstrom, while our Southern Sisters sang sweet songs into his ears and fanned his fat behind with palmettos.

It felt to me as if the prairies were on fire—not for Lincoln, as the newspapers said—but from sadness and futility. There's the rub. The nation was heading toward ruin. The peacemakers in our own Party asked me to deliver a statement that would reassure the South. There was nothing I could deliver. The South was holding a pistol to my ear, as I had informed the folks at the Cooper Institute, and I didn't intend to pay any tribute to some highwayman.

Suddenly that new appellation of mine seemed fit, since the Rail Splitter had hacked the Republic in two. I couldn't have wandered into the Deep South in my stovepipe hat and walked out alive. There were rallies against the Rail Splitter in Richmond and Mobile, and Manhattan endured the same unrest, as Mayor Fernando Wood, I'm told, talked about marrying up New Yorkers with King Cotton.

The Democrats didn't need a Rail Splitter—they chose suicide, split up into two warring wings, but I longed for an election, not an *embalmment*, and not a wake, where half the country wouldn't have minded to see me dead.

Billy tried to pull me out of my own mordant humor. He knew I would have the *hypo* if I had to remain locked up in Springfield like a convict, with two whole months before Election Day, and he lassoed my generals into agreeing to a little public tour of the hinterland that September—I could be seen in public at the fairgrounds—at the very edge of Springfield. I thought I would smile a bit, shake a couple of hands, and juggle my hat. But no one could have appraised the crowd; folks had come from everywhere to meet the reclusive candidate. Billy and I rode to the grounds in my carriage; we couldn't find a bit of breathing space in that thicket of people. My faithful old mare shied and snorted and stamped her feet. "Whoa, Cricket," I muttered, "whoa."

We must have had enough voters at the fair to fill five counties. A razzle of young Republican *Wide-Awakes*, looking like phantoms in their black oilcloth caps and capes, ran through the grounds with rails topped with torches of burning rags to celebrate the Rail Splitter— they almost set a little girl's hair on fire. The sheriff might have locked them up as public nuisances if Billy hadn't intervened and got some of the Wide-Awakes to give up their burning rags. Their friends and accomplices shouted, "We want the Rail Splitter—speech, speech, speech."

I wouldn't roil these folks at the fair, wouldn't alarm them with any talk of a dire future. I climbed onto the footboard and screamed as loud I could, "I'm sworn to silence. It has been my purpose, since I have been placed in my present position, to make no speeches."

"Aw, Abe," someone shouted, "you can make an exception for us."

And others picked up that refrain. *Exception—exception—exception!*

A woman with burning red eyes under her bonnet asked, "What are we gonna do about those boogers in Alabam?"

And that refrain was picked up. *Boogers—boogers—boogers!*

I tried to calm that crowd. "Alabama's still in the Union, last time I heard."

Another woman cried, "We love ye, Abe, we really do."

Folks shoved closer and closer to the carriage. I watched men and women whip their heads from side to side like religious penitents. Several Wide-Awakes climbed onto the footboard; the carriage rocked. Cricket reared and bucked at the men and women behind her. Some of these same Republicans slashed the carriage roof with their pocketknives and near took out Billy's eyes. They hadn't lost their presentiment or their vigor.

"We love ye, Abe, we really do."

It was like swimming around in a pond of people. I couldn't breathe, but Billy kept his cool. He grabbed one of the pocketknives, sliced through Cricket's reins, and while people pawed at me, their thumbs perilously close to my eyes, he shoved me through the carriage's metal bars, and right over Cricket's rump, held me until I could clutch her mane, launched me with a light kick, and leapt off the carriage.

"Lincoln," he said. "Run for it—I'll manage."

I saw him stumble, and I scooped him up onto Cricket's back, and we rode like Injuns through that crowd, with people getting more excited as we passed—*the Rail Splitter, the Rail Splitter*—until I lost count where we were riding and who I was and what I wanted to be. I could feel the heat of burning rags, notice the top of a tent, as I rumbled in and out of lucidity. I was a pale rider rather than some Presidential candidate, and I had to calm Cricket or she might have crushed a child. We rode like that, through time and eternity, on a fairground that would never end.

THE DISTRICT
1861

19.

Victory Ride

IT WAS ARCTIC weather when we climbed aboard the train, with a freezing wind that could knock off a man's hat and send it sailing across streets and alleys covered in black mud. The depot was as dark and hangdog as some ancient world with blood on the moon, yet half of Springfield had crowded onto the boards to bid farewell to the Rail Splitter. They could have been spectral creatures in that dark wind—the depot rocked as if a devil lived right under the boards, and the trees swayed with a somber music, and I had to wonder if we were riding into a whirlwind.

These folks hadn't come to harm the Lincolns. They carried signs and sang to us, banged their drums and blew on their cornets, and I had to hush them up a little.

"My friends—here I have lived a quarter of a century, and have passed from a young to an old man. Here my children have been born, and one is buried. I now leave, not knowing when, or whether ever, I may return . . ."

"Abe," said one old man, "you'll be back in no time. We won't let that damn District keep ye too long."

The cornets started up again, with their bleat crashing into the roof of the depot till it sounded like a series of wails. Mother shivered. I couldn't find much happiness on her face, and that mystified me. Ever since she was a child in Lexington, she had dreamt of becoming Mrs. President, but somehow she was reluctant to leave Illinois, where half the country had courted the Lady Elect. She worried about Bob, who'd come down from Harvard to be on board with us, worried about Willie and Tad, who were dressed up like little field marshals and might lose their hides in the District. Atlanta's own newspaper, *Confederacy*, could see the Potomac "crimsoned in human gore," and Pennsylvania Avenue "paved ten fathoms deep with mangled bodies," if I or any other Republican baboon was sworn in.

The Presidential train belched a bit of smoke and then churned out of Springfield on that morning of black mud, banners flying in the wind. Folks were lined up all along the tracks, looking like some serpent in Sunday clothes that went on for miles. We had our own private car, replete with crimson curtains and a carpet as complicated as Ali Baba's den. My lips were trembling. My mind was playing tricks. I could see myself, a live man sitting in a bier that could have been a rowboat on wheels, while men in white war paint surrounded my strange ambulance and let out a deafening huzzah.

There had been rumors that the Rebels would seize Washington and the White House before I had the chance to arrive—and my own inauguration would rocket out into the wind. I felt like a wild man communing with his own wild fate, the President Elect of a nation about to evaporate into smoke. Union commanders wanted Mary and our boys to travel on a separate train—the five of us were too much of a target, they declared—but Mary refused. She would stay in the *line* of danger, with me. I was caught in the middle of this tug, but finally these commanders were overruled by Winfield Scott, the Union's

General-in-Chief. Old Fuss & Feathers wired from the District that Mary and the boys would be a perfect camouflage. It was much safer, he insisted, if I was surrounded by my family. That didn't prevent him from hiding sharpshooters along the Presidential route—the riflemen sat in their own invisible aeries, but they couldn't hide the rifles, with that incessant gleam of their long silver snouts; it seemed much more sinister than anything the Rebels could produce.

Willie and Tad had a walloping time with every soldier and civilian on board. They couldn't stop exploring the cars. Our college boy was more reserved. The ride and all its fanfare was a damn intrusion. His classmates at Harvard had poked fun of him as the Prince of Rails, and he couldn't have had much tranquility under the Presidential glare. I'd never met a boy as secretive as Bob. He stood in the corner and whispered to his Mama a whole lot. He could have been conspiring against the Union, and I would have been the last to know. He must have been born in some sweet-water well that didn't have much truck with politicians and reporters.

I couldn't coax Mary into coming out onto the rear platform of our car at all the little stops, but folks kept insisting. "We want all the Lincolns!"

So she appeared on the platform with our three boys and waved one of her little hands, while I hopped around like a jackass. Mary was frightened of this fuss—local dignitaries crowding into the Presidential car, stroking the curtains and stomping up a storm. The constant banter terrified her. She saw Rebels lurking everywhere. Mother had pictured the Lady Elect as a new kind of Republican queen, but the politicians on the train weren't partial to queens.

Mary was much more at ease when we stopped at some governor's mansion, and she could wear one of her new dresses at the governor's ball ... and dance with Bob, the Prince of Rails, who was photographed as much as his Pa. His secretiveness was suddenly gone. He chatted with reporters, flirted with the prettiest gals. He wore the finest clothes, and he didn't scoff at my own irregular rigging.

So I trusted Bob, let him guard the Presidential satchel, the oil-cloth bag that contained the first and last copies of my inaugural address. But Bob had flirted too much, had had too much to drink. He came to me one morning with bloodshot eyes.

"Father, I lost your satchel."

I couldn't believe there was malice in him, that he'd lost the satchel on purpose to vex his own Pa, poke at my innards with a stick. He hid behind his Harvard shellac—that's what bothered me the most. "Father, you mustn't worry. I'll buy you another satchel."

"That's damn foolishness," I said. "Told you what I was carrying inside."

He must have seen the anger in my eyes—and for the first time in his life, Bob flinched. I was half a trigger away from striking my boy. I'd inherited Pa's *hate*, that penchant to flair up and hurt whoever was in front of him.

"I'm awful sorry, son. But when did you last see that gripsack of mine?"

"Sir, I left it with the hotel porter—I think."

So we rushed downstairs to the lobby, Bob and I, and rummaged through all the bags behind the manager's desk, but my sack was gone. No one, not even my escorts, dared look at me. Folks moved as far as they could from the President Elect. I didn't have the heart—or the enterprise—to rewrite that address.

And then a porter appeared. He'd found my gripsack behind a chair. I rummaged inside and recognized my own scrawls.

"Boys," I said to *everyone* in the lobby with a smile, "that darn thing contains my certificate of moral character, written by myself."

Bob wasn't fooled. All that reserve of his had come back. He'd sniffed out something he'd never seen in his Pa, and he was mortified.

He put a Harvard ribbon round his neck and wore it for the rest of the ride, like some talisman that would protect him from his own Pa.

I HAD TO HEAR from the tap of a telegraph clerk that Jeff Davis was inaugurated while I was still riding the rails. It was an uncommon insult. I'd have to wait until the fourth of March to be sworn in. So it seemed like some savage delusion that the country—or part of it— had a new President, housed in Montgomery, Alabama. Folks on the Victory Train figured I might not be inaugurated at all—that a bomb might explode, or our car could be derailed by a team of saboteurs. I didn't want my boys to suffer on account of their Pa's foolish wish to seek out the Presidency. Seems there was a plot afoot in Baltimore to assassinate me after our entourage arrived. Even Baltimore's marshal of police was involved in the plot. Was the whole country *gambling* against me? That's what some of the railroad men believed.

"Where did you get such candid information?" I asked.

"From Allan Pinkerton," said a vice president of the B&O line.

"And who in thunder is this Pinkerton feller?"

A detective in a derby hat, with a cigar in his mouth, said, "I am."

I had heard of Pinkerton—and his accomplished fleet of spies— who protected the railroads from every sort of sabotage and broke many a skull. But I was stupefied when I learned that this pugnacious detective and his spies had been summoned by the railroad to protect my life and limb.

It turned out that the Presidential train was loaded with *Pinkertons*; Tad and Willie even played with a couple. And a journalist who pretended to be in the employ of *Godey's Magazine & Lady's Book* was a Pinkerton, too. She was a rough, rawboned creature who advertised herself as Mrs. Small. The boys took a shine to her, and she was the one female on the Presidential tour who didn't arouse Mary's jealous nature.

Pinkerton used her as a "firefly" to prey on certain nefarious men. Mrs. Small, it seems, had slipped into Baltimore and insinuated herself inside that little band of plotters, who had their own militia company. She'd become *intimate* with the leader of the plot, a Corsican barber named Cypriano Ferrandini; he was a captain of the militia who worked at Barnum's Hotel and was sympathetic to the South. It disheartened me to hear that tale of Mrs. Small lending her body and soul to such a rascal. Allan Pinkerton seemed to take some pride in her sacrifice, but Mrs. Small was much more sensitive than her boss and noticed my dilemma.

She blushed behind that hard bark of hers. "It was dreadful, Mr. Lincoln, being around that skunk."

The barber and his band meant to meet our train at Baltimore's Calvert Street Station, where the Presidential car had to be pulled across town to Camden Street by several teams of horses and connect up with the Baltimore & Ohio train to Washington. The barber would create a scuffle at Camden Street, divert the marshal of police and all his men, and while our party drove through Baltimore, the barber's men would attack the Presidential car and tear us to pieces.

It had all the ardor of *Beadle's Dime Novels.*

"Forgive me, Mrs. Small, but even the barber's name is difficult to swallow."

I'd offended this lady detective, I could tell. I kissed her hand, but she wasn't looking for gallantry. Mrs. Small rolled up one sleeve and revealed where the barber had scratched her arm with a razor—it was an awful funny way of handling her.

"That's how he wanted to buy my devotion," she said.

Then Governor Seward's own son appeared at my hotel in Philadelphia with a note from his Pa and General Scott, who watched over the Union from his headquarters in the District. The note mentioned that infernal barber and the marshal of police. Baltimore had been given over to the rabble, according to Seward and Scott. The *Secesh* would soon be in a position to strike, and if the whole of Maryland fell, the District would be in danger.

"Mr. Lincoln," said the railroad detective, with that cigar still in his mouth, "you'll have to leave Philadelphia at once—under cover."

But I had to address the Legislature tomorrow at Harrisburg, and I wasn't going to shift my plans on account of a rebellious barber and his accomplices in the police, not while the Union was unraveling right in front of my eyes.

"We'll leave from Harrisburg," I said. "But I'll have to tell my wife."

"Sir, you cannot tell a living soul, or our own plans will run awry."

"I'll still have to tell my wife."

So we summoned Mary to our salon at the Continental Hotel. She could read our faces before I said a word. I showed her the report from General Scott. Mary plummeted into a chair.

"I will not leave my husband alone, not during such a calamity. Bob can look after Willie and Todd."

"Madam," chortled the railroad detective, "there are Confederate spies in Philadelphia this very moment, watching our every move. We'll have a disaster on our hands should we signal to them any change in your husband's itinerary."

It was then Mary must have noticed that Mrs. Small, who sat in the salon with us, wasn't a journalist from *Godey's*.

"I suppose you're covering this event for the *Lady's Book*, Mrs. Small. Well, you can ask me all the questions you want on our clandestine ride to Baltimore."

"Mother," I said, "be quiet."

Mary sat seething in her chair, while I turned to the detective.

"And what will happen when the Presidential train arrives in Baltimore with my wife and three boys on board? That barber could hold them hostage."

"Not at all," said Allan Pinkerton. "By that time the cat will be out of the bag."

I had to travel in a soft felt hat, with an unfamiliar coat hunched around my shoulders. We left Harrisburg like thieves in the night, on a special two-car train, with not a single light turned on. My sleeping berth was much too small for my legs. So I had to sit up half the night with my two detectives. I learned a lot from Pinkerton. He told me that every other damn train in the area had been *stalled* until ours got through. And the telegraph lines going in and out of Harrisburg had been cut, so the Confederate spies would be *wireless* until I reached the capital.

Pinkerton and his lady detective were smoking pitch-black cigars. They cleaned all their armaments with a little rag. I could see that something was pestering Mrs. Small.

"I listened to your speech at Trenton," she told me. "And you said you were the humble instrument in the hands of the Almighty, and his almost chosen people. Now why is it we were *almost* chosen?"

I could have spent half my canvassing on that single word.

"I'm not so sure. We all see ourselves as the chosen ones. And it ain't the evil of slavery that separates us. The foul smell is in all our bones. Perhaps it will always be there, on both sides."

※

WE ARRIVED IN BALTIMORE at 3½ in the morning. The sky was black as a coal bin without a bottom, but with a gray edge like the mouth of a furnace lit long ago and with a residue of ash. The Calvert Street Station was deserted, except for one man—the marshal of police. He stood there all alone, with silver notches in his uniform. He was very tall. He must have been looking for some train that had been rerouted. He was clever enough to realize we might have come in under a secret schedule.

Pinkerton didn't panic. He sent Mrs. Small out to greet the marshal, who recognized her as one of the barber's sweethearts. But what was she doing here at this haunted hour, stepping off a train that wasn't even lit? He was about to blow his whistle when Mrs. Small cracked him on the head with a slung shot that was a kin to the kind Duff Armstrong liked to carry around his wrist.

That marshal dropped to the platform like a bolt. Mrs. Small hid him behind a gigantic bin. Then the barber arrived out of nowhere— in a cape, like Prince Hamlet. Cypriano Ferrandini was trussed up with pistols and knives and bullet pouches. He hadn't come alone. He had five of his militiamen, who were also trussed up. The barber had a broad mustache. He couldn't have been older than thirty. He pecked at his teeth with a metal pick. I'd never seen a feller with so much sauce. He bowed to Mrs. Small and clapped his hands.

"Bravo, my sweet. I took you in. I branded you, like my own little cow. None of my boys ever laid a finger on you. And this is how you reward me? You're a government tart. I should have figured as much."

Pinkerton clutched my arm. There was a harsh fire in his eyes.

"Don't move," he said. "You'll get her killed."

"But he'll butcher her on the spot," I said. "I won't be able to bear it."

"Lincoln, sit still!"

And he kept me there with the curious cadence of his voice. I was caught in Allan Pinkerton's spell. He was master of this car, not the President Elect. I peered through the window. The barber had plucked a razor with a pearl handle out of his coat. Mrs. Small wasn't under its sway. She smiled at the barber.

"Cyp," she said with a soft growl. "It won't be the first time I've been cut by a man."

Her smile immobilized the barber and unmanned him for a minute. Then all his meanness came back. He strutted around Mrs. Small with the weaponry he was wearing. He cut her once with the razor—it was the lightest of nicks. I was mortified. I was witnessing some kind of lovers' spat. He nicked her again. I knew the cuts would grow deeper and deeper.

I shoved Pinkerton aside and climbed out the car.

"Captain Ferrandini, I'm the feller you're looking for."

The barber was bewildered.

"Almost didn't recognize you without your tall hat."

"That little lady is a friend of mine," I told him. "And if you touch her again, you'll swallow your own razor before I'm finished with you."

Mrs. Small was shivering. It wasn't on account of the barber. She'd been paid to protect my life. And I'd come waltzing out of the car, but the barber had forgotten her—and that was fatal. He'd never even noticed the sailor's awl cupped in her hand. I could see it flash in the dark like a silver tooth before she dug it deep into his neck. It startled him. He couldn't seem to get rid of that silver tooth. He caressed its wooden handle and wavered in the dark while Mrs. Small whispered to me, "Get back into the car."

I stood there. The five militiamen froze as the barber twisted about and fell. And then they ran. I got back into the car with Mrs. Small. She wouldn't allow Allan Pinkerton to wipe the blood from her face.

"Mr. Lincoln," he said, "you must never repeat a word of what happened here. That barber doesn't exist."

If anyone yapped about the plot, Pinkerton and his agents would be compromised. They'd never break into another gang. The B&O would have to admit that it couldn't protect a President Elect along its lines. And General Scott, with all his medals, would seem like an impotent child.

Teams of horses suddenly appeared; trainmen attached them to our car.

We rode out of the Calvert Street Station in the middle of the night and traveled past houses that looked like rotting teeth. The moon was out, and Baltimore could have been a cavalcade of meandering avenues and roads. I didn't see much sign of a mob, just trails of black mud, as we had in Springfield. One lamp was lit, but mostly we moved in the dark. We arrived at Camden Street, where a train was waiting; our own little car was hooked up to it. The ride was smooth as the Devil. I couldn't even hear the harsh *sting* of the wheels. I kept thinking of that Corsican barber and the nicks he left on Mrs. Small, like crazy wounds of love.

20.

Listen to the Mockingbird

Poor, poor Buchanan.

Our bachelor President was a stout sort of feller who had his own niece at the White House, Harriet Lane, or Miss Hallie, as she was known in Washington circles. She was an orphan who had lived with her uncle since she was eleven. Miss Hallie was tall and blonde, with violet eyes and a handsome bosom that breathed like a wild bird. She'd gone with Buchanan to London, when he was our minister over there, and Queen Victoria was so taken with Miss Hallie that she called her Madame Ambassador. Harriet wasn't much different at the White House, where everyone knew her as Buchanan's First Lady.

It was a signally somber mansion. Miss Hallie had remodeled the whole shebang, but it was still like a cavern with a whole lot of staircases. A gaggle of young men fluttered about in soft collars and black coats. I couldn't tell if they were Buchanan's messengers or secretaries. They whispered in the President's ear and wouldn't welcome me or my Secretary of State, a little man with a long nose and rumpled gray scalp. Seward had brought me along to meet Miss Hallie and the President. Before I could introduce myself, a dog that was bigger and fatter than a prairie wolf lumbered down the stairs on monstrous paws, growled at us, and lay down next to Buchanan, with one eye open and one eye closed, just like his master.

Turns out Buchanan had a terrible squint. Seward had once sat in Congress with him, but that wasn't much of a recommendation—the President had a Cabinet full of traitors who were feeding arms and ammunition to the *Secesh*. Buchanan and Miss Hallie would have preferred Seward in my place. He was a gentleman, but Seward had much more sand in him than a President who coddled Southern Senators and let the Union slide into the wind.

The public never took to Buchanan ... and never tired of his niece. Women named their daughters after her, copied her copious hair. They stood in line to greet Miss Hallie. That lonesome tune "Listen to the Mockingbird" had been dedicated to her.

> *I'm dreaming now of Hallie*
> *Sweet Hallie, sweet Hallie ...*
> *Listen to the Mockingbird,*
> *Still singing when the weeping willows wave.*

Harriet Lane kept staring at me like some White House witch, with that wild bird beating under her throat. I was startled by the contempt in her violet eyes, her "gracious chill," as others called it. She clung to Buchanan with her own big hands; the President had a sizable paunch and a shock of silver hair.

Hallie harped about my scrape in Baltimore. "Good Lord, you were nearly scalped."

Pinkerton must have told the President and Miss Hallie about that mad barber. And she was chattering like that mockingbird in the song—*sweet, sweet Hallie with the sour face*. I wanted to light out of there and avoid the witch. She curtsied to me and Mr. Seward with a strange air of triumph. Then Miss Hallie whispered—in a rather loud voice.

"Mr. Lincoln, sir, be warned. The Confederates have their own sharpshooters now, and they mean to disrupt Inauguration Day— they're coming up to the District in droves."

My Secretary of State was furious. "That's idle gossip."

"Not according to General Scott."

"Then we'll hear it from Scott," Seward said, scowling at Miss Hallie.

Buchanan was eager to vacate the White House, but not his Hallie. She loved the chandeliers her uncle had installed, paid for out of his own pocket. She was mistress of the levees and government balls. She got along with the Cave Dwellers—the capital's upper crust—and must have looked down upon Mary and me as nincompoops . . .

General Scott was next on Seward's list. We visited him at the War Department. The tallest man in Washington at six foot five, and also one of the fattest. Old Fuss & Feathers was seventy-five years old. He received us while napping on the biggest sofa I had ever seen. He snored with one eye open, like Buchanan's great big dog. It took two of his aides to rouse him from his slumber. But he was alert as Moses once his eyes weren't shut.

Told him how chagrined I was about having to sneak into the District in a slouch hat.

"Ah," he said, suddenly serious, "but you couldn't have come in any other way—*alive*." He had sent his sharpshooters to Baltimore— they were crouched in the rafters when our night train arrived at the Calvert Street Station. But I can't recall one of 'em firing a shot at the barber and his cohorts.

Seward's bushy eyebrows commenced to twitch with alarm. "That is yesterday's news, General Scott. What about the inauguration? There will be spies *everywhere* in the capital—and an abundance of lunatics who have promised their brothers that Mr. Lincoln will never be sworn in."

"Ah," said that oracle from his sofa. "But the President's safety is now in my hands. I may have lost some soldiers to the *Secesh*, but my sharpshooters are loyal to me. I'll bottle up Pennsylvania Avenue with our cannon, and if those Rebels raise a stink, I'll blow them to hell."

All his bluster couldn't seem to calm Mr. Seward. He had sensed the danger long before I ever did. Seward did not want to see the Republic ripped apart by wolves. He was much more worried about my welfare than the bachelor President and his niece, or Old Fuss & Feathers with his cannon and his company of sharpshooters.

"Mr. Lincoln, I am not so sanguine about General Scott's sharp-shooters as he is."

"Seward, neither am I."

I couldn't get Miss Hallie's tune out of my head. We'd become a nation of mockingbirds, full of malicious chatter. I wondered if Hallie had put a hex over the White House. So I was awful curious when a cavalry officer in a blond mustache scuffled with my body-guards outside my door at the Willard. This officer wasn't carrying any papers—or a weapon in his sleeve. He couldn't have been much of a sharpshooter, but my bodyguards still knocked him about. He had one of Miss Hallie's calling cards in his possession. I sent the bodyguards away while the cavalryman commenced to tear off his mustache—it was Hallie herself. And she looked much sadder away from the President's rooms.

"Please forgive my little masquerade. But I would have been mobbed if I hadn't worn a mustache. And I must speak with you, Mr. President."

I didn't know what to think of this sudden visitation. She'd become a vagabond, dislodged by her own conspicuousness. A revenue cutter was named after her, the *Harriet Lane*. Songs about Buchanan's niece were as loud as any cry for war. She was a prisoner at the White House who couldn't go abroad without creating a stir.

"Your uncle's still President, Miss Hallie. I'm nothing but the next sucker in line for his chair."

I felt like a *sucker*. Buchanan's incompetence, his downright disappearance from the Presidency, had encouraged the Disunionists, led them into open rebellion.

"But I had no right to be so rude," she said. "And I was *unforgivably* rude."

"What's eating you, Miss Hallie?"

It was the *Secesh*. Folks blamed her Uncle for not holding the country together. She had tried, but whenever she sat Unionists and the *Secesh* at the same table, they flung food and crockery at each other until she and her uncle had civil war at the White House.

Better the White House than the nation.

I didn't say that to Miss Hallie. She and Buchanan swept calamity under the rug—had their shindigs and let our Southern Sisters slip into their own masquerade of a "union." Now we had hell to pay. And I had to stand in the dark, with blood and rain about to piss from the sky.

"I should have been more generous," she said. "That's my flaw. I'm much too possessive. I didn't want to share Uncle's abode with you and Mrs. Lincoln. You shouldn't blame him. He can't abide the District. I'm the one who's happy here, minding my uncle and his *store*. That's what it is, Mr. Lincoln—the nation's store, where everything under the sun is up for grabs. And I *worshiped* every minute—the politics, all the little flirtations with Uncle's generals. I am a horrible flirt."

I wanted to shake Hallie like a rag doll. Her damn insouciance had blinded her to everything.

"You don't have to move out, Miss Hallie. You can board with us at the White House. Mrs. Lincoln will look after all your needs."

She didn't understand a word I'd said. She started to laugh, and then I saw the harsh lines under her violet eyes, like a revenue cutter out of control, the *Harriet Lane* in hostile waters.

"Oh, I couldn't leave Uncle to his own devices," she said, clutching my hand. "But I wasn't fooling about those *Secesh* sharpshooters."

I promised Miss Hallie I'd be careful, not to assuage her guilt, but to let her have her little dream of destruction. She'd conjured up half those sharpshooters in her head, and there wasn't much I could do about that other half. She put her mustache back on and her cavalryman's cape. I kissed her hand, like some bittersweet adversary, and my bodyguards let her out the door. She hadn't conjured up *all* that destruction—there was violence in the March wind, in the sway of the trees, in the blue hiss of the lamps . . .

The entire District was still a contagion of mud and dust. God help man or beast caught in the mud. And here we were supposed to have a Presidential parade. Dusters requisitioned to sweep the avenues found a quagmire instead. The army had to arrive with caissons and a company of sappers, else that mud would never have been removed in time.

The morning was overcast. I didn't have the least notion to descend into the dusty heart of the District. A note had been slipped under our door at the Willard.

If you don't Resign we are going to put a spider in your Dumpling and play the Devil with you.

Mary commenced to scream. "There are assassins in the house! You will never arrive on Capitol Hill."

"Mother, hush up! You're scarifying the boys."

I put Bob in charge, appointed him grand marshal of the Lincolns, and I strode downstairs in my shiny black boots and white kid gloves, my speech and spectacles in my pocket. Folks curtsied and bowed to me in the lobby. The moment I appeared on Pennsylvania Avenue, a band arrived and tootled "Hail to the Chief." I climbed aboard a barouche and sat opposite Buchanan, who hid behind the curtains like a wizened boy. He must have known we were hurtling toward a bloodbath that none of us could escape. Coward that he was, he smoothed his own feathers and wouldn't even wrassle with the rogue States.

The President seemed very pale. "Lincoln," he said, "if you're as pleased to inherit the White House as I shall feel upon returning to Wheatland"—his country manor in Pennsylvania—"you, sir, are a happy man."

I looked up and saw riflemen crouching on the roofs along Pennsylvania Avenue. They were wearing green coats. *Lincoln green*—like Robin Hood.

I was startled by the boldness of these men, who hopped from roof to roof with their long rifles, and without the least fear of falling. Some of them leaned over the lip of a roof to hail the *two* Commanders-in-Chief in the carriage. It must have confused them some to have a pair of Presidents in the same car. I waved back with my white gloves. I couldn't see much of the parade. Other riflemen in Lincoln green swarmed around the carriage. I espied Old Fuss & Feathers on Capitol Hill, in all the finery of a General-in-Chief, with silver tassels and gold epaulettes. He was sitting on a horse that swayed under his immensity. His own artillerymen had to clutch his saddle, else the horse might have collapsed.

I STOOD IN FRONT of the tiny speaker's table on an enormous wooden plank that jutted out from the eastern portico of the Capitol. My boots creaked. I pulled out my spectacles, turned for an instant, and could spot sharpshooters in the Capitol's windows, like a band of green crows.

My voice shot across that plain of people with its own high pitch. I argued that no State *upon its mere notion* can lawfully get out of the Union. If it could, we would live at the edge of anarchy. *The Union is unbroken*, I said. I did not mention the Confederacy, could not. But I promised the people of the Southern States that a Republican administration would not rob them of their property or peace of mind.

There needs to be no bloodshed or violence; and there shall be none, unless it is forced upon the national authority. Yet I was disingenuous, a little. I had the premonition of blood. Seward *complained* for peace. I could not.

Still, I pleaded. *I am loath to close. We are not enemies, but friends*, I said to the Southern people. The mystic chords of memory that stretched from every battlefield to every human heart would heal our wounds—restore our bonds of affection—when touched again *by the better angels of our nature.*

I believed in those better angels, else I would have lived with the prairie dogs, or run off to the moon, and abandoned mankind. But I was forlorn as I looked down that hill. I could smell the mud and silt of the Potomac, and I wondered if some Rebel demons were crouching on the far side of the river. I was already in a muddle. I remember the first words I ever writ—in the sand outside Pa's Kentucky cabin. I felt the power in my fingernails to brand the earth with my own scrawl.

I am Abraham

There was a mystery in the letters of my name. A-b-r-a-h-a-m. It was beyond a little boy's reach. I was still that same man-child, with some kind of an electric touch. I lived in words and would be buried in their fire. Who in hell was this here Lincoln, President of the United States? I didn't know the critter. Likely I never would.

21.

The Belle of the Ball

THE SHINDIG WAS held on the night of my inauguration, not in some massive tent on the White House lawn, but in the rump of City Hall, a dank, cavernous room that reminded us folks from the frontier of a snake charmer's paradise. My secretaries called it the White Muslin Palace of Aladdin, because it was festooned from ceiling to floor in white draperies with a blue trim—and it was a palace of sorts, bathed in a curious, flickering light from five huge gas chandeliers.

Mother had been in a fury from the moment we arrived at the White House. Not a single one of my secretaries or our servants had salaamed and called her Mrs. President. But something else was gnawing at her insides. Perhaps she didn't feel beautiful enough, or fine enough, in her own mirror. She'd gone over the guest list and wanted to *disinvite* Seward and Chase, and Chase's *delicious* twenty-year-old daughter, Miss Kate.

"Mother, do you want to provoke a Cabinet crisis? Both my *prima donnas* will resign if I lock them out of the Union Ball."

"Good riddance," she said. And she let out a childish laugh. "Husband, we will bargain together. You may have your pair of Judases, but not Miss Kate."

Now that she was naughty, her rage was gone. She didn't have much faith in my Cabinet, thought she deserved to be my Treasury Secretary *and* Secretary of State.

"Mary," I muttered, "should I tell Chase that his daughter's been disallowed?"

"Not at all. *I* will notify him."

Suddenly she was satisfied with what she saw in the mirror, as if her beauty was coupled with the coils of a snake, and she had the power to bite—or mesmerize the Cave Dwellers and other old-line families of the District.

But Bob had witnessed Mary's tantrum and he stepped in.

"Mother, if you persist in this *vanity* of yours, I will leave for Harvard this minute, and to hell with your Union Ball!"

Mary wouldn't bother listening to me, but she'd never trade blows with her boy. She retired to her own room to take care of her habiliments, while Bob stood against the wall and fingered his watch.

"You were harsh with your mother," I said. "I would have calmed Mary down."

"Father, you spoil her," said my Harvard prince, stroking the edge of his mustache. He stood there like some indoor hunter, with the watch fob trapped in his fist. Then he grew reckless. Bob reached up and pecked his own Pa on the beard.

"I am proud of you, sir. That was a magnificent speech on Capitol Hill."

It was damn hard for him to admit that, to praise his own Pa. I was the backwoods lawyer who happened to be President. He must have pondered over that miracle with his classmates. Mary had visited Cambridge, supped on peach flambé, watched the Harvard regatta, and I'd never been near that citadel in my stovepipe hat.

SHE WAS THE REAL SPOILER that evening in a blue silk gown, with a magnificent blue feather in her hair. She wore the pearl necklace I'd gotten for her at Tiffany's, that highfalutin shop in Manhattan, where all the nabobs outfitted their sweethearts, sometimes even their wives. I paid hard cash for the pearls; it was a victory present for the hard times we'd had, and for putting up with such a wanderer all these years.

Miss Kate snubbed the Union Ball, as it turned out. She had twisted her ankle, she claimed, and was a virtual prisoner at the Willard. "I am in such despair," she scribbled in a note to my wife. "I was so much looking forward to your quaint little palace."

With Miss Kate out of commission, none of the demoiselles could outshine Mary that first night of her *reign* as Mrs. President. She had a radiance no other woman possessed in Aladdin's White Muslin Palace. *Scintillatin'* is the word. Mary scintillated. She curtsied and smiled while I shook hands with every sucker in the Palace. She chatted with the Premier, as my secretaries called Mr. Seward—and Seward was in her thrall. There were one or two Cave Dwellers nosing around, spies from the District's posh inner circle. They were hardly indifferent to Mother's Lexington manners and musical voice. They had a certain foreboding about *their* limited life in the capital. The Cave Dwellers had a formidable foe in the White House.

Mary entered the ballroom arm in arm with Senator Douglas, while I had the mayor of Washington as my partner, the Hon. James Gabriel Beret, and the Marine Band played *Hail Columbia, happy land!* Mary danced the mazurka with her old *flame*, while the gaslights flickered and their shadows crept along the white draperies on the walls. Every little Washington lord wanted to dance with my wife. But Mary seemed to dance only with Dug—polkas and waltzes and whatnot. It was obvious to everybody that Dug was a sick man. The election had broken him—riding the rails like some demon Democrat, while Southerners mocked the Little Giant and pissed in the wind wherever he went. Now Dug coughed into a handkerchief. He couldn't contain or control that muscular glide of Mary's feet. So he had to sit in Mayor Beret's velvet chair, as a new partner revealed himself—and Mary's eyes were shot with wonder.

It was Bob who went with her through the different hops of a mazurka, Harvard style. It petrified me just to look. They were such a gorgeous couple. Luckily Bob didn't have my outlandish height or my naked shins. Had to crucify my feelings, or admit that I feared my own boy—feared his manhood and his moodiness, as if I had let some strange critter slip into the house. I left the ballroom near midnight, all pinched out from watching them strut. The last glimpse I had was of Mary doing some foreign fandango with Bob and a company of other ladies and gents. She had all the grace of a princess who had wandered into Aladdin's den and overwhelmed every cavalier at the ball.

My marine bodyguards, ablaze in fancy, red-lined cloaks, were dancing with their sweethearts, and I didn't have the heart to pull them out of that shindig. So I slipped away from the Muslin Palace and walked back to the White House alone in the dark; wasn't a lantern lit. Soldiers at the gate barely recognized the new Commander-in-Chief in his stovepipe hat. The moon was down to a sliver, and the Mansion with all its porticos looked like a wall of hollowed-out eyes.

22.

Mother & the Mantua-Maker

MY FIRST MORNING as Commander-in-Chief I found a despatch on my desk from Major Robert Anderson at Fort Sumpter—or Sumter, as everyone else seemed fond of calling that embattled sandbar at the mouth of Charleston harbor. It was the Union's last little *island* in South Carolina. Anderson said the fort was running low, and unless we could refurbish him, he'd have to surrender in six or seven weeks. Seward was very hot on having us abandon the fort. If we mounted an expedition to aid Anderson, he said, Virginia and the border States would bolt from the Union. I'd have abandoned the White House—lived in a shack—to hold on to Virginia, but I didn't really trust Seward as a peacemaker. There wasn't much peace to be made.

He wanted to hold the first Lincoln Levee at his mansion on Lafayette Square. Seward was like a manor lord with his fine Arabian mares, while Mary and I were strangers in the District. But Mary insisted that the Lincoln Levee be held at the Lincoln White House. She had her own mulatto mantua-maker now, Elizabeth Keckly, a former slave with fiercely lit dark eyes, a full figure, and hands that moved with the melody of a swan when she sewed one of Mrs. Lincoln's gowns; she wore five thimbles—five—and they glittered like pieces of silver while her fingers fluttered in the somber light. She had once worked for Mrs. Jeff Davis, who would have ransomed her own skin to keep her, but Elizabeth wouldn't move down to Montgomery with Mrs. Jeff, no matter how kind she was. It would have made her too sad to live around the *Secesh*, she told my wife. And Mother "kidnapped" Keckly from all the Cave Dwellers in the District, stole her right out of their hands. She got along exceedingly well with her mulatto seamstress. They spoke a curious kind of patois—like friends from some long forgotten past. Elizabeth had her own shop in the capital, but she created a second shop in Mary's bedroom.

I happened to come in while Elizabeth was dressing her. They were haggling about the price of this or that. I sat down and fiddled with my gloves.

"*Lizabeth*, I can't afford to pay big prices. We're just from the West, and we are poor. I believe my husband will concur."

The two of 'em must have sensed my *blue unholies*, seen my hollow face. I kept thinking of Major Anderson having to starve all his men at Sumpter, and I had to blot it from my mind. And so I preempted my wife's call to poverty.

"I guess we can afford Mrs. Keckly, for a little while."

My wife wasn't pleased; her mouth went bitter all of a sudden; her eyes blinked. I'd interfered in her bartering. She'd bartered all through our marriage—with butchers, grocers, Irish maids—and the White House was no different. She had that look of a battalion commander in her eye.

"Oh, Mr. Lincoln, you are a child in matters of money. We'd be in the poorhouse if I listened to you reckoning."

I could see how uncomfortable Keckly was, and so I sashayed onto another subject.

"Mother, you look charming in that dress."

"Flatterer," she said, but her eyes had stopped blinking, and she purred like a prize cat. Mary did look like an *apparition* at the first Lincoln Levee in magenta watered silk, as Keckly called it, with a wreath of red and white roses in her hair. Folks gawked at her. I shook so many hands, my fingers numbed up. And when Seward wanted to host our first State dinner at *his* mansion, considering how dark and forlorn the White House was, Mother bristled at him.

"Madame, it's a hapless hotel for Presidents. It has no charm."

Miss Hallie must have rifled the place, ripped it raw, taken some of her uncle's furniture back to Wheatland, because the White House did look like a barn with chandeliers. That didn't stop Mother. She had an upholsterer come in, borrowed whatever she could from Keckly's clients, and shoved Seward aside. But Mary hadn't calculated on Miss Kate.

She sat like a beautiful bird of prey, swiveled her long white neck as she eyed the chips in the silverware and the markings on the walls. Miss Kate didn't even bother to hide her contempt—my wife was an insignificant article to her. *She* deserved to occupy the White House with her Pa, Secretary Chase, and not a yokel from Illinois and his upstart wife. And when she spoke in that melodious whisper of hers, the whole damn dining room was wrapped up in Miss Kate.

"The pheasant is scrumptious, Mrs. Lincoln. My father and I might have to steal the White House staff for one of our own dinners."

"Goodness," said my wife, fondling a twisted rose in her hair. "You can *have* our major domo. He isn't worth the salt on your plate. But he is a kind fellow."

That huntress peered into Mary's blue eyes. "It's not the major domo who interests me. I must compliment you on your couturière. Mrs. Keckly says she has no time for mere mortals. She has much more pressing concerns at the White House."

That's what stuck in Mother's craw. The majestic tone of Miss Kate, that air of invincibility about her, as if nothing or no one could ever cut her down. She was twenty-one years old, and tycoons from every town were crawling to kiss her hand. But Mary had her own strong wind, her own fizzle-sticks, even if she was much stouter than Miss Kate, and loved to lie about her age.

"Ah, but I will recommend Lizabeth to you—as a personal favor from me and my husband. And you must come again, Miss Kate."

Kate rose up with that swanlike neck of hers. "My dear Mrs. Lincoln, I shall be delighted to have *you* call on *me*, with your major domo at our dinner table!"

Chase and his daughter had moved out of their apartments at the Willard and into a brick mansion on E Street. An invite to one of her dinners had become the most precious ticket in town. *Old Washington*, with all its Cave Dwellers, flocked to her soirees. The only one who remained loyal to my wife was Mrs. Keckly. And when I felt the *unholies* coming on after one of our Cabinet meetings, I would cross the hall to Mary's headquarters and listen in. I couldn't save the Union flag in Charleston harbor without putting our men in the middle of a firestorm. So I crossed the hall and listened to some *creole*. It wasn't hard to catch. They were talking about what Mrs. Jeff had told Elizabeth before she vanished with her furniture and her hatboxes and her husband's prize horses. *Lizzie, I would rather remain in Washington and be kicked out, than go to Alabama and be Mrs. President. But as soon as we go South, we will raise an army and march to Washington, and then I shall live in the White House.*

The two Mrs. Presidents had never met, and they were still involved in a war over the White House. Elizabeth seemed to brood as she sat on Mary's divan, while I could imagine the Rebels sneaking up from Alabama and bivouacking in Lafayette Park. I lit out of there—I had to be alone. The White House was packed with office seekers. I rushed out the rear door and wandered into the wild lands beside the Potomac.

I wasn't alone very long. The twigs crackled—a man crept up to me with a gun in his hand. I figured he was stalking Presidents. I couldn't holler my way out of this scrape. Then I recognized his derby and that trim beard of his—it was the railroad detective, Allan Pinkerton. Mary must have voiced her fears to General Scott, and the General had asked Pinkerton to guard the grounds as a special favor. I was wrong about the little detective. Pinkerton was carrying that gun for his own protection. He wanted to consult with me in private.

"Mr. President, that modiste who belongs to your wife . . ."

He meant Mrs. Keckly, but he had a damn detective's way of declaring it.

"She's invaluable, sir. We'd like to borrow her from your wife and send her to Montgomery on a special train."

But Mary had chased Pinkerton out of her boudoir, called him a rascal for even suggesting that her mantua-maker spy on Mr. and Mrs. Jeff. That little tale cured my *unholies*, as I imagined Mother ripping into the railroad detective. And I left him there, in the wild lands, with his silver-handled Colt.

23.

A Mountain of Dust

I WATCHED THEIR WHITE tents bloom like malignant blossoms as I climbed up to the roof of the White House—as if we were the interlopers, and they were the real owners of the District, gathering their Parrott rifles and other ten-pounders and biding their time. They wore ragged homespun coats dyed deep yellow or butternut, and they looked like circus trainers with hatchets and long knives rather than soldiers of some identifiable army; and this randomness only added to the general gloom, because there would be no *reason* to their attack; they would come at us like savages in their piebald coats, that butternut color bleeding in the sun.

And that afternoon was the first time I heard the banshee cry of these wild men—their Rebel yell. It could crack your bones right where you stood, and make a man piss blood. They whooped and yawped with an unnatural glee that had nothing to do with the sounds of war. There were several Comanche among them who wore the same ragged butternut coats. They didn't do most of the howling. I espied several dwarfs. They stood on other men's shoulders with their red signal flags and kept signaling into the wind. I'm not sure the flags made much sense, but out of what cave or hill or perverse apple orchard did these dwarfs and Comanche and butternut warriors come from, with their hatchets and howls? Some of them had servants who lathered their beards, or carried ammunition belts and poured red wine from dented silver flasks, and howled along with the rest.

I had my own armed guards—Willie and Tad. They'd built a little fort on the roof, with a few broken rifles and blocks of wood, but we had no Comanche in our ranks, no dwarfs with red flags.

"*Paw*," Tad said, shivering in the sun; the Rebs must have scared him in the right way, because his own little song wasn't imperiled by his lisp. "Ye think they were born in hell? They're like bloodhounds with boots and tents."

I imagined those Rebel demons capturing the Long Bridge, crossing the Potomac, and massacring children on the White House lawn.

I shook myself out of my own disaster dream and scrutinized the Potomac with my telescope. I couldn't see any signs of a rescue mission, no transports or barges filled with troops. "Where are they?" I muttered, collapsing the telescope and trying not to alarm Willie and Tad.

Our General-in-Chief was racked with rheumatism, but he surveyed the District from an ambulance, and was disheartened by those Comanche yells. He had no one on hand, nothing but his Silver Grays, as he called them, old recruits from some earlier Indian war. They didn't even know how to yell. The tents on the far side of the Potomac flapped in the wind like grounded white birds. I worried more about Mother than Willie and Tad, who could ride out this insurrection on the roofs. But Mary kept *seeing* my assassination; it traveled with her, a nightmare that meandered like a river's bloody wake. Shadows grew out of my beard, my fingers were tall as a tent—Mary's bosoms flew under her bodice like bowling balls.

General Scott insisted that she evacuate the capital with our two boys. He could insist until his head caught fire. Not even all the *Secesh* on the other side of the bridge could have told Mother what to do if she didn't want to do it. Scott had cured her hysterical fit.

"General," she said, with that Kentucky tartness of hers, "attend to your Silver Grays, and I will attend to my husband."

Mother followed me often as she could, and the two boys became her accomplices. Tad would interrupt Cabinet meetings, sit on my lap, peruse every face, and then saunter out like a Comanche—not a Rebel in a butternut coat, but a real Comanche, who might attack you at your own peril, but wouldn't have joined up with the *Secesh*. He'd race up and down the stairs, ring all the buzzers in the attic, and the servants would collect in a panic, believing the First Lady had summoned them. He had Mary's hot temper and caprice. He'd stop a maid on the stairs and collect tribute from her, like a highwayman. He'd even harangue my ministers.

"Pay or die," he'd growl, with a tin pistol that couldn't have fired a plug of spit. No one dared disobey him, not even his Pa, who was nothing more than a captive President on that planet Tad had created in our halls. The District had tightened into a couple of staircases and an attic where he could count his coins. Willie never joined his brother's escapades—he didn't have Tad's piratical streak.

Tad still had to contend with other pirates, like General Scott's Silver Grays, who foraged in the deserted streets, stole whatever food they could, and decided to protect the White House on a whim. They camped out in the East Room, scratching their backs against the carpets. These recruits looked ferocious in their frontier uniforms, with feathers in their hair and war paint on their sunken cheeks—yet they serenaded Mary with their own gnarled voices. And it helped lift her. She forgot about the danger we were in—unprotected and utterly isolated from the North—and blushed near the Silver Grays.

"You gentlemen have a lot of sauce—serenading the President's Lady."

She brought them little gifts from the pantry, invited them into the Crimson Room, which was *her* parlor, and talked to them about their kin, while Mrs. Keckly served the last little cakes that were left. Mary was in her element now—she had an audience of raw old men who worshiped that Southern singsong in her voice.

"It's kind of you to camp here and protect Mr. Lincoln and our little boys."

They weren't kind at all; they were bigger rascals than the butternut warriors across the bridge, but they couldn't have menaced a flea. They didn't even carry any cartridges, and I'd wager that their scalping knives had never *breathed*, and were kept in some snug portion of their pants. Meantime a pair of stragglers from a lone Massachusetts regiment snuck across the railroad bridge, wandered into the White House with the yellow eyes of wounded animals, and wolfed down whatever scraps we had.

I looked at them with bewilderment and muttered, "I don't believe there is a North! It can't exist. You Massachusetts boys are the only real thing left in the world!"

And just as the *unholies* were hitting hard, I heard some light thunder outside my window, that telltale rat-a-tat of regimental drums. I went to the window. I couldn't see anything but a mountain of dust on the *Ave*, as locals loved to call Pennsylvania Avenue. The mountain of dust commenced to move. Then I could make out that thickening tread of an army—patches of blue emerging from the dust on their coats. The 7th New York had arrived. Somehow I couldn't heed this parade. I'd lived with those Rebels a little too long—their piebald coats seemed much more real.

I scampered up to the roof with my telescope and tall hat. And what I saw stupefied me. The white tents had scattered like macabre trees on a windy plain. The dust cleared a little, and the dwarfs I had imagined with their red flags were child buglers; else it's possible the dwarfs had disappeared and were replaced by children with wrinkled faces, their bugle cries much more plangent than the Rebel call. Black servants ran across the fields with piles of ammunition on their shoulders. The Parrott guns were gone, and there was a great flurry of butternut coats, and not a single one of the horses I saw had a rider. The horses leapt into dust clouds with their rippling flanks—every muscle as secure as silver. It was my first Rebel retreat.

24

Spotted Ponies

C UT ME TO PIECES after what folks in the District started to say about Mary. They called her the *Traitoress*, just because some of her brothers and half brothers had decided to join the insurrection. Mrs. Keckly was kind enough to act as my secret agent in matters that concerned the welfare of my wife.

"They're vicious," she said, "these high-blood Washingtonians."

Her nostrils flared up, but neither of us had the perspicacity or the power to keep my wife away from the bear traps those highfalutin ladies had set for her, or the traps she sometimes set for herself. The White House had fallen into ruin under President Buchanan and his niece. Miss Hallie had the finest chandeliers installed in the public rooms, but she paid no mind to the President's quarters, which had all the idle charm of a second-rate hotel. The oilcloth on some of the floors creaked and was just about as unpredictable as a swollen sea; the walls were peeling, the lamps were chipped. The furniture looked like refugees of some old curiosity shop. And it troubled Mary's own esteem.

Congress had set aside a whopping sum of twenty thousand dollars to *prettify* the Mansion, and she meant to eat into that fund as much she could. In May, after the District was secured, Mary decided to visit Philadelphia and New York with one of her little cousins and William Wood, our new commissioner of buildings. She was in some kind of *duel* with her mortal enemy, Miss Kate, who had already gone to Manhattan to buy carpets for her father's E Street house.

Mary had put on her war bonnet—she was screaming for a fight. I'd kept her out of politics, she said, shoved her to one side. Mother was once my secretary of war and peace, but I would have been crucified had I allowed the First Lady to haggle with my Cabinet and General Scott. And she was wild to see Bob, as she always was. She'd visit him at the tail end of her shopping tour. I missed my child-wife after she left for the depot with all her sundries. I paced that creaky oilcloth in my office.

I found a pair of spotted horses in the White House stables after my wife returned from the trip—ponies they were, for Willie and Tad.

"Oh, they're anonymous gifts," she said.

I knew what *anonymous* meant. Mother had done some serious horse trading on her own, without considering how it might compromise me.

"Who gave them to you, Mary?"

We'd had our quarrels, but for the first time in our marriage she avoided my glance, like a scheming little girl.

"I can't recall," she said. "I was at a dinner with some bankers and I happened to mention that we might have to sell the manure in our stables—that's how strapped we were."

I wanted to slap her for such an outright lie, but I was haunted by the image of my father's angry red face—like a poker iron that was piping hot. She shouldn't have made up that tale about manure. Mother counterattacked, said I was handing out postmasterships and other prizes while we lived like paupers with holes in our carpets. I deflected her attack, or we would have had to discuss every damn scoundrel at our door.

"Now what did you promise these men?"

"*Nothing.* I said they could write to me. They had my permission. They're friends of Mr. Wood's. And they would be obliged if Mr. Wood received a *permanent* appointment as commissioner of buildings."

"And is that why you got the ponies? On the promise of that appointment?"

"I promised nothing," she said.

I wanted to return the twin ponies to these bankers, but it would have made even more of a ruckus. And I didn't want to undercut Mother's rôle as Lady President. The boys would have been heartsick without their new ponies. I thought at least I'd get something, that Mother might have some news from our older boy.

"And what about Bob?" I had to ask. "Is he still enamored of Harvard?"

She looked away again, like a waif now, not a scheming child, as if I'd caught her in some skullduggery.

"Oh, I didn't have time to see him. There were too many dinners, too many things to buy. And Bob just couldn't break away from his classes. But he promised to come down to see us—the moment he has a chance."

Hadn't realized how much I'd been looking forward to hearing about her visit with Bob, the cream cakes they had, the lobster bisque, the chats with his tutors and all his chums. What could have held her in Manhattan? Midnight suppers with War Democrats? Yachting parties with bankers and publishing tycoons? Bottles of perfume and swatches of drapery from some owner of a dry goods emporium? She'd always made time for Bob. Manhattan must have been too much of a *thrill*, even for Mother, who had to use up some of her charm to secure twin ponies for Willie and Tad.

25.

The Picnic War

H E WAS A general with a gigantic appetite—could fart like
a furnace and eat six roasted quail at one sitting—but didn't
have much of an appetite for war. He'd rather feast at Gautier's with
his *family* and their brass spurs, or spend the night at his favorite
bawdyhouse. Half the town seemed to know his battle plans; that's
how many Rebel spies we had in the District. There were no secret
maneuvers in the dark. McDowell left in the early morning, on the
sixteenth of July, under a blazing sun, and he didn't leave *alone* with
his thirty thousand troops. He had a wagon train of followers—six
United States Senators, ten Congressmen, a gaggle of journalists and
Washington wives with their own carriages and supplies—umbrellas,
opera glasses, and picnic baskets. Every available wagon had been
hired in advance of the battle. The capital's caterers charged a fortune
for the simplest baskets and hampers they had, with or without a
bottle of wine. There was a kind of giddy joy that we were stopping
at Manassas Junction to duel with the Rebels a bit and then march all
the way into Dixie Land. I couldn't deal with *romance* in this first real
engagement of the war. We had one mission—to dislodge the Rebels

from their works behind the meandering mud of Bull Run Creek and break their will, else the insurrection would fall into some distant romance and never end.

I despised a wagon train that could turn war into an opera in the countryside, but I couldn't discourage all the carriages. The excitement of the ladies was like a terrible plague. They'd be out picnicking while men died. But the Senators had their war committees, the journalists their sketchbooks, the photographers their *Shadow Boxes*, and I was back home in the White House with Mary and the boys, far from the thunder and flying red spit.

For one darn moment I wished I was aboard that caravan, moving into Virginia, past the deserted farmhouses and dusty roads in the wake of war. There weren't only fools and Senators on the wagon train; there were soldiers' sweethearts and wives, with bandages and rum, and *vivandières*—young female sutlers—carrying fresh pies and the colors of some company that had adopted one or two of them. Yet I didn't want to be on some hill overlooking the battle around Bull Run, with all the Senators and the Washington wives with their opera glasses and roast chicken, like spectators at a bloody game of bowls.

The despatches that came in over the wire talked of one little victory after the other, as the Rebels were pushed back deeper and deeper into the woods. No one talked of bedlam, and the impossible tug of war. And that's what scratched at me, all the hurrahing and the hoopla. There were runners who posted each new despatch on the Willard's front door and read the despatches aloud while folks predicted McDowell and his men would break through Manassas Junction and arrive in Richmond tomorrow. They dreamt of Mr. Jeff Davis roped up on the White House lawn like a monkey on display.

The Rebel yell couldn't have had much shrift at Manassas. We all expected a rout. I went to the Navy Yard with Willie and Tad, to talk with the yard's commander about our gunboats. Sailors saluted us as we went into that maze of sheds and dismantled ships. Willie and Tad wanted to carouse among the torpedoes, but I couldn't carouse. There was a message from Secretary Seward waiting for me at the White House.

The day is lost.

I couldn't make much sense of it all. McDowell had smashed the Rebel line. How could battle lines leap around like that? I didn't rush to headquarters. I waited a bit. General Scott wasn't snoring on his gigantic couch. He looked very grave in his gold buttons and feathered hat. The Rebel cavalry arrived from nowhere, swarmed out of the woods in a lightning raid—like ghosts, it seems, and swept our boys right out of the battle. Some of the Rebs were wearing Union blue. And that's what befuddled our boys, who expected the strict neutrality of butternut or blue that would allow *any* bluecoat to leap right into our lines. Others swore that these diabolical cavalrymen were all black. I dared not believe it.

Scott explained the tactics behind that puzzler. Officers often rode into battle with their servants on the same horse. And such servant might thrash about with a wooden saber and blind some Ohio boy. I'd never understand *modern* war. Black Hawk might have scalped soldiers and civilians, but he wouldn't have dressed his braves in soldier blue, or had his own white prisoners and slaves carry toy tomahawks. He wouldn't have demeaned a man like that.

Scott read one of the despatches. "The routed troops will not reform. Save Washington and the remnants of this army."

I'm not sure how long I stayed at the War Department, with McDowell's wires recounting the chaos. His army had become a confused mob. Soldiers fled with that broken caravan of Senators and Washington wives in what was soon known as the Great Skedaddle. Some of the boys must have gone berserk; they were carrying dead men's boots in their arms like leather babies while they hopped around on hardscrabble with their toes peeking out of torn socks. A drummer boy with a bloody eye beat a wild tattoo that sounded like a devil's dance; no human could have marched or run to that rat-a-tat. Women and wounded men dropped near the roadside, begging for a drink of water. That dazed caravan passed them right by. Soldiers sang their regimental songs in a hoarse whisper, but couldn't recollect most of the words. A Congressman was captured and led away to Richmond, in a wooden cage no less. Fancy hats, jars, umbrellas, and opera glasses were strewn along the road, as grim reminders of that picnic war, but it was even harsher than that—crinolines and umbrellas caught fire in all the panic, and one of the ladies burned to death in her gown.

I didn't have to wait around for any more of those despatches.

I returned to the White House. It had the familiarity of a morgue. I could hear the rattle of ambulances filled with wounded men. I saw them from my window—listless, half-dead men leaning over the sides of ambulances, like the parched crew of a whaler, wearing knotted handkerchiefs on their heads. I went out in the middle of the night to meet with some of the soldiers, giving them cups of water and whatever grub I had. Felt as if I myself had managed this war with a picnic basket, watching the battle at Manassas on some imaginary hill.

I could hear the random roar of rain on the roof, like the drumrolls of an incoherent army. Soldiers kept returning in tattered coats; a whole lot of them limped into Washington without boots. Old Fuss & Feathers arrived early at the White House. His eyes were swollen, and his hands shook. He stuttered in the cavernous tomb of the East Room. Took him a whole minute to collect himself. He wiped the spittle from his tongue. As the nation's General-in-Chief he'd assumed the right to assemble Mary and the boys. He told her flat out that the Rebels could be rushing to Washington this minute. It was no longer safe for her to be here with Willie and Tad.

"Mrs. Lincoln, I'll have members of my own guard ride with you to Philadelphia, if you prefer."

Mary was wearing her war bonnet with strings she had knotted with her own hands. She'd made a tent for Willie and Tad, clutched them under her shawl, as if that little dark tunnel might deliver them from the *Secesh*. She was worn through, hadn't slept since Manassas, and couldn't even answer the General. Mary turned to me.

"Will you go with us, Mr. Lincoln?" she asked. She knew I'd never skedaddle, not after the rout at Bull Run, with soldiers caught in the drizzling rain. But I was a little formal in front of Old Fuss & Feathers.

"Most assuredly, Mrs. Lincoln, I will not leave at this juncture."

She was just as formal, though her eyes darted, and I could sense she was at the limit of whatever little control she had left.

"Then I will not leave you at this juncture," she said, and marched upstairs with my two boys under that tent of hers.

26.

Yib

THE WHITE HOUSE had its own schoolroom, but the boys were always playing tricks on their teacher, swiping his hat or setting one of his shoes on fire. That damn school became a sore spot between Mrs. Keckly and me, and the subject of our first altercation. The children of our servants often played with Willie and Tad, and were part of their own little band, the Union Jacks. And once, after this wild band took possession of the attic, Keckly came to see me. I was in my office, scratching around with the kitten she gave Tad as a gift, though that kitten, I suspect, was as much a gift for Tad's *Paw*. She must have sniffed my isolation, that singular loneliness of a Commander-in-Chief after Bull Run.

"Madame Elizabeth," I said, "I was about to call on you. I'm in need of your opinion. It's about this colonization business."

I could see that startled look in her mournful eyes.

"What colonization business? Mr. Lincoln, are you asking slaves and freedmen to *volunteer* to leave their homes for some forlorn spot in Africa?"

Suddenly I felt like the main attraction in a monster show. "But Lizabeth," I pleaded, "we'd be sending them back to the land of their fathers."

"Most of their fathers were born here, as you must know—I was born in Virginia, Mr. Lincoln. I learned to read and write as a slave. My master, Mr. Armistead Burwell, took my mother as his concubine, only I never discovered that until the day she died. But I'm a Virginian, sir, and all the wealth in the world couldn't get me to say otherwise."

I was like a lonely dog looking for a lick of affection.

"What did you want to ask me, Madame Elizabeth?"

"It's the classroom at the White House, sir. I was wondering if I could make use of it? It has a chalkboard and such. And I'd like to help the housemaids' little boys to read and write."

She never even asked if the White House tutor would give private lessons to these little boys, or if they could come and join Willie and Tad's class. She wouldn't trespass upon Washington manners. All she wanted was to *borrow* the chalkboard.

"Elizabeth, you can borrow the chalkboard *and* the tutor."

Keckly was wearing black for the first time. I figured she'd lost a favorite aunt. And once she secured the rights to the chalkboard, Elizabeth commenced to teach her own special class to all the colored children at the White House. She was much better at tutoring than the tutor we had. My own boys volunteered to join Keckly's class. She's the one who taught Tad how to spell. After a month he talked like Hamlet with a slight stutter. He scribbled poems to his *Paw*. Keckly was attached to that boy. He called her *Yib*, which must have been his own personal corruption of *Elizabeth*.

I WAS DRAWN TO KECKLY'S hint of melancholia, but I was also frightened of Elizabeth a little, I had to admit, frightened of that *lash* of pain I could feel around her eyes. Tad was more familiar with Elizabeth than I would ever be.

"*Paw,* how come Yib don't move into the Mansion and stay with us, huh? She could sure use another son."

I had to learn about Yib's bereavement from my own ten-year-old boy. Keckly had a son—George Kirkland—killed at Wilson's Creek. I had to pry all the particulars out of Mary, who was loath to give Elizabeth's secrets away. Born in Virginia, as she said, Yib was fair game for any aristocratic tomcat once she arrived at the ripeness of a girl. And she couldn't fend such tomcats off forever. One of these "persecutors," as she called them, was a profligate young merchant from Hillsborough, North Carolina, Mr. Alexander Kirkland, whose own wife was pregnant at the time, and who forced himself upon Yib when she was seventeen or so. And Yib gave birth to a little boy, a *ghost child* who belonged to her mistress, Anne Burwell Garland.

After her mistress moved to Missouri, Yib established herself as a mantua-maker, and was able to buy her freedom in '55. She removed to the District several years later, and was soon the most sought-after seamstress in town, working for Mrs. Jefferson Davis and Mrs. Robert Lee. The finest ladies of the District would have *devoured* Yib if she'd given them half the chance. They all wanted to keep her on consignment. Meantime her son went off to a colored college in Ohio and tried to enlist after the war commenced, but Ohio didn't have room for black volunteers, except as mule drivers. So he joined the 1st Missouri with several of his mulatto classmates, not as mule drivers, but as raw white recruits. He had some supernatural luck as the 1st Missouri's chief scout. He'd walk through a burning apple orchard like some invisible waif, the last man alive in his scouting party. He carried a crazed colonel across Rebel lines, his own tunic on fire. He'd disappear during a raid, and appear again with a cache of rifles and the Rebel flag—until he was shot to pieces at Wilson's Creek, in a skirmish with a renegade Rebel militia.

I seized Keckly's hand and kissed it the next time I saw her in black.

"I am so sorry for your sacrifice, Madame Elizabeth."

For the first time I could feel in my bones that she thought a little less of me. And it was like being scalped as I looked into her eyes.

"It wasn't a sacrifice, Mr. President. If I had been younger, I would have disguised myself as a man and joined his regiment. I wouldn't have fallen in his place. That would have rubbed out the dignity of his death. He had the honor of fighting for his country, Mr. Lincoln, even if *that* country couldn't recognize the worth of who he was. He wouldn't sit out the war at some haven in Ohio. That wasn't in my George's nature."

She didn't want to be consoled. All she wanted was a classroom. So I was determined to sit in on one of her classes, not to spy on her, you see, but to get acquainted with Yib and her chalkboard. She didn't seem startled when I entered her classroom in the basement and sat down on a tiny stool next to Willie and Tad and the servant boys. I'd just come back from the War Department and was still wearing my chapeau. It was unconscionably impolite, and I placed that stovepipe hat on my knee, like a toadstool or a writing desk. Desks were in short supply, and all her pupils had to sit around a rickety table with their tablets and black lead pencils, while Elizabeth, still in her mourner's black gloves, scratched a word on the chalkboard with all the flair of a schoolmarm.

Turpitude

She made us all pronounce that word on our tongues with the trill of an opera star.

The boys scratched their heads. "Tur-pee-tude," Tad muttered. "That sounds like a fine pickle, ma'am."

"Take a stab at it, Mr. Tad."

He was stumped, like all her other pupils, and Yib turned to me, as if I were a philosopher—or a fireman who could solve a difficult flame.

I told her what I thought. "I'd say it was a vile blister in the human heart."

And she asked us who suffered from such a blister.

Bradley, the butler's boy, said, "All the generals in Virginia and all the Johnny Rebs."

His accomplices in the room punched that rickety writing table and it just about collapsed. "Hooray for Brad!"

Keckly stared them down. "What if Varina Davis—or her couturière—was teaching a similar class at the Rebel White House? Wouldn't Varina sing that *our* generals suffered from the same vile blister?"

"Then she would be wrong," said my Willie, with a troubled look on his blond brow. "Ain't that so, *Paw?*"

I realized the pickle I was in. "Yes—and no. A general who believed in his cause, no matter what side he was on, wouldn't have to suffer from rascality. But he could still have a ruinous heart . . ."

Luckily there was a knock on the door. One of my confidential secretaries said I was late for a Cabinet meeting, and that Mr. Seward might kill Mr. Chase, or vice versa, if I didn't come upstairs immediately and end their tuffle. So I excused myself, and realized I ought not intrude upon Yib's domain again. I didn't know her and probably never would. I had to fight my own Pa to learn the alphabet, but I hadn't endured what she had to endure as a child. And yet we were alike in a way—quick to wound and slow to heal. She'd risen out of nowhere, without book learning or a blab school, and was mistress of the needle and the chalkboard. Fortune had put us together somehow and made Yib a curious acquaintance of mine. She was half an ally, and Lord knows what the other half was.

27.

Little Mac & the Lady President

W E WANTED A magnificent rider to lead us, not a man who couldn't even mount a horse. So I summoned General George B. McClellan—handsome, robust, thirty-four years old—to the District that same July, a week after the disaster at Bull Run. He'd already trounced the Rebels during a skirmish in the backwaters of western Virginia. He came from a distinguished Philadelphia line, had entered West Point at fifteen, the youngest cadet in his class. I needed a feller who didn't creak along with arthritis. I couldn't afford another fizzle. He wouldn't have raced home from Bull Run like a general with a bunch of nanny goats. McClellan had too much pride—and too much precision.

Our one war hero, he arrived in Washington on horseback and waited for nobody, not even a member of his new staff. Galloping across the capital, he rounded up all the deserters and stragglers he could find, tossed soldiers out of brothels and bars, and returned them to camp. He gathered this little growing army of deserters behind his black horse, some of the boys wearing corsets out of a brothel, others dressed up like bandits in red scarves, or disguised as carpenters and grocers—it didn't matter to McClellan. He tamed them all. These very stragglers developed a deep affection for their new general and called him *Little Mac*. He'd gone into dark alleys and other hellholes to dig them out, fought river pirates and brothel keepers with a bullwhip, while his black horse—Dan Webster—waited for him, whinnying once and stamping his foot in the dust.

That horse was as vain as he was. McClellan went into the back streets in full dress, stopping to comb his reddish brown mustache. We housed him in his own mansion at the corner of Lafayette Square. The bottom floor served as his headquarters and telegraph office, and he himself lived on the second floor. "I feel that God has put a great work in my hands," he told his fellow officers.

And he opined that there was little room for General Scott in God's great work. McClellan ignored our General-in-Chief, who couldn't seem to move from his divan on account of the dropsy in his feet and legs. He'd once been Scott's loyal aide, had admired his love of battle, but ridiculed him now. He wouldn't even meet with Old Fuss & Feathers, and locked him out of his own headquarters. "I'm the only one who can save the Union," he proclaimed. He surrounded himself with junior officers who were loyal to him, pontificated like some preacher, gave a hundred interviews, met with Congressional committees. The Democrats adored "Little Napoleon," as the papers dubbed him, and would have preferred a military man as the nation's Commander-in-Chief, but I had to suffer his pompous ways or I couldn't survive.

He humiliated Scott once too often. "Excellency," he said to me, "must I endure that old idiot? I cannot lead an army with him rattling in my ear." Scott wasn't his only target. McClellan called me "the original gorilla" behind my back, but I had been called worse than that. Scott had none of McClellan's lightning, or at least no lightning left, and when I asked Little Mac if he could head the Army of the

Potomac and also become our General-in-Chief, he pulled once on his brand-new chin beard and said, "Excellency, I can do it all."

So I had to drop Old Fuss & Feathers, allow him to resign, and put all my faith in that bantam rooster. He built a ring of forts and camps around the capital and sometimes he would survey his own army from a hot-air balloon. We'd never had another general remotely like him. Washington wives loved to watch him sail in his balloon. He'd stand in the gondola—alone—while it rocked in the wind and rose above the White House, the wives clutching their hearts at the sight of this marvel, who could have been emperor of the District in a floating sedan chair. He wasn't interested in these elegant ladies. He loved his wife, Mary Ellen, the daughter of an army engineer who'd become his adjutant. He wrote her religiously twice a day, I hear. I'd hate to imagine what was in his letters. He must have attacked me relentlessly as a civilian nincompoop. Half of 'em were treasonable, I suppose, but there was no one else who could get us out of this scrape. And I kind of envied that gondola of McClellan's, wished I could fly over cow pastures and Rebel terrain with his damn insouciance, but I was grounded in my own terrain, without tether cords or the ballast of a black stallion.

Mother had given him a bouquet when he first arrived. It was her way of introducing herself to that bantam in blue. He handed the bouquet to his father-in-law, turned on his heels, and nuzzled his horse—and now Mary had an unpopular opinion of him.

"He is humbug," Mary said.

"What makes you think so, Mother?"

"Because he talks so much and does so little."

I couldn't blame him for that. He could conjure up an army with the force of his personality and a few words. Six months ago we were a phantom village, with our telegraph wires cut, and not one car that could connect us with Baltimore, and now we had a hundred thousand men in a maze of forts that was like a dark, impenetrable illusion. Little Mac would ride from fort to fort, without a single guard, as if he were challenging the Rebels to *trouble* him.

Problem was he had a damn big mouth. "We have to dodge the nigger question," he said. Fugitive slaves had little chance with Little Mac as General-in-Chief. It did not matter who was hiding them, or where they were hid. Little Mac rooted them out, riding his black horse, and had his commanders return them to their masters. "Excellency," he said, "I'd rather not poison the waters."

I didn't quarrel with him. He was the master engineer. I think he meant to scare the Rebels out of the war with the might of his army. I visited his troops riding on a borrowed horse, with my feet scraping the ground. He kept stroking his mustache and palavering about the one *epic* attack that would break the Rebels all at once. He was gallant in his uniform, with a silk scarf around his throat. His boys never even looked at me—I was the scarecrow in a stovepipe hat who happened to be President, and he was a god who strode among them and wasn't even as tall as other generals; he might ask a boy about his sick mother, or contribute to the funeral of a soldier's *Paw*. They stood in the snow for him, in wind and rain, dazzled if they could touch Dan Webster's silky flank.

I'd see him every morning from my windows, magnificent on his black stallion, hooves trampling the dust on Pennsylvania Avenue, while he strode across the District like some grand marshal of war—only Little Mac wasn't making war; he was collecting blankets and ammunition dumps. So one night in the middle of November— 1861—I went to see him with Mr. Seward and my confidential secretaries, Nicolay & Hay. We strolled across Lafayette Park with the wind in our mouths, the trees bending like live bullets with branches and chipped bark, the ground swelling under our feet as we stopped in front of the little general's palatial home and headquarters with its clique of armed guards.

We were shown into the parlor. Little Mac was at a wedding and wouldn't be back for a while. We decided to wait. Nicolay & Hay commenced to burn while my Secretary of State smoked one of his Havana cigars. An hour passed. I could feel the *unholies* coming on. Someone should have run to that wedding and notified Little Mac—I began to wonder if I was his general, or he was mine. McClellan appeared in his military cape, shuffled right past us without a smile or the briefest hello, and bounded up the stairs to his living quarters. We waited another hour, with the *unholies* riding through my blood—I wanted to drag him through the sawdust by his chin beard. I sent word up to Little Mac.

His aide climbed back down and shrugged his shoulders with some of McClellan's own arrogance.

"I'm awful sorry, Mr. Lincoln, but the General is indisposed."

"Then you might *dispose* him," I said.

"I can't, sir. He's retired for the night."

So we left that armed palace, Nicolay & Hay twitching with anger.

"That's the insolence of epaulettes. Soon he'll ask you to water his horse."

My lips were trembling. "I'd water his horse and hoist him into his saddle if that could produce some victories."

I returned to the White House, leaving Mr. Seward at his doorstep.

Little Mac's allies in the Senate kept reminding him that he ought to be Dictator, while I could remain in town as his puppet President. I didn't want to *wrassle* with him right now. I could have lopped Little Mac off at the knees with a stroke of the pen and tossed him into the Dakota Territories, but it soothed folks to have *their* general ride through the District on a black horse. And the Rebel chiefs in Richmond must have shuddered a bit when their spies whispered to them how Little Mac rode from one camp to the next—the lord of his domain—while the Union Army swelled up like a beast.

I could hear the rattle of dishes in the Crimson Room. Mary was having one of her soirees—the laughter rang like a rifle shot. I was glad she hadn't called me down to greet her guests. The winter season had started in Washington in spite of the war—no, even the war was now *delusional*, thanks to McClellan and Mr. Dan Webster. Folks felt safe in their beds, surrounded as they were by so many bayonets, but somehow I'd have to get that pretty little man to fight.

MOTHER'S COUNTER CABINET convened in the Crimson Room, and like my own Cabinet, its members were all male. It included the White House gardener, John Watt, an unsavory man who collected tribute from our servants and picked their pockets from time to time. He had a terrible thirst for money and should have been treated like a bandit, but Mary seemed to admire him so. She had a fondness for adventurers who quickened her blood. Among them was a New York Congressman, Daniel Sickles, who had shot a man to death for being a little too *amorous* with his wife. But Sickles never sat in jail. His kingpin lawyers convinced the jury that their client had suffered from a fit of temporary insanity.

I shouldn't complain. I would have worked that jury the same damn way. And now Sickles had tea and crumpets in the Crimson Room with Mary's other scoundrels. Her favorite was the Chevalier Wikoff, who'd been a spy in several European capitals and had a habit of running off with other men's wives and tossing them away at his convenience. He was a great flatterer, this Chevalier, but he didn't try to peddle any of his stuff on me. Still, he was always around. He had free run of the White House, thanks to my wife. I could find him dozing on some chair in the corridor, a silk hat over his eyes.

God help us all, but he had become Mary's social adviser. The Chevalier introduced her to other *aristocrats*—other silken peddlers—like himself. The Crimson Room was full of that lot. My secretaries could hear them talk up a storm about *love, law, and literature.* I would have thrown them onto the manure pile, but they kept Mary occupied with their *lust* for literature—and other matters. Whenever a new adventurer arrived—a fallen duke, a penniless colonel, a Harvard man who'd gone to rot—Mary would welcome him into her Counter Cabinet with a bouquet from the White House's glassed-in garden.

I let them clatter around until her Cabinet intruded upon mine. She would come to me with her "womanly intuition," inspired by the Chevalier and his little circle, who loved to play politics. Perhaps the Chevalier wanted to become my new Secretary of State. I ain't certain, but it seemed like that.

She was shrewd enough not to mention Wikoff, but I could figure out which cabal had been coaching her. I was stretched out on my rattan sofa, reading the *New York Times*, which hadn't left off crucifying me and my Cabinet, when Mary sauntered in, wearing one of Keckly's creations, a silk gown that blossomed on her like the plumage of some rare bird. She was all breathless in her gown of feathers. She started with an attack on my Secretary of the Treasury, Mr. Chase, who'd been caring for wounded soldiers in his E Street mansion. Miss Kate had converted his parlor and study into a sanitarium after Bull Run; there were no more midnight suppers on E Street.

"Father," she said, without a bit of rancor in her voice, "I do wish you would inquire into the motives of Mr. Chase. He belittles you behind your back."

Mary had pushed right up against my spleen. "Is that the Chevalier's opinion?"

Her face went white as the powder on Willie and Tad's chalkboard. "What Chevalier? Father, you must be delirious!"

And she gathered up her silken feathers and the wondrous folds of her gown and marched out of my office. That wasn't the end of it. She mounted another campaign within a week. Mary wanted me to rescue a militiaman named William Scott. He was a Vermonter who had fallen asleep while on picket duty and was about to be executed for dereliction. Mary gathered her own little army in her behalf—Tad. He came to me in the middle of a Cabinet meeting, but it wasn't to slip onto my lap.

"*Paw*," he said in his vernacular lisp, "if it was your own little boy who was just tired after fightin', and marchin' all day, that he could not keep awake, much as he tried to—would you have him shot to pieces like some buzzard, would you, *Paw*?"

I had to retreat. I couldn't fight so eloquent an advocate, even if I didn't enjoy interfering in McClellan's military matters. After I was done with the Cabinet, I raced downstairs. The Chevalier was dozing on a divan. I couldn't drag him along the Potomac on a rail. It would have damaged Mary's pride—Wikoff was her confidant and her protégé.

I scrambled over to Little Mac's headquarters. As usual, he was much too busy to meet with the President. I walked right past his phalanx of aides and went into McClellan's private office. His blue-gray eyes seemed to startle out of his head. The little general had never seen me in such a shivering rage.

"General," I said, without a particle of politeness, "I'm the one urgency you have—not Richmond, not the Rebels, but Abraham Lincoln. And I'm a man who does not relish barking at his generals."

He was still kind of stunned.

"I'd like you to issue a Pardon for Private William Scott of K Company, the Third Vermont Infantry."

Finally he spoke, but in a subdued voice. "On what grounds, Excellency?"

"Any damn grounds you want. But you could give as a reason that it was by request of the Lady President."

He pondered that. *The Lady President.* One Lincoln had been quite enough. And now he had to contend with the Chief Executive's wife. He'd misjudged Mary's worth, never bothered to notice her intelligence or her stubborn streak.

While he was pondering, I left him there with his books and his maps. I saw a red streak of railroad lines, around Manassas Junction, and a bunch of poker chips—white and blue—that could have marked out Rebel formations and munitions depots on one of his maps. He must have spent half the day shoving those chips around, when he wasn't riding his horse from camp to camp, or peering down at us from his gondola in the sky.

28.

Flub Dubs

SHE'D BEEN FINAGLING with that White House gardener, John Watt. They moved around funds they didn't really have. I should have shaken her like a petulant child. Things were complicated in the middle of an insurrection. Members of the White House staff had to have some kind of military appointment or they couldn't be paid. Mary conspired with my Secretary of War to have her gardener appointed to the cavalry and stationed at the Mansion. I was *powerless.* I wouldn't block one of the Lady President's own commissions. I was glad she hadn't assigned the Chevalier as Captain of the White House Watch—he was near the Crimson Room often enough to command some kind of post.

She was more interested in the gardener now—John Watt. She had his wife appointed as White House steward. Most of Madame Watt's salary went to pay Mary's creditors, I imagine. I'd catch her huddling with a Washington upholsterer, or a minor prince from a dry goods palace, who was always accompanied by mysterious men with hats over their eyes. A dozen footstools appeared one day, and were gone the next. Draperies arrived, and were never installed. The

East Room was like one of Little Mac's encampments, where a whole *battery* of furniture kept shifting around—nothing was safe, not even the spittoons. I couldn't rest my eye on a single marker; Mary suffered from some terrible affliction, like a madwoman bartering in her sleep. In less than nine months Mother had swallowed up that twenty-thousand-dollar fund Congress had given her to refurbish the White House with carpets and all the other *flub dubs* that were dear to my wife. And she still owed another six or seven thousand dollars.

I wasn't blind to her predicament. Mother had to drive the rats out of that maze of rooms in the cellar before the whole Mansion was infested. She had to buy new china and Parisian wallpaper. She couldn't have a Crimson Room without crimson carpets. I'd catch her in the middle of the night with a hammer in her hand. She had to nail down some carpet, or fix the leg of a favorite chair. She'd gone to Manhattan with that gardener of hers and spent six thousand dollars on curtains, sofas, and hassocks. I hadn't been President more than a couple of seasons, and still Mother worried about my prospects. The little sultans who let her borrow to the hilt would demand payment in full once I had to vacate the White House. I learned all this from Nicolay & Hay, who were like my own detective bureau.

While they spied on the Hell-Cat, as they called her, she angled to get them fired. And she almost did. In the end, with no more means to hide her misconduct, Mary came to me. I was glad she didn't bring my boys into the fracas and have Willie or Tad sing about the high cost of chalk in their classroom. She wore a simple black gown with long sleeves and only a single feather—kind of a mourner's costume—without a particle of decoration in her hair. She'd been crying. But she wasn't crying now, and she didn't aggrandize herself, tempt me with the ghost of Dolley Madison.

"Father, I overspent."

"We'll manage," I said. "But, Mother, it would stink in the land to have it whispered that the money for furnishing this house was tossed into the wind by the President when soldiers are freezing and don't have proper blankets and shoes."

Mary blinked at me. "Wind," she said. "I didn't . . ."

"I'll never approve the bills for *flub dubs* for this damn old house."

Her shoulders shivered under that mourner's costume. There was a wall of frozen pain on the side of her face, like a momentary paralysis. Her mouth twitched. She had a worse stutter and lisp than Tad—and a terrible pout. Her temples throbbed. I knew what she was trying to pronounce. So I pronounced it for her.

"*Flub dubs.*"

And her old flare of anger came back. She no longer had a lisp.

"Mr. Lincoln," she said, "I'm not in the habit of buying *flub dubs*. Mr. Buchanan and his niece turned the White House into a wilderness. Miss Hallie tinkered with the East Room and left our own quarters uninhabitable. I will not have my boys live in a field of rats. I spent more than I had the means to spend. But the task was prodigious."

I meant to kiss Molly and hold on to that sweet musk of hers, but I couldn't. Was I jealous of the Chevalier and his *lust* for literature? Did I want to tear down the Crimson Room with its Parisian wallpaper? But she shouldn't have been *that* foolish, to turn a gardener into a finagling cavalry man, and fill the Mansion with some sultan's carpets while I had to hold the Union together with the flat of my hand.

I let her wander away, the skirts of her gown gliding against the oilcloth with a strange *whish* while I stayed there, in the dumps. Tad's kitten leapt onto my lap. Tabby commenced to tear at my sleeve, and pretty soon it had a tiny batch of thread in its paw—I could feel that little cat unravel me. I stuffed him in my pocket, while I was raveling out somewhere on some private moon.

29.

Noel 1861

I COULD HEAR THE church bells clap like a melody of thunder in this first year of war—and the rumble of men returning
from battle without their boots on, ambulances caught in the ruts of
a road, boys with blood on their faces trying to outrun a cannon's
brutal song. I'd just come back from McClellan's camp with Mary
and the boys to offer little gifts to the soldiers in their winter huts. We
couldn't stay long—there was an epidemic of measles. But Mother
and her White House sewing circle had knit socks for the soldiers.
And despite the measles, Mary traveled from hut to hut, with bundles
of woolen socks until she looked like some strange martyr. She asked
every single soldier his name and where he was from. Mother could
see how gaunt they were; she had nothing from her garden to give
them in the December frost, so she dug into her bundle, and they
kissed her hand as she delivered the socks.

"Bless you, Madame President."

We could only bring a pittance for them. I was feuding with the
War Department. A clever little band of foxes in Manhattan were

making a fortune speculatin' on this *conflagration*—the war was like a burning barn, and we were saddled with half-blind horses and pistols that shattered after the first shot. Soldiers went into the field with gimcrack guns that could make them lose a hand or an eye and might get them killed. I couldn't even complain to Little Mac. He fell ill with typhoid fever just before Christmas. No one was permitted to see him, not even his generals.

"The bottom is out of the tub," I told my secretaries.

Bob had come down from Harvard in his crimson cravat, and I felt impoverished in front of him with that little rope of silk around my neck. He'd run away from home as a little boy. It was Mary who found him hiding under the porch. I was out on the circuit, in one of the far counties, while Bob must have been dreaming of a far county of his own. He was an outrider, like his Pa. We had a similar streak of *terrifying* loneliness.

We managed to put on a good show in front of Mary and Bob's little brothers, who idolized him. Tad ran through the corridors like an Injun.

"Bobbie's back, Bobbie's back."

He sat with Mary, held her hand. Her eyes began to wander. She wasn't fooled by Bob's civility. She could feel his absence, and she had to fight her own hysteria.

"Robert, do tell us about the Cambridge societies, and all the fun you've had. I still recollect that soufflé we shared at one of the Harvard clubs."

"Mother," he said, "there's little to tell."

He knew how to cut her to the bone. He wasn't cruel, just remote. And when he saw her tears, he relented and allowed his mother to stroke his hair.

"I'm popular," he blurted out. "Oh, the other fellers are so curious about you and Father."

Mary perked up. "Curious about me? I declare, that's a *curious* curiosity. What ever do they ask?"

"About Camp Mary."

Mary ruffled her nose. "That little thing? I was visiting a field of tents, handing out bonbons and handkerchiefs, and a colonel with a goatee cracked a bottle of champagne over a carriage wheel—it was a regular explosion. And he bowed to me, this colonel with the goatee, and said, 'Madame President, I christen these grounds as *Camp Mary*, in honor of your war work.' That's all it was."

Bob wasn't even listening. He kissed Mary on the forehead and promenaded out of the family parlor. I found him in the corridor.

"Father," he said, "I want to go to war. The other fellers are joining up, and I can't. I feel like a piece of crystal—*the President's boy*—too precious to run off with some regiment. It isn't fair."

I should have encouraged him to run off, but the news would have killed his Ma. The mere sound of a fizzle-stick or the boom of some carriage could set her mind to fly away with assassination plots. She was fearful whenever I left the Mansion, fearful that some disgruntled office seeker might rip me apart in our own public rooms. She assigned Willie and Tad as my bodyguards, and then worried that the boys might get hurt *bodyguarding* me. Her eyes were in a constant glaze. I had to reassure her half the time that Bob was safe at Harvard.

"I'm glad, Son, but it would break your mother's heart."

Bob's eyes went cold. He bowed to me, like one of my own ambassadors. Then he hurried down the hall. I couldn't get near him after that—Bob was like a coyote in a gentleman's jacket. He pulled away from all of us, though he did play Christmas games with his brothers on the White House lawn, utilizing leather pouches as bowling balls.

And he would watch them ride their ponies.

The White House stables had multiplied with the war. Little Mac housed some of his own horses with us, and the boys' ponies were now government horses, too. Half the cavalry used our barn. Little Mac could have usurped our stables for his cavalry, but he didn't. He shared the premises with us. And until he caught typhoid fever, he rode through the President's Park with his usual fury.

It was Christmas Eve, and some drunken soldier must have dropped a lantern, and soon the whole barn was ablaze. We didn't lose one horse, not even the ponies. The stable hands slapped their rumps and led them out of that conflagration with rifle shots. But nothing could control them away from the barn, no matter how hard the soldiers *hee-hawed* and waved their wet blankets. We had a stampede—a hundred riderless horses raced across the capital's streets, overturning carriages, ripping off the signs of hotels with their flanks. One horse bit a man—chewed half his coat as he was coming out of a saloon. You could hear the horses' neighing for hours, and it was a bloodcurdling call.

The snow fell right in the middle of that stampede—as if nature was conspiring with McClellan's horses. The flakes rode the wind, like a crystal cloud that followed the horses' tracks. Tad and Willie were worried about their ponies. I had to put Mother to bed.

"Mr. Lincoln, you won't let our boys loose—like the ponies."

"No, Mother."

"And why is Robert so distant all of a sudden?"

"That's the habit of a Harvard man," I explained.

Bob and I went down to the stables in our winter boots. The cinders were still flying, and we had to cover our faces. Bob's coat suddenly caught fire, and I had to slap at him with my sleeves until the flames relented a little—and then I hurled him to the ground like a potato sack and dug him into a pile of snow. He looked up at me with the flakes in his eyes—a porous mask, pocked with jewels.

I wasn't pondering the war, not even the soldiers in their huts. I was thinking of my son—how he was vanishing into his own wilderness, and I couldn't catch him. Bob looked like a creature created in a curtain of fire and snow.

We heard a gentle noise, like a child whimpering. And Little Mac stepped right through that curtain of snow without his britches. He was wearing cap and boots, with his field jacket over his nightshirt, and clutching the reins of two spotted ponies.

He tipped his cap and handed both pair of reins to Bob. Then he saluted me.

"Good night, Excellency. I still have the fever—I'm going back to bed."

He was another snowman, flushed with wind and fire.

"Wait," I said, in a panic. "You haven't been properly introduced to my boy."

He smiled, stroked his chin beard, as grand as any general in a nightshirt, grander even, with his spurs on.

"Oh, I've met with Bob before," said my General-in-Chief. "While I was riding in your park—we talked artillery."

Bob knew more about Parrott rifles than his own artillery captains, according to Little Mac. I was stupefied. Bob had never talked artillery with his own *Paw*.

Parrott rifles, Parrott rifles rang in my ear like some military tune. I heard a heartless pounding in my ear—like thunder in the snow. And then the whinnying of animals, wild yet familiar, like a mournful wail. McClellan stood there—didn't move a muscle. And those delinquent horses, two or three at a time, suddenly appeared like children with wet manes, bumped their noses against Little Mac and made no other sign. Bob and I might as well have been invisible as the riderless horses returned. McClellan whistled once, and a dozen horse soldiers arrived with blankets.

He went from horse to horse with a blanket, whispered, "Whoa,

Rider, whoa, Tom," and walked into the snow with his little troop of cavalry horses; some had bruised eyes and bloody ears, others limped on broken hooves. I'd misjudged the man and his hauteur; he wanted a world of soldiers, where he and the *Secesh* could meet, general to general, battle in the sun and then smoke a cigar with some lost brother from West Point—civilians didn't count, only horses, his men and boys, his encampments, reconnaissance balloons, and artillery trains. I wasn't sure where he'd stable his hundred horses tonight; perhaps in some other cavalry barn, or at his own headquarters, where he'd croon Christmas carols in his nightshirt, this singular man, who was part magician, part fraud . . .

Mary and the boys were already asleep when I returned to the Mansion with Bob. We walked through the ceremonial rooms like a pair of stragglers in the semidarkness; one chandelier blazed above our heads, and the halls could have been some vast echo chamber. The night watchman was snoring in a gilded chair. I could tell that Bob's mind was on those wild horses that only Little Mac could tame, like some circus master. I didn't have that talent. But I didn't want to lose my boy to this circus master. I squinted hard into the last glimmers of light and could see that Bob's lazy eye was trembling.

"Goodnight, Son," I said.

He trod upstairs on Mother's Manhattan carpets. The watchman's stentorian snores sounded like the thunder of horses' hooves.

"Goodnight, Father," Bob replied from the top of the stairs, his voice wafting above the watchman's rumble, like some sweet serenade, while I stood there, a President with black snow on his boots.

THE DISTRICT
1862, Winter–Spring

30.

The White House & Vinegar Hill

BLACK MAN WAS found frozen in his tracks on Vinegar Hill that January, like a hunter who had nothing to hunt—took half a day to dig his legs out of the ice. Folks trudged all the way from the Willard to have a look at the frozen man. It was the bitterest January in years, and Tad's spotted pony had to wear leggings and a winter hood in a barn that still smoldered. Vinegar Hill had been a haven for free blacks until Army engineers pilfered their land to put up Fort Massachusetts, but McClellan's engineers didn't have to bust up little farms and let these farmers freeze to death.

I could have gone to Vinegar Hill with the War Department, but I decided to visit on my own, without a White House detective on my tail. I climbed on Old Tom and rode along the Seventh Street Pike, with rifle pits everywhere I looked. Hotels were boarded up near this part of the pike—it was meant for military traffic. And I realized for the first time that most of Vinegar Hill was gone. It was swallowed up by rifle pits, an ammunitions dump, a blockhouse, and Fort Massachusetts, built right out of the bones and timber and orchards of the old farms. The farmers were still around; they lived in the ruins near the fort—many of them were women who had nowhere else to park their feet. They wore rags in winter, and leggings cut from strips of paper. I met a farmer lady, who had an infant in her arms. Called herself Aunt Bertha, and she had every right to cuss at me. My troopers had destroyed her farmhouse and driven her off her land. I told her she could stay in the fort with her child whenever the wind was riding hard.

She ignored my summons and offered me a hunk of johnnycake. Her teeth were chattering, her lips had turned blue. I rounded up all the farmers I could find and stood under the ramparts of the fort with them.

The engineers must have forgotten to build a gate; you had to climb the ramparts if you wanted to get in. "We're coming up," I had to holler into the wind.

The commandant called down to me from the ramparts, wrapped in a cape that covered half his mouth. "You can't bring in the niggers, Mr. President. Those are orders from the General-in-Chief."

"Son," I had to shout, "Mr. McClellan works for me."

I climbed up to the ramparts with these colored pilgrims. I could see clear to the White House in the wind. The District had become one huge military camp, alive with a metal gleam that looked like a labyrinth of rifle pits and Parrott guns mounted on little silver trucks.

The commandant was a young captain who couldn't have been more than twenty-five. I told him to feed the farmers and their children and to house them best he could, and if there was the least bit of bellicosity from Mr. McClellan, the captain was to remind the general that this fort was part of the President's own domain.

I bid goodbye to Aunt Bertha and went back to the White House, where I got into a scrape with my new Secretary of War, Mr. Stanton, an irascible sort of feller, with the long unruly beard of a prophet. He commenced to tear into me at a Cabinet meeting.

"Sir, the Lady President can do what she likes with her own clique, but I will not sign up unqualified men. Are you fond of this Wikoff?"

Mary must have tried to palm off the Chevalier on Mr. Stanton. "Mr. President, why is he always *here*? I keep running into him on my way to our meetings."

"Well, he's kind of Mary's major domo."

He was also a rogue reporter sent by the *New York Herald* to spy on the White House. The *Herald* had the largest circulation in the world, according to its editor, Gordon Bennett, who idolized Little Mac, and wanted to see this general in my chair. Bennett would have used his considerable power to ruin me, and he must have pulled Wikoff out of some old shoebox. The Chevalier was a relic *before* he came to Washington. He advertised himself as Louis Napoleon's friend and Queen Isabella's confidant, but Isabella couldn't keep him out of jail in Italy or Spain. He must have visited every bordello in the District, but that wasn't why he was here.

Suddenly I started to see peculiar tidbits in the *Herald*—my own private words and whispers. If I'd been a lady and not some sucker with long elbows and a beard, I would have gambled that Wikoff had crept right into my boudoir. I'd been working on my annual address to Congress, and the notes were locked away in a drawer, but whole paragraphs had been ripped out of that address and appeared in the *Herald*.

Congress decided to look into those damn leaks, and Mary was furious when the Chevalier was *invited* to appear before the Judiciary Committee. She put her hot little hands over her eyes and said Congress was picking on her protégé. Should have scolded her like a child, even if she was the Lady President . . .

Wikoff appeared before the committee next morning and said it was Major Watt, the White House gardener, who had rifled my drawer. I knew it was a lie. No one but Mary could read my scrawl.

So I climbed up to the Capitol and met with the Republicans on the Judiciary Committee in one of their private chambers—it was laden with spittoons and hissing lamps. I had to squint through a miasma of cigar smoke to make out each member of the committee. They were flabbergasted to see me in their headquarters—the Capitol was far from a President's haunts.

"Friends," I said, "you'll have to forgive me for coming here, but I'd be obliged if you released Wikoff. The longer you hold him, the more of a scrape I'll be in—it's a family affair."

I didn't leave them much choice, even if a few Congressmen tittered at my remarks. But they wouldn't have wrecked the Party's chances over one Chevalier. Mary welcomed him back to the White House like some prodigal son who'd wandered from the grasp of evil jailors. She fed him champagne. I knew she'd also fed him my speech, word for word, and I didn't know why.

While Mary reveled one floor below, Nicolay & Hay tiptoed into my office. I couldn't always trust my little detective bureau in matters concerning my wife, but they'd found the Chevalier's diary.

"Nico, did you pick his pocket?"

"We'd do anything to protect our Titan," they said. "But he was vain enough to leave his little book lying around."

It troubled me to read a man's private words—reminders to himself. But these were more than reminders. They were a battle plan. And the Chevalier's scrawl was much clearer than mine, like a child's script.

He wasn't only writing for the *Herald*, it seems. The Chevalier had been in touch with Rebel spies. He was a hopeless amateur and couldn't have harmed us much. But his impressions of Mary hurt the most.

I own that little woman. She'd run off to the moon if I ever asked.

I had to quit reading. I called in my own pair of bodyguards from the Metropolitan Police—they liked to pose as stewards.

"Please march into the Crimson Room and bring me Wikoff."

"Should we knock, sir? The Lady President might be upset."

"Just bring him to me."

I kept thinking of Aunt Bertha and the other pilgrims left out in the cold by McClellan. I'm the one who had asked him to build a ring of forts around the capital, and so he'd usurped property in my name. But each of those farmers was worth much more than Wikoff, who lied his way into the White House and bamboozled my wife.

I'd dealt with fakers before, one-eyed men who sold cures for every affliction under the sun, and carried little hatchets in their back pockets, if ever they had to flee, spoke like minstrels and wandering players with honey under their tongues, but could turn into a viper at any moment. I'd met them in Springfield, or at country inns, while I was traveling the circuit. And I expected the Chevalier to be much the same, even if he'd practiced his craft abroad.

Wikoff was wearing a Prince Albert coat with buttons made of bone. He had a supple ash cane and a silk hat. Metropolitan detectives couldn't seem to bother him. I hoped he would come upstairs shaking a little. But he was petulant, and annoyed. He had a purplish knot in the middle of his forehead.

"Mr. Lincoln, do you have some use for me? You've interrupted my affairs. I was performing some shadow tricks, *Monsieur.*"

I didn't take kindly to him *monsieuring* me. I felt every bit a backwoodsman, and it threw me off the mark.

"Chevalier," I said, "shut your mouth and listen."

He laughed. He had wined and dined with courtesans at Versailles, and here he was in an office covered with oilcloth. It wasn't like the Crimson Room downstairs, with Parisian wallpaper that could remind him of Louis Napoleon's palace. He sniffed about with an air of contempt. He could have wiped me off the map with one of his looks.

"The Presidential chair means nothing to me. I won't be quiet. You're a commoner, Monsieur. And I'm a titled man. Why did you summon me? I was looking forward to a marvelous game of hearts with your wife."

"It's the last game of hearts you'll ever play in this house."

His laugh turned into a sinister bark. "Are you threatening me, Monsieur? I have the whole *New York Herald* behind me. I'm their star reporter."

"No—you're a spy."

"*Ha!*" he said. "I've been called a secret agent many times. And I've sat in many jails. But my friends are much more powerful than my enemies. You will discover that on very short notice."

He was starting to wear me down with his palaver. I was glad I'd never faced him in court. He could have won a jury over with his aristocratic ways, but he was in Lincoln's court right now—all alone with the Titan, without Mary to help him. And I wasn't partial to *furriners*. It was a frontiersman's prejudice, I suppose. Only Wikoff wasn't a *furriner*. He was born in Philadelphia, had gone to Yale and had studied the law on his own, like me, but abandoned his studies and wandered through Europe as the heir to a private fortune. He was a libertine and a liar, according to my secretaries.

"You should have been more careful with your little black book."

He wasn't scared. "Ah, one of your own agents must have picked my pocket—it's not even safe in the President's hotel. And why should you be interested in my ramblings?"

"You've been in touch with Richmond."

He danced on his toes. "You're the one who should be frightened, Monsieur."

He reached inside his coat and pulled out a packet of letters, roped together with a black velvet ribbon. It wasn't the letters that unmanned me, it was the ribbon—it had come from Mary's own ribbon box.

"Excellency, shall I recite some of Mrs. Lincoln's best lines? She writes a *beautiful* letter. She has all the ardor of a well-bred Southern lady. I imagine you wouldn't want Mrs. Lincoln's lines to stray too far abroad. The *Herald* is dying to have a look. But mind you, I'm not a rattlesnake. I might let you have the whole bundle for ten thousand dollars—and an appointment at the War Department. I wouldn't mind being a colonel near Mr. Stanton's desk."

I seized the letters, shoving them back inside his coat.

"Chevalier, whatever Mrs. Lincoln wrote you, she wrote as a friend. And you shouldn't be selling her letters to a damn newspaper in Manhattan."

He wasn't a battler, like Jack Armstrong. He didn't have Jack's princely grace. I twirled the Chevalier around with my left hand and carried him to the door. Down the stairs we went, while White House workers stood inside their cubbyholes and Mary wandered out of the Crimson Room with a puzzled look.

"What on earth is going on?"

She could see the wildness in my eyes—and she panicked, stood there in a frozen trance. No one could rescue her now, certainly not the Chevalier. He'd never been bundled up like that by someone who could wield an axe in either hand. I left him on the lawn.

"Chevalier, don't you ever come here again."

I walked back inside the White House. Mary was still standing there. I wouldn't release her. I kept seeing that delicate rope of ribbon from her ribbon box, imagining it in her hair, and I had the worst case of the *unholies* I'd ever had. There was no cure. I locked myself in my office and wouldn't see a soul, not Willie, not Tad, not my Secretary of War, not McClellan's senior generals—the country hung on a strange cord, where every article and action was suspended, waiting for the President's perusal or signature. I stared out the window, beyond the Washington Monument with its marble mask, and onto the mudflats, and felt like a sleepwalker. I was furious when I heard a knock on my door.

"Who is it?" I growled.

"Mrs. Small. I once rode with you into Baltimore, sir."

That lady Pinkerton entered with her rough, rawboned look. She had nasty scars on her cheek from where that barber had nicked her with his razor. I remembered the pearl handle, could see it still. She'd rescued me from the barber and that rogue marshal in Baltimore. The Pinkertons were now in McClellan's employ as Union spies.

I was much more comfortable with Mrs. Small than with McClellan and my Secretary of State—she was no damn aristocrat. Allan Pinkerton had told me all about her. She'd grown up in one of Illinois' poorest provinces without a Pa, her face marked with smallpox, and moved to Chicago as a pickpocket by the time she was twelve. She taught herself to read and write while riding the cars Pinkerton had been paid to protect. She was nineteen when he found her with another man's wallet. He didn't handcuff her. He saw her talent and claimed her as his first female detective. I'm not sure what name she had. Pinkerton dubbed her Mrs. Small, though she was never married or even engaged to a man. And she'd been a ghost in his service ever since.

She put Mary's packet of letters on the table, roped up with the same velvet cord.

"Sir, the Chevalier Wikoff tried to load off these letters on me. Someone must have told him I was a Rebel courier."

I was silent for a moment. "Did you show that packet to McClellan?"

"No, Mr. President."

I couldn't read her face—it was like a dim lantern in the raw light of the room. My question must have troubled her. She was in Little Mac's secret service and should have reported to him.

"But you're my Commander-in-Chief," she said, and suddenly I could catch a smile on her scarred face. I was feeling mighty low.

"Did you read my wife's letters, Mrs. Small?"

"I would have been derelict if I hadn't, sir. I was *your* courier now. I had to memorize whatever was writ, in case circumstances obliged me to destroy the packet, sir. I couldn't let it fall into Rebel hands."

There was another matter, a little more complicated. She wasn't that fond of McClellan, I could tell, but she wouldn't have been disloyal under normal circumstances. Little Mac was a Democrat, supported by the *Herald*, and she knew what would happen if the *Herald* ever got its hands on Mother's letters to Wikoff. I couldn't have lasted out my own administration.

She must have seen how bereft I was, how lost—a husband with his wife's secret sentiments sitting on the table.

"Forgive me, sir, but Mrs. Lincoln doesn't have the right sauce for the District—it's filled with imposters, like the Chevalier. All she ever did was hold his hand on a carriage ride to Silver Spring, surrounded by four or five other phony dukes. I wouldn't imagine they were ever alone for a minute. And Madame wrote some silly things. She sounds more like a fifteen-year-old convent girl than the Lady President. Should I burn the whole caboodle?"

"Yes," I whispered, but I preserved that rope of ribbon, remembered it around Mary's neck, or knotted in her hair. And I couldn't have borne to watch it sizzle and smoke.

The lady Pinkerton and I tore into that packet and threw every last shred onto the fire in my office. I was stunned to hear myself sniffle. I still had that rope of ribbon in my hand.

"Ma'am, I could be the one who doesn't have the right sauce for this town."

The lady Pinkerton chided me. "That's balderdash, Mr. President. The likes of Mr. Buchanan would have let the Republic *slide*. But we're still the United States, thanks to you."

And she was halfway into the hall before I had the chance to thank her.

"Mrs. Small, won't you stay and have some supper with me and my boys?"

Her face was in the shadows again. I couldn't tell if she was mocking me a little.

"Mr. Lincoln, I was never here, and we never had this conversation. I'm not listed in the logbook downstairs. Little Mac would have a fit if he ever knew I was here. He's kind of solicitous about his property. We're his agents. And he doesn't like to lend us around."

I was quick enough to clutch her hand.

"My, my," she said. "A body might think I was a baroness."

And then she was gone.

I invited Willie and Tad into my office, had the butler bring us up some provisions. We dined on apples and cheese and water from the White House well. Tad asked about the mysterious lady with the pocks on her face.

"*Paw*, she rode out right with the wind. Wasn't she in the cars with us last year?"

I couldn't tell him much about Mrs. Small, else he would have started his own pickpockets' society at the White House. She'd been in some kind of paid bondage to Allan Pinkerton ever since he nearly arrested her in a car outside Chicago. And now she was McClellan's slave and a spy for the Federals who had stumbled upon Mary's letters and didn't reveal them to Pinkerton or McClellan. It was like having a pockmarked angel in my camp—a secret agent who could guard the President's secrets and steal into the White House with an invisible cloak. Pinkerton had trained her well, even if he damn near robbed her of her life

.

31.

Suitors

I SCRATCHED A NOTE to Mary, put it *and* that slice of ribbon she had presented to the Chevalier in an envelope with the President's seal, and handed that package to Willie, who often served as his mother's messenger. The note read,

> *MY DEAR WIFE: I am returning your ribbon. You must have misplaced it somewhere.*
>
> *Affectionately, A. LINCOLN*

I knew my words would cut, with all their strict neutrality. I shouldn't have involved Willie in my scheme. That wasn't fair. It haunted me, but not as much as the Chevalier holding hands with my wife on some clandestine carriage ride. I didn't give a hoot how many other witnesses were on board; they could have all been Rebel spies, compatriots of the Chevalier. Did they smile at Old Abe, mock me and my injudicious wife, infatuated with one of their own fakers? I felt like Titan, prepared to devour the World, but Titan couldn't even tie his shoes, or solve the riddles in his own house.

I met with no one. I planned nothing. Wouldn't see my own secretaries. I skirted around petitioners in the corridors, had them all scat. I had a sudden itch to travel, to roll down the Mississippi in a flatboat, with nothing on the horizon but mud, water, and bald patches of sky. But it wasn't so easy to light out of here. The Titan was too damn tall. I couldn't even hunt for catfish in the canal without being mobbed—and I'm not sure why, but I had a hunger to see Senator Douglas' widow, Adèle; she'd become a recluse after Dug died of the typhoid last year, a little after my inauguration. But it wasn't the typhoid that finished him. The Little Giant was tuckered out. His heart was kind of broken. He hopped across the country, campaigned with his chronic sore throat, and still couldn't hold the *Locofocos* together—that's what we called the Democrats, after a certain kind of friction match that could fire up in your face. If the Democrats hadn't sputtered out of control, he'd be sitting *here*, and I'd be picking spiders off the windowsills of my Springfield office with Billy Herndon.

I had tried to visit Adèle once before, out of respect for Dug. I'd gone to his mansion with my Secretary of State, but Adèle wouldn't even honor Mr. Seward's calling card. I was more determined now. I skipped out the servants' entrance, with my bodyguard asleep on a bench, and hightailed it out of there while folks gawked at the Titan. I didn't have a penny in my pocket—Tad carried all my cash. I climbed onto a horsecar but couldn't pay the fare. The conductor didn't question my right to travel on the cars. I *chawed* with a few of the passengers, signed autograph books with a butcher's pencil, and almost missed my stop. But I climbed down on Jersey Avenue, near the old munitions dump, with its sunken sheds and abandoned privies, and footed it to "Eye" Street.

The Little Giant had once held levees with a thousand guests snaking right onto the street. The mansion still looked like a run-down morgue with shuttered windows and a slanted roof. I rang the bell. I nearly startled the maid's eyes out of her head.

"Could you announce me? I *jest* want to holler hello to Mrs. Adèle."

I stood in the vestibule while Adèle's maid scampered upstairs in her muslin skirt. I didn't have to stand around very long. The widow arrived in a black gown with a crucifix near her neck and a liquid rhythm in each of her steps. I was struck by that singular beauty of hers, even with her long neck. Adèle had been Dug's secret hammer during our seven debates. Her quiet presence, the way she twirled her parasol and smiled at all those querulous folks, had blunted my attack. Adèle didn't seem bothered at all to find me at her mansion-morgue.

"How kind of you to call, Mr. President. I haven't had many callers ever since Dug died. People tend to cut a widow when they can't wheedle a whole lot of favors out of her."

"That's a misappropriation, Mrs. Adèle. My wife has invited you to every one of her shindigs."

"Oh, I did not mean the Lady President. She has sent me flowers from the White House conservatory on more than one occasion. How is Mrs. Lincoln?"

"Tolerable well."

There was no point involving the widow in my scrape with Mary, though I would have liked to confide in someone other than a phantom secret agent—I couldn't reveal my distemper to Adèle.

So we sat in the parlor, with dust all over the place. The mansion had its own ballroom; but I didn't see a hair of it in those windy rooms. And the divans and tables were covered in ghostly white cloth.

"You ought to know, Mr. Lincoln, that my husband really admired you. You're one of the few honest politicians he ever met. He called you the rarest of rare birds. And he suffered over some of the things he said during the debates—I suffered too. I couldn't sleep at night over his remarks about the colored race. That wasn't Dug. It was the monstrosity of politics."

"But he won the canvass, ma'am. I did not."

Now her eyes went pale, as if she were absent and present at the same time. Adèle had withdrawn so deep after Dug's death that it was hard to hold her in one place.

"Did he really win? He crucified himself, I should think. And he was so fond of your wife. Wasn't he one of her first beaux?"

I didn't know how to answer Adèle. It wasn't clear how much of a beau Dug had really been. He was a young politician on the rise, and may not have wanted a plump little wife from Lexington, and Mary may not have wanted him. I like to think she had her sights on another man—a rawboned lawyer out of New Salem without Dug's deep voice and oratorical skills. It *seemed* important to Adèle that the four of us were connected somehow, and it also comforted her that Dug had been Mary's beau. Perhaps it fired up her fancy and kept a particle of him alive . . .

"The very first," I told her.

Her eyes lit in that somber room. "There!" she said. "That makes us cousins, of a sort."

Cousins. The Little Giant would have hatcheted me if I'd given him half the chance. I barely escaped Illinois with my own skin, but he was the loyalest adversary I ever had once I became President Elect. Dug and Mary never lost their bond of affection. I remember how they danced at the Union Ball, how much of a couple they were, though I could sense that fatal fatigue in him, as if he were on the verge of vanishing in the middle of that dance. He'd *imagined* himself as President and savior of the Republic, but when the country spiraled in its own direction, without him and his dreams, Dug couldn't save himself—or Adèle, and I wanted to bring his widow into our entourage.

"Couldn't we invite you to one of our levees?"

Her mood turned dark again.

"Oh, Cousin Abraham—I mean Mr. President—I never leave this house any more."

We had coffee from an unpolished urn, and cake as hard as a soldier's biscuit.

I shouldn't have waited this long to visit Cousin Adèle. I should have *courted* her, a little, seduced her out of that solitude, come by with Tad and his pony, but I hadn't come soon enough. Her eyes started to wander. She mumbled to herself. The maid covered her shoulders with a shawl. I kissed her on the forehead—like some forgotten suitor—and left that morgue on "Eye" Street.

I SAT IN MY OFFICE, slicing up an apple with my jackknife, when I heard the rustle of silk. It was midnight, and Mother had arrived in her nightgown like a somnambulist, with that rope of ribbon in her hair. I skipped all the niceties and preambles.

"He wanted to sell your *love letters* to Richmond."

She went meek, like a lost child. It was as if I had slashed her with a razor—from ear to ear—and she was all bled out, like a butchered hog, but with her own pale beauty.

Her tongue was as twisted as Tad's. She couldn't even pronounce *love letters*.

"They—they were the smallest souvenirs," she said. "They meant nothing. The Chevalier flirted with me. He was a member of my court."

"*Souvenirs.* Can you imagine one of your letters in the *Charleston Mercury?* We'd all have to run for the hills. Mrs. Jeff Davis could move right back to the District. The Rebels have always considered our capital as their own. We're sittin' in their seats."

And a rage built up in her like a burning eye.

"It wouldn't have happened—if you hadn't locked me out. You trust that little hyena, Seward, more than you ever trusted me. You should have married him. You're at his mansion every night—I imagine he would make an excellent bride."

I pulled that ribbon out of her hair, twisted it in my hand.

"Molly, please listen. Seward does not give my secrets away. He does not peddle his influence—for a pair of ponies."

"I did not . . ."

She'd once been the queen of my campaigns. She'd read all my speeches, helped me recite them in front of a mirror, but I locked her out, as she said, didn't even seek her counsel. And it rubbed her raw. I couldn't have survived for a moment with Mary as my general. The damn country would have crucified me. She had a lust to be the Lady President, *almost* like McClellan. She was the prisoner of protocol, a queen without claws. She wasn't meant for conservatories and sewing circles. Mary wanted to intrigue, like all the men around her. But as Lady President, she was banished to the little country of her own quarters, and all she had left was to intrigue with scoundrels like the Chevalier. I'd abandoned her to this big white barn near the Potomac, my child-wife. So she went on mad sprees with Major Watt, bought enough hassocks to outfit an apple orchard, and the dark veins deepened above her eye, as if some permanent crease had entered her life. I couldn't bargain with her. I had to woo her away from that glut of buying.

"Puss, I saw Adèle."

She ruffled her nose, as if some sudden attack had come from another quarter.

"Which Adèle?"

"Dug's *Widder.*"

"But I am stunned—Mrs. Adèle sees no one."

"Well, she saw me. And she said how we were cousins and all, on account of Dug being your first suitor."

Now my Puss began to purr.

"Good gracious, he wasn't the first. I had so many suitors, my feet nearly fell off from sashaying on such hard floors."

So much of the bile had bled out of me. I put that hunk of velvet back in her hair, but I couldn't hold her very long. The vein was beating over her eye, with bits of blue thunder. "Why," she said, like a creature who had walked out of the forest in a feather dress and had learned human manners in a day, "I never did dance with Mr. Wikoff. I haven't replied to one of his letters, one of his pleas. I suspect the Chevalier is stranded in Baltimore without a pinch of currency to pay his hotel bill. And I wouldn't dream of inviting him here."

Then she stroked my arm like some Secretary of State. "We ought to sell the Mansion to Mrs. Jeff. She'd have to pay a pretty price. We could move into the Willard with Willie and Tad. Mr. Lincoln, it would be much simpler to talk peace if President Davis lived across the lawn."

I didn't even try to dissuade her. She'd forget about Mrs. Jeff in another hour, find another strategy, meet with Major Watt. I'd have had him guillotined if he couldn't smooth Mother's feathers from time to time. She marched across the hall to her headquarters, her mind swollen with secrets.

32.

The Dead Prince & the Demented Queen

MARY DID HAVE one male accomplice at the White House—Willie. With his brownish-blond hair and blue eyes, Willie had attained a certain stature at eleven. He'd become the Young Prince President, as Keckly and others called him. He wasn't a wild Injun, like Tad. He didn't steal pillows and pens, or add to the general mischief. He often went on some ride with his mother and Mrs. Keckly to the finest hat and cloak salons in town. Mary would remain in the carriage with the Young Prince President, while her seamstress negotiated with the shop girls; these girls would bring the shop's goods out to the carriage, and the Lady President would try on different hats and cloaks, with Willie holding up a mirror in front of her eyes.

"Mother, that's the one!"

He had a habit of dressing in her clothes. Mother didn't seem to mind; she encouraged Willie. He must have served as her private mirror. When the boys created their own circus up on the roof, charging a penny or two—Tad wore my spectacles and pretended to be a tyrant, which he often was, and Willie wore one of his mother's lilac gowns, very low at the neck. I forked over two cents, like some of the other suckers at the spectacle, heard Tad sing, "Old Abe Lincoln came out of the wilderness," while Willie danced in his boots and gown.

I wasn't the only one under his spell—he could crush you with all that blue ice in his eyes. The prime minister of Morocco visited our Mansion and presented the Young Prince President with a new pony, and that damn gift was far more legitimate than the spotted ponies Mother had picked up in Manhattan from some banker or dry goods baron. Willie pranced around, giving rides to all the servants' boys at the White House who'd never been on a horse's back. He went riding in the mudflats near the Potomac and caught a chill—that chill turned into bilious fever. He shouldn't have gone out where all the dead cats were buried. He'd suffered through a bout of scarlet fever two years before and still had a weak constitution.

Mother had to put her prince to bed while his fever climbed. He vomited and had the runs, and ofttimes he was delirious, screaming for his pony. I would have rid *Duke* up the stairs of the White House and right into Willie's sickroom if that would have cured him of the fever. Mary was going to annul the grand gala she had planned for the fifth of February—an evening ball where you couldn't get in without a ticket—but Willie's condition improved, and the very best doctor in the District said our boy would be fine. Mary still stayed with him most days and nights, slept beside him. Keckly or I would relieve her for a spell, and I was feeling chipper after Willie opened his blue eyes and said, "*Paw*, are you taking care of Duke?"

"Rubbing him with my own hands," I said. I liked walking down to the stables after Cabinet meetings—it cleared the mind of fluff. And I could be certain that Duke didn't have any saddle sores . . .

I sauntered into Mary's boudoir a few hours before the big soiree.

Mrs. Keckly was doing the final touches on Mary's gown. My wife was wearing white satin, with lace twisted into little black flowers that were part of a very long satin trail.

It was Mrs. Keckly who minded our sick boy while we went downstairs to a ball whose tail had been cut short—*La Reine*, as my secretaries sometimes called Mrs. Lincoln, had outlawed dancing for the night. Mother feared that all the chomping around in the East Room might disturb her Willie, but the Marine Band still played "The Mary Lincoln Polka" while our guests arrived.

Folks were flabbergasted; they'd never seen such vittles in all their lives—neither had I. Mary's gala had been fixed up by Maillard's of Manhattan, the finest caterer in the land. And folks could feast their eyes on silver tubs of partridge, quail, duck, foie gras, oysters, and beef, accompanied by a *battlefield* of champagne glasses, and a spun-sugar gateau in the shape of Fort Sumpter, while I pictured wounded soldiers in their ambulances without a bite to eat.

The dinner lasted until three, but Mother and I hardly touched a morsel. We took turns sneaking upstairs to the sick room. Mary had a bewildered look under her black-and-white headband when she returned to the soiree, her eyes darting from guest to guest. She could have been out on the China Sea. I'd have to rein her in.

I loped up the stairs, two at a time. Mrs. Keckly was wiping our boy's temples with a wet rag. I clutched Willie's hand.

"*Paw*," he said. "Lightnin' struck the barn. I was there, *Paw*. The smoke and fire made my Duke blind. He fell down, *Paw,* and there wasn't a body to pick him up. I'll never be able to gallop with him again."

I tried to nudge Willie out of that damn dagger of a dream.

I could hear that constant roar from the dining room below. Folks had started dancing in spite of *La Reine*. The staircase rumbled, and a lone chandelier rocked and left a shadow on the wall. I wondered if Willie's delirium about Duke's blindness was the mark of some strange perdition.

The wailing went on and on, as if Willie's delirium was an eternity of screams that rose above the chandeliers and hid inside the rafters. What troubled me was that his sounds could have been an erratic bugler's call, the melodies of war. He sang of sick cows stranded on a battlefield, of soldiers with cups of blood in their caps, of worms crawling out of the water, of Parrott guns with eyes and ears. It was a revelation listening to Willie. He could have been creating his own Bible, chapter by chapter.

Yet he couldn't seem to *heal*. He would rally for a few days, smile at Mary and Tad, converse with his *Paw*, then return to his bugler's call, with each delirium deeper still. His songs no longer made much sense, and his fever was like a tornado ride. Mary grew morose as she watched Willie worsen. Soon Mrs. Keckly had to look after her and our boy; she had to hide the blood on his nightshirt from us. Willie's eyes turned clear as crystal the sicker he got—it was the same pale blue that enriched the air right after a thunderstorm. I could feel the Almighty lurking in that pitiless color, as my son was *wrassling* with the angels.

Leslie's Illustrated Newspaper had lauded Mrs. Lincoln after her gala as our Republican Queen. But another paper printed up "The Lady-President's Ball," a poem about a dying militiaman in the capital who can *feel* the flickering glow of the White House from his hospital room.

> *What matter that I, poor private,*
> *Lie here on my narrow bed,*
> *With the fever gripping my vitals,*
> *And dazing my hapless head!*
> *What matter that nurses are callous,*

And rations meager and small,
So long as the beau monde revel
At my Lady-President's Ball!

I pitied that poor boy, but was disheartened by the *unfairness* of the poem.

"Mary, you've visited a hundred privates like him in their hospital beds. You even have a camp named after you."

"And a polka," she said. "The Lord is punishing me now for my pride—and my expensive frills. I've been remiss. Those who urged me to that *heartless* step of having a ball now ridicule me for it, and not one of them has asked about Willie. *I have had evil counselors!* And all of them will have to pay. I will lock the public rooms. We will never have another levee, or another gala."

She took to wearing a veil, and she muttered prayers to herself, used incense she kept in a fiery silver ball—it was to scarify the Angel of Death hovering over Willie's sick room. She wasn't that eager to have Willie's best friend—Bud Taft—visit the White House, but when Willie woke from his delirium, he was lonesome without Bud, and I couldn't get that little boy to go home.

"Gosh, Mr. Lincoln," Bud said, with God-awful red eyes, "I couldn't abandon Willie just like that. He'll start to cry when he wakes up and finds me gone."

After it got late and Bud fell asleep near Willie's bed, I picked up the boy, wrapped him in a blanket, and had my own *bodyguard* carry Bud home. Tad couldn't visit his brother because he, too, now suffered from the same chills and high fever.

I returned to the sick room and found Mrs. Keckly standing by the bed. She was taking care of all the Lincolns now and practically lived at the White House. My wife couldn't have borne the burden of two sick boys without Elizabeth. Mother would keep vigil all the time, wandering from Willie's room to Tad's, like a sleepwalker with a wet rag. She kept wiping her hands, wiping her hands, and wouldn't stop. Elizabeth had to tug at Mary to get that rag out of her hand.

Now she tugged at me. "Rest up, Mr. Lincoln. I'll mind the boy."

"But he might call for me, Madame Elizabeth."

And the sliver of a smile broke through her sorrow.

"I'll know where to find you, sir, even in this big house."

The stewards were very quiet, not wishing to disturb our boys. The maids curtsied and kissed my hand. Bob had come down from Harvard to be with us during our double affliction—two boys with bilious fever. He helped Elizabeth with her chores and was the only one who could calm my wife. She listened to Bob, like his own child.

"Mother, go to bed!"

For once, he wasn't even wearing Harvard's crimson cravat, nor did he say a word about gallivanting off to the army with Little Mac. He seemed to summon a strength none of us had. I sat with him in the sick room, while he held Willie's hand. Little Mac's own surgeon arrived to look after our boy—a major in McClellan's medical corps. He had blood on his tunic from the operating table, and he was so damn tired, the color had bled from his eyes, like a salmon trout on a silver hook. He listened to Willie's heart with the twisted tubes of a stethoscope, then took Bob aside, talked to him near the window, and vanished with his medical kit and the sour perfume of blood.

"Bob," I whispered, "what did that damn sawbones say about Willie?"

"He'll survive the crisis. The Doc gave his guarantee."

Guarantee. Our boy had had five or six surgeons, with their fancy syrups and hacksaws sticking out of their pockets, but Willie never stopped coughing strings of blood. He drank and drank, yet his mouth was all blistered. His eyes wandered from Bob to my beard, from my beard to the wall, as if he could suck meaning from every single glance.

And then his hand went soft and the wandering stopped. His throat made one tiny rattle and a couple of chirps, each one faint as the last. The wind went out of him—and Willie was gone. My oldest boy wiped Willie's eyes and took charge. He summoned Elizabeth and had her wash and comb his dead brother.

I watched Yib undress my blue-eyed boy, pluck off his nightshirt, and I was terrified—not of the dying, that I understood, but of his swollen belly and the pale shine of his skin. He had no flesh on his arms, no flesh at all.

Bob recalled what had happened when Little Eddie died twelve years ago, and his mother had surrendered to her nervous fits. He'd been around her while I was out on the circuit, his classmates poking fun of Cockeyed Bob—the two of us still had that lazy eye.

He combed her hair with loving strides of the brush and sang to her, kept her out of the sickroom, so she wouldn't see Willie's pale mouth and ravished body. He was gentle to his mother, even gentler with me. I should have been the one to console him. I couldn't.

"Father, it was the typhoid. Nothing would have helped."

My stranger-son took me in his arms and stopped my shivering.

"And if the same thing should happen to Tad?" I moaned, utterly unmanned.

"I'll watch over him—I will."

I let my boy go about his *bidness*. I was hampering him, like some melancholy aide. I wandered into the sickroom—a death room now—and watched Elizabeth wash and dress my blue-eyed Willie. She was bent over, moving with a marvelous, mournful rhythm, as if her hands could drum a little life into him.

I looked at my dead boy—his crystal eyes shut now, his shoulders as narrow as pins.

I covered my own face with my hands.

"It's hard, hard to have him die."

          ❧

THE EMBALMER WAS a little man with a derby and a general's goatee; he had the delicate fingers and musical gait of a dancing master; his apprentice, who couldn't have been older than Willie and had *some* of Willie's blond hair, carried all his embalming fluids and other tricks of the trade in a satchel that dragged at his feet— the boy could have been lugging cannonballs around, and nearly stubbed my toe.

The embalmer cuffed him on the ear. "Careful, careful. That's the President's foot."

The boy seemed so harassed that I wanted to rescue him from the embalming business. The embalmer dove into his satchel and plucked out a portrait of Willie with blond hair and blue eyes painted in.

"Mr. Lincoln, is that the likeness you and the Lady President are looking for?"

The question troubled me; I didn't know what to say to this ghoul, who was about to manhandle my own little boy and suck the juices out of him. Bob had to rescue his *Paw*.

"Sir, we do not want my mother to be shocked by what she sees. That is the sole purpose of your visit."

The embalmer smiled; he was much more comfortable around my older boy.

"I understand perfectly, Mr. Robert."

He tipped his derby, grabbed his satchel in one hand and his apprentice in the other, and disappeared inside the Green Room. I heard the lock click; the embalmer had bolted himself inside. He worked for six solid hours and communicated with no one. Then the lock clicked again, and he emerged from the Green Room with his apprentice, their own faces embalmed with a waxen look, as he bowed and ushered us in like a ballet master.

I was scared to look. All I could remember was that pale skeleton with sunken cheeks—but the skeleton was gone. Willie had the sweetest smile. That embalmer must have engineered flesh with his balls of wax. Willie's fingers were polished; his cheekbones weren't sharp as knives; the apprentice had washed and combed Willie's hair. And now I understood the embalmer's art. He used a live boy to groom a dead one.

I got them out of the Mansion as quick I could. While Willie lay there in his silver casket, Bob summoned his mother; she descended in her black veils and didn't want to enter the Green Room. Bob had to entice her, lure her in, and get Mary to look inside the silver casket.

"That's not my Willie," she said. "It's a wax boy. His cheeks are all rouged."

Bob kept her in the Green Room, and we had our own private service—there were no prayers. Mother was decked out in her widow's weeds—layer upon layer—until most of her was obscured under her veils, but the little I could see of her mouth was white as chalk. We couldn't control her wailing—no one could, not even Bob—but he kept her afloat with his quiet power.

She couldn't bear to face other mourners, she said, and wouldn't attend the funeral. "I won't parade in public with my Willie gone." So Bob delivered her back upstairs while the casket was shut tight with its silver screws.

The services were held in the East Room, where my wife had presided over the Lady-President's Ball. I remember how the caterers had arrived from Manhattan two whole afternoons before the ball—Monsieur Maillard with a platoon of chefs. We all stared at pastry guns that could sculpt nougat mountains and spin sugar into beehives or revenue cutters and mermaids leaping out of waterfalls composed of charlotte russe, while Mother babbled with Monsieur Henri in French. She waved her arm like a magic wand and yet another piece of confection appeared. Both our boys had a candy mountain named after them, even if they were too ill to feed on their mountain, and Mother herself would become the first *fatality* of her own ball . . .

The Capitol had shut down for the day in remembrance of Willie. Willard's canceled its afternoon tea. The bordellos of Marble Alley wouldn't accept a single client. Little Mac arrived at the White House in his brocaded uniform and embraced Bob—he looked like a popinjay in his yellow sash. He'd come with his wife, Nell, who didn't have his hauteur in her hazel eyes. She was, in fact, much *prettier* than McClellan in a black cloak without a warrior's ribbons. She clutched my hand and didn't have to say a word.

The roof rattled like a lumbering barn and the chandeliers shivered—a terrific storm seemed to rip right through our attic just as the general's aides filed into the funeral with all the majesty of their polished chevrons. They might have smirked if they hadn't promised Miss Nell to be on their best behavior. Their loyalty was to the General-in-Chief and his bride. A window shattered somewhere in the house. Mary's own preacher talked about Providence. I didn't listen to a word—I found myself in a carriage pulled by two black horses with silver bells on their bridles, and Bob right beside me. We were riding to a chapel vault in Georgetown.

Our carriage rocked under the assault of the whipping rain. I saw a building collapse—its roof spun in the air like a murderous projectile. An uprooted tree was in the middle of the road. The ground seemed to saunter like a swollen snake. The wind curled the horses' manes. A rocking chair in the grass could have been the relic of some lost battlefield.

"Father," Bob said, "we may have to put her away for a while."

"Put who away?"

"Mother," he said. "Her mind is clouded."

I stared at this general, who was planning his line of battle.

"Bob, it's been a great shock, and we're not over it. We've both witnessed Mary's *dry* spells."

"But this is worse," he said. "We may have to lock her up at St. Elizabeths."

I was pretty much silent after that, with the rain pelting our leather carriage like live bombs. I'd visited the government asylum, a brick castle across the Navy Yard Bridge; St. Elizabeths sat on its own hill—the castle had a crenellated roof and cages in its back yard that served as a storage bin for tigers and elephants from the Smithsonian—you could hear the elephants trumpet their own sad cause from the Sixth Street docks. I took Tad and Willie to see the tigers once; their coats were covered with sores, and they had drugged eyes; they weren't much better off than the lunatics inside . . .

※

MOTHER GOT RID of Willie's toys and clothes, tossed them into a barrel—wouldn't even offer a trinket to one of the White House's colored boys. She couldn't bear to look at his picture or one of his poems. The least mention of Willie would have her fly into a rage. Not even Keckly, who was mistress of her wardrobe, could escape Mother's wrath. She'd become a Juggernaut—you were overrun if you got into her way. I wouldn't have been bothered much if she hadn't hurt our other boy. Tad must have reminded her too much of Willie. She cackled at him, nearly struck him, too, her fist flying out from within her welter of black crêpe and veils.

"You're not my son. You're some impostor who happens to live here—go away, or I'll kill you."

Molly couldn't have meant that, but Elizabeth and I still had to watch over Tad.

"*Paw*, is Yib my mama now?"

I didn't know how to tell him that his mama wasn't *right*. She hated the corridors where Willie had walked, the servants who had looked into Willie's eyes, the very walls that had witnessed his pranks with Tad, and she must have hated herself for being alive while Willie's bones were in a crypt. God had punished her in a furnace of afflictions.

I would catch her biting her own fist. And she would flail at me.

"*Mr. Lincoln.* You were dancing downstairs with Miss Kate while our boy had the fever. You kissed her, had both your hands inside her skirts. You brought a strumpet into this house. That's why God has abandoned us . . . while the *beau monde* was reveling at my Lady-President's Ball."

You couldn't reason with her, and I didn't try. I let her whack at me until she got a little tired. She would withdraw into her bedroom in the crêpe of a demented queen, with Keckly as her companion and nurse—she had no other friends in the capital. Sometimes she would wail for Willie half the night, with the sounds *ripping* through the walls.

"Where's my angel boy? Who stole him from me? Was it that *chocolatier*, Henri Maillard? I'll smother him in his own charlotte russe."

Bob called her a candidate for that hospital on the hill, but he had much more patience than his Pa. If she passed him in the corridor in her mountain of crêpe, he would peck his mother's hand and survey her with his own *mountain* of pity.

He wouldn't leave while Taddie *tossed with the typhoid*. It was Tad who kept him here, not his mother's mourning. Tad would only take his dose of medicine from Bob's hand, or mine. And the moment Tad's crisis passed, Bob had to pack. His jaw was bristling with emotion. He was a boy who never cried, not even as a *little-un*.

He offered to skip a semester at Harvard, stay here with us, but I wouldn't allow it.

So I watched over Tad. He would sit perched on my shoulder at Cabinet meetings, like some obligatory owl, or would hide under my desk when I had some writing to do. Then I would carry him down the hall, with his head ducking under the chandeliers, and both of us would sleep on my narrow bed.

Still, matters got worse once we went into April; the lamps sputtered as Molly wandered around in her veils and slapped a couple of servants for bringing up Willie in her presence. So I crashed into her headquarters in my old subaltern's shirt that I used as a dressing gown. She was sobbing with Mrs. Keckly at her side, aswim in black crêpe.

"Mother, you cannot hide Willie's death under your veils."

I could see her mouth sucking against all that black silk. I'd startled her. I must have looked like some crazed Cossack.

"Father," she muttered, as if she were in a trance, "everything appears a mockery when my idolized one is not with us."

Took her gently by the hand and led her to the window.

"Mother, do you see that large red castle on the hill yonder? Try and control your grief, or it will drive you mad, and we may have to send you there."

Molly was silent for a moment, like a general gathering the last troops she had left. Her eyes blazed—then she gave up the battle. She dug at her heart, as if she were about to stab herself with a sharpened silver spoon. And a kind of clever smile erupted on her mouth as she chanted to herself about the *beau monde* and the Lady-President's Ball.

❦

I COULD HAVE BEEN a sleepwalker, like my wife. Weary as I was, I put a shirt over my subaltern's gown, decked myself in a green shawl, and walked out the Mansion well after midnight. It was no idle march. I saluted the armed guards who never questioned one of my rambles, and was nearly run down by a barouche full of drunken officers. The carriage lurched to a halt. And then an officer leapt down from the roof with the slight contempt of a cavalry man for all noncombatants, clicked his heels, and said, "It was unconscionable, Mr. President. Our coachman was blind. But I don't blame him. I should have noticed ye, and I did not."

I could tell from his swagger that he must have served with McClellan. And there was no getting free of him now. He insisted that I ride with him and his fellow officers, who had none of his flair. I wouldn't get into his military car. I hung from the coachman's handle, like some silver wraith with hair on his chin.

"The Patent Office," I said, and we flew into the wind, up past Willard's and onto F Street. It was the first moment of delight I'd had since Willie's death. I was unencumbered, unshackled, clutching that handle on the outside of a car. And then the Patent Office rose out of the fog, like some benign monstrosity that covered an entire block—half the town could have lived inside its marble pillars. My Secretary of War had moved all the Patent Office examiners to a back stairway, and converted the building into a barracks and a morgue—and a military hospital in three compartments under the ornate ceiling of the second floor. I had no trouble gaining entry, even in my unusual garb. The male nurses and chief surgeon saluted me. The chief's name was Mallory. He'd suffered a nervous collapse during Shiloh, after presiding over the amputation tables for thirty-six hours, until his gown was one great smear of blood, his face a grim mask, and his fingers nearly ruined from the mark of his own scalpel and hacksaw—and still he cut, until his aides had to subdue him, and he returned from Shiloh with a slight tremor and half his thumb gone. And now he was stationed here, a chief surgeon who no longer amputated limbs, but could guide the hacksaws of younger surgeons like a maestro and rally nurses who'd been on the wards without a moment of rest. He wore carpet slippers, like the President of the United States. He was the gentlest sort of man, and I could imagine what all the hacking had done to his constitution.

He still wore his surgeon's cap, like some great thinker out of the Bible.

"Mr. President, I'm so sorry about your loss. We worshiped the young prince."

I couldn't talk about Willie, couldn't even thank the chief surgeon for his remembrance of my little boy.

"I hope I'm not intruding. I'd like to stroll the wards, even if the boys are asleep."

"Ah, they'll be in rare form, sir. It'll liven up their spirit to see the Commander-in-Chief."

So we went out upon these curious wards, which consisted of a narrow passage between two mountainous glass cases packed with miniature models of inventions *patented* at the Patent Office. No one human mind could have absorbed the sheer variety, taken all these inventions in; fire trucks with ladders that reached some unimaginable sky; silk balloons with tentacles rather than a single tether; muskets with three rifled bores, like a man born with multiple thumbs; a saber that doubled as a harpoon; a pocket pistol with a lamp imbedded in the grip; metal fingers that could replace a severed hand, &c., &c. I couldn't walk among these cases without sensing some new and defiant wonder, but I hadn't come here for that.

The chief surgeon had a bottle of rich red wine poking out of his pocket, and I reckoned he'd become a tippler after his collapse. I was prepared to prop him up if he did his own curious dance on the wards, but it wasn't wine. He was carrying a bottle of blackberry syrup for all the sick soldiers, who lay in a double row of cots along a gallery as deep as a cornfield. There were water pails near every cot and scraps of muslin for boys who were coughing up blood and phlegm. The groans grew quiet when these boys on the ward noticed their new guest. They sat up straight as they could, even those swathed in bandages. Several of the boys cried as the chief surgeon mixed the blackberry syrup with sweet water and handed out his *brew* in tiny tin cups. They couldn't swallow the syrup for a couple of moments.

"We mourned the young prince, Mr. President. Chief Mallory had us light a candle on the day he passed. We were preparing to writ you a letter, sir. But Nurse ran out of paper and ink."

Not a single boy would talk about his wounds, or his suffering, and the bloody rags piled near his bed. I was caught in my own well of emotion, but I wouldn't break down in front of these boys. They kept asking about Mother and Bob and Tad and how I was holding up.

"Tolerable," I said.

The surgeon didn't have to look at the little tags strung to the cots; he knew the name and rank of every single soldier.

"Jonesy, do ye have anything to ask Mr. Lincoln now he's here? You may not get another chance."

Private Jones of the 5th Massachusetts couldn't sip the blackberry solution from his tin cup; he'd been wounded in the neck and shoulder, and was all wrapped up in muslin; so he had to suck in the syrup through a glass tube. "That's scrumptious, Chief."

He coughed up syrup and blood; and suddenly I couldn't find one darn nurse on the ward, not even a volunteer, so I patted the boy's mouth with a strip of muslin. He'd been a clerk at a dry goods store in Newton and never even owned a saddle, but the first question he asked was about a horse.

"The Young Prince President, sir, what was the name of his pony?"

Duke.

The memory of that little palomino cut under the skin like a scalpel. If Willie hadn't gone with Duke near the mudflats, he might never have died of the fever. But that hospital ward was like a telegraph service, and the palomino's name traveled from cot to cot on its own magnificent wire. And before we arrived at the middle of that deep corridor, Duke was the most celebrated palomino in creation—at the Patent Office.

Then a murmur broke through the silence of the ward—not the tick of a telegraph, or the flutter of wings, but that peculiar honey of the human voice when it didn't rise up in anger. And I realized where all the lady nurses had gone; they hadn't abandoned the hospital clinic. They stood at the end of the ward in their gray and green garb, with hymn books in their hands; accompanying them was another nurse with an accordion, and a little choral of convalescent soldiers who'd climbed out of their sickbeds to sing with the nurses.

> *It came upon the midnight clear*
> *That glorious song of old,*
> *From angels bending near the earth*
> *To touch their harps of gold . . .*
> *And ye, beneath life's crushing load,*
> *O rest beside the weary road*
> *And hear the angels sing!*

Their sounds rose to the barreled ceiling, and then sailed back down, with an unbroken melody that disarmed us, not with the sweetness of those angels in their chant, but with an accordion that wheezed like any *convalescent,* with soldiers who could barely hold a tune, and nurses who had the rough contralto of some wild man; and still all the singing meshed in that long gallery under the roof, and we mourned as soldiers mourned, not for some fine prince of peace and war, but for the broken earth in battles yet to come, for the living and the dead we would never meet, for a lone palomino who sat idle in his stall, waiting for a rider who would never come.

SOLDIERS' HOME
1862, Summer–Fall

33.

Summerland

MOTHER HAD CRASHED out of *jail*—that self-imposed asylum in her bedroom—and started to shed her winter veils. Her mood hadn't shifted much. She locked up the Green Room, where the embalmer had worked on Willie, and kept the key. She appeared one morning in Tad's room like a stranded mermaid, without her crêpe, or a stitch of clothes, and hugged him as if nothing at all had ever happened. Elizabeth had to cover Molly in a blanket and lead her back across the hall, but Tad was overjoyed. He came marching into my office like a trooper and sang in front of my whole darn Cabinet.

> *Mary Lincoln's my Maw again,*
> *Mary Lincoln's my Maw again!*
> *God save the Union, hurrah, hurray, hurroo!*

I had to dress him most mornings. He wouldn't sit still long enough for me to get him into his socks. But he had a new house to explore—the Presidential cottage at the Soldiers' Home, an asylum for disabled veterans with its own secluded splendor, along the road to Silver Spring. I didn't want to tell my boy that I was one more *disabled veteran*, desperate for a little break from the sad eyes of the telegraph office's cipher clerk—with his cavalcade of dire news.

The Soldiers' Home had the advantage of being in the hills three miles north of the capital, where no one could see Mother trot around *nek-kid* in front of her little boy. And we could avoid that thunderous roll of wagons carting night soil from the canal. The diggers on board would sing their drunken songs about some favorite harlot and topple off their wagons. I'd find them in the morning, under a tree in the President's Park. And so we skedaddled to the Soldiers' Home the second week of June; there were no drunken diggers or dead cats in these hills, no carcasses of rotting horses—just four cottages and a central asylum with a grand tower, where soldiers would lean over the ledge like circus devils and signal with their semaphores to the encampments down below. Tad often shared mess kits with some of these *active* soldiers. They dubbed Tad a *3rd Lieutenant*, and made him part of the Presidential detail—the War Department had even conjured up a uniform for him.

The Presidential cottage, with its gables and chocolate-colored trim, was near the site of our first *national* war cemetery, and I could see that field of white stones and markers from my bedroom window. The casualties of Bull Run were buried in this tranquil retreat, but that relentless chip of the shovels wasn't tranquil to mind or ear. We had new arrivals every week, more than thirty—boys who'd survived Bull Run with some horrendous wound and lay in a forgotten ward until they stopped breathing; other boys with brittle eyes who *disappeared* all of a sudden, and still others who had to be dug up from some distant cemetery and delivered to the Soldiers' Home in a funeral truck or military ambulance.

The diggers sang to themselves—not bawdy songs, else Mother

would have chased them from the grounds—just tunes about some sweetheart or lost Kentucky home. And ofttimes Tad would wander over to the graves in his uniform and bring them a piping pot of coffee together with Mary's finest cups. But I couldn't beat my own son to the checkerboard. The minute I descended the stairs, I'd discover Tad at the great big cloth board I'd carried from the White House, with the checkers all lined up, and Tad sucking at Bob's Harvard pipe, without a pip of tobacco in its bowl.

"*Paw*, will ye take a game?"

I didn't have my heart in it, not with the diggers who seemed just next door, with coffins that could have been varnished crows, and that chipping music in my ear, and Tad like a little general at the board, puffing on his pipe, while he leapt over my checkers with the merciless exuberance of a hussar.

"King me, *Paw*."

I crowned a couple critters until I had to stare at a brace of checker-kings and wonder if I had any moves left. I couldn't *hive* the enemy now, couldn't own the board. A Commander-in-Chief was like a flatboatman who had to pilot his vessel from point to point and couldn't set his course farther than the eye can clear. But I wasn't much of a river pilot—or President—against Tad. He could have shucked me into the corner day and night, with his relentless leaps.

❧

MOLLY WOULD STROLL the cottage grounds with a black-eyed Susan in her hair. Mind you, it wasn't a sign of merriment; no country air could cure her of Willie's death. She'd gone way inside where civil strife couldn't interrupt her mourning. So I was stunned when Mary came up to me in her nightshirt with some of the old razzle in her blue eyes and that black-eyed Susan in her hair.

"Mr. Lincoln," she said, "I've *seen* our boy."

"Which one—Bob or Tad?"

"*Willie,*" she said. "Our beloved boy. He visited me last night, kissed me with his angel lips. He said I shouldn't cry just because he had crossed over. We'll all meet in Summerland, he said. And so I have been picking flowers, dear, to pass the time. *Susans for Summerland.*"

"Summerland? What's that, Mother?" I asked, kind of jealous over her visiting rights with our Willie. "Is Summerland another cottage at the Soldiers' Home?"

She wouldn't allow my heathen heart to ruin her joy.

"Why, it's heaven, dear. It's where I'll meet up with my two lost boys. And we shall never be lonely again. Father, the fightin' would be done in a minute if you wore a posy in your hair."

And she was even amorous after that. We hadn't kissed in months—longer, not since Willie took sick and died. I'd been hungering for her, and never even noticed. But Molly was no mourner under her nightshirt. I hadn't sniffed her flesh in such a long time. I was randy as a goat after she unbuckled my belt, and licked that gorge between her bosoms. She lay there like a luminous ghost, never moved once, but moaned with a child's delight. And I had to thank Willie's apparition for it. *Wasn't Willie.* It was those damn mediums who hit us like a plague of locusts in the summer of '62.

Mrs. Keckly had introduced my wife to the world of mediums. She herself had once been part of the same spirit circle. So I caught up with Keckly, while she was delivering a satin dress to Mother. I met with her *in camera*, on the porch.

"Madame Elizabeth," I whispered, like a man holding a pistol to her head, "do you believe in all that spirit stuff?"

"Yes."

Keckly looked me in the eye, and was bold about it.

"That stupefies me," I said. "My wife is gullible enough, and she'd shake the world apart to have what she imagined was a glimpse of her boy."

"Well, sir, has she suffered from it? Mrs. President has been getting rid of her veils, hasn't she? She's been visiting soldiers at the hospitals, putting flowers on their pillows, acting as their scribe. . . . Hasn't she been more of a wife to you? It sweetens her temperament to talk to Willie. Where's the harm?"

Mrs. Keckly hadn't been curtained off as a child in a Lexington mansion, like my wife. She'd been whipped and beaten, preyed upon by her master's son and abused by other men. She still had welts on her back. She couldn't have bought her own freedom without some hard sense, looked after her boy, and earned her keep as a couturière. She ought to have been a bit more skeptical about a place called Summerland.

"Madame Elizabeth, what's it like—Lord Colchester's little paradise?"

Keckly was much too clever to fall into one of my bear traps.

"It's not his paradise to win or lose," she said with a flutter of her lip.

I rolled my eyes and pretended exasperation when I was as calm and regular as the wind on my porch—it was much easier to make a point if some folks figured you were half insane.

"Will a body tell me what Summerland looks like? Is it an endless field of goldenrods where children who have crossed can romp without a single chore?"

"Mr. Lincoln, sir, it's not a farm or a field. No mortal can imagine it, not even you. But it's where I'll meet my dead boy the moment I cross. And if it has horsecars for coloreds and horsecars for whites, I'll kill those cars and bring my boy back down."

Keckly didn't vanish from our hill. She went back inside the cottage. Then other women came, the wives of certain Senators. And a few men marched up the hill, shady characters who hid their eyes under a hat. I couldn't do a thing. They all had a pass from the Lady President. Then a stoutish man arrived, much more regal than the rest. He climbed out of a carriage and kept fingering a felt hat. I didn't have to consult a medium to imagine who he was—Colchester, the charlatan himself . . .

Mary wasn't amused—I'd invaded her sanctuary, and she didn't like it. She was sitting around a long table I'd never seen before; it must have come from the attic—else that charlatan had borrowed this *spirit table* from his hotel. It was like a flimsy vessel that could seat twenty voyagers. Colchester's table reminded me of a sinking barque. All the women were dressed in black, and wore their veils. Mrs. Keckly was with them, near my wife, while the charlatan's male conspirators kept their hats tilted over one eye, like the Devil's own dominion.

"Mr. Lincoln," my wife said, without her Southern lilt, "have you strayed into our hall?"

That old fork of irritability appeared above her eyes. Soon her whole face rippled like a barn on fire. But Colchester calmed her down—as if she were his unruly colt. He had blue veins on both his cheeks and advertised himself as the illegitimate son of some baron.

"Mrs. Lincoln, I'm delighted to have the President. We have nothing to hide."

"But he cannot sit at our table," she said. "He will weaken our chain, and the electrical spark will never, never pass—Willie won't talk to me with my husband in the hall. He will remain in the ether, lost to us. And I won't allow that to happen."

"He's an intruder," said one of the bereaved wives, her tongue poking through the veil like a pink spoon.

"Nonsense," said Colchester, like some unctuous snake. He reminded me of Mother's other confidant, Chevalier Wikoff, but Wikoff wasn't half the scoundrel Colchester was. Wikoff didn't prey upon bereaved mothers, didn't pull on their purse strings and suck their blood. "We're not a closed society—please sit with us, Mr. President."

So I sat down between Keckly and the charlatan on one of the cottage's cane chairs. There were no lectures or introductions, no wanderings of the piano, and not a single spirit rapped on the wall. We didn't have to sit in the dark—the angels in Summerland weren't shy about sunlight, it seems. Colchester asked us to clutch each other's hand.

"That is paramount, Mr. President. Once our chain is broken, the spirits will slip right through your fingers."

So we held onto each other and swayed a little, like *wrasslers* warming up for a tug-of-war. A couple of the charlatan's little men moaned. But the moaning wasn't loud. Colchester never asked us to shut our eyes, so I watched Mother and Mrs. Keckly—I was like a Pinkerton at the table sifting for clues. Mother's eyes shone with a liquid light, as if she were locked inside some rapture where not even a husband could intrude. I didn't feel some electrical cord winding through my body, not a pinch of power. And then one of the women shouted from under her veil.

"I can see my Tommy," she said. "The sun is out, Lordship, and he's still on the battlefield, with blood all over."

And that's where Colchester chimed in, with his voice hopping out of the chandeliers like some revelation from the cottage's own burning bush.

"Mother, what did Tommy say?"

"That I shouldn't fret. His wounds didn't hurt him none. He's already crossed."

"But he's still on the battlefield," Colchester said while I squinted at the chandelier.

The woman was sobbing now. "The battlefield's a mirage. He's crossed over, blood and all."

I looked at Keckly; she must have caught the shiver of some electrical charge, but she didn't squeal or moan like Colchester's little men and she didn't have Molly's bliss in her eyes.

"Mother Keckly," said the charlatan, "has your boy been visiting with you too?"

She was silent for a second, but she near took off my arm with the current inside her. And I wondered if I was just another casualty of Colchester's spirit wars.

"The Bluecoats tried to set fire to my George, said he shouldn't be in Summerland. But George don't have to listen. He's content."

"Mother Lincoln," said that buzzard, "what about your own dead boy?"

Suddenly that allure was gone, that brilliant blue of her eyes, and there was a look of pure terror. Molly was caught in that chain. She couldn't clasp or unclasp her hands.

"I can't, milord. Not . . ."

Colchester could have been perusing a worthless child. That's how hard he stared at my wife.

"Now, now, mustn't whisper. Speak up."

"I can't. Not with Mr. Lincoln in the room."

I wanted to rip Colchester from his chair.

"But we'll break the chain if Mr. Lincoln leaves," he said, in the unctuous voice of an animal trainer. He prospered in such a brutal time, where the living had to *live* with the dead. He must have struggled until the war as a sharper, and now he was a *spiritualist* who had his own little order of heaven. "And where will you be, Mother, without your Willie?"

"Lost," she whispered, her body undulating to some rhythm inside her head. I had a hunch that this charlatan was performing for me, that he wanted to show how useful he might become in managing Molly, and should be a member of my own political circus.

"Mother, can you see him now?"

"*Yes.* He's right here, at the cottage. He's walking on the roof . . . and wearing the uniform of a bugler. He borrowed it from another boy—in Summerland. He's so blond, milord."

I wasn't even surprised to hear that knocking on the roof. His conspirators at the table must have had pedals and clackers at their feet that could hurl a sound into the air, or something similar to that. His humbug irritated me, but I was as vulnerable as any other *Paw* who lost a boy to the fever. And for a second I could glimpse Willie with a bugle in his hand and the sun in his eyes. There was so much pain attached to Molly's pleasure of conjuring Willie out of this hocus-pocus—she had to worry that he might slip right off the roof. A boy who leapt out of the ether could still crack his skull. Summerland wasn't all that safe.

Molly's shoulders heaved as she began to sob, and the charlatan was alarmed. He couldn't afford to have his star client out of control. He had to keep her snug inside his own little peg. "Mother, what's wrong?"

I ain't certain what she saw. I had to catch her words between every single sob.

"Milord, do they have embalmers in Summerland? My boy is tottering on the roof—he'll fall. And Willie doesn't have wings."

I was still trapped in the séance, with rumblings on the roof. And then the rumblings reverberated right above our heads, in the attic. That damn attic had some missing floorboards, else our ceiling must have been porous and besieged by termites, because a man crashed through the ceiling and fell right onto the table in a whirl of dust. He had every sort of instrument strapped to his middle—hammers and bells and tuning forks that could have re-created the fiercest wind or the echoes of the living and the dead. He stared at us like some delinquent child, though he must have been fifty. Colchester tried to disown him, pretend he wasn't there, but Molly had had enough of her new confidant. She undid the chain with a violent pull, and that whole spirit circle fell apart. One of Colchester's henchmen landed on the floor. Molly stood there, muttering to herself. The others were petrified, even Elizabeth. The Senators' wives commenced to shriek. I calmed them down like petrified ponies and had the charlatan pack all his apparatus. He and his henchmen lit out of there with their little boxes. They scurried to his carriage like a band of mountebank mice. I could have chased them down the hill, or locked them in the guardhouse, or had them quarantined for a week at the Willard or the National. But his Lordship wouldn't be returning with any of his trickster mechanics to our roof. He'd read the wrath in my eyes, witnessed my swollen cheeks, and he was no fool.

34.

At Harrison's Landing

I WENT ON A Presidential *picnic* in July to meet Little Mac at his new headquarters, while Mary went to Manhattan—her favorite arena—with Tad. My little boy was allowed to wear his 3rd Lieutenant's uniform on the train. He traveled with soldiers rather than civilians. And I boarded the *Ariel* with a bunch of marines at the Navy Yard, and we hightailed out of the District, while the hospital ships were arriving with their terrible cargo. I couldn't see a soul under the heavy canvas covers, but we could all hear the wailing that seemed to ride above the river with its own palpable presence—a *dirge* for the living and the dead. Then a tarpaulin was raised, and a nurse in a wrinkled blue jacket appeared from within the bowels of one boat; I watched her climb onto the wharves with a slow, mournful dance and a deranged look—all that wailing could have been inside her own head.

The *blue unholies* hit, and I stood frozen in my summer shawl. My spirits lifted with the morning fog, and I never felt more peaceful than I did on the *Ariel*'s deck—away from bloodstained bandages for a little while. Our steamer approached Harrison's Landing right at sunset, with the wharves under a brilliant red sheen—the tents on the hill and the boats in the harbor blazed up for McClellan, as if the sun had conspired with the general's own wizards. His camps were always a marvel of engineering. At City Point, I saw some kind of soldiers' Jerusalem, a new town—with hospitals, artillery, tents as tall as a sail—that stretched for miles. His new headquarters at Harrison's Landing wasn't as bountiful, but it was sculpted right out of the riverbank, with his *boys* part of the same pristine sculpture. No one could have guessed that they'd come out of battle two weeks ago with blood under their fingernails, their tunics ripped, their caps lost in some woeful field, with the shriek of a dying brother still in their ears.

McClellan was waiting for me on the wharves, one hand inside his military tunic; his mustache and chin beard had a raw red gleam that was almost ominous in the near dark, while his aides hovered around him like circus animals, half wild—and utterly timid. All his senior officers had their own chin beards—replicas of Little Mac, they strutted like him and recognized no other god. Yet his own boys couldn't find him in the thick of battle on the Peninsula. Little Mac rode off on Dan Webster's back, without leaving anyone else in charge; his generals had to scoot for themselves. And here he was two weeks later, twice as arrogant, rubbing his chin beard as if nothing at all had happened. He'd been four miles from Richmond, *four miles*, and now he preened in his military paradise on the James, with a host of sutlers' tents and an embalmers' shed—none of his officers would ever die *unremarked*; a special detail would carry them off the battlefield in their tunics and bring them right to the embalmers' table. He had the cadavers shipped home in a metal coffin, each little agony of war erased from their hides.

He didn't have his usual dreamy menace, or that sardonic laugh of a high-pitched hyena.

"Excellency, glad you could come to my quarters," he said with a grin. He lived with his *family* in a mansion on a hill above the embalmers' shed. I saw an endless scattering of white tents as we climbed that hill—the tents seemed to rise right out of the water and cover the encampment like a series of humpbacked snakes. I could hear a soft tumult come from the tents, like the murmur of siege guns. The soldiers on the hill were much more ragged than McClellan's honor guard at the wharves. They hobbled in and out of their tents with frying pans, coffeepots, and lanterns that looked like a swelter of swollen eyes.

Little Mac had turned the old brick mansion into a barrack, cluttered with his generals and all their toys—riding boots, unsewn epaulettes, cigar tins, spaniels that accompanied them into battle and slept in a shoebox. We sat in the parlor, which he had converted into a map room and a mess hall, and he offered me champagne his spies had stolen from the wharves of Savannah.

He began to pontificate after his first sip of champagne.

"War, Mr. President, is the finest form of art men have ever had. It must be conducted upon the highest principles known to Christian civilization. And radical views, especially upon slavery, will be the ruin of our men. We are churchgoers, sir. We don't attack civilian populations, we don't steal crops, or give our own shirts to niggers."

A Christian war, he said, a little cavalcade between white folks on one side of the river and white folks on the other. But we couldn't play McClellan's game much longer, a game in which we staked all, and our enemies staked nothing.

"*General,*" I said, in a room that bristled with officers and their hot breath, "we cannot win the war you describe. The rebellion has gone too far. We must strip the South of *all* its resources, and the greatest resource it has are its colored soldiers."

McClellan plucked his chin beard. "Excellency, we didn't knock down any colored boys on the battlefield. There isn't one solid nigger captain among the *Secesh*."

His generals laughed and plucked their own chin beards. They would have stripped off my clothes and sent me howling into the wilderness, if Little Mac had given them the word. They were sore as hell after I relieved him of his command as General-in-Chief. But I couldn't really get rid of Little Mac. I had to let him stay on to lead the Army of the Potomac. Yet I still seethed a bit about an old *war* wound. Little Mac had been vice president of the Illinois Central during my seven debates with Dug—a Democrat and a Douglas man, he was the one who ordered his conductors to lock me out of the saloon cars. So I'd always had an urge to whack him around the ears, even when he was my General-in-Chief.

"It's preposterous, Mr. President," said one of his lackeys, Harve Haverstall, a lieutenant colonel with my own affliction, a lazy eye. "Jeff Davis wouldn't arm his colored population. He's scared to death of a nigger uprising. Lord, having a slave army among the Rebs would be our biggest ally. But it will never happen, sir—no, no, they're fiddlers and barbers and drummer boys."

"And stevedores and nurses and ammunition carriers that are as good as soldiers," I said, "because it permits Mr. Jeff to parcel out his fighting men . . . and keep his army afloat."

The generals squinted at me as if I'd fallen off the moon.

"Are you saying, sir," muttered the tallest general, "that you would like the aforesaid colored boys to fight on our side?"

"That's exactly what I'm saying."

"It would hasten our demise, sir, not theirs," said the lieutenant colonel, who must have been the family philosopher and court jester. "Our boys won't fight with coloreds at their side. They'll lay down their weapons, sir, and run home to their farms."

I'll risk that, I wanted to hurl into their teeth. They were convinced

I would smash to pieces, wouldn't last the war, and that Little Mac would prevail. So I had to deprive them of their little illusions once and for all.

"Gentlemen, I ain't going anywhere. I expect to maintain this contest until I die, or am conquered, or my term expires, or Congress or the country forsakes me."

I watched the glee curl around in Little Mac's eyes.

"And what if the army forsakes you, sir?" asked one of the generals.

"Then I'll find another."

And now the lieutenant colonel rasped at me. "And who would train this mystical army? Colored boys from the Cotton States?"

"Hush up, Harve," said Little Mac, utterly pleased with himself. He had his pack of wild dogs soften me for the kill. Now he could pick at my carcass with his own paw.

"Excellency, you're correct. It's hopeless—we cannot win. But for another reason. I'll tell you a tale I heard from my own spies. When President Davis appeared at Bobbie Lee's camp for the first time, the general asked, 'Who's in charge here?' 'You are,' said Mr. Jeff. And Lee answered, 'Then I'd like it a lot better if you rolled right back to Richmond.'"

The generals yawped like a bunch of lunatics, while Little Mac paraded in front of them.

"Excellency, I mean no disrespect. But unless we are guided by conservative and Christian policies, the war will linger on to a miserable end. A declaration of radical views, especially upon slavery, will disintegrate our present armies, and you will have no other, I swear to God."

He must have had spies in the President's House who read my every scratch. I was thinking hard on "a declaration of radical views," much more *radical* than he might have imagined. I couldn't crush Mr. Jeff without disinheriting him of his army of slaves.

"Mr. President, I may be on the brink of eternity, with all my warriors, so I can allow myself a little bluntness. You will require a Commander-in-Chief of the Army, one who possesses your confidences." He paused to cup his chin in his hand. "I don't ask that position for myself, but I am willing to serve in such position as you may assign me."

He was a master of finesse, like an aeronaut in his balloon, surveying every corner of the landscape, but he forgot that I was holding the tether cords and could rein him in.

"Mr. McClellan," I said, "I shan't be appointing any dictators this season."

The parlor was poorly lit, and I watched his generals smolder as they moved in and out of the dark like shadow men. Seward had warned me not to tangle with Little Mac on his own territory, that his generals were capable of any kind of revolt. Was I supposed to hide from Little Mac at Harrison's Landing, not come here at all? I'd wounded his vanity, a little. His mustache was quivering.

"And what if the country should demand it of you?" he asked in a contralto's nervous pitch.

"Well, there's one Commander-in-Chief, far as I can tell, and you're looking at him."

He was absent from that moment on, his face stark white in the shadows, while we supped on a rabbit stew prepared by his family, absent while we went on a midnight parade in front of his adoring *legions*, boys who would have done anything to touch Dan Webster's flanks, and that's why I kept him, even while he ran off the battlefield like some brat, because I didn't have another general who could hold the heartbeat of entire regiments in his hand. And when we returned to the old red house, it was Lieutenant Colonel Haverstall who accompanied me up the stairs with a candle; I could feel the malice in the tread of his heels—how he would have loved to pitch me over the banister and into the dark ruin of the stairwell. I heard him sniffle as the staircase rocked under our feet like a decrepit cradle. He delivered me to my bedroom in one piece, lit the lantern on the bureau. But his body writhed with emotion, and went stiff, like some gigantic claw.

"You have maligned him, Mr. President. He's the best darn general in the service."

He bolted out of there with the candle in his fist, and the clump of his boots haunted my sleep like hammer blows on the head.

35.

Jackson & the Little General

H E CARRIED HIS Bible with him into battle. Stonewall Jackson suffered from dyspepsia and had to suck on lemons all the time. He rode a gelding, Little Sorrel, but wasn't much of a sight on his chestnut horse, slumped down in a ragged tunic, like some old-clothes man, with the bill of his cap nearly blinding him—that's how low it sat. His eyes went bad, and his orderly, whom the general had taught to read, now had to recite passages from the Bible, or that dyspeptic man in his ragged coat couldn't fall asleep.

Yet he wasn't dyspeptic on the battlefield. He crept behind our lines in late August and found a treasure at Manassas Junction—all our damn supplies were sittin' in the sun. That deacon sat on Little Sorrel and watched his boys have a Bacchanal. They gorged themselves on lobster salad and rinsed their throats with Union champagne. They wove around in feather hats and crinolines that must have belonged to some Union general's war wife. They battled over jars of pickled oysters. They guzzled whiskey until the deacon-general confiscated all the whiskey they had and broke bottle after bottle against the side of a railroad car. He took nothing for himself. But he allowed his boys to escape with *some* of the spoils. He burnt and blew up whatever remained until that railroad junction resembled a vast funeral pyre.

I could smell the smoke from my country cottage—I assumed it was a *signal* that Richmond was on fire. I should have reckoned it was the first sign of our ruination. Jackson decided he would have one more funeral pyre. His men snuck back into the woods—and John Pope, who led our brand-new Army of Virginia, started his attack, confident that reinforcements would arrive from McClellan, but Pope's boys wouldn't fight; they loved Little Mac—and McClellan's relief corps was nowhere to be found. He wouldn't budge from his new headquarters at Annapolis. His horses were going blind in the sun, he said. And Little Mac telegraphed the War Department: "We have to leave Pope to get out of this scrape & at once use all our means to make the Capital safe."

Jackson was like some apocalypse in a ragged coat who could mow down all the men and matériel between Manassas Junction and the District while sitting on the back of Little Sorrel. Our citizens waited for his gelding to appear on Pennsylvania Avenue with all those marching madmen in crinolines and feather hats. Willard's wouldn't let in any *unfamiliar* guests. The hotel's habitués had steak and onions for breakfast, pigs' feet and gingerbread for lunch, and sat around the Willard's curved bar with hatchets under their coats, waiting for the barbarians. Families carted their possessions around in wheelbarrows, not knowing where to run; I could see them move in narrowing circles near the canal—their barrows looked like beetles. Some fancy girls from Marble Alley stood on the Long Bridge with *Secesh* flags until marines from the Navy Yard carried them off to Old Capitol Prison. The B&O station on Jersey Avenue was packed with people who would have given a month's wages for a railroad pass out of the District—they clambered aboard military trains and left their baggage at the depot, while wounded soldiers wandered the streets.

My Cabinet screamed for McClellan's scalp, but I couldn't pull commanders out of my hat. The Rebels had Stonewall Jackson and Little Sorrel. All we had was Little Mac, who built encampments like a pharaoh, entombed himself, and never sought the muck of battle, but his men didn't have much morale without him.

In early September, in a torrent of rain, as the last of Pope's troops trudged back to the District, some of them without shirts or shoes, others limping in paper boots, Tad and I walked out the White House to greet them with a basket of little cakes. The soldiers moved in some kind of reveille, as if they couldn't rouse themselves from the dream of battle. Their mouths twitched; their eyes fluttered to some private tune where pomp and circumstance failed to matter. They clutched the soggy cake and saluted Tad. He wasn't a 3rd Lieutenant now, the pampered son of a President. The rain had lent him the illusion of a real officer, who just happened to look like a child.

"Greetings, sir. God protect ye."

These soldiers saw something else in that torrent—*their* general, Little Mac, riding his black stallion through the blinding rain. These men couldn't have mistaken him for Stonewall Jackson and his sorrel. He didn't have tattered sleeves or a cap over one eye. He wore his full dress uniform, with a commander's yellow sash. But the sash seemed much darker in the rain. He wasn't some cockerel preening for his generals. His pain was much too raw; the horror seemed imbedded in his brow. His hand shook for a moment; and then this cautious, calculating general rode along that ragged line on Dan Webster and saluted every soldier with his cap. I watched him lean over the bridle and converse with a particular man, ask about his wife and children— it was hard to talk with rain in his mouth, but he swallowed the rain and didn't cough once.

He removed his cape like some cavalier and put it around a shivering soldier. The soldier started to cry.

"I can't take that, sir. It's much too precious."

"Son, it won't get lost. You'll know where to find me. Keep it as long as you like."

Little Mac remained there until that line thinned out to nothing. Then he cantered over to me and Tad. He saluted my boy with that same wet cap.

"Lieutenant Lincoln," he said, "I might need a bugler one of these days."

"But I can't bugle, sir."

"Your *Paw* will learn ye," he said in my Kentucky accent. He wasn't mocking me. He was trying to play with my boy.

The pity was now gone from his eyes. McClellan was furious with me and my Cabinet. We had interfered with his notions of war. He didn't believe much in willful ruin. He would have sat outside Richmond forever with his siege guns until the Rebels swallowed their own hides. War had little to do with chaos—it was, according to him, a contest between Christian generals, a dance as particular and patterned as the quadrille. But there were no ladies involved, just generals and their Christian soldiers. And he didn't leave much room for Presidents and other civilians in this scrape. I was supposed to provide him with men and matériel and hold my tongue, while the Christian generals danced their quadrille in some far corner of the map. But he knew I would never buy that ticket. So he bent in his saddle, bowed to me, and rode off without another word, his stallion taking perfect steps as the rain lashed and lashed.

A BITTER WIND SWIRLED around the Soldiers' Home. Mary caught a chill; Tad shivered in his nightshirt. And one afternoon, in mid-November of '62, we abandoned our summer cottage, and with our cavalry escort right behind us, we moved back into the President's House. It felt like an army of our own, all that crashing around in the dust.

That same army crept inside my skull, as it strove in the corn. I'd landed in some Inferno where a great battle was fought over and over again. Cavalry from both sides charged about, beheading stalks. At first I thought it was a kind of brilliant exercise, that this cornfield was a training ground for cavalrymen. Then they whirled about and attacked their own horses. And the horses neighed with a horrible melody that carried across the field like the cries of children.

Bodies rose up from the crushed corn. It wasn't much of a resurrection. They wandered about amid the blades of corn. And it didn't seem to matter how hard I wept. I couldn't save these wanderers. Then someone else rose out of the corn, a bugler with Willie's light hair. He had blood all over his face, but I could recognize my own dead boy. I must have been right there with him, in that field of carnage, since he said, "*Paw*, do you miss me, *Paw?*"

I was confused and filled with every sort of wonder. I had no philosophy to deal with this, nothing I could ask my Maker about—if we had a Maker and hadn't come out of a broth of little devils. Had heaven and hell swirled into one during the rebellion, and was war itself a spiritualist's dream? Summerland had become a battleground of corn, with ambulances and bloated horses, and with my dead boy as a bugler—without his bugle.

And that's when I saw him, the far rider with a Bible in his saddlebags. But he didn't have his sorrel with him. He was struggling in the corn, his bony knees rising up and disappearing again. He could have had some piston in his back—that's how regular was the rise and fall of his knees. He plucked his Bible out of a pocket, and he read from Revelation, as his knees rose and plunged.

And I saw heaven opened, and behold a white horse; and he that sat upon him was called Faithful and True, and in righteousness he doth judge and make war.

He was a horseless rider, a prophet in a rumpled coat, who sang about the white horse of war. All the wanderers were gone—and my Willie. The prophet was alone with his Bible and straggly black beard. He didn't have his army of fanatics in their crinolines and feather hats, boys who went to war with their frying pans lodged inside their muskets, so they would have more room for gunpowder in their haversacks. He must have been a lunatic, because he danced and sang in the corn without the least bit of shame.

I heard the voice of harpers harping with their harps . . .

The bloated horses were gone, the cadavers with clamped fists and startled eyes, the ambulances with missing wheels, the haversacks, the muskets, the frying pans, as if that white horse had swept through the cornfield and wiped out the carnage in its wake. The prophet kept pumping with his knees, and it wasn't madness at all. He was communing with the dead. And I realized what that rising and plunging meant. He was his own sorrel, horse and rider in the crushed corn.

THE DISTRICT
& ENVIRONS
1863 & WINTER 1864

36.

Emancipation Day

I T WAS MARY'S first official appearance since Willie had passed, and she wore a black bonnet and a dress of dark silk that New Year's Day, but she didn't waver once while we stood in the Blue Room and welcomed our guests, didn't whisper in my ear about the spirit world. My white gloves were soiled after a solid hour of shaking hands, while Mary's eyes commenced to wander. I could see that worrisome fork in the middle of her forehead, like a load of lightning under her skin, as we approached the anniversary of *our* little soldier's fatal illness. She still communed with Willie most nights, and I tried not to listen when she wandered through the halls in her nightgown, looking like Ophelia in the candlelight, a child with a woman's round lines, humming nursery songs to the little soldier, while her mouth puckered into a half-mad smile. And then the humming would stop, and she'd grip her own head in her little hands, as if she had plunged into an apoplectic fit. The *blinders*, which grew worse the nearer we got to Willie's deathday, on the twentieth of February, could cripple Mother and contort her features into a swollen mask. But I didn't feel a *blinder* coming on.

She started to chatter with a covey of my commanders and their wives. She relished the idea of playing Mrs. Commander-in-Chief.

"General Joe," she chirped with icicles in her eyes, "don't you think we should have crossed the Rappahannock *upriver*, where the bombardment wouldn't have been so fierce, and the Rebels couldn't have rained so much fire on our heads with such rapidity? Those devils came roaring right out of the fog, and our pontoon bridges swayed so hard, half our army could have drowned."

And before the general could answer, she turned on the soft heels of her slippers and said to the general's wife, "Mrs. Joe, will my husband sign his Proclamation, or will he leave it to rot under a pile of maps on his desk? How much are you willing to wager?"

I had to intervene, or there might have been a rebellion in the ranks: my commanders didn't much care for that Proclamation, said it would sow discord among our troops.

"Mother, we wouldn't want to saddle Mr. Hooker and his wife with such highfalutin matters on the first day of the year."

She still had a river of ice in her eyes. "Father, I have a million things to ask Mrs. Joe."

"*Mother*, you'll have to ask her another time."

She grew quiet, but I could feel the rage rise up in her against me and my generals. She'd have dashed off to the front if I'd allowed her to do so. And we stood in the reception line, while Mary bowed and I clutched more hands. The generals all sneaked out to some shindig on Lafayette Square. The White House gates were opened, and the *wild geese*, as Mary called them, flooded through. They weren't wild at all. They were ordinary folks of the District, men in mechanic's coats, with mud on their boots, and their wives decked out in brilliant-colored bonnets and shawls. Mary winced as they marched across the tiny hills that the corduroy sleeves had made in the carpets, but it was *their* Levee, and they didn't want that much of me—a toast for the New Year, a touch of my hand, and a word with the Lady President.

The reception wasn't over until well into the afternoon. I kissed Mary and climbed upstairs to my office. My Secretary of State arrived with his son Fred and a finished draft of my Proclamation in his pigskin portfolio. Fred was his Pa's Assistant Secretary of State, and he carried that portfolio under his arm. No one else but Fred and his Pa had perused the final draft. He had black side-whiskers and dark bags under his eyes, like Seward himself.

"Mr. President," he said, "this will be the most historic moment of the war."

I could see how nervous he was. "Fred, hold your horses. I haven't signed it yet. My generals consider me insane. They call that document the Great Rebel Backbone Breaker, and swear that it will only fire up the *Secesh* if I nick them of their slaves."

Seward must have signaled to his son, because Fred was quiet after that. He unrolled the parchment for me, but my hand trembled, and I couldn't seem to sign the document.

"Mr. Lincoln," Seward asked, "is something wrong?"

Didn't he know that a President could panic, like any other man? The Proclamation was a Bone Crusher, and that's what I meant it to be.

I do order and declare that all persons held as slaves within said designated States . . .

"Fred, if my hand shivers, anyone who examines the document hereafter will say, *He hesitated,* and I wouldn't want that to happen."

So I waited a little while and then scratched my name on the parchment without a single shiver. Seward also signed, and Fred rolled up the parchment and returned to the State Department with his Pa and the pigskin case. And I snuck out the door, convinced I had made a failure in my first two years as President.

I strolled through the gates, and watched the lights of the Willard across the road, with a sea of carriages in front of the portico. Willard's must have been at the *tail* end of its New Year Lunch—the roar from across the *Ave* was like a deafening bolt. But I looked again, and realized that the roar wasn't coming from Willard's. The front gate was surrounded by negroes who hadn't been invited inside to the Levee. They weren't decked out as fine as Mary's *wild geese*, but they still had splendid bonnets and parasols and winter cloaks. They must have heard about the signing from one of my own butlers. A couple of White House guards wanted to brush them away with their bayonets.

"You *cain't* bother the President."

"Stop that now," I said. "Nobody's bothering me. These are my guests."

One of the guards was a brazen fool. "Well, I didn't see 'em at the Levee."

"Son, we're having our Levee right here."

That still didn't satisfy them. They'd have stuck to my skin like horseflies if I hadn't sent them off to Willard's on some wild chase.

The black men kneaded their soft hats against their chests. They could have been stevedores and mechanics, or ditchdiggers. The women did the same with their bonnets, crushing them against their winter coats. The men didn't wear coats in January, but short jackets.

"Mr. *Lincoln*," said one of the women, "could I *tech* your hand?"

I held her hand in mine, and it startled her—no, frightened her a little, because she hadn't expected me to grip her like that. I felt like some two-legged horse in a stovepipe hat who happened to be President. I went among them, gripping hands. These mechanics had a firmer grip than mine. They didn't ask questions like a lot of tricky Senators. I knew about their quarters, the *Nigger Hills* they inhabited, always at the edge of some neighborhood, or near some abandoned slave pen, or burnt-out market, where no one else would live, with hogs rooting at the side of the road, leaving long runnels of pigshit, and children playing with pieces of catgut. I'd noticed everything, and pretended not to notice at all.

"Bless you, Father Abraham."

And then they dispersed—like some strange shot, as if they had apportioned their time with me, had parceled it out with a sugar spoon, and left in the blink of an eye, and I stood there alone, beside one of the old privies that served as a guardhouse, and couldn't find a trace of them on the lawn.

They considered me their Great Captain, but it wasn't true. I struggled over that Proclamation to expedite the war. As I scribbled to Horace Greeley: "If I could save the Union without freeing *any* slave I would do it, and if I could save it by freeing *all* the slaves I would do it; and if I could save it by freeing some and leaving others alone I would also do that." We could no longer win the war without black troops. So I was the poor man's Machiavel, the grand manipulator. Jeff Davis threatened to hang captured negro troops and their white officers. And I warned Mr. Jeff that I would repay his barbarisms with some of my own. I'd rattled his feathers, robbed him of his greatest commodity—the South's inexhaustible market of slaves—with one stroke of the pen. If my generals wouldn't ride to Richmond, then I'd ride there with my *writs*.

37.

Blinders

No one knew when Mary's *blinders* would rip. A *blinder* might come when she was at breakfast. The first inkling of it would be the spoon that fell out of her fist, or the rattle of her egg cup. She could be in the middle of a conversation, and her right eye would twitch. Then her lips would purse, and there would be a confusion of speech. She never babbled, but she might whisper, "*Please—find—Keck-k-k-ly.*" And then she'd fall into a swoon that was close to an epileptic fit, and I'd have to rock her in my arms and watch her eyes flutter in some electric storm—as if the furies were locked inside and could never be expelled.

Elizabeth would glide down the attic stairs, clutching a candle, while her shadow crept up the wall and the candle's eerie light licked at her cheeks and mouth until she looked like a spirit come to visit with us awhile. Mary had given her a *palatial* room—a doll's closet—which had become her private quarters. Sometimes I'd listen to the patter of her feet as she wandered through that dollhouse-dungeon of hers after midnight, and wonder why she put up with the Lincolns. She had her own apartment near the Powder Magazine, her own

little couturière's shop, and clients far richer than the Lady President.
Yet she moved all her operations into our attic, with spider webs and
mice as her confreres.

She wore a nightgown, and it startled me how beautiful she was,
as if she had bathed in silver. None of us could grasp the *pantomime*
that went on between her and my wife. Mary's eyes stopped fluttering
the second she saw Elizabeth. Mother scratched at her like a petulant
child and pointed to the ceiling.

"*Upstairs—Lizabeth—upstairs.*"

Elizabeth had to scold her. "Shame on you, Mrs. President. You're
much too weak to gallivant around. A body could lose herself in all
the cobwebs, and Mr. Lincoln would have to call the militia."

She mewled like a baby and continued to scratch. So Elizabeth
wrapped her in a blanket, fed her a cup of water, and I carried my wife
up the attic stairs, with Tad tight on my tail.

"*Paw*, are gonna move in with Yib?"

"Well, we may have to one of these days."

The banisters creaked, and Tad held on to my pocket—I thought
the stairs might collapse under our weight, and we'd tumble into
the well, but we all landed in the attic alive. Elizabeth had installed
a sewing machine in that maze of little rooms, and some kind of
regal chair with sunken upholstery and crooked legs, where Mary
could rule in the middle of a *blinder*. She'd take flight, disappear into
this attic kingdom, with Yib as her accomplice and companion. She
might sit with Yib during her *monthlies*, or descend into that basement
boudoir known as The First Lady's Confinement Room, a rathole
with a miserable chair, its carpet covered with water buckets and
cotton scraps—Tad called them *soljer's bandages* on account of all the
menstrual blood. Here she would hide when she had a headache or
her cramps, though she preferred the attic.

Still, she couldn't find much peace, not even in her little warren.

Her head started to sway as she sat in the chair, one hand cupped over her eye.

"Lizabeth, be an angel and get my carriage. We'll have a picnic on the Potomac. And if my husband's soldiers stare at us, we'll perform our own little tricks."

"But that carriage bounces like the Devil. Wouldn't you rather stay here, Mrs. President?"

Mother froze in her attic chair. "You're a scavenger—you live under my roof without paying a penny, and I won't tolerate your sass."

Yib grew silent as Mary scolded her like some *lesser* sister.

"You dress me in rags and guard all the profits, grow rich on my miserable bounty. And you wag your tail at Mr. Lincoln. You'd poison me if you could and live with my husband in the attic."

It was pitiful to see her cuss at Mrs. Keckly, as if she were ripping at herself and unraveling in front of Tad. Her ire would only get worse. Not even the ghost of Henry Clay could have reasoned with Molly during one of her storms. The *blinder* had come back, and she uttered a shriek that whistled in my ears and dug like a hammer's hook between my eyes. I didn't know what to do. I carried Mother down those treacherous stairs and into her bedroom, with Tad still on my tail.

The doctor had to be snuck in through the servants' door, with his medical kit under his coat. Mary didn't want her *blinders* advertised. So the tonic that the doctor prescribed would be in Keckly's name; it was a white powder that permitted Mary to sleep while the *blinder* ripped. Often she had to bite into a stick, and her mouth bled from all the biting. Elizabeth would wipe the blood with the skirts of her nightgown. I was puzzled by her devotion to Mary, which seemed absolute—and irrevocable. She didn't have to sleep in an attic. And yet she was upstairs almost every night. Mary couldn't have paid her much more than a pittance—she was a prized couturière. And the District's finest dowagers must have offered a princely sum to lure her to their mansions. Yet she stayed, this woman with her invisible White House address, who never used her cachet to capture other clients.

Mary hollered at her half the time, and it didn't seem to bother her none. And once, after a wallop of a *blinder*, where she had spent a long vigil with my wife, I tried to offer her a pittance of my own. She wouldn't take a nickel.

"Mrs. Lincoln is my friend."

"But you have to feed yourself, Elizabeth."

I kept staring at the blood on her nightgown—from that stick Mary had to bite. "Oh, I have plenty of rich clients, Mr. Lincoln. Mrs. President pays me whatever she can."

"But at least we could find you a regular room—on the family floor."

She looked at me as if I were some imbecile fresh out of a circus.

"Doesn't she have enough trouble, sir, without having a mulatto lady sleeping on the same floor? I'm fine where I am—up in the attic. And when she has her *blinders*, I sleep in the chair right next to her, or let her come to the attic and be my guest. She loves that ol' attic chair."

Elizabeth turned away from me. I couldn't even tell if she was crying.

"I have a powerful affection for Mrs. Lincoln—and Taddie—and Bob—and even you *sometimes*, when you aren't crawling up the shirts of those slavers in Kentucky. But I won't discuss politics while Mrs. President is ill."

Elizabeth brought her own royalty to the attic—not the noisome kind that paraded around in their costumes and titles and ornaments of silver and gold. She tutored the servants' children, tied Tad's laces, fed him when he forgot to eat, and attended to Mary like some strange midwife who could absorb every tantrum, every shriek—as if every damn blow in the universe rained down right off her head with no more harm than a scatter of pumpkin seeds.

38.

Apollonia's Boy

TAD HAD BLACK hair, black eyes, and the brooding look of Lord Byron—Byron as a boy, in a 3ʳᵈ Lieutenant's uniform, but without the clubfoot. He brooded more the closer we got to the anniversary of his brother's death, and it took an ugly twist. He set fire to the shoes of a boy in Mrs. Keckly's class, ransacked the closet of a maid who lived in the attic, stole some coins from the purse of Mary's prize gardener. Mary couldn't tame him—nobody could, not even Yib. So I sent for him. Tad loved the stables, which were rebuilt after the last fire, when Little Mac came marching out of the snow with a pair of spotted ponies. My generals didn't house their horses with us any longer; they had their own big barn near the Navy Yard. But Tad would carouse with the stable boys, show them magic tricks—he wasn't with the stable boys. The moment I was ready to sound the alarm, Tad walked into my office in his crumpled uniform.

I couldn't have killed the wildness in him. I wouldn't know how, but we did what we always did when both of us had the *bleeds* and were feeling blue. We marched right past Senators and salesmen who besieged the second floor and would have ripped my coat to bits, begging for favors I just couldn't grant—a captaincy for some cousin, railroad passes for a tribe of sisters—and we skedaddled, wandered off to Apollonia Stuntz's Toy Store on New York Avenue, a few hundred yards from the White House.

It was our favorite retreat, where we could gorge ourselves on tidbits from the penny counter—licorice as black as McClellan's coal-black horse, buns in the shape of unicorns, jujubes that could gum up your teeth—and we walked among the toy soldiers on the tables that Apollonia's husband, Joseph Stuntz, a veteran of the Napoleonic Wars, had crafted with his own hands before he died; there was a certain remorse as we fondled the soldiers in their *tricornes* and bandoliers, since we'd come here last when Willie was alive; he kept a whole battlefield under his bed, with cannons and horses and carts from Stuntz's center table.

Tad stared at another prize, hanging from the wall, a soldier that had been hanging there even before Sumpter fell and wasn't like any other toy in the store. Apollonia had dubbed that soldier Jackie Boy and refused to sell him at any price. Jack was a puppet without strings, a doll made of wood and cloth; bits of glass were wedged into his eye sockets with all the precision of a jeweler. Jack wore a uniform, but with no discernible rank. He could have been a general, else the rawest recruit. He was about a foot and a half tall. Apollonia had stuffed him herself and sewn up his innards. She sat near the window in a shop that was like a narrow cave filled with miniature warriors, and she watched Tad watching Jack. She was a war widow, even if her husband hadn't died in battle; he'd lost a leg at Austerlitz, and had become a *toy soldier*, sitting with his wooden leg on a stool and carving little ghosts of the battles he'd been in. That's why my own generals coveted Stuntz's toys, with their genuine *stink* of war—startled eyes and soiled trousers. She still wouldn't sell them Jack.

Yet she must have sniffed the agony between Tad's shoulder blades, must have tasted his want, because she got up from her chair, unwound Jack from his peg on the wall, and gave that puppet to my boy.

"But I can't pay you, Apollonia."

I didn't even carry a purse. And I couldn't ask Tad to dig into his collection of coins. It wasn't proper for a President to borrow from his own boy. But I'd misread the proprietress, who wasn't in the mood to part with Jack for money.

"I'm lending him to the White House, Mr. Lincoln, on a kind of permanent loan. Tad and my Jackie will make good soldiers together."

Tad saluted Apollonia, clicked his heels, and marched out of the shop with that doll cradled in his arms. I was hoping Jack might provide my 3rd Lieutenant with a little companionship, and he did, but that damn doll didn't draw the meanness out of him. Jack aided and abetted Tad's own flair for savagery. That boy and his doll went on *razzias* in the White House and upset every protocol with their plundering. They pilfered soap from the maids, squandered gooseberry pies from Mary's kitchen, and set up headquarters in the attic, where Tad could appraise his treasure in peace.

I couldn't bear the notion of corporal punishment. I'd never spanked Tad once in my life. I kept waiting for all the banditry in him to burn out. Yib wouldn't let him into her classroom with that piratical puppet. So his speech grew wild. But Tad wasn't *deef.* He could hear the terrible tattoo of the drums at Fort Stevens, as recreants were rapped right out of their regiment and had to walk through a *firing line* of officers who beat them like donkeys with their batons. Such disgraced soldiers, who might have stolen cash from their own corporals' fund, couldn't walk into a tavern in the District, or put on their regimental colors again. They would become walking ghosts, condemned to wander in the midst of war. That tale and the tattoos had touched my 3rd Lieutenant. His own rampages stopped. He quit his headquarters in the attic, and asked my secretaries for an official appointment with the Commander-in-Chief. He was somber and subdued when he came into my office, his black hair slicked down, his cap over his heart. He must have realized that he couldn't deploy a puppet, that Jack had his own terrifying inertia. Or else Jack had disobeyed one of Tad's commands—there could have been a thousand arguments between a puppet and a boy.

He knew I could pardon any soldier, save him from being drummed out of his regiment with a scratch of my pen. Tad wanted me to pardon Jack.

"Taddie, what has Jack done?"

"He's *derelicked*. He won't get up when I tell him. He won't do his chores. But I'd like you to pardon him on account he's Jack."

I did pardon Jack on a piece of Presidential paper, but I saw the same turmoil in Tad's eyes, the same deep reverie. The heart had been torn out of him. He suffered Willie's absence somewhere beneath his bones.

Reporters wrote about him as the First Child who watched over the White House. They never understood how alone he was, with some *razzia* raging inside him that couldn't be calmed by Stuntz's toys. He saw the wounded soldiers, heard the tattoos, and he echoed the carnage around him in his rampages—there wasn't much room for little boys in a rebellion.

I was the one who discovered Jack the very next day hanging from a tree on the south lawn. There was a piece of paper attached to Jack's leg, like a rooster's tag. Nothing was written on it. Tad's *derelicked* soldier couldn't bear to be pardoned, else Tad couldn't bear to pardon himself. It might have been much simpler than that—the

First Child getting sick of a soldier stuffed with straw. But I didn't cut Jack down. I left him to dangle, like some grim reminder of a dangling war—there wasn't a damn finisher among Jack and all my generals. And then, after a month or so, I cleaned up Jack's sooty britches, and returned him to Mrs. Stuntz's store.

39.

Old Capitol

I T WAS LIKE some insane turkey shoot without turkeys, as officers and raw recruits attacked contrabands—runaway blacks—
in the streets of Washington, firing a couple of shots over their heads
or hurling stones at them, and tossing children into the offal of the
old canal. Invalids, returning to active duty from some military clinic,
beat the tar out of black dishwashers at the Soldiers' Retreat, that canteen on the Sixth Street wharf. No ambulance arrived to deliver these
broken dishwashers to the Colored Hospice near the Poor House;
they were left to rot in the rain. And while they groaned on the docks,
a black angel appeared, dressed in bombazine like a war widow, and
carted them off in the Presidential carriage.

The town was bewildered by this mysterious lady in a widow's
black veil, who arrived out of nowhere that March of '63. She rescued
wounded contrabands, pulled them out of the mud in Mary Lincoln's
own cabriolet. That angel in bombazine was Mrs. Keckly, who
wasn't just a couturière and a schoolmarm at the White House. She
would flit across Washington like a lunatic in widow's weeds—it was
Keckly's way of disguising her mission. Pickets and boys from the

military police wouldn't chase a widow down, even if she was carting contrabands. Besides, these pickets were reluctant to stop the Lady President's white horse, and interfere with her tiny silver carriage.

As President of the Contraband Relief Club, Elizabeth would pluck endangered runaways off the *Ave* and bring them inside the wooden walls of the camp on Boundary Street, where they wouldn't starve; but the camp was overcrowded, and an entire tent city rose up outside its walls. And when the Sanitary Commission started to whisper about a smallpox epidemic at the camp, boys from the Provost Marshal's office arrested the black widow as a provocateur, shackled her like a slave, and sent her to the Old Capitol Prison with deserters, prostitutes, and prisoners of war.

That was enough to wake Mary out of whatever mournful slumber she was in. She hurried to Old Capitol the moment she heard of Elizabeth's incarceration. But the sentinels wouldn't even let her past the outer hall. It was a Federal facility, they said, and Lady Presidents had no jurisdiction there.

I had half a mind to shut that jailhouse and toss the sentinels into the Potomac.

"Mary, what did you do?"

"Shout," she said.

Then a captain arrived who was a touch more cautious—said the prisoner was being interrogated and would return to her bunk, with all the prostitutes who'd been corralled that week. *Our little mamzelles,* he called them. Mary would require a special license from the prison's own magistrate to meet with the black angel—but the prison was out of licenses, he said.

So we climbed into Mary's carriage, sailed down Pennsylvania Avenue, and stopped in front of an old brick barn on A Street, across from the Capitol, with a great arched window above its medieval metal door. I could see a panorama of prisoners in the broken window panes—men and women with wild hair and mottled red cheeks, standing like florid ghosts on display. That brick barn with wooden slats across every other window had been a boardinghouse for Senators that ran into ruin. It had no proper prison cells—its rooms weren't even locked. Old Capitol had to rely on its sentinels, who patrolled the area around A Street and every corner of the yard with their blackjacks and their clubs. They had mean little eyes like killer hogs. Their hands were gnarled, their faces ripped raw of sunlight.

They met us in the outer hall—sucking at the blisters on their lips as they stroked truncheons that could have split a man's skull.

They bowed to Mary in their own mocking manner. I wanted to bite their throats. A body could disappear in this endless cave of unwashed walls, with curtain after curtain of spider webs. They were the monarchs here, but they should have been kinder to my wife. I looked into their mean little eyes and played a little Presidential poker.

"We're forming a new regiment, boys. The 13th Ohio. Daredevils. They like to hop around with mud and cartridge powder on their faces, like wild Injuns. We'll drop them behind enemy lines. And I'm including all your names. You look like worthy souls."

That malicious grin was gone, and suddenly their Superintendent arrived, William Wood, a stocky little man who'd once been a private in the Union Army, and loved to lord it over the imprisoned officers at Old Capitol. Wood was a favorite of my Secretary of War, who told me how the Super would come crashing through the corridors and yell to the prisoners, "All ye who want to hear the Lord God preached according to Mr. Jeff Davis, go down to the yard; and all ye who want to hear the Lord God according to Abe Lincoln, stay right where ye are."

Prisoners with cash in their pockets, or a friend in high places, didn't have to eat the usual prison slop. They were given a special card, which allowed them to wash in the sentinels' own sink, and to buy grub and tobacco from the prison commissary at piratical prices. I watched these star boarders shuffle around, as if they were at some indoor plantation rather than a prison. They swaggered in their winter cloaks, saluted the sentinels, and shoved other prisoners aside, while I was filled with a melancholic rage.

I didn't reprimand Wood in front of his own men. I tried to stay civil. Told him I hadn't come here to inspect his damn hotel, but to free one of his prisoners, who shouldn't have been here in the first place.

The tallest of the sentinels cupped his hand over Wood's ear, and they whispered back and forth like buzzards, while Wood's face turned a lunatic red.

"Mr. Lincoln, I'm afraid there's been a malaprop—Mrs. Keckly is missing."

Mother nearly swooned under her own bombazine. "Father, they've killed her."

"No, no," Wood insisted. "She must have wandered somewhere. There are no locks and keys at Old Capitol. But I'll find her, Madame President. You have my word. Please come with us."

Mother grabbed my elbow, and we went deeper into that brick barn, marched up a flight of stairs with the Super and his sentinels. The staircase was lit with one gas lamp gouged into the wall. Our shadows climbed like wanton sheaths. We passed bald rooms that had an unbelievable stench—like the sting of cats' piss. None of the rooms had a reliable door. I watched Rebel officers walk round and round a row of bunks—there was nothing left in their eyes, not pride or fear or sorrow. But they marched to the beat of some monotonous music inside their skulls.

I'd come to the house of the dead.

I recognized clerks who had talked treason, businessmen who had blown up a bridge—saboteurs and lunatics, and other political prisoners, who had their own stark room, Number 16, an enormous closet, really, with a mound of straw, like a manger littered with bedbugs and lice—this *seat* at the center of Old Capitol had once been used by Congress and had all the gallantry of that great arched window above the prison's main door. Number 16 had a triple tier of bunks that reached the ceiling and looked like it was about to topple on our heads. One of the lunatics ran out and accosted me. He kneeled down and clutched my shinbones.

"Oh, pardon me, kind sir. I have done nothing that would cause alarm. Help me, Captain!"

"Imbecile," the Super said. "You're talking to the President of the United States."

The man grinned at me. "Is that Abe the Cock-a-doodle? Or Captain Tenafly? Didn't ye arrest me for trying to bomb the B&O? It wasn't sedition, sir. I have a grievance against the railroad. One of its detectives threw me off the cars and stomped on my hat. That was unkind, sir."

"I'll look into it, son."

He slid off my shins and hopped back into that huge hole in the wall, while his compatriots in Number 16 stared at me in the feeble gaslight with the yellow eyes of wounded animals. And I wondered what harm I had done that had caused so much grief? But I hadn't been honest with that lunatic. I'd outlawed sedition *everywhere*, and my Secretary of War had dragged editors, government clerks, matrons, and railroad men into Old Capitol if they had ever been a little too vociferous in their sympathies to the South. I had little choice. We couldn't win a war while there was a fire in the rear, with the flames licking at our coats. Stanton had arrested the mayor of Baltimore at my command. The mayor started up his own militia, and was fixing to turn the town into a Rebel fortress. I had him dragged right out of Baltimore . . .

We passed another room, where Union officers sat in their own filth. What crime had they committed? Had they led some charge down the wrong hill? Massacred some of their men? Criticized one of my generals? What horrible sin tore them from their regiments and earned them a card to Old Capitol? I had to crucify my feelings, or I would never have gotten to Elizabeth.

"Super," I shouted, "will you find these officers some fresh uniforms? Whatever they've done, they're still ours."

"But Stanton said that—"

"Damn my Secretary of War! Get them some uniforms. They can soil their britches as often they like. Stanton will pay for it—out of his own pocket."

I had the Super bring me one of the officers, a young captain of the 2nd Ohio who had been stripped of his rank and all his insignias; his tunic sat on him like a rumpled nightshirt. He seemed reluctant to approach. He kept twisting and untwisting the bill of his cap. He had the dark red *insignia* of squashed bedbugs on his sleeves. His name was Robertson.

"Come closer, Captain."

"I can't, Mr. President. I shit my pants."

"Well, Captain, my little boy shits his pants every day of the week, and I've managed to survive."

He shuffled a little closer in his prison slippers. "But Mrs. Lincoln, sir . . ."

Mary was much braver than Wood and all his sentinels, who pulled back from the powerful sting in their nostrils. She fondled the captain's tunic where his shoulder boards had been. I could feel the sweetness of her touch. She cradled her arm in his, and strolled with the captain in that infernal corridor. I saw him smile. Half his teeth were gone, and his gums were like black pits. He kissed Mary's hand and sauntered back to me. I watched him rub at his tunic until his fingers were raw. I didn't have the heart to interrogate him.

"Captain, you don't . . ."

His eyes seemed to twist right out of their sockets as he hopped on his toes with a violent rhythm and commenced to croon. "*An-tiet-am*, sir. I was attached to the general. I watched him pace his tent. He was near undone when he had to lose lives. So I figured I'd stay healthy on account of the general. We loved to see him ride black Dan . . ."

McClellan, always McClellan. It was as if I had no other generals. I could picture him charging up the stairs on Dan Webster's back and rescuing this boy captain from the Super's abominable sink.

"I was in the middle of an apple orchard, with the Rebs fifty feet away, and I couldn't fire my gun. A Rebel captain rushed at us with his colored orderly right beside him, and they were whooping and cawing like crazy crows. Next I remember I was in the Provost's hut, with two of his adjutants kicking at me, and saying I led my own boys into a death trap. They never convened a court. I didn't merit one, they said. They sent me here in a cattle car filled with Rebel prisoners . . ."

It was one of Stanton's tricks. He'd rather *warehouse* lost souls in the prison yards at A Street than surrender them to a court-martial that might rain down some bad publicity on the War Department. And if I interfered with that little gnome of a man who had all the wrath of Jehovah in his long, scratchy beard, I could wreck my own war machine. Truth is I preferred this boy to stay here than risk sitting on his own coffin in front of a firing squad. But that didn't make me less angry at Wood, who was in cahoots with my Secretary of War.

Mary brushed the boy captain's cheeks with the soft bump of her hand, and he went back inside that squalid room, while I deliberated how to smash Wood's little kingdom at Old Capitol. I'd never win. There'd always be *another* Wood with sentinels who seemed to have bands of leather and rough bark screwed tight into their skin.

"Mr. Wood, you can tell your master at the War Department that if I don't have fresh uniforms by this afternoon, you'll have to strip in front of your sentinels and offer that boy captain your clothes . . . now *find* Mrs. Keckly."

We turned the corner and entered a corridor that swarmed with as many harlots as that Whores' Lane just west of the White House. When Little Mac still ruled the District, he would chase the harlots to Boundary Street on one of his colossal *whore runs*. I could watch that roundup from my window, the harlots shrieking as Dan Webster flew right past, and they tumbled to the ground in their crushed crinolines. Didn't seem to matter how often Little Mac made his runs. The harlots always reappeared in their petticoats, with the high-stepping kick that had become their hallmark. And here they were in the corridors of Old Capitol, with the same high kick that was halfway between a walk and a dance. They were not alone. They had their gentlemen callers—cardsharps in tall hats, confidence men, clairvoyants, even a Confederate general, who must have escaped from that officers' asylum on the other side of the hall in his slouch hat. He couldn't have noticed us. He clapped his hands, and one of the harlots raised her petticoats to the sky and revealed her quim—couldn't see much more than a flick of her unwashed thighs in that somber light, and neither could my wife.

"You cockroach," Wood roared, "the Lady President is in this house—with Mr. Lincoln," and he threw his baton at the general. The whole corridor emptied in a whirl of petticoats, and that poor general had to fend for himself. He stood on one knee and doffed his slouch hat. He was no general of the line, but a logistics officer who had been captured while sitting on a supply train.

"I am inconsolable, Madame President," he muttered. His eyes couldn't seem to focus. One of his own commanders must have left him on that train, half out of his mind. He knew Mary's people in Lexington and wouldn't stop yattering about great aunts and prize peacocks and a duel over some damsel who lived down the road on Short Street.

"Father," Mary whispered, "we must find Lizabeth."

So we abandoned the general and marched into that enormous barrack where all the harlots had fled. It was as big and wild as the President's Park—Number 19, where the commissary was situated and all the bartering was done—copulation was the prison's prime affair. Number 19 was populated with an armada of curtains and privacy screens, where the prison's prostitutes assembled with their clients. The Super couldn't even suppress such business while Mary and I were there; it was beyond his purview, like the shifting chaos of battle. Yet Mother didn't trouble herself about this *charivari* of grunts and groans.

We had to survey Number 19, walk among the harlots in their cloaks and stockings rich as blood, but we couldn't find Elizabeth in the general uproar. I glanced across that room like a chicken hawk on the prowl, went into every corner with my lazy eye.

"Lizabeth," Mary shrieked, "Lizabeth, where are you?"

No one could have heard her in all that din.

"Mother, wait here."

Now I went from curtain to curtain, trying not to bother about the copulations, but I had a peculiar lesson in *geography*; most of these harlots had painted their nipples and their quims with lip rouge; their eyes were camouflaged with charcoal. Some wore chains around their middles like Christian martyrs. They didn't copulate on some old mattress. They clutched a curtain rod or the rails of a privacy screen and stood with their arses in the air, while their clients rutted them from behind, their faces half hidden. Else they danced in front of a feller, while he plucked on his own red root. And it kind of interrupted my search—I was caught in the sway of these prison house Salomes, with all their shivers and undulations, the tiny turns of their hands, the sweet pendulum of their breasts, and I might have plucked at my own root on another occasion. But I wasn't as mottled in the head as that supply general. I noticed a Senator and a couple of Congressmen who must have entered Old Capitol through some private door. They were so *inflamed*, with their eyes squeezed tight, that I probably looked like one more shadow in Number 19.

Then someone scratched at my sleeve—it was the mayor of Baltimore with nothing on but his boots; he had scars under his heart that looked like arrow heads, and I wondered if it was the price he had to pay for some scalping party. I should have realized that my Secretary of War had incarcerated him among all these slobbering fools.

"Lincoln, you and that damn *writ* of yours. Stanton stole my life away."

I didn't want to deal with him now, listen to his drumroll of complaints.

"I have no time for you."

"Then you had better make some time," he said and clung to my sleeve like a shoofly. So I had to stand there and jaw with him in that monumental harlots' house.

"You're a monster," he said, "tramplin' on the law and suspendin' habeas corpus. Judge Taney called you a tyrant and a maniac."

"Well," I said, jabbing at the mayor, like a stick in his guts, "I might have the Judge keep you company at Old Capitol, *jest* like that."

The wind went out of him. "You can't arrest the Chief Justice. That's obscene."

I twisted free and shook him like a great rag doll. "What's obscene, sir, is asking for troops to protect your little enclave in Baltimore, when all the while you plotted to kill me and my wife in bed."

His shoulders slumped and his mouth twitched with alarm. "How did you . . . ?"

Allan Pinkerton had planted a spy in the mayor's office and read all the *traffic* between Richmond and Baltimore, or we couldn't have squandered him and his plot.

The mayor commenced to sob among all his cronies. But he might as well have been silent in all that squealing behind the curtains.

"It ain't right. These yards are your monstrosity, Lincoln. Your footprint is in every room."

And he wandered off. I did feel like some kind of dragon in his own lair. *Old Capitol.* Yet I hadn't dragged Mrs. Keckly into these yards. I hadn't hired sentinels with bullet ears and mean little eyes. I hadn't built a *locomotive* heated up by harlots and their privacy screens. Every screen could have been painted by some prison artist, with castles and cornfields, lighthouses and ships of the line, hurricanes and desert storms, as if some biblical creature had reinvented the world at Old Capitol. But I didn't want to reinvent the world.

I overturned the screens, kicked at them, and finally found Elizabeth behind a curtain, hugging her knees, as she shivered on the floor. She was wearing some sort of smock that looked like a monk's shirt; her hands and feet were filthy. Her hair must have been shorn by some sentinel who fancied himself a barber. There were bumps all over her scalp. She had bruises on her face. I couldn't even tend to her. I had to give my autograph to certain ladies of Number 19, who kept their souvenir albums tucked inside their bodices. They gawked at me as if I'd tumbled out of a dream. They touched my beard while I tried to gather Elizabeth in my arms. She sat there frozen, her teeth rattling all the time. I whispered in her ear like some kindly serpent.

"Elizabeth, we have to scatter, or this old jail might come crashing down on our heads."

She mumbled something, and I had to lean down on my coattails to catch her mutterings. *Mr. Lincoln—I can't move.*

And that's when Mother arrived, amid all the copulations and a cacophonous din. She wasn't even bothered by the groans and farts, the frenzied maneuvers around her.

"Lizzie, get up. Goodness, you can't sit here in all this filth. You'll die."

Keckly stood up like Mother's own marionette, but she started to totter. "My legs have gone *daid.*"

"Nonsense," Mother told her.

It took Keckly five whole minutes to collect herself. She scrutinized that endless parlor as if she had landed in a forest of privacy screens, and wiped her face with Mother's silk handkerchief.

"I'll never get out of here, Mr. Lincoln. I'm on the Provost's list."

⚜

His name was Rosecrans, like one of my generals. But this magistrate was a colonel with the Provost's office. He sat in his own little court on the second floor. He could have been my age, though it was hard to tell. He wasn't deformed, or anything like that, but he did have a tiny hump on his back—a war wound, I reckon, and that's why he was stationed at Old Capitol. He had little concern for my Presidency. But his eyes rattled in his head when I entered his courtroom with Elizabeth and Mary and two sentinels. I'd seen him once before, riding through the District with George McClellan, on one of his mad dashes from the Powder Magazine to Lafayette Park, Little Mac flying out of the dust with his retinue, while half the city was agog and still worshiped him; Rosecrans was there, in his duster, as Little Mac and his family flanked the White House and rode across the Long Bridge, into Alexandria, went from camp to camp.

"Mr. Lincoln, why did you come into my court with the prisoner?"

"Her being here is a flat mistake."

He sat on a very tall bench, and I had to stand on my toes if I wanted to catch his eye. He rifled through a drawer and squinted at a sheet of paper with a magnifying glass.

"Isn't she Elizabeth Keckly, who's been aiding and abetting criminals and deserters at a so-called contraband camp? We caught her flat out. She had the cheek to sabotage our investigations, sir, to hinder us from capturing such criminals. We don't even have to charge the lady. We're at war, sir."

He smiled to himself, like the petty tyrant he was. "Are you defending her as an officer of this court?"

"Yes," I told him. "I'm licensed in Illinois."

"Illinois don't mean much in my court. This here's a prison for soldiers and crimes connected to soldiering and sabotage."

"You have no authority over her. This woman works for me. Her contraband camps are a cover."

I'd scratched at his curiosity. "Cover for what?"

"A training ground for future black officers."

He started to slink in his high chair. This magistrate had barked at prisoners and junior officers, at prostitutes and tramps, at bomb throwers and editors of seditious material, but not at a man who could bark right back.

"I never received any notice about such an institution," he muttered from his high chair.

And now I prepared to break him, like some gullible alligator.

"Rosecrans, you're a magistrate, not the Secretary of War."

He started mumbling to himself. "And do these camps have a code name?"

"*Yes,*" I spat. "*West Point.* These officers will command a regiment one day."

He slipped further and further into the well of his high chair. "Black regiments, sir?"

"Some black, some white."

I'd crushed his belief in the world. He couldn't bear to look at Elizabeth. She'd become a sign of his unworthiness. He stamped her release form. We might never have left that maze without his signature—dead or alive. Prisoners had a habit of getting lost at Old Capitol, which had its own gallows and mortuary. We climbed down the stairs, past the Rebel officers, who trudged back and forth in a trance, and the traitor-clerks, who screamed their oaths of loyalty into the walls, past the paupers, who congregated here until they could be sent to the Poor House, past the harlots and matrons who had spied on us and sat in a corner until some *repatriation boat* carried them to Richmond, past the child murderers, who wandered about in their chains, and the sentinels, who herded prisoners from hall to hall. Keckly shuddered, as the stench grew worse and worse. The sentinels hissed at me—a President didn't have much quarter here—but they wouldn't question the magistrate's stamp.

Elizabeth blinked into the bald light once we entered the yards. "Shame on you, Mr. Lincoln—bamboozling that poor magistrate."

And she corralled me with my own lies.

"Would you like to visit *West Point?* We can ride through one of the contraband camps . . . and you can appoint a couple of colored cadets."

I *jest* couldn't do it. My generals wouldn't have tolerated a little college for colored cadets. They'd never serve with black officers.

We'd have open rebellion in the ranks. I could shout until blood came leaking out my ears, and we still wouldn't have been able to go on with the war. Richmond would have crept across the river like some land-and-sea monster, with Rebels swimming right on our porch . . .

Elizabeth fell asleep against my shoulder on the trip back to the White House—we rode past Swampdoodle, a marshland of privies and shacks, where the Irish lived; most sane men avoided that swamp; enlistment officers rarely entered the Irish enclave, looking for raw recruits. We rode past an ambulance delivering certain fine ladies to the wharves—these were Washington matrons who'd been a bit reckless in their sympathies to the South; they sang "The Bonnie Blue Flag" smack in the middle of Union country.

> *We are a band of brothers and native to the soil*
> *Fighting for the property we gained in honest toil*
> *And when our rights were threatened, the cry rose near and far*
> *Hurrah! For the Bonnie Blue Flag that bears a single star.*

There wasn't much of a melody in their eyes. I noticed the *bracelets* on their legs; they were lashed to that ambulance. And they weren't raucous with Mother and me.

"We're going to Richmond. Should we give your regards to Mr. Jeff?"

The ambulance was gone before I had the chance to utter a sound. I couldn't stop thinking of those Belles Dames and their Bonnie Blue Flag. They must have dreaded that repatriation boat, a little. Still, they hadn't woken Elizabeth—she was sobbing in her dreams.

"Father," Mary said, "you must shut down that rotten sink, or I will shut it myself."

"And where should I put all the prisoners? Stanton will store them in your flower garden."

"Mr. Lincoln, those were a poor excuse for prisoners. Strumpets parading with Senators. Soldiers who should be in an infirmary, or a mental ward. Half-blind saboteurs who kept bumping into walls."

And might have murdered Taddie in his bed.

Mother wasn't wrong. Old Capitol was a rotten sink and a circus for profiteers. I doubted Stanton collected a penny for himself. He must have realized that a penal house had to be run like any other business—with canteen cards and privacy screens. I couldn't afford to shut it down, else we'd have to jump onto the repatriation boat with the Belles Dames and flee from all the chaos.

Mary pouted for a while and then broke her silence with a smile.

"Father," she said, with a playful twist in her eyes, "do you think a black officer will ever command a white regiment?"

"I doubt it."

"Not even in Taddie's lifetime?"

"No. Not ever."

We rode along Pennsylvania Avenue, past the Willard, where every room was lit, and entered the reptilian darkness of the President's grounds—the front porch had a single, sputtering flare; the stables looked like catacombs. I wouldn't let the coachman handle Elizabeth. I carried her through the gate. Mother didn't want her sleeping all alone in the attic, so I set her down on a divan in Mary's headquarters and covered her with a blanket. I watched her breath for a little while, watched the flutter of her hands. The Locofocos liked to harp about the Miscegenation Balls we had at the White House, how the Lincolns lived *incestuous* lives. But their evil gossip couldn't corral the feelings I had for Elizabeth; she was like an irascible sister you loved in spite of the quarrels you had, an angel in the attic, even without her bombazine.

40.

Gettysburg

MY SECRETARY OF WAR had requisitioned a special four-car train that November, with sharpshooters and a tiny cannon, put there for ceremonial sake. I traveled with my confidential secretaries, my valet, and Mr. Seward. Much as I tried, I couldn't seem to finish my remarks for the dedication—how could one lone man in the White House, who sent boys off to their doom, find the will to *represent* these fallen boys? I scribbled on scraps of paper, using my stovepipe hat as a desk, but I couldn't find the words to capture the living or the dead. It was as if I'd suddenly gone *deef* and dumb to the constant tattoo inside my skull.

I sat in the personal car of the B&O president, like some ceremonial king, with my own bedroom and private privy, with lamps that lit up the second we approached a tunnel, with Venetian blinds, and carpets soft as quilt, but all that luxury couldn't inspire me none, or dress over my remarks. I was approaching a battleground where the Commander-in-Chief hadn't played the littlest part, where row after row of hospital tents had straddled every orchard, where the sting of excrement and rotting carcasses had remained for months, where one sleepy village and all its farmland had turned into a vast slaughter yard.

I didn't want it to feel like a circus, but it did. Medicine men hovered around the tracks with every sort of moonshine; children hawked balloons; and counterfeit soldiers in motley uniforms cradled war souvenirs in their arms, but not everyone belonged to the same menagerie. I saw nurses with that genuine remorse in their eyes of women who must have lived for weeks around wounded men. And others, like myself, recalled the battlefields as best we could, and were confused and uncertain and more than a little shy the nearer we got to Gettysburg.

I arrived at the tall depot on Carlisle Street as the sun was going down—it burnt the walls of the car a soft and luscious red. But I couldn't relish that color very long. The platform of the depot was lined with row after relentless row of coffins—the very last interments before the dedication, I suspect. Diggers would probably work half the night on Cemetery Hill . . .

We gathered next morning at the *Diamond*, as citizens of the town called their central square, with hundreds of souls packed into that space, perhaps a lot more—I hadn't come here to count. I was vertiginous after a while, as people moved in great numbers and shouted, "Lincoln, Lincoln, Lincoln." A soldier had to help me onto my horse, or I might have been landlocked somewhere and missed the ceremonial.

I towered above half the world and rode to the cemetery that morning in the midst of a procession that included firemen, reporters, soldiers, and politicians. People kept trying to clutch my hand. Up Baltimore Street I went on my bay horse, my shoes slipping out of the stirrups, my meager remarks in my pocket. I wore a black band on my hat to remember my dead boy—and the dead boys of Gettysburg, some of whose bones were still scattered in the fields, with the carcasses of horses and cows. I didn't see any broken buildings on Baltimore Street, or collapsed roofs, but several of the walls along our route were riddled with bullet holes. I'd heard tales of the Rebel yell being much more reckless than a cannonball and halting a courier's horse in its tracks. And of Lee's *foragers* hunting for Gettysburg blacks—mainly women and children—in the midst of battle, forcing them out of their homes like the worst kind of kidnappers and thieves, and hauling them back to headquarters as their own little *battery* of slaves . . .

I was pulled right out of my reverie by the folks who were selling souvenirs—little relics of war that included bullet pouches and broken cannonballs. They lurched out at us with their plunder; one of them had a Rebel captain's uniform on a stick, and brandished it like a scarecrow, with painted eyes and whiskers.

"Five dollars," he said, running beside me with that wicked semaphore, as if he were signaling to his own army of ghouls. "Mr. Lincoln, four dollars—you can give the uniform to Tad. I pressed it clean."

I had to knock that stick out of his hand, or he would have followed me past the ragged line of houses, to the Baltimore Pike, and the top of Cemetery Hill, where every grave, every marker, could be seen from my saddle. We had to cross a *pinched* piece of battleground, and I was bewildered by what I saw—belt buckles, bits of cracked glass, torn insignias, a tattered shirt, an officer's whip, the rusty barrel of a gun, all strewn about, as if some madman were leaving vestiges of his mayhem, or a tornado had struck without warning, desiccated the land, and went on to destroy another hill.

We cannot dedicate—we cannot consecrate—we cannot hallow . . .

The ground was pocked with wound after wound, and I felt like some lost pilgrim who might stray into a hole and never be found again, or perhaps it was simpler than that.

A part of me wanted to remain here amid all the punctures. *Now I heard the timpani in my skull.* I belonged with the dead, with the stray caps and an occasional boot, and with the cartridge belts hanging from the branches of trees, like grim bracelets. Souvenir seekers hadn't yet managed to pick the place clean. Dead horses rotted in the sun, their broken reins bleached a bloodless white. The rat-a-tat-tat grew stronger in my ears, as if I could listen to the music of a battlefield, not the Rebel yell, and the roar of Parrott guns, not the clack of hooves in the Peach Orchard, not the groans, not the *scratch* of body parts flying into the air, not the raw stink of terror, but the soft, incessant rap of boys marching against their own brothers, knowing they would never see sunlight again.

That Boston orator, Mr. Everett, arrived late, wearing kid gloves and a silk cravat. He was a touch under seventy, and had a stooped back. There was a quiet rage in his eyes. He'd endured a bout of apoplexy that marked him with a slight tremble. He was still the finest orator in the land, but his wife had gone mad. He had to lock her away.

He peered out at us, sucked us all into his gaze, like some Merlin in a silk cravat, and said, "Standing beneath this serene sky, overlooking these broad fields, and the graves of our brethren beneath our feet, it is without hesitation that I raise my poor voice to break the eloquent silence of God . . ."

I wondered if my own courtship would end on the same car with Everett's mad wife. Mary's fits grew worse and worse. I'd seen her whack one of the gardeners. I heard her cuss a maid. Then the fits would pass, and she was fine—for a little while. And it would start all over, like some seesaw of the fates.

She was on much better behavior when Bob was around. But I couldn't hire him as an adjutant to his own mother. And I had nightmares about Mary and Bob—in my dreams Mary wore an old gown, with Bob hovering over her in some kind of a uniform, like a horsecar conductor. But it wasn't a horsecar. It was the back room of an asylum. And Bob wasn't calling out stations and stops. He wasn't harsh. He wept and tried to calm his mother's nerves.

"For consider, my friends, what would have been the consequences to the country, to yourselves, and to all you hold dear, if those who sleep beneath our feet, and their gallant comrades who survive to serve their country in other fields of danger, had failed."

He sang to us for two hours in a silver voice that shot across the cemetery, while I glanced at my own speech, scribbled on White House scratch paper. I didn't have his poetry, his rhetoric, his musical lilt.

His music didn't matter to some folks, who covered their faces with mottled scarves, scattered in the middle of his speech, and went searching for souvenirs on the battlefield, while all the others clapped and cheered, and didn't want Everett to leave the platform. They were restless after he was gone, with wandering eyes, waiting for another fine oration, and I had nothing to give. I strode up to the platform in the black broadcloth of a mortician, while photographers fiddled with their Shadow Boxes in front of me, like a crooked line of crows. My mouth was parched. I had my scratchings, sentences I had strung together without Everett's silk. I put on my spectacles and plucked the little speech out of my pocket. I couldn't recognize the sound of my voice—it seemed to ricochet from someone else's throat.

" . . . We cannot dedicate, we cannot consecrate, we cannot hallow this ground. The brave men, living and dead, who struggled here, have consecrated it far above our power to add or detract."

People muttered a bit, poked each other, clapped, and waited for the fireworks, but I didn't have Everett's flair. I had a tin box that couldn't even rise above the trees.

I spoke for two minutes and returned to my chair. The crowd was a little ruffled by the *briefness* of my visit. They had expected a much longer serenade. No one clapped or whistled. I was startled by that sea of silence, as if folks were waiting for me to duck into Everett's private tent, rinse my throat in salt water, and return to the platform with a resounding song.

"That speech won't *scour*," I whispered to an old friend on the platform. "It is a flat failure, and the people are disappointed."

Most of the damn reporters at the consecration agreed. I watched them scribble in their notebooks and scurry among themselves. "Silly stuff," murmured the boy from Harrisburg. "The Pres ought to be ashamed." He glanced right past me, and walked over to Everett with a look of exaltation in his eyes. Others rambled across the cemetery, hunting for souvenirs. I couldn't blame these boys. They were exploring a battle circus. I looked beyond the stone wall, into the darkening fields, with its broke-back trees, its pocked earth, its shiny shards of glass, as if I were tethered to this ground, tied with some primitive cord, and while the wind licked at my mortician's coat, I could feel a tug at the seat of my pants. I wasn't one of Little Mac's reconnaissance balloons. I couldn't float above the battlefield, like some aeronaut of Gettysburg. I had to fend for myself on the cemetery floor—the dead can't whistle. All I could hear was the rattling sound of souvenir seekers and the rustle of red leaves.

❀

FARMERS STOOD ALONG the rails, staring at me in soldiers' caps plucked from the battlefield. I took ill in the cars, and my teeth clattered in my head like a cannonade. My manservant, William, wrapped me up in my green shawl, but I had the chills and couldn't move my legs by the time we landed in the District; one of Stanton's sharpshooters had to summon an ambulance from the Navy Yard, and I rode to the White House lying on my back, with people along the *Ave* looking under the canvas roof and wondering if their President had been shot.

I did have my own souvenir from the battlefield, it seems—*varioloid*, a milder variation of the smallpox. I must have contracted it while I was riding up Cemetery Hill with those other pilgrims. I could still hear the music of the dead, that strange tapping in the wind. Whenever I had a nightmare, Mary would enter my room like a ghost in a white gown and sing me back to sleep. Mother refused to wear a mask, and neither would Elizabeth.

Everybody else at the White House had to wear one—servants and Senators alike. Tad fell in love with this profusion of white masks. He would wait outside my door and watch the generals and chief clerks congregate in their masks, but he loved my barber best. William would arrive promptly at ten with his razor box, looking piratical in the white mask that covered his mouth, Tad plucking at his arm.

"Will Johnson, are you ever gonna razor me?"

"Soon as you grow side-whiskers, Mr. Tad."

He'd stride into my room with a roaring laugh that nearly ripped away his mask. I'd come to depend on Will. He couldn't get along with our other servants, who were ashamed of Will on account of his very dark skin. Mary scolded them, but he was still pretty much of a pariah.

Will came down with varioloid a week after I did, and was confined to the colored ward near the old canal. He couldn't collect his pay while he was in quarantine, so I had the greenbacks sent to him in an envelope with the White House seal.

DEAR WILLIAM: The current White House barber will bleed me into oblivion if you don't get well soon.

One of the nurses on Will's ward acted as his scribe. "President Lincoln," she wrote in her fine hand, "Mr. Johnson says that if that barber ever scrapes you again, he will not live to scrape another man. Johnson will see to it himself."

Will died that very afternoon, and I had a dream that night—wasn't about the barber, wasn't about Will. It was about my child-wife. The White House was under attack, and we removed to the attic. Mary was the barber now, though she didn't have much of a razor. Taddie was her assistant, her lather boy—kept heaping foam out of a pail with a stick. The barber chair was an old rocker. I had seen it out on the lawn—rotting in the rain. There were no other women in Mother's attic barbershop. It was loaded with army officers. I could hear the little noises of battle down below. But those pock-pocks couldn't invade the attic. Must have been twenty officers in line—ready to be razored by my wife. My own damn officers whistled at her and made obscene calls.

Mother was wearing a nightgown, like a little girl. The nightgown had a very low neck. And it troubled me, scraped my mind. I wondered if this barbershop was a brothel. I had no proof, no hard evidence. Still, I wasn't keen on Mary scratching at some officer's lathered-up whiskers with the blade of her hand—it was more like a caress.

"*Aw*, Miss Mary, that's very nice."

I kicked the pail out of Tad's hand, but I couldn't crash through that line of officers with lather on their chins. I could see the *plop* of Mary's breasts under her silken gown. And then I couldn't see her at all. Some silly officer had plunked the pail over my head. I was pushed into a corner, and I sat there like the attic dunce, sat for a little eternity—until I woke with a scream.

Yib came rushing into my bedroom. She wore one of Mother's morning robes. Her hair wasn't all trussed up. It lay around her shoulders with a silver shine. I could sense the alarm in her eyes.

"Mr. Lincoln, I didn't mean to intrude. But I heard . . ."

"Is Molly all right?" I asked like the shiest of suitors.

"Mrs. President is asleep, sir. She had her tonic."

I kept seeing that picture of my wife as the lady barber in the attic.

"Elizabeth, how well did you know Will Johnson?"

"Your late barber, sir? We never talked much. Sometimes I mended his clothes."

"I don't understand. Why would you . . . ?"

She smiled at my befuddlement. But it wasn't untender.

"I am a seamstress, sir. And Will was also your valet."

"I still don't . . ."

"Well, sir, Mrs. President couldn't have your valet coming into the Mansion with a frayed cuff. So she would ask me to fix him up—from time to time."

"But I could have bought him a new coat. All he had to do was ask."

"He wasn't a beggar, sir. He had his wages."

I pricked my ears and heard Mary moan in her sleep—it was a soft cry, like a lover's whistle. It wakened a little wildness in me.

"I'd best return to her bedside, sir. Mrs. President is cranky if she wakes up and doesn't see me sitting in my chair."

And she vanished into Mary's bedroom, shutting the door behind her—Yib's feet were bare. I imagined her mending William's coat with her magic thimbles, a couple of stitches at a time. And then Mother arrived in the very nightgown she wore in the dream, with the same low neck, and I didn't know what to believe. I saw the little ripe *roseola* around her nipple, like a pink harvest.

"Father," she said with a deep pucker in her brow, "I'm so sorry to hear of Will. We couldn't even visit him on account of the quarantine. I did try. Some damn major in the Medical Department said I had no business being near the colored smallpox ward. So I had to shout across that infernal room, while the medical staff was gone, and Johnson told me about the scrape he had in the cars."

"What cars, Mother?"

She looked at me as if I'd suffered a sunstroke in the middle of my bedroom.

"Why, the cars out of Gettysburg."

No one had bothered to tell me until now. The conductor was a McClellan man, and ridiculed my speech on Cemetery Hill, called it trash. Will dragged him along the aisle, and dumped him into that little *socket* where Stanton's sharpshooters liked to sit when they weren't protecting me. The conductor would have pressed charges if I hadn't taken ill.

Mary's mind began to drift. She cupped her hand over her nipple, as if she were examining some exotic merchandise, and she chattered about the draperies in the East Room, about the mice in the attic, about Taddie's lisp—a songbird that could dart from subject to subject. I couldn't get her to sit still. And when I touched her hair to calm her, she bolted out of the room, and I was left with the memory of Will shouting across the ward to my wife, rekindling my own time at Gettysburg and the dead who seemed to bestride that village in ghostly blue caps.

41.

The Rebel in the White House

I WAS STILL IN quarantine when I heard the tale of Little Sister's travails, and it rubbed at me like a raw wound. Emilie Todd Helm had been living on potato peels and rotten collards with her little girl. There were food riots in Selma, and robber bands ravaged the town on ponies that cried out their pangs of hunger. That sound tore through whatever spirit she had left—it was worse than a child wailing under water. A renegade with a red rag around his throat nearly chopped her head off with an axe while looking for a handful of butter beans. Emilie was Mother's favorite half sister, and she might not have survived another week in Alabam. She'd crossed the mountains and come to Selma to be near her husband, Ben, but a courier dressed in rags knocked on the door and told her that Ben lay dying at a hospital in Atlanta. She couldn't have gotten onto the cars with her little girl if Ben hadn't been a brigadier general. Officers in rumpled tunics and great slouch hats fed Emilie and the girl scraps of food from their despatch cases—soda crackers, a dried plum, and discolored lemon drops. The cars arrived in Atlanta a little too late. She went through every ward at the hospital in her white veil, while wounded soldiers called her a *livin' wraith* and clutched at her hand, but she couldn't find Ben—until one of the surgeons accompanied her to the morgue.

He was lying on a table with dirt and blood on his red beard; there were bruises under both his eyes. Emile couldn't even kiss him and wash his beard, as the morgue attendants kept shuffling bodies from place to place and growled at the little girl, who sat alone in a waiting room. Emilie ran out the hospital with her Kate and felt more and more like a vagabond. Suddenly she had a new status—the widow of Brigadier Ben. She wanted to return to her own people in Kentucky, but she couldn't get there without a transit card through Union lines. A Rebel general in Atlanta wrote to one of my generals—Mary's name was mentioned—and *Little Sister,* as we called her, was awarded her own private ambulance. She arrived at Fort Monroe with a lot of fanfare. She had lunch with the commandant, but his captains insisted that she swear an oath of allegiance before they let her through. Emilie was petrified. She couldn't disavow the Rebels right after her husband died. The captains bullied her, said they would keep little Katherine at the fort, and send her to Richmond on a mule. But they should have reckoned with Mary's half sister. She threw a Kentucky tantrum, and the captains had to retreat. They wired the White House, and I wired back.

Send her to me.

She and Katherine came in the middle of the night, with their sunken cheeks and wiry hair, and we fed them in the kitchen. I was mortified—the little girl's hands hopped like wounded birds. We couldn't console mother and daughter. But having Little Sister and Katherine around was an elixir for Mary, who could play mother hen. She wore a black dress, but it was for Little Sister's sake; she was awful fond of the brigadier and his red beard. And I watched her cry—and laugh. She'd stroke Little Sister's cheek, stuff her with morsels of pickled shad.

Just two weeks ago, she dropped her serving spoon in the middle of a meal, clutched her forehead, and disappeared into her headquarters, with Elizabeth as her sentinel. Nothing could draw her out—until Little Sister arrived. She went on carriage rides with Emilie. I couldn't accompany them; I was only a day or so out of quarantine. But Tad had a playmate now. He'd rush up to the roof with Katherine, and they'd stare at the Potomac like accomplished sea captains. They turned the staircase into a toll bridge, demanding tribute from whoever passed their little booth. And that look of famine fled from Katherine's cheeks. But she got into a ruckus with Tad over politics and the rebellion. Tad kept carrying around a portrait of me.

"Pa's President, Cousin Kate. He could hang Bobbie Lee if he put his mind to it, or pull Mr. Jeff out of the Rebel White House, and execute him on the spot, without a court-martial."

Her shoulders whipped like a windup doll, and she tumbled about with disjointed steps, as she stole a glance at me.

"Then your Pa is the Executioner-in-Chief, and Mother and I won't stay here another minute."

She packed her own little bag and stood on the south porch, waiting for some phantom carriage to whisk her away from the Mansion. And I had to humble myself in front of that child, or risk losing her whole regard.

"Well, Missy, I might spare Mr. Jeff—and I might not."

That captured her curiosity; and her eyes softened a bit, though she still pretended not to notice where I was.

"And what would persuade you, Uncle Abraham?"

"The color of the sky," I said, "the path of the moon—and how nice you are to me."

She licked her tongue with short, deliberate swipes. "And suppose I wasn't nice? Would you give me to your generals and have them feed on my carcass?"

"Missy, I'd sign the order myself."

She giggled, plucked at her little bag, and moved back into the White House.

She was our star boarder, who gobbled her vittles greedily, hiding buns and slivers of cake in her lap, while she fell in love with one of Mary's prize china inkwells—you couldn't find another like it in all the land. Then we had a robbery on the second floor, and that inkwell vanished from Mary's satin box. Mother shrieked at the servants, called them lazy no-accounts, and wanted to fire every one. But before she had the chance to wreck our tranquility, Tad found the inkwell stuffed inside Katherine's pillowcase. I wasn't happy about his little treasure hunt. He shouldn't have gone sneaking into that little girl's room.

Emilie flew into a rage. She seized Katherine's skinny arm and shook it like a pump handle. "Ungrateful girl, plundering your relations like a common Yankee thief."

I worried that she would rip Katherine's arm right off at the root in that temper of hers. But I couldn't intervene. Molly had to calm her own sister like a Kentucky mare.

"Oh, Em, I promised Kate that portion of China. It was a pact between her secret angel and mine."

Little Sister stopped cranking her daughter's arm. But the little girl, herself a casualty of war, couldn't even trust her own good fortune.

"Auntie, is that angel of *yourn* a liar or not?"

"Child, angels never lie—not in this house."

I didn't want a lot of folks learning we had Mary's Rebel half sister in the Mansion. But my wife bandied it abroad—to gardeners and tradesmen, and whoever else would listen. In her mind, we managed to *steal* Little Sister from the South. Mary invited a pair of confederates from her old Crimson Room salon—General Dan Sickles and New York Senator Ira Harris—to the White House. She just couldn't understand how *suicidal* it was, and destructive to her own sister. Harris, who occupied Seward's old seat in the Senate, had a boy in the Army, risking his life for the Union, and would have been pretty raw about the widow of a Rebel brigadier in the White House. And Sickles had lost a leg at Gettysburg—it was shattered by a cannonball, but he went on fighting in a wheelbarrow until he fainted, and his men carried him from the field. General Dan was Mary's favorite rascal; he's the one who'd been declared momentarily insane after murdering his wife's *admirer* in Lafayette Park. He hopped around on that wooden leg of his, and frequented every bordello in the District; that stump had become a legend at the Ironclad, the Blue Goose, and other high-class houses. Mother relished his tales, but she never bothered to notice his mean, brooding twitch.

Both he and the Senator were bilious at the first sight of Emilie in a black satin robe, mourning her dead brigadier. I was at their little séance in the Crimson Room. But since I hadn't fully recovered, I could afford to lie down on Mary's divan with one eye shut. Both of 'em were skilled at attack and counterattack. They pretended I was some silent witness in the salon; neither one would disturb the President's sleep.

"Mrs. Lincoln," said the Senator, "my little niece met your Robert on Boston Commons the other day, says he's in tiptop condition."

Mary was purring like a pregnant cat. "We're proud of him," she said.

I knew the trap was set. But Mary was blind to the whole business.

The Senator barked like a seal and commenced to swoop. "General Dan and I are eager to learn what regiment Robert will join. He should have gone to the front some time ago."

Mary turned pale; her mouth quivered. She was looking for me to defend Bob, but I wouldn't enter the fracas with one closed eye. Mother patted her mouth with a silk handkerchief. Perhaps I wanted her own confederates to punish her for the foolishness of bringing them here.

"Robert is making his preparations now to enter the Army," she said. "He is not a shirker as you seem to imply. If fault there be, it is mine, dear Harris. I have insisted that Bob stay in college a little longer, as I think an educated man can serve his country with more intelligent purpose than an ignoramus."

Now the Senator turned to Emilie with a masked smile.

"We have whipped the Rebels at Chattanooga," he said. "And I hear, madam, that the scoundrels ran like scared rabbits."

Emilie bit right back. "It was the example you set at Manassas, when the Yankees had their Great Skedaddle."

She ran out the room with Mary right behind. And I was left all alone with the patriarchs. But I shut my mouth while Sickles leaned over the divan and looked at me.

"Sir, you should not have that little Rebel in your house."

He could have been some winter fly—that's how I swatted him away, but that didn't rescue Little Sister. She couldn't even celebrate Christmas with us. General Dan and his cohorts would have crucified her; they published poisonous letters in all the local papers about Little Sister and her fallen brigadier, Ben Hardin Helm. My own Republican stalwarts tossed mud at the Presidential carriage whenever the two *Traitoresses* rode through town. And I could see that frozen look descend upon Mary as her sister was about to depart. She felt forlorn, loved by neither North nor South, and Little Sister had soothed that raw nerve.

They hugged and kissed for half an hour, and then Mary vanished into her room, while I accompanied mother and daughter to their carriage; my wife had packed the coach with candy and dolls for her little niece, who might have to spend her Christmas in a railroad car.

"Brother Abraham," Emilie whispered in my ear, "it was bitter to see my Ben in that little charnel house—with blood all over his beard. If he had looked in your eyes one last time, he might never have . . ."

I couldn't bear to see her shiver and cry. "You know, Little Sister, I tried to have Ben stay with the Union. I wanted to make him our paymaster. But he refused."

"I couldn't stir him," she said, daubing her eyes with one of Mary's silk handkerchiefs. "He saw his star in the South. And it pained Ben, brother killing brother—he was half Yankee himself."

"And I suppose I'm one quarter Rebel. But you shouldn't tell that to Senator Harris. . . . It was good to have you and Katherine here. Mary's nerves have gone to pieces."

There was a divide of eighteen years between the two sisters. Mary hadn't watched her grow up. She ran from Lexington while Emilie was a child. But she sort of adopted Little Sister after we got married—and no war in the world could have broken that bond.

"Mary does seem excitable," Little Sister said. "And once or twice when I came into the room the frightened look in her eyes appalled me—if anything should happen to you or Bob or Tad . . ."

I knew Mother was dancing at some edge, on her velvet slippers. I didn't want those slippers to crash—and imagine her in the madhouse. She felt the whole country had abandoned her, and all she had was her headquarters in a borrowed house. But she was less of a fugitive with Little Sister around.

"You'll come again," I muttered like some hermit in the midst of a hurricane. "Come when you can."

The blush had gone out of Little Sister in her widow's bonnet. She seemed frail, distracted—wounded by Mr. Lincoln's War. She must have blamed me, a little, for her husband's death. Still, she had a much sweeter temperament than my wife. She'd once been the most seductive creature alive—with a perfect oval face and brilliant eyes. A hundred men had courted her—at least a hundred. She'd ruined the season for a lot of Southern belles, but sadness had warped her mouth, twisted it to one side—must have happened after her Ben died and she had to scrounge for food in Alabam.

I kissed little Katherine and hoisted her up into the carriage with her china inkwell in a satin box. The coachman kept muttering how it wasn't his fault if he didn't get to the depot in time. His name was Tim. He was always quarreling with my wife, always driving her to the fashionable shops. He was a great—big—wild sort of feller.

"The cars will leave without us, Mr. Lincoln."

I'd scribbled Emilie a pass for her voyage to Lexington. I also prepared a Presidential pardon, but I knew she'd never take the oath, not with her husband—Brigadier Ben—still boiling inside her head. But no one would dare stop her in the cars, not with my *seal* in her pocket.

I reached into the carriage and hugged my two Rebels for the last time.

"Missy, you watch over your Mama, hear?"

Little Kate wagged her finger at the Executioner-in-Chief.

"I will, Uncle. And you stop hurting people. And tell Tad that it's all right to carry your picture around. I forgive him. And don't forget me, hear?"

The three of us were war-torn stragglers, without a planet of their own. The rebellion had ruined the fabric, unwound the string that tied us all. Little Kate had given me too much credit. I was more like chief plasterer, I suppose, building a whole bunch of wet walls.

"I feel as though I shall never be glad again," I said, while the coachman nattered at me.

"The cars, the cars, Mr. Lincoln. They'll leave without us."

His horses stood in line with their sturdy legs, snorting against the grip of their reins. He administered one lash, and the carriage lurched forward, went through the gate with a horrible, squealing noise, and fell right into the morning fog.

42.

February Fire

IT WASN'T MUCH of a Christmas without Emilie and Miss Kate. We crossed into the New Year like a little band of orphans careening blindly in a broken truck. Mollie had a blue spell most of the time, wishing the war would go away and she could be with Little Sister again. And then, in February of '64, while dozing in my office I heard the rattle of the fire alarm. I ran downstairs in my slippers. I could sniff the smoke. It wasn't coming from our rooms or the servants' quarters. I hopped onto the porch. Acrid smoke was coming from the Presidential stables, which stood behind a hedge near the great granite box of the Treasury Building. But the Treasury was shut at that hour, and the night watchman hadn't smelt the smoke. It was the second damn fire in two years—some witch of war was against the White House.

I lost one slipper as I ran to the stables—there were six horses trapped inside, including Tad's spotted pony and the one that had belonged to our Willie. I leapt over the damn ledge and lost my second slipper. That frightened call of the ponies dug like a stick under my heart.

The fire brigade had arrived; these volunteers chopped at the stable door with their hatchets; but I could tell from the feeble grip they had that their hatchetings wouldn't amount to much. Nothing but splinters flew from the door. I relieved a fireman of his hatchet and ripped the door away with two blows. The fire roared right into my face, and the flames licked at my eyebrows with some kind of tantalizing touch. I stood there, in the fire's sway, like a man stuck in the middle of a bewildering waltz. But something pushed me out of my little fire trance. I had the awful taste of kerosene on my tongue. I could see the cracked blue *corpse* of the arsonist's bottle.

The ponies were behind a wall of fire. I wanted to rush inside and rescue them, but these volunteer firemen grabbed my arms and legs and hurled me onto the ground.

"I'm President of the United States," I hurled back at them.

"Sir," said the chief of the fire brigade, "that's why we're protecting you—from yourself. The horses are goners. No one can save them now."

We all stood there at that little requiem for ponies that were still alive, and we were utterly unmanned, as we heard hooves beating against the walls of the barn and a faint whimper through the constant crackle of fire.

THE PROVOST MARSHAL wandered through the grounds with a bunch of Pinkertons, moving across a cradle of smoke. They talked of sabotage. Allan Pinkerton questioned the entire household staff, even my confidential secretaries. The culprit wasn't hard to find. He was arrested the next day—a coachman Mary had sacked the morning of the fire. I felt a rage in me. I had this urge to shellac my wife. Her *violent* quarrels with the coachman had precipitated the violent death of all six horses.

Mary never uttered a word about the fire. It was as if she were floating in some tranquil balloon where nothing could encumber her, neither horses nor husbands nor her own little boy. I caught her at a fitting with Mrs. Keckly, who had a bunch of pins in her mouth. Mary kept looking into her mirror, and the face that looked back seemed to have an absent, silver sheen. She had as many pins in her as a porcupine.

"Mother, you shouldn't have quarreled with that coachman."

"What coachman?" she asked while plucking at the pins that could have been some portion of a martyr's shirt.

"Timothy—Tim. He set fire to the stables."

"But that wasn't *our* Tim. Tim and I never quarreled. It was another coachman."

I couldn't reason with Mary, make her sense her own participation in the fire. I returned to my office. I could still hear the hot breath of those dying horses, as they kicked against their stalls—the strange, soft whinnying that rose above the fire with all the little plumes of smoke. Mrs. Keckly knocked. There were no more pins in her mouth. I took a little of my rage out on her.

"Madame, has Mary sent you here to make peace?"

I could see the disappointment—and the hurt—crawl onto her face. She'd been kind to Tad, could tear right through the flaws in his speech and understand every syllable. I shouldn't have tanned her hide.

"Mr. Lincoln, Mrs. President doesn't even know I'm here. She cries all the time, but she's too ashamed to tell you. She lent the coachman money, that awful Tim. He'd gamble it away and ask for more. That's why she got rid of him."

"Why didn't she tell me? I would have tossed him out the window."

There was a pause, as if Keckly had a speech defect of her own.

Then she revealed how Tim had been part of Mother's spirit circle. He'd drive her and Mrs. Keckly across Rock Creek, sit with them at séances in Georgetown. But he took advantage of Mother's kindness, went on drunken brawls, raced down Missouri Avenue to Marble Alley, with a *regiment* of strumpets in the car.

"Mrs. President cannot sleep. She keeps hearing the dead ponies in the night."

"Then I'll calm her myself. I'll . . ."

"You mustn't. She'll realize I betrayed her, and she'll only feel worse."

"Then it's our secret, I reckon."

Elizabeth returned to my wife. The fire continued to crackle—I could see the sparks slap at the horses' flanks and sail into the burning wind. A minstrel song started to roll around in my head—humming always seemed to sooth my nerves.

> *To Dixie's Land I'm bound to trabble*
> *Look away! Look away! Dixie Land*

I could feel the *unholies* coming, and even while I hummed, the stables went on burning. I could hear terrified ponies whimper through the wall, like the last, agonizing cries of battle. Then the whimpering got closer and closer, and I wondered if these phantom ponies had come right into the house.

I looked up—Mary stood there in her velvet coat of quills. But she wasn't wounded—it was the sunlight dancing off the pins in her back.

"I was reckless with Mr. Tim," she muttered, without looking into my eyes. "And now I have no peace. I keep hearing the ponies call for help. I must be mad."

I wanted to tell her, *Mother, I hear 'em too—the ponies*. But I couldn't resolve the mystery of dead horses that neighed like dying boys in hospital wards, and in some broken field. I couldn't resolve anything at all. I knew I'd keep on hearing the ponies in time and in eternity, and I'd never reach some *bourne*, where I might be safe from their soft, persistent cries.

THE DISTRICT
& ENVIRONS

1864 & WINTER 1865

43.

Grant

FRED, WHO WAS all but fourteen, had been to Vicksburg with his Pa, had lived through the siege and final surrender of the town, had seen the Rebels hurl hand grenades from their parapets, and watched his father's men dart out of a rifle pit to catch a grenade and hurl it right back. His Pa intended to "out-camp" the enemy, which he did. Cannons couldn't topple this little fortress town, the general told his son. "It can only be taken with the pick and shovel." Grant surrounded Vicksburg with seven miles of tunnels and rifle pits, and waited while the town starved. "Whatever they have on hand cannot last always." Fred saw the first surrender flags, and the elaborate caves that civilians had carved out of the dark red earth on the hillside. They'd abandoned their homes under the parapets—that's how frightened they were of General Grant. His Pa did a kind of Indian dance in the privacy of their quarters. "Son, the fate of the *Secesh* is sealed. We control the Mississippi from its source to its mouth." Ulysses Grant had not always been that sanguine. Fred had to watch over him during his drunken withdrawals, while the general stared at some chandelier for hours and wouldn't eat a morsel.

His Pa was jittery about coming to the capital, where he would be fêted as the first three-star general since George Washington; Congress had revived that rank for Grant, who hated every kind of celebration. They'd never been to the District before, and the general wasn't interested in any of the sights. He had a reservation at the Willard, but no one recognized him in his worn duster. What was this modest little man doing at the hotel of Presidents and diplomats? The clerk assigned him a tiny garret right under the roof. And then the little man scribbled his name in the register.

U. S. Grant & son, Galena, Illinois

The clerk started to tremble. He hadn't recognized the hero of Vicksburg. Grant had attacked through the swamps with a python's grip and nothing but a toothbrush in his pants. He walked into the dining room with Fred, cloaked in the anonymity of a little man with crooked shoulders, lusterless eyes, and a light brown beard—until someone at the next table noticed him. "There's the general." The whole dining room cheered. Fred was embarrassed for his Pa, whose eyes darted from wine bottle to wine bottle at the different tables. Guests at the Willard banged the tabletops with their fists, while the wine bottles wavered, and Ulysses bowed to each guest. He looked more like a grocery clerk than a general . . .

He dozed in the middle of the meal—trench warfare could awaken him, not the Willard. He wouldn't talk about Vicksburg at the dinner table. He signed a dozen autograph albums and went up to his room with Fred. He'd rather have slept on dark clay with his men than have his own suite at the Willard. Ulysses put his son to bed, but he couldn't find the key to his trunk. He walked out of the Willard in his old travel uniform with missing buttons and a frayed cuff, crossed the miasma of Pennsylvania Avenue, and wandered into the Mansion.

Nicolay & Hay hadn't expected Grant until tomorrow. And here he was in the middle of a White House gala with mud on his boots.

Folks swarmed around him—gloves were lost, crinolines collapsed, and shoes were trampled on in that swarm. It was like an invading army in our own salon. And that's how I first met Ulysses Grant. I looked into his blue-gray eyes, and could feel that sense of *risk* I hadn't been able to find in my other generals. *He fights, he kills.* He stole the Mississippi from the Rebels. And now he'd come to the capital in his rumpled uniform, a commander who made sure his mules were fed.

He seemed uncomfortable amid that blind thrust of people in the Blue Room. Ulysses blinked as he was shoved along, sweat pouring from his forehead. I loped toward him, grinning like a jackass. He was a soldier who could disappear into the swamps and survive without a servant or a camp chest or a caravan of clothes.

He didn't have much use for shindigs and chandeliers. He could have had McClellan's old headquarters on Lafayette Square, but he'd have to suffer a season of soirees, with Senators barking down his back. So he decided to make his headquarters at City Point, beside his war tents and his troops.

We all wondered why Ulysses hadn't brought his wife—he was always with Julia. The Rebels had tried to capture her during the Vicksburg campaign, when they raided one of Grant's supply depots; she outfoxed those butternut boys, disappeared from the depot in a squaw's blanket, and managed to join Ulysses at the front. Julia wasn't a great belle—she had a horseface and a permanent squint in one eye, but she was devoted to Grant. Yet he hadn't brought her to the White House on the eve of his anointment as lieutenant general. She was cleverer than Grant *beyond* the battlefield. And she didn't want to compete with Mary on Mary's home ground.

Mother was delighted with the general. She wasn't shy around this shy man. She kept nudging me with her elbow, while she looked at Ulysses.

"Father, we can't have him leave the capital without a dinner in his honor. It isn't fair. Invite him for Saturday. And don't you fail!"

Swamped by politicians, he had to stand on a crimson sofa, or he would have vanished in that morass. The general blushed like a little girl as women leapt out of their lace shawls to clasp his hand.

"Speech, speech," they shouted under the chandeliers. "Hurrah for the hero of Vicksburg!"

He turned ashen all of a sudden—that little girl's blush was gone.

I could tell how mortified he was, and I invited him to climb down. He was no McClellan, who loved to pontificate on the littlest maneuver. Grant killed *quietly* and wouldn't talk with civilians about the fake romance of blood.

We went upstairs to my war room. He sat in Mr. Seward's Cabinet chair, lit up a cigar, and shut his eyes; there was a slight tremor in his eyelids. I was silent until he opened his eyes again.

"Grant, I never liked to interfere with my generals. It's a bad policy. You can't run a war from the White House. But I didn't have much choice."

Folks said I ought to fear him—as a rival, like Little Mac. But the general with the gray eyes was my wild card, perhaps the only card I had left. My own Party wanted to ditch me; my precinct captains said I'd never win another election—without Grant. I couldn't read much into that ash gray color while he puffed on his cigar. I watched the smoke rings multiply, mesmerized a little. I'd made him my General-in-Chief—and I didn't want those honors to bite my own back. No one could say when that Presidential grub gets to gnawing at a man, and I didn't know if there was one gnawing at Grant. Yet that wasn't what gnawed at me. Horace Greeley wrote that if I couldn't find some prescription for peace, we would all drown in *new rivers of human blood.*

But I could not preserve the Union without these rivers of blood. And I needed Grant as a great military captain. I still found it hard to talk to this quiet killer.

"My wife says you cannot leave the District without a dinner in your honor. Does Saturday suit you?"

He shut his eyes again, with a deep tremor in his eyelids, and he said in that slow drawl of his that he couldn't dally—each dinner he attended would cost us.

"We can't excuse you, Grant. It would be the play of *Hamlet* with Hamlet left out . . ."

I'd been jousting with him like a juggler, a common clown. He must have seen the dilemma in my eyes, that supercilious smile.

"Mr. Lincoln," he said, gripping my hand across the table with all the camaraderie of a very private man. "I've *liquored* up a lot, and it's no secret. There must have been a torrent of detraction from every quarter, yet you stuck with me."

I took a shine to Grant. He didn't hide behind his own war paint, and the flags of his men.

"Well, Grant, if I had listened to my Washington friends, who fight with their tongues, the Rebels would still be roasting chestnuts on the banks of the Mississip, with our gunboats dead in the water."

He was still in some sort of agony. "You named me General-in-Chief before we ever met. Weren't you gambling with the nation's chips?"

"General, a man who feeds his mules before he sits down to supper is someone I'd be willing to wager on—with my life."

None of his aides arrived in the morning, not one solid general from his staff, not even a plumed horse. He rose early, without Fred, and toured the District in his slouch hat. No one accompanied Ulysses. First he marched to Old Capitol, where the sentinels gawked at him and got out of his way. He went upstairs and sat with Rebel officers and Union men, calming them with his own deep quiet. Next he walked down to the Navy Yard, sat with sailors, not admirals and the commandant. He didn't ask one question about ordinance at the yard. He looked at the machine shops and the sheds, at gunboats in disrepair, and scribbled a few cryptic lines on his cuff. He was forever at some *front* deep inside his head. I pitied Grant, a little. He was reborn on a battlefield, and couldn't go back to selling saddles in a saddle shop.

He wandered into the Soldiers' Retreat, near the wharves, and had an apple and a fried egg. The soldiers and sailors in the canteen were bewildered by his presence: a three-star general who didn't even wear shoulder straps. There wasn't a gold button or bar on his uniform. He was all slumped over, like someone who had been defeated in battle. They fell into an eerie silence while he finished his meal, but whistled and clapped when Grant stood up from his tiny table and acknowledged them with a slight twist of his slouch hat.

Crowds gathered as he loped up Georgia Avenue to the Orphans' Asylum; soon he had a little tail of soldiers and civilians that tucked itself right behind him; he didn't rouse the asylum, raise it from the dead. He met with orphans in the chapel. They asked him wondrous things about the war. And he spoke to them with a fluidity he didn't have with his generals. He plucked the toothbrush out of his pocket— it had broken bristles. "Boys, I do my best thinking whenever I brush my teeth."

It wasn't like the days when McClellan first rode into the District on Dan Webster, capturing the town with his golden strides and the dizzying flight of his reconnaissance balloons. Grant didn't have an aeronaut, not even a coal-black stallion. He came alone and promised nothing. But there was the quiet of a man who appeared without drums or regimental banners, without the fanfare of military campaigns, just a soldier with his mules and his supplies, wading through the swamps with his men, and arriving under the parapets of Vicksburg, almost by accident, but with deadly design.

44.

Mad Friday

I KNEW THEY STOOD some wayward boy on a barrel with a knapsack crammed with bricks and wouldn't allow him to budge through roll call and reveille; then his sergeant would bang his toes with a hammer until he swayed and danced and toppled off the barrel with his bag of bricks. He wouldn't be ruined, but he'd have blackened toes for life. Or else they'd sit him on a chair with a rifle thrust between his legs and toss him into the Potomac. *Sink or swim* was their motto, and none of the boys ever drowned, but they often returned to shore with blood in their eyes and ears and ended up in the infirmary with acute catarrh.

Then the desertions got real bad. And there were no more *punishment chairs* and knapsacks of brick. My Secretary of War said we couldn't control this epidemic of desertions without the *ritual* of a firing squad. A soldier would sit on his own coffin in front of a firing squad dressed in short capes, with his regiment looking on—until the boy's commander rode onto the grounds, raised his sword, and there would be a fusillade that echoed through the camp like ruffled thunder; it took a full minute for the puffs of fire and smoke to clear;

and then they saw the boy lying on the coffin, with his head pulled back, half his fingers ripped off, his tunic torn to bits, and a wall of blood on his chest.

And when I could hear that terrible clatter of bullets—a merciless, ungodly *rip*—from a military camp nearby, I knew it was the mark of mad Friday. Deserters were always shot on that day. I pardoned as many as I could. "It would frighten the poor devils too terribly, to shoot them." That's what I told my generals and my Secretary of War, but they were adamant about deserters. And I couldn't add to Stanton's troubles. The pressure upon him was immeasurable. Without Stanton the war would grind to a halt. We'd have no horses and ammunition—and supply trains would land in the wrong depot. I couldn't really complain to Grant. He'd fled the capital a week ago, and I didn't want that burden on him.

So I dreaded Friday mornings. And as I scraped around in my slippers, I noticed a man come out of the Prince of Wales Bedroom, wearing one of my nightshirts; it was much too large for him. He swam inside that shirt, the sleeves hanging down to the floor like elephant trunks. I didn't recognize him at first; he had the matted gray beard of a fallen patriarch, with scratches and welts all over his face. It was Billy Herndon, my law partner, whom I had left behind in Springfield. Billy wasn't fat, but he had a fat man's dreams, like the Falstaff I had seen at Grover's. Billy loved to carouse, like Sir John, loved to be in his drams. He also knew how to run a campaign. But I abandoned Billy, let him twist about in Illinois with holes in his pockets . . .

I ordered up an egg, toast, and tea for the two of us and signaled for Billy to wander into my office. Meantime I found Mary floating around the corridor, in her satin nightgown.

"Mother," I whispered, "what is Billy doing in the Prince of Wales

Bedroom? I thought you banned him from our living quarters. How did he get upstairs?"

"The coachmen had to carry him," she said.

"Was he inebriated?"

"Oh, it was much worse than that. I couldn't leave him stranded. Billy was the best soldier you ever had."

My own 3rd Lieutenant, I muttered to myself, as Mary told me what had happened. He was discovered outside the Willard last night by a clerk—he'd been in a brawl. But the hotel wouldn't receive him in such a state. He had no money in his purse, and nothing but a letter from me in his wallet. The Willard sent a message to the White House. And Mary herself had fetched Billy while I was at Grover's with Tad.

"That was mighty kind of you," I said.

"It wasn't kindness. We couldn't have Billy sleep in some pauper's paradise, while he has a letter from you in his pocket. He was once your partner, for God's sake."

"Still is," I said.

"But he has to be out of here by noon."

Billy must have had a bad angel in matters to do with my wife. He could never get on her good side; it was like being sick with poison ivy every season of the year. But they were more alike than Mother imagined. They were always socking people. Something gnawed at them—a terrible want, as if they meant to control the world through one of their rages, and finished up eating their insides.

I went into my office with Billy and shut the door. I could still hear the burst of rifles from Fort Stevens—the sound grew fainter and fainter. Billy watched me wince with each soft clap.

"What is that?"

"Deserters' Day," I said.

For a second I thought Billy was gonna flatten me. He hunkered down in that fighting stance of his, and his eyes shrank into his skull. But Billy must have changed his mind.

"Couldn't you put an end to it? You're the President. You can stop an execution anytime you want."

"And have my generals revolt? That would murder morale. And Stanton would run into the hills with all his railroads. I have to show a little discretion."

"That's not what I hear," he said. "You'll sign any pardon, if a mother cries to you about her boy."

Our breakfasts arrived in a pair of tin trays; we used our pocket-knives to crack open the eggs. Billy's knife shivered as he buttered his toast; and then the toast fell to pieces in his hand.

"What happened at the Willard?"

Billy got into a scrape with a Democrat—while they were having a dram. They quarreled inside the bar, and then out on Pennsylvania Avenue, in front of all the carriages and horsecars and military ambulances.

"And what was that quarrel about?"

"Your wife," he said.

I liked the idea of Billy defending Mother's honor at the Willard. That Democrat had called her unconscionable things, he said. I had to stare him down until he spat out the details.

"He called her a harlot and a Rebel spy who harbored Jeff Davis' own whore in the White House."

"I'm the harlot here. Mary's Rebel sister had nowhere else to go. I let her stay with us a while. So your quarrel with that Democrat was about a little dust."

Billy had the ragged look of a renegade general. And he once had the merriest eyes in Illinois, but Lincoln & Herndon meant nothing in the middle of a rebellion. The war had beggared Billy, made him into a wanderer with nowhere to go.

We both sucked on our eggs, the way we had done at my law office when we didn't have more than a minute to spare; soon our nightshirts were stained. It wasn't that simple to suck on an egg.

We drank our tea in silence. We couldn't talk politics any longer. One civil war wasn't enough for Billy. He wanted a different kind of war—*bloody revolution*, as he called it, where the South would be reduced to rubble and the border States would have to give up every single black. Maryland, Missouri, and Kentuck had poisoned the Union in Billy's mind, and we had to rid ourselves of all the paraphernalia of slavery. Otherwise we'd have a slave culture another hundred years. Billy wasn't so wrong. Slavery anywhere in the Union was an *affront*. Yet I had to woo *our* slaveholders gently until we finished the war. Julia Grant still had her own slave. She was a good Missouri gal. Billy might have forgiven Julia, but he wouldn't forgive the South. And I couldn't save the Union by turning the South into a vast prison farm. I was no jailor, and neither was General Grant.

Billy broke the silence with a short breath. "It wasn't only about your wife," he blurted out. "That Democrat said you had a harem in the White House—that you slept with all the maids and with Mary's seamstress, a mulatto gal—that you sired a devil child, half boy, half dog—that he lives in the attic, and presides over a Miscegenation Ball. That's when I hit him, hit him hard."

I didn't know how to comfort Billy. I wanted to touch his face; but he was covered with welts and his beard was gnarled as a blackberry bush.

"Mr. Lincoln, are you ever coming back to Illinois?"

"I may be back sooner than you think—if the Democrats prevail."

"I've kept your chair the way it was, close up to the wall," he said.

"And your couch, with all the piles of paper. People are always coming in to have a look. I have to chase them out. 'It's not a shrine, for God's sake.' That's what I tell them. 'It's where Mr. Lincoln worked, and where he'll work again.' "

I could have found a sinecure for Billy—some fat office in the Interior Department. But he would drink his way into oblivion, fight with his superiors, and I'd have to clean up the mess. I had no time for Billy.

He finished his tea and toast, and walked out of my office. I wouldn't have followed Mary's mandate, and hurled him out at high noon. I'd have let him heal up in the Prince of Wales Bedroom. Perhaps he had never intended to come here, but had been waylaid by Mary's coachmen after his drunken brawl. He gathered up his clothes, scribbled a couple of lines to my wife, and left the White House at a quarter to nine, in a hat with a tattered brim . . .

I heard the rifles from Fort Stevens well into the morning—that strange, almost silent bark, like the sound of pathetic, tin dogs. My hands were shaking, and I had the worst blue spell in a long while when my confidential secretaries knocked and entered with a brand-new folio of court-martials from Stanton at the War Department. I noticed the hollows in their cheeks. Nicolay & Hay were as melancholy as their Titan about the fusillades at Fort Stevens.

"Damn my Secretary of War!"

I took that folio and tossed it against the wall—my secretaries blinked as all the dossiers flew out like paper orphans and landed on the oilcloth.

The Titan is having a fit.

They stooped and picked up the different dossiers and piled them on my Cabinet table. I looked upon these court-martials as little sagas. I perused the first one. It told the saga of a farmer boy from Missouri who deserted, took care of his crops, and enlisted again.

"Why shoot that boy? Let him fight."

I pardoned him with a scratch of green ink. After that the tales grew more entangled and more complex. A raw recruit murdered his own captain, but there had been bad blood between him and the captain, who was brutal with all his men; then there was the deserter who signed up with the Rebels, collected his bonus, ran back across the lines, joined another regiment, and did the same maneuver five or six times; or the colonel who left the battlefield and slashed his wife to pieces on his own little holiday from the war. These sagas started to molt inside my brain, and to preserve my sanity I scribbled on the dossiers: *Send to Dry Tortugas.* It was where McClellan had banished all his bad soldiers—the military's isolation camp on the Dry Tortugas, where none was ever heard from again.

"The Dry Tortugas, sir," said my secretaries with great reluctance, "is not the same as a firing squad. You can either pardon a soldier or . . ."

Send him to the Tortugas.

The barking at Fort Stevens had stopped, and I moved on to the next dossier, with a bitterness in my heart, not against my generals and their rules, but at my own culpability as the mad king of war.

45.

An Evil Hour

I HAD TO ENDURE a summer's worth of Mad Fridays, as a blue haze rose off the river and the canals and seemed to *stifle* the sky, while a vast army of pigs rooted along the avenues and rushed through the back door of the Willard, frightening cooks and the hotel's clients. Marines, who were called in from their barracks, chased the pigs down to the Potomac flats with their batons and rifle butts, and lost them in the blue haze of swamp gas.

Mary and Tad got out of this swamp, and escaped to Vermont that August with a caravan of hatboxes that filled an entire baggage car. I was all alone at our summer cottage, in the worst damn summer of the war. A few drunken soldiers may have lurched here and there—shots were fired—but the Rebels sat within their ramparts at Petersburg, and we couldn't pierce or break Lee's line. Grant had despatched his own best general to invade Georgia and hurl the Rebels right into the sea, yet Tecumseh Sherman couldn't be found anywhere on the map. His army had vanished into some mythical wood. We were stuck in *an evil hour*, according to my critics. Republican and Democratic papers sang the same tune. "The People are wild for Peace." And the

Locos had their *Peace* candidate, McClellan, who sat in his cottage on Orange Mountain, in New Jersey, and sulked because I wouldn't give him another crack at a command. "The wish of my heart is to lead the Army of the Potomac in one more great campaign," he told reporters and whatever general would listen. Meantime he connived with Copperheads—those Northern reptiles who wanted us to *surrender* the war—and other poisonous snakes. Stanton warned that any general who turned politics into *a game of blood* ran the risk of getting gored. And still McClellan intrigued, spurred on by his own battle fever. Convinced that every soldier in the land would vote for him, he conspired with the McClellan Legion of veterans' clubs to deliver that vote. There were torchlight parades up the mountain, with Copperheads and Legionnaires, who despised each other and scuffled all along the mountain road. The Legionnaires arrived first, with broken lanterns and torn battle blouses; and while one side of the mountain lit up like a meteor, McClellan men did rally under a single banner.

Time to Swap Horses.

And then, one night, just after the convention in Chicago anointed Little Mac as the solitary soldier who could distance us from the dread *arbitrament* of war, I grew restless rambling on the grounds of the Soldiers' Home, and called for the Presidential carriage, with its solid silver lamps and silvered steps that always seemed to sway. The coachman arrived, and I was alarmed. It was Tim, that recreant who had set fire to the stables and burnt our ponies alive. I could still listen to their lament sometimes, before I fell asleep.

I was startled to see his haggard face and ropey hands, his eyes like little pink buttons.

"Timothy, weren't you arrested?"

"I was betrayed, sir. It was a false accusation. I would never harm your horses—I fed them every morning, combed their manes. I took much pride in their handsome coats. It was one of the gardeners, sir, who started that fire. He stole some cash from the Lady President. She got rid of him, and he took his revenge on the ponies."

I searched those pink buttons, but the coachman's eyes didn't reveal a thing. I climbed into the carriage and told him to take me to the Willard. I didn't want to rush over to the War Department and sit around with the cipher clerk—it would only have added to my gloom. I wanted some company, the pleasure of seeing a kind face under the soft blue hiss of the hotel's gaslights.

We rolled down from the hills, passed one of our earthworks, with Tim clucking at the horses. The little fort lay abandoned; there were hats and old shoes lying around, and the rifle pits were all unmanned. We passed a row of privies that resembled a staggered, leaning platoon; a howitzer and a Parrott gun lay in the middle of the road on little trucks without wheels. And Tim had to steer around these *impediments*, or we might have spilled into a ravine.

I'd never traveled on such a forlorn route, where no picket challenged our right of passage, no colored farmers carried watermelons on their little trucks. I couldn't recollect meeting one human eye, and we got to the Willard in record time. I clambered down silvered steps that stuck out like bristles and near broke my ankle.

"Shall I wait for you, sir?" he asked from his kingly chair.

"Go about your business, Tim. I'll sleep at the Willard tonight."

The Willard was as somber as that earthwork on the hill. I'd watched it flicker like a burning barn on most other nights. The doorman wasn't even there to greet me in his high hat. I went into the lobby and fell into a blaze of light. The divans shone under the chandeliers, bristled like peacock tails. I was surrounded by an assembly of clerks.

"Mr. Lincoln, what a pleasant surprise!"

Bellboys hovered around, volunteering to be my runners—they would have delivered messages to Richmond, or to General Grant, would have scoured the whole of Dixie Land for a trace of Tecumseh, my missing general, and his missing men.

"Boys," I said, "no traffic tonight. Not even to the telegraph office. I'm on a little holiday—at the Willard."

I was served Maryland oysters and a drop of wine at my own little table in one of the Willard's private parlors, though it wasn't so private, and I wasn't all alone. A voice shot out at me, like an electric bolt.

"Enjoying your midnight supper, Excellency?"

I peered into the shadows; an officer was sitting on a divan, his chin resting on the pommel of his sword. I recognized his silky mustache, and the military cape he was wearing in this infernal heat. Why wasn't he on his mountain, where he belonged?

"General, what are ye doin' at the Willard?"

"Oh, I'm having a little respite—from Stanton's damn detectives. They've been following me everywhere."

And you shouldn't have been fooling around with Copperheads.

He sat humped in the shadows, with his chin on that sword; couldn't see much more than a hint of his eyes. He'd always been a man of shadows, contemptuous of everyone who wasn't part of his military family—and that included other generals.

"Excellency," he whispered from his divan. "You can't fool me with your killer in the long hat. *Unconditional Surrender Grant.* Well, I believe in terms—good terms, fair terms, not unconditional carnage. But Sherman is lost in the woods, and Grant's beard will turn silver in the middle of his siege. I'll sack them both first chance I get, send them to fight the Sioux."

"And what fate have you prepared for me?"

I heard him titter in the dark. "You can become the President of a colored college—I'll collect some cash, give you the first hundred dollars."

"And I suppose you'll send a peace commission to meet with Jeff Davis."

The hate in him was palpable—I could feel it flutter around, a half-mad missile. Little Mac was like a secular bishop certain of his own divine sense, and I was the gadfly who got in his way.

"Excellency, you should have given me back my old command, and then you wouldn't be in this pickle, staring at the man who's going to steal your chair and send you flying back to Illinois."

He brushed his mustache and chin beard with a little amber comb, as if he were posing for some invisible camera in the room. Little Mac was the *prettiest* general we ever had, and he would have been the first to acknowledge that. But there was a lilt in his left eye, a wayward slant, that left him with a deeply troubled look.

"I should silence Stanton, shut him up, before he slanders me again. You believe his canard that I met Bobbie Lee on the battlefield . . ."

Stanton loved to flesh out the old fable—that the two generals got together at Antietam, talked of peace while sitting on their mounts, that McClellan's boys helped Lee skedaddle with his war wagons, let him race back across the river. But that fable didn't wash. Lee took a spill from his horse and had to wear splints on both his arms. He was carted around in an ambulance during the whole battle. Even if he'd had the time or the inclination to meet with Little Mac, Lee wouldn't have wanted a Union general to catch him lying flat, in an ambulance.

McClellan continued to swagger. "Excellency, I don't care a tit what you think. West Pointers will have to decide our fate, not your conniving Secretary of War. I'll break that man once I get to the White House."

I had to skin him a little, disturb his silk mustache.

"And what if I delay the elections, and you can't get in?"

He was silent for a moment, like some befuddled bear in a yellow sash. Then he broke from the shadows with a violent thrust. His chin beard twitched with rage. He'd never forgive me for having removed him from headquarters—with his horse no less.

"You wouldn't have the brass. You're good for emancipating colored people and telling vulgar jokes. You can't even read the terrain on a map. You don't have the stomach to stall the elections."

Either I had to tamp his feathers down or spit some oyster juice into his wayward eye.

"General, did I ever tell you about my Harvard boy? Bob was of a scientific turn as a child. I bought him a microscope. Bob went around experimenting with his glass on everything. And one day, at the dinner table, I took up a piece of cheese. 'Don't eat that, Pa,' said Bob. 'It's full of *wrigglers.*' But I took a huge bite and said, 'Son, let 'em *wriggle.* I can stand it if they can.' "

He wouldn't stop perusing me from the heights of his chair.

"Are you demented, sir? What do your damn wrigglers have to do with me?"

"Nothing, General. I was *jest* in dire need of a joke."

He gripped his sword, and he had such a demented look that I was fairly certain he was about to present me with my own ticket to hell. That's how much bitterness and contempt he had with his sword held high. What would it have taken him to cleave me in two? I just sat there and sipped my wine. That enraged—and unraveled—him even more. He must have *imagined* my own blood as he slashed at the pillows and the curtains beside me, until the parlor was filled with feather dust, and his entire face had a fierce glint. Then he sat down again with a tiny mark of satisfaction, and a macabre grin.

"I could have gotten rid of you," he said. "I had a million chances. My officers begged me to do it. Even now they beg me, even now.

And people would stop me at the side of the road—good people, plain people, not politicians. They idolized Dan Webster, loved the black silk of his coat, said we were the lords of Pennsylvania Avenue, Dan and I, and you didn't have one token of legitimacy. I should have marched on Washington and had you clamped in irons with your mad wife. Who would have stopped me?"

"No one," I said.

And now he started to smile, with all the menace and the *meat* of it. "I wouldn't have bothered your little boy with the lisp—I kinda like him. He could have served me wine at my headquarters, in that uniform the War Department allows him to wear—3rd Lieutenant Tad."

Exiled in New Jersey, stripped of his colors, and without men and boys to lead, he must have had an *infinity* of battle plans inside his head that maddened him beyond repair.

"Excellency, you ought to kiss my boots. *I* gave you Gettysburg. Your own officers said that 'McClellan's ghost' won the battle, because the boys wouldn't have fought with the same valor if they hadn't assumed I was still in command. But you don't have that *ghost* any more in your arsenal. All you have now are your nigger troops. And you dance with them while the nation leaks treasure and blood."

He rose up on the pommel of his sword and left with all the clatter of a general; I could hear his spurs jangle across the parlors, their echo like a nightmare of splintered glass. I wondered where he would show up next. Would I encounter that splintered glass while I was on the privy, or when I carried Tad across the White House on my back? McClellan's *madness* would always have a hold on me.

I walked through the Willard, my tall hat nearly bumping into the chandeliers. I couldn't find much company—there wasn't a soul to be seen in the women's parlor. The rugs were cluttered with scraps of paper, cigar stumps, and spilled spittoons. I went out into the night, with that strange rattle of McClellan's spurs still ringing in my ears.

46

Mother's Mission

I T WAS DESOLATE at dawn, with its clock tower tolling in the wind, its ticket office half shuttered, its ladies' saloon in disrepair, full of debris. The stationmaster fumbled about with a big brass key in his fist, while troopers stood on guard in rubber raincoats. No one could get onto and off the cars without a government ticket or a special pass from the B&O. We crossed the depot, Keckly and I, and strode onto the platform of the main car shed, with its crumbling granite pillars and porous tin roof, and there she was in her pale gown, without the sign of a slipper or shoe, as if she'd strolled out her bedroom, and hadn't traveled in her bare feet with a hatbox and a footstool to a stucco railroad station, north of the Capitol.

It was but a week after I'd met Little Mac at the Willard, and Mother had just returned from Maine. The wind yapped like a mad dog in that long tin tunnel, but she didn't panic. She had a look of absolute bliss, like an eager child who had just made some startling discovery. Her reddish hair glowed in the tinny light. And for a moment she wasn't even my wife, but Miss Mary Todd, a Lexington belle with a willful streak, and then I noticed the hatbox with its bruised cover, and her footstool, crouching like a gigantic mushroom, or a mottled toad.

"Mother, where are you going?"

"To Richmond," she said, like a moody child. "Father, I'm delirious with joy. The stationmaster has promised me the next car will come along. I can ride to Virginia with one of your regiments. The *Secesh* wouldn't dare disturb Mary Lincoln's car."

There were no cars to Richmond. And the stationmaster couldn't have produced one even if the whole damn war depended on it. He must have coddled my child-wife, watched her come into the depot like a distracted barefoot queen, and wanted to get on her good side. But nothing I said could break Mary's own conviction.

"A car will come—if I wait long enough. I have a rendezvous with Mrs. Jeff Davis. We're the only ones who can stop this war."

Mother had some powerful logic—wives were as worthy as generals in this scrape. I should have kept a cool hand at the depot, but seeing Mother like that in her flimsy gown, with goose bumps between her bosoms, unsettled me and I began to cry. That startled my child-wife.

"Husband, it's the only way to bust loose from the Locos and Little Mac."

I couldn't *smash* that spell of hers. Mother was on a peace mission. She might have waited until the next full moon for a car to Richmond. I had to depend on Elizabeth, who jolted Mary with a little pack of lies.

"Mrs. President, isn't it a shame about Mrs. Jeff?"

My wife scowled at Elizabeth. "Lizzie, are you saying the cars won't come?"

"They'll come, Mrs. President. But Mrs. Jeff won't be there to meet *your* car. She's been at the hospital all night, helping to bandage up children caught in the fire and smoke from Mr. Grant's siege guns."

Mother put her fat little hand over her heart. "Poor, poor Varina and her hospital children. If they expire, they'll be all alone in *immensity*, like my little son, and there won't be a soul to sing to them, or my Willie. Father, we must have Senators and Stanton's clerks, and all the reprobates from Old Capitol, every one, on the train to Richmond. . . . Lizzie, round up all the contrabands you can find and all the colored maids, and Grant must come with us and beg forgiveness to Varina and the children. Father, summon the Butcher, grab him by his straps . . ."

She fell silent, exhausted by her own melodic chant. Elizabeth took Mother by the hand and led her away from the car shed and across the depot, as the stationmaster curtsied with the key in his fist. "It was an honor to have the Lady President at the B&O. I trust we'll be seeing Madame again."

I could have lashed at him for selling my wife a song about some spectral car to Richmond, only what would I have done in his shoes, if the Lady President walked into my terminal in her nightgown, and with *nek-kid* toes, like some Ophelia of the plains? I might have sold her the same song about the Baltimore–Richmond line. I strode out of the depot with Mother's hatbox and footstool. That recreant, Tim, was waiting for us on Jersey Avenue with our carriage, and we lit out of there, the coachman clucking at his horses like a gifted marriage broker. The wind on her face must have refreshed Mary.

"I'll have to wear silver," she said. "I won't have Mrs. McClellan dancing around me with her good looks, not when silver is so exceptional on my skin."

I didn't know what to do. Mary's *seasons* were as variable as monsoon weather. But Elizabeth and I returned to the Mansion and tucked Mary in. Mother didn't talk about the cars, and her jaunt to Jersey Avenue in the middle of the night, like a somnambulist with her eyes wide open. I knew she couldn't rest at night, that some dream of our lost boy wandering in *immensity* would startle her sleep. That's why Yib came down from her attic workshop and slept beside Mary on a vermilion sofa.

As I clutched Yib's hand, I felt that same electric pull we'd had at the séance in the Soldiers' Home, with Lord Colchester.

"Lizabeth, if a calamity should occur—anything—promise me you won't abandon Mary and Tad, that you'll look after them. I mean, I might run into a Rebel sharpshooter at the B&O, or some lady spy could poke me at the the-*ay*-ter with a pocket pistol . . ."

She was silent for a second. "Sir, I'd never leave Mrs. President and the boy."

"But she won't always be *Mrs. President*. And it will be hard for her without that mantle . . . and a load of servants."

Elizabeth didn't try to steer me away from death and destruction. We could still have been in Colchester's spirit house, roaming with all the angels, the good *and* the bad, looking for the perpetual corn and lilacs of Summerland. I should have realized that Colchester's orchards and fields were battlegrounds where all the blood had cleared, and all the groans of the wounded had washed into the ether.

"I won't leave her, Mr. President."

Then all the electricity left my hand. And she did a strange thing. She shut her eyes and caressed the contours of my face with her own two hands—my chin, my cheeks, my bony brow—like a blind woman encountering a death mask. And she went back inside Mother's headquarters without another word.

🙴

MARY WORRIED ABOUT Little Mac's *deepening* presence. The war wouldn't last a week after he was elected, he told the *London Times*. He was photographed with his Nellie in her handsome silk bonnet.

People bowed in front of their carriage. Stanton called them a pair of traitors, but it wasn't true. Nell had been kind to Mother after our Willie passed, her robust blue-eyed blondeness hidden under a veil she wore out of respect for Mother's grief. She was like one of Mary's half sisters, eighteen years younger, and that's what troubled Mother during the canvass, that she had a beautiful young rival, with a piercing blondeness that trivialized her own plump look. And so everything to do with Nellie and Little Mac filled her with terror now, and she would fly into a fit at the least mention of *McClellan*. But that didn't mean Little Mac was a traitor. It was the usual flimflam of Presidential politics. His posters were set in bleached brown, with his silken mustache looking severe, his dark eyes contemplating the Presidency, his hair combed high on his forehead, his buttons bristling, his general's cape curled around his shoulders.

McCLELLAN is the MAN

I couldn't compete with that stunning image, not in my stovepipe hat, my sallow face half a mountain of hollows, and Mary made matters worse with all her vitriol. After shellacking Nell and calling her a *blonde toadstool*, she went after Little Mac like a thirsty shark. "He'll declare Richmond the new capital of the Republic after he sits down with Mr. Jeff at the Rebel White House." I couldn't rein her in. It was as if her life depended on the canvass, and perhaps it did. I knew she owed money to a certain dry goods baron in New York for the little hurricane of hats she acquired on her last trip to the metropolis. And she wouldn't have been able to bargain with him once she lost her mantle as Lady President. I could have exiled her to that little room in the basement where she passed the worst of her *monthlies*, but Tad would miss her. So would I—and Bob. He'd come down from Harvard to be with us. Her barrage of bitter remarks—and the mad pulse above her eye—troubled Bob. I could tell how embarrassed he was from the little twitch of his mustache. He would shout at her in the middle of a tirade.

"Mother, you must stop this. It does not become you to be a harridan. Mr. McClellan is not a convict, for God's sake, and Nellie is not his whore."

She would vanish into her headquarters and return after an hour with a *suspicion* of red paint on her cheeks, and all her mad trembling gone—that's how susceptible she was to Bob.

Serenaders showed up every night. We stood on the south porch, Mary in a black silk dress, Tad with some engine of destruction in his hand—a penknife or the ripped pieces of a captured Confederate flag—and Bob, in a splendid suit, his arms crossed, like some champion, his mustache neat as a general's.

That's how the serenaders saw him, as my general in civilian clothes.

> *Who's the prince we love the best?*
> *Bob—our Bob—the Prince of Rails*

The serenaders begged him for a little speech. Bob blushed. He wasn't much good at speechifying. But he addressed the serenaders with the merciless tap-tap of a telegraph machine.

"I'm here to help my Pa," he said.

His mother still kept him on a string. He studied law on her account, stayed clear of a Massachusetts regiment. He preferred his cramped quarters at Harvard to his *suite* at the White House, which must have reminded Bob of how he'd always been caged in by her emotions and moods and her *beau ideal* of him, the Harvard gentleman from Illinois. She couldn't cure my rotten habits—welcoming guests with my shirttail sticking out, reading with my elbows on the floor, jabbing at my vittles with a knife, cussing like a mechanic. She cured Bob, but it only made him wilder. He had perfect diction. He could perform a duet at the dinner table with his knife and fork. Still, I never saw my son smile. And he told me once, half in jest, that he'd rather run away with a circus than study the law. But even clowns and acrobats had to enlist. And almost every circus died during the insurrection.

His hands were trembling as he waved to the serenaders.

"Bobbie," Mother said, "Bob," in that teasing voice of hers, like a piece of silk with a ragged edge, "shouldn't you *engage* them a little, tell people about your plans after the canvass. It would be a kindness to me and your father."

He turned from her, like that little boy who ran away from home when he was six, and now there was nowhere to run. He'd never attack his mother or Tad, but he might gnaw off his own arm, if I wasn't careful with him.

He stopped me in the hall after the serenaders had gone, pleaded with his Pa. My Bob would rather be the lowliest private than the Prince of Rails. He couldn't fight Mary alone. *She smothers, she overwhelms.* I tried to comfort him, to touch his arm, but he pulled away, as if I were a water moccasin.

I had to help Bob, or I'd lose him to some *insane* circus without a single acrobat. But I couldn't do a thing until the canvass was over . . .

My managers cautioned me about McClellan, hinted that I should fetter the soldier vote wherever I could. But I wanted soldiers to vote. "We are as certain of the soldier vote as we are certain of the sun," McClellan's managers said. I didn't care. I couldn't ask a soldier to gamble life and limb and then turn around and pilfer his right to vote. I had my Secretary of War devise a plan to help soldiers cast absentee ballots in the field. My critics swore I was prepared to carry around a carpetbag and collect the ballots myself. Indeed, I might have done so with Tad. But my 3rd Lieutenant was already involved in the canvass, him and Gulliver, his pet turkey. This fine turkey, with full black feathers, and a solid white breast, had been sentenced to the dinner table—until Tad purloined him and defied his Pa and the White House cook. He'd run around the Mansion, teaching his turkey every sort of trick. When the Pennsylvania boys camping at the White House started to cast their ballots, Gulliver mingled among them and interfered with the commissioners at the polling station. The commissioners were querulous at first. They couldn't conduct their polling with a live turkey in the same precinct.

"Son," I said, "is your turkey a Pennsylvanian? Does Gulliver intend to vote?"

"No," Tad whipped right back. "He is not of age."

The commissioners all laughed. But I was haunted by that image of McClellan in his cape, as if he could straddle the world in one great stride. And on the very eve of the election, I saw a flickering light in my window and heard a low hum, as if some angel were trying to console me. I went to the window, and there was a damn sight—a parade of candles across the lawn, like the rising up of the dead; soldiers lost on the battlefield had come to curse their President. Perhaps I needed cussing. I'd *spent* their manhood and hadn't delivered much. I could catch the hollows of their eyes, the broken boot tips, the wasted limbs.

They tossed their caps into the air when I waved to them. And one of these silent serenaders shouted, "We ain't for no damn Jersey general. We're for Ol' Abe."

Then they danced, blew out their candles, and disappeared from the lawn. I was left with the fury of my own wants and the taste of gall on my tongue—a Commander-in-Chief who was hostage to every act of carnage, every bit of battleground, and every single cavalry charge in his name. Grant and Sherman didn't have McClellan's flair to build fortresses a hundred miles from the front, but they knew how to kill. And I couldn't preserve the Union without those killers of mine . . .

McClellan came down off his mountain and swaggered here and there with his young wife—certain fancy folks took to calling her Mrs. President. He was welcomed in Philadelphia and New York as the nation's commander-king. His managers talked of using my skull for target practice. They maligned my wife, said she was the secret queen of Richmond—that's what stuck in my craw, and Little Mac promised to ride to the gates of the White House on his beautiful black stallion, with the soldier vote behind him, but it was a lot of *tin*.

There was *civil war* in the District between McClellan's supporters and our own Elephant Clubs, with competing torchlight parades. The McClellan Legion had a hard time finding raw recruits in the Republican precincts, while the Elephant Clubs marched through the streets with howitzers and military ambulances and lit-up transparencies—one of General Grant and another of myself in a stovepipe hat and long tails that seemed to flare up and shoot sparks into the sky. As the Elephants marched past Democratic headquarters at Parker Hall with their bits of fire, a banner of McClellan strung across the *Ave* burst into flames, and *McCLELLAN* shriveled and turned to smoke. The Legionnaires were furious, but they couldn't muster many Locos among the troops. They called the Elephants "abolition traitors," and had to retreat into Parker Hall in a storm of cobblestones. Some of the Elephants wept, even as they hurled the stones. They belonged to the Army of the Potomac, and still loved their old leader, but could never vote for McClellan.

His own boys turned against him when the Democrats talked of peace while soldiers were dying in the fields. A young Vermonter, who was a McClellan man *clear to the bone*, said he'd rather rot under Rebel ground than vote for *dear George*.

A week after the canvassing was done, Mary came to me, swathed in black from head to toe. She looked like a creature of cold, hard chalk under her veils. But there was nothing *pale* about her blue eyes. I wondered if Mary was on another mission.

"Father," she said, "we will have to do something about Robert. He can no longer tolerate his portion—he's quitting law school. You must use all your influence to find some light task for him in the military. I will not have my son ending up as cannon fodder."

My Ophelia wasn't waiting for some spectral car to Richmond, wasn't in bare feet. She was made of chalk this afternoon. But I couldn't sacrifice other sons for her sake.

"Mary, I'm Commander-in-Chief. I cannot shield my own boy."

Then all that veneer suddenly broke down, and her little chalk house commenced to crumble, and I saw a hollow in the veil where her mouth was, as she made little sucking noises like a child under duress.

She'll go to the cars again, stand under that tin roof in her sleepwalker gown, and my heart will tear—one thread at a time. I won't survive that second ride to B&O.

"Mr. Lincoln," she said in the rumbling voice of a petitioner, "if Bob goes to the front, who will do his *wash*? I'll have to get a chit from Ulysses Grant. There must be accommodations for mothers and wives. I'll live with the sutler women, sell chocolate to the soldiers. And I'll have to take Lizzie, hear? And one of the other gals. Tad will want to come see his brother. The District is dead this time of year."

"Mother, for God's sake—stop!"

She ripped off her veil with one savage sweep of her hand. Her eyes were swollen. Her mouth was twisted at the corners into a snarl, as if some demented bear had bitten her. And then that forlorn mask disappeared.

"Goodness, other mothers have sons in the war. We'll pack a picnic for Robert. He loves the pickled ham they serve at the Willard, and poached eggs on a sliver of toast."

"Molly," I whispered, soft as a serpent, "I'll find a way to shield Bob."

I didn't want to wound my wife, just to calm her down. And I didn't want Bob to chaperone his mother to the government insane hospital, not in his last act as a civilian. But Mary hummed to herself, and her eyes raced with rapture over Bob. She was as cunning as a gifted, petulant little girl who loved to bribe and be bribed. She strolled into her headquarters under all her widow's weeds, while I went into my office, stood near the window, and could *see* the end of the war in the chipped glass, as if it were a general's translucent map. As I looked deep into the glass, it flashed like a mirror in the sun. I was frightened of my own face. It wasn't my sunken cheeks. I was getting used to that. I'd become a bag of bones. It was the *terror* on my brow—fierce and unfriendly as an open sore. My face was a silent scream that suddenly cracked open, shook the chandeliers, and shivered right through the glass.

47.

Captain Bob

January 19, 1865

LIEUTENANT-GENERAL GRANT:

Please read and answer this letter as though I was not President, but only a friend. My son, now in his twenty second year, having graduated at Harvard, wishes to see something of the war before it ends. I do not wish to put him in the ranks, nor yet to give him a commission, to which those who have already served long are better entitled and better qualified to hold. Could he, without embarrassment to you or detriment to the service, go into your military family with some nominal rank, I, and not the public, furnishing his necessary means? If no, say so without the least hesitation, because I am as anxious, and as deeply interested, that you shall not be encumbered. . . .

I would have volunteered in Bob's place, gone into battle with a bent bayonet and my pockets stuffed with hardtack, slept on the ground like General Grant, and carried the slop of an entire regiment—rather than use my office in the service of my son. I hoped—in secret—that the general would deny my request, and hoped that he wouldn't. He didn't stall, as I had done, but wrote back in two days, never once flaunting his power. "I will be most happy to have him in my military family," he said, and suggested that the rank of captain would be just about right.

I went to Mary with the general's despatch. I couldn't find one particle of joy on her face, none of the bliss she'd had at the B&O, waiting with her hatbox and her footstool for a phantom car. I couldn't *enthrall* her with the news about Bob.

"Father," she said, wrinkling her nose, "Grant shouldn't be that near our boy—his Butcher's habits might spill onto Bob. Couldn't you find something for him with the quartermaster, or else your Secretary of War, where Bob would be billeted in Washington?"

My feet were always cold. I had to warm them near the fire. I'd lope from shiver to shiver as I went through the corridors in my green shawl. And now my hands were shaking, too. I'd picked up Mary's affliction—I was becoming as mercurial as my wife.

"Mother, he doesn't want to be billeted in Washington. He's had enough of us. He wants to see the war after *five* years at Harvard. He's entitled to that, at least. You cannot keep coddling him."

She'd arrived at some infernal bridge that could be crossed once, and only once, or she'd never come back with a moment of peace from that frayed edge. I had to bring her down, woo her off the bridge, but she would have smelled a whopper, so I couldn't tell a bald-faced lie.

"A general's family isn't always near the front—Bob won't have to follow the whistle of *every* bomb."

"I'm still not glad about it," she said. But that fork of dissatisfaction had disappeared from her forehead. And we had an extended truce until Bob arrived—in his captain's bars. Mary showed him off wherever she could. Poor Bob had to escort her to shindigs in the Blue Room while she corralled some Senator in the hall and sang him a song. She bloomed like a winter flower around Bob. Her cheeks were always flushed. She had an inexplicable red rash at the back of her neck. She'd rub his sleeve and stand with her head on his shoulder, her satin slippers all curled out, like a ballet dancer. She called him *Bobbie dear* and *darling Robert*, sometimes even called him *Abraham*, and she'd cover her mouth like a little girl and commence to giggle.

"Robert," she sang aloud, "your mother is losing half her mind—Lord knows what *wisdom* will fall from my mouth next."

I was like a stranger, it seems, who happened to be her husband and President of the United States. I couldn't break through that curtain Mary wove around Bob—nothing could. Finally she came to me, with all the bustle of her black silk flounces, in a moment of despair, her fat little hands moving like ferrets, her eyes unable to hold a strict gaze.

"You must write to Grant," she announced. "You are the general of all his generals. I won't be trifled with—or trampled on by that Butcher. I must have Bob for another week."

She returned to her headquarters across the hall. I loped down the stairs in my winter boots, went out onto the lawn, the bite of February in my bones. I found Bob standing under a barren, wind-swept tree in his captain's blouse. His throat was uncovered, and his gullet bobbed up and down, while his shoulders were weaving in the wind. He happened to glance up and I could see the furor in his eyes. And for a moment he looked like his mother—half mad.

"Father, I will not dance with her again—I'd rather set my uniform on fire, burn every patch."

"It gives her so much pleasure, Son."

"But it is *unnatural*. My brother officers will mock me. I have to rush from soiree to soiree, with my own mother on my arm. I'm not blind. All the Senators and matrons she wants to collect have begun to titter behind her back. And what must they think of you, Father, to allow it?"

I didn't care a pin what they thought, all those leeches who sucked blood out of the war, with their government contracts and goose liver from Gautier's, where my own generals loved to dine—except for Grant, who always dined in the field, with his men.

"Father, I could have joined some anonymous regiment. I didn't need a special favor."

"The favor was for me," I said.

"No, no—you begged the general for Mother's sake. To keep me close to the general's skirts. But that's what I am, Father—his puppy. Everyone's careful around the Prince of Rails. Takes years for other men to make rank, and I was born a captain. I have had no training. I've never been under assault. I'm not even sure I could fire a gun."

It was the longest conversation I'd ever had with Bob. I wanted him to laugh again. I took a gamble with Bob.

"Well, Son, consider yourself a *political* captain, sort of my eyes and ears—at Grant's headquarters."

He gave me one of Molly's quizzical stares. "Your spy, you mean."

"We're all a bunch of spies, if it comes down to the essential business of rebellion. I wouldn't want you to spy on your own general. I trust Grant. And you wouldn't have to report to me, not on a regular basis. But you might give your Pa a little perspicacity, from time to time—about the war."

"*Perspicacity*," Bob muttered, and wandered out from under the branches that swayed in the wind. Then he turned to me with a flick of defiance. "Father, perhaps I could tell you a thing or two about headquarters—from time to time."

SHE WOULD WANDER ABOUT, whirl like some caged animal—in her crinoline. No one dared interrupt her thoughts. She was as silent as General Grant, and even more mysterious. Her own powerful intuition must have told her how *ruinous* she had become on Bob's little furlough to the White House. She wore a salmon tulle sacque on the day of his departure, and a headband garlanded with purple violets, like a giddy bride. She never clung to Bob, but she did swipe at him with her handkerchief on our carriage ride to the wharves, to get at a speck of dust near his eye.

There seemed to be an infinite parade on Pennsylvania Avenue, as procession followed procession. Officers rode in marvelous silver carriages with their concubines, as if the war had become a muffled drumbeat at some macabre bazaar—or harlequinade. Men in handcuffs marched along the *Ave* with large red labels tagged to their chests—*I am a Pickpocket and a Thief*—while members of the Provost's squad prodded them with sticks and batons. Unlike these policemen, who had a scrofulous look, the pickpockets wore satin trousers and jackets of burning red silk, and were very bold and very shy. They paused on their march and bowed to Mary.

"You look *immaculate*, Madame."

The policemen tripped them with their batons. "Desist! You cannot address the Lady President. It is illegal."

Mary stood up in her salmon-colored tulle. "You must give them water," she said, while our carriage proceeded with a jolt, and she watched her headband sail into the February wind.

"Timothy," she shouted to the coachman, "I will have you flogged."

We passed a cavalcade of hospital trucks loaded with nurses in dark tan traveling dresses; they looked like waxen creatures until they noticed Bob, and then their eyes filled with all the wonder of sweet fire. "Nan, Nan, there's the young prince."

Bob was panicked by this sudden notoriety. He would have liked to remain *invisible* in his seat. He scratched his mustache and ducked deeper into the carriage, as we cantered right onto the wharves, the horses' hoofs sounding like celestial hammers on the hard wood—and it was as if we had entered some vast the-*ay*-ter on Sixth Street. The piers were packed with people—mechanics, carpenters, and clerks from the Navy Yard, wounded soldiers left on the wharves until an ambulance arrived, sutlers with their gunny sacks of goods, preparing to leave on the same small gunboat, clad in tin—the *Juno*—that would carry Bob to Grant's headquarters at City Point. Then there were the captains' *wives*, waiting to board in bell-shaped skirts; and roustabouts who loved to wander near the sheds and watch the constant flow of traffic.

All the bluster came to a sudden stop as Bob stepped off the carriage. Every eye was on Bob; the whole damn wharf could have come to celebrate his *crossing*. His face was like some variable mask where the emotions kept shifting. He couldn't seem to locate who he was near the tinclad that would surrender him to City Point. It wasn't fright or uncertainty. He must have sensed in his own deep *timber* how tied he was to Mary, how volatile they were, how *unanswerable* to anything but their own turmoil. He had Mary's feline nature. He wasn't like Tad or his Pa. Tad's sense of banditry was just under the surface. He was a buccaneer out of loneliness. But Bob loved to prowl.

And here were my two cat-creatures, who couldn't decide whether to purr or claw each other to death. Mother wouldn't have joined him on the *Juno*, with her hatboxes, like some captain's concubine, but she could have annihilated him on the spot with that ferocious love of hers. They stood on the wharves together, Bob still gallant. He kissed Mary on the forehead, rubbed her cheek. And when her mouth trembled, he kissed her again and strode along the docks without a word.

Bob climbed onto the ironclad with all the concubines and sutlers and several other officers. A whistle shrieked across the morning wind; the twin smokestacks on board belched some black fire. Bob waved to us and went below.

We stood there as that tin tub broke away from the dock with a rattle that left a sting in my ears and then churned downriver— wasn't much of a tub. It shivered up such a storm, I thought it would sink. I followed the *wounds* it left in the river, as if all that tin could cut deep. Mary was like a little general; she waved even after Bob went below.

DIXIE LAND

1865, March & April

48.

The Boy from Milledgeville

WE HAD BECOME the capital of butternut and gray, as deserters flocked into the District in tattered uniforms and cardboard shoes. They lined up at Lafayette Square, to take the oath of allegiance, hundreds in a single afternoon. I could see them on my way to the War Department, boys unraveling in front of my eyes, with black teeth, and black toes that shoved right out of the cardboard shoes, as nurses fed them sweet buns and let them have licks of coffee from a communal cup. They were neither soldiers nor civilians any longer, but lived in some no-man's-land between North and South. Wagons would take them to some forlorn shelter at the Marine Barracks, where they would be shut away for the rest of the war, while they performed menial tasks for one of our departments. Grant didn't want these *shooflies* to march with him. He considered half were secret agents put here by the Rebel White House, and the other half were worthless louts. The general was a bit disingenuous though. He knew the Rebels were *leaking* a regiment a day, and couldn't override such a desertion rate, even if they took cadets out of their military college and conscripted boys of fourteen into their *junior reserves.*

I couldn't recognize the town in this *fifth* year of rebellion. The generals no longer dined at Gautier's; they'd all deserted us and gone to Grant. His headquarters on the James had become the new war-time capital and a Federal city all its own—with tents and houses for my commissioners and clerks, while we had the peculators and stragglers and little ghosts of war: hospitals where men lay groaning in darkened wards, caravansaries like the Willard and the National, where tycoons sucked on oysters in and out of season and made fortunes selling merchandise *borrowed* from Union stores, backstreet dens where deserters who didn't take the oath lived in squalor, and sometimes haunted old, abandoned woodsheds and alleys beside the canal with impoverished *vivandières*, who had run out of festering pies to sell.

It was Mary who went among these desolate souls, fed them scraps from the kitchen, and gave the *vivandières* a portion of her clothes—a vast pile of outmoded skirts and bonnets from Springfield that had accompanied her to the capital on a separate car; she also had some old jackets and shawls for the men. I was dismayed at the habiliments Mother had collected—she couldn't get rid of some ravaged ribbon box or a shoe with a splintered spine, but she would ramble through her boudoir at the White House and *rescue* some of her own garments, while she, Tad, and Elizabeth delivered her bounty in a wheelbarrow. I would catch them from my window, with Tad and Elizabeth steering the little truck, and Mother right behind them, her black veils like a flag in the wind. Mary seemed to have a desperate stride. She shuffled toward the Potomac in a mournful daze. Mother was marking time. Nothing could console my wife, who missed Bob without measure. She never talked of another furlough, never complained, never plotted some strategy to recapture Bob. She sat around and moped whenever she wasn't with her refugees near the river.

So I was delighted to receive an invitation from the general, prompted by his wife, Julia, to come downriver. "Can you not visit City Point for a day or two? I would like very much to see you and I think the rest would do you good."

Mother revealed nothing as I read her the invitation from Grant; not one muscle moved in her face, as if she had learned to disconnect herself from her own joys and desires—it astonished me, and troubled me, too.

Mother wouldn't take Mrs. Keckly along—Keckly would have calmed her, but perhaps she didn't want Julia Grant to see how dependent she was on her own couturière. So she brought one of her servants. We left in the middle of a squall—the twenty-third of March—arriving at the Arsenal Wharf in the early afternoon, with Tad and my bodyguard, Mr. Crook, and like good troopers, we climbed aboard the *River Queen.*

That night, while I was in the President's stateroom with Mary, I dreamt that the White House was on fire; the oilcloth crackled and buckled up like breakers; the windows burst; the carpets in the East Room left a plume of smoke that traveled across the Mansion. I'm not sure why, but I took a certain pleasure in it all, as if I were the architect of this fire—the Arsonist-in-Chief.

I couldn't keep quiet. I told Mary about my dream. I was the biggest damn fool on the Potomac. Mary started to moan. She never much trusted my dreams, but this one, she said, was an omen. She had two telegrams sent to the capital, and didn't stop fidgeting until she heard from Mrs. Keckly.

There isn't the littlest trace of a fire, Mrs. President.

My wife wasn't reassured until Bob appeared at City Point in his captain's bars. She marched down the gangplank with him, unable to mask her shiver of joy; it was Mary's first smile in a month. But Bob couldn't squire his own mother around. He had to return to headquarters—and from that moment, as Bob receded up the hill to Grant's cabin—without her—Mary remained in a surly mood. Her mouth quivered, as she kept perusing that hill. Nothing could please her, certainly not the two other prominent ladies at City Point, neither Mrs. Grant nor Mrs. General Ord, who was much younger than my wife, with saucy red hair and a *piquant* nose. She had warm, gentle eyes, and Mary didn't take a shine to her at all. My wife expected to be surrounded by her royal subjects. It was some kind of *disillusion.* And she was chagrined when neither lady would bow to her.

Bob was embarrassed when he saw how imperious his mother could be as a guest of Julia Grant, while he himself was half in love with Mrs. General Ord. That much I could tell, and I could also imagine him dancing with her at one of the camp soirees. Mary wouldn't allow poor Mrs. General Ord to say a word at dinner, interrupting her all the time. Her real target was Julia Grant, who had to squint constantly out of her walleye. Mary couldn't forgive Julia for inviting me here, as if it had diminished her somehow, exposed her crazy desire to be around Bob. And when General Ord asked what should be done with Jeff Davis if he was ever captured, Mary broke in with a growl. "Why, whup him like a dog, for stealing our boys—whup him until the bleeding never stops."

Then she turned to Julia Grant with a cherubic smile. "Suppose we ask Mrs. Grant. She ought to enlighten us. What ever shall we do with Mr. Jeff?"

Julia was far more diplomatic than my wife, and wouldn't fall into one of Mary's snares.

"I think," she said, licking her lip as she looked into my wandering eye with her own walleye, "Mr. Jeff can be trusted to the mercy of our most gracious President."

That silenced Mary; she sat with a vacant stare, clutching her knife and fork until her knuckles turned red, but in the middle of our plum pudding, she started in again. "Mr. Grant, I'm told you can run into George Washington *anywhere* in Richmond, find a portrait of him on every street corner. Now isn't that a queer thing?"

"Not so queer," said Ulysses. "After all, he was from Virginia."

"And beloved by North and South," said General Ord.

My wife wasn't satisfied. "His face is on their currency. They *use* Washington to legitimize their tyrannical impulses. Mr. Jeff calls him father of the *second* Revolution, forgetful of the first."

Mary was right, of course. The Rebels claimed that Washington— or his spirit—would have bolted from the Union and fought on the Rebel side. It was another example of their piracy and plunder. They wanted to drag France and England into the conflict by invoking the one real Father we had . . .

Mary couldn't stop there. She babbled about my Secretary of War and Grant's positions at Petersburg; she chattered on and on—until I had to slow the engine down.

"Mother, that's enough. You'll mix up General Grant—until he can't think about the war."

The general was much more magnanimous. Perhaps he could feel the pain of a woman who mourned her husband while he was still alive and lived in a constant state of fear—that *fear* had deranged her, a little, and obliged Mother to put on an arch mask when she also had a lot of sweetness in her nature. Grant saw right under the mask.

"Mrs. President isn't bothering me at all. I'm always mixed up before a battle."

And we managed to return to the *River Queen* without any more scrapes.

Mary's sullenness was gone once we met with the wounded soldiers. One of them looked like little more than a skeleton. He watched
me with an air of cautious hostility. He didn't have a tooth in his head.
It took me a while to realize he was a Rebel. "What's your name, son?"

"None of your business, grandpa."

A wounded boy in the next cot tossed a broken boot at him.

"Hey, Johnny, show some respect to the Commander-in-Chief."

"He's not my Commander," the Rebel muttered. "Not today, not
tomorrow."

There was no use having this tug of war. I'd never win. But then
Mary came over and charmed that skeleton out of his hospital shirt.

"You mustn't be unkind to Mr. Lincoln," she sang in that Southern
lilt of hers. "He might have a nightmare and scare the bejesus out of
his own boy. Where are you from, soldier?"

"I'm from Milledgeville, ma'am. And we'll never forget that
maniac, Wild Bill Sherman—he burnt the Oconee bridge, burnt the
Statehouse, burnt the penitentiary, burnt the arsenal, and left us with
nothing but a fistful of sand and rye."

I couldn't pretend I was *deef.* I knew what Sherman had done
November last, with his lugubrious eyes, his crooked mouth, and
sixty thousand boys that Grant himself said was like a monster that
could brood and think. Milledgeville wasn't much—just a watering
hole where the monster could slake its thirst and breathe a little on
the way to Savannah. And the foulest part of the monster's foul breath
belonged to the foragers—or *bummers,* as everybody called them, and
the *bummers* called themselves. They were jaunty boys in buckskin
shirts who left camp every morning on foot and returned on a mule
or a Rebel captain's horse, with their own store of goods they had
pilfered from a farm, a supply train, or some Rebel scouting party.

According to this wounded boy, the *bummers* crept into Milledgeville near midnight and set fire to the north side of Statehouse

Square, their faces covered with gunpowder and black earth, so that they looked like creatures who'd rumbled right out of the ground. They didn't stop their pillaging when the State militia appeared, fourteen-year-old boys who hadn't even finished their first season at the military academy; their hands shook so hard, they couldn't hold on to their cartridge cases.

That's when Wild Bill's cavalry rode into town, their forage caps tilted over one eye, as they pursued the militia halfway across Milledgeville, cranking up their sabers like madcap windmills and nicking the boys' arms and legs until blood and horse piss mingled into a deadly sweet perfume, and Wild Bill himself had to stop this mayhem pell-mell, round up these junior reserves in their ripped coats, lock them inside the chapel, and have his own surgeon attend their wounds.

The governor had fled a week before with all his clerks, and while the fire *reveled* in the November wind, the lunatics walked out of the State asylum in their nightgowns and wandered into the governor's mansion. They tore the chandeliers from their sockets and marched through the halls, like chamberlains—and magicians—from the new Republic of Georgia. They might have triumphed, if they hadn't been trapped in the flames. They stood in line and leapt out the windows with their gowns on fire. Their sad bleats resounded from roof to roof like some terrible war cry that froze Wild Bill and his cavalry. But the *bummers* dove into the fire with wet handkerchief masks, uncovered a back stairway, and coaxed the lunatics down the stairs, one by one, with hoots and lies and bawdy songs. Still, a dozen lunatics perished in the fire, and the *bummers* went right on ransacking the town; they gallivanted along Liberty Street, stole bags of flour and jelly jars from frightened widows, stripped every bed and cupboard at the hospital, raided a peacock farm at the edge of town, plucked those birds, and filled an enormous sack of peacock feathers worth a fortune.

"They were scalp hunters, too," said the boy from Milledgeville. "They wore charm bracelets strung together with bits of ear as black as tar. Wild Bill rode with these devils, and he had a squint that could melt a man, and pocks in his face the size of a peanut. He went on a tour of ruination through Milledgeville with his *bummers*. They took our church and made it into a barn, filling it with their cavalry horses and *our* cattle. What kind of war is that, frightening folks out of their wits, settin' up their own legislature in the Republic of Georgia, and declaring Yankee rules and Yankee laws? Destroying our church organ, pouring molasses into the pipes out of devilment, tearing up our railroad tracks and twisting the rails onto the roof of our depot, like a mockery of the Cross and a sign of their own black deeds, what kind of war is that?"

Colossal Destruction, but I didn't have the heart to tell him. Grant had given Wild Bill the license to make war on people and property, and I had licensed Grant. We had to punish the patriarchs in Richmond, punish the whole of Dixie, else the war might drag on and on, through weal and woe. But I couldn't mock this poor boy, tell him that the *raking* of Milledgeville had been one of my own ideas. I had to watch the skeleton writhe in Mary's arms, as he told her his name, and his mother's name. He had a wound in his gut and could digest nothing but a watery potato soup that had less nutrition than a peach pit, and wasn't half as succulent. And seeing him suffer like that, I had a *tear* in my gullet to tell him the truth.

"Son, you ought not blame Wild Bill. I gave the order to bust up the town."

The boy glanced at me and commenced to cackle. His ribcage shook so hard, I worried he might crack in two. Then he calmed down a bit and clutched my hand in his skeletal claws.

"Will ye feed me, grandpa? I want to get my vittles from the Commander-in-Chief."

So I sat there on his rumpled cot, worried that it might crash right out from under me, and gave him a sip of that watery soup. It was edifying. Not on account of him being a wounded Rebel who wouldn't survive this cot, and City Point, and the war—it was the replication of that unpolished spoon, how peaceful it was, like a metronome, or the tick of a clock. All the shiver had gone out of my hand, as I fed him sip after sip, and my legs didn't feel cold in that field hospital near the front.

The surgeon whispered in my ear that this might be the boy's last meal. But the boy was awful pleased with himself when he had Mary take down all the little reverberations of his last letter home to Milledgeville.

Ma, you could never guess in a million years who's feeding me now at this dog's hospital in Yankeeville. It's Grant's own war chief, him with the warts on his face and his high hat that's the living dream of every sharpshooter in our Republic. Well, I hate him and I don't. But his wife is from Kentucky, and I promised her some home cooking after the Yankees pack up and leave. Don't you break my promise . . .

I didn't have to hide any tears. I wouldn't have wanted that sick boy to see me cry. Mary finished the letter—Grant's postmaster would send it right to Fort Monroe, where Rebel couriers would ride it down along a particular route. I could fancy some courier galloping in Wild Bill's wake, along a road of sacked farmhouses, smashed bridges and culverts, wrecked depots and deserted hamlets, with a bonnet on a blackened windowsill and the bloated carcass of a cow blocking the courier's path.

49.

Lincoln's Folly

AFTER SEVERAL DAYS of parties and a *flotilla* of dances, I accompanied Grant on horseback to review General Ord's troops at Malvern Hill, four miles from City Point. We had to cover some bitter ground—swamps and woods and swollen fields, where men from the graves division wandered about like ghouls in the debris of battle, looking for the dead in some hidden ravine, or the hollow of a tree. I should have sat in my saddle with the Lady President right on my lap, but Grant insisted that she follow behind us in her own ambulance, with a military escort, and Mrs. Grant to keep her company.

So we took off for Malvern Hill, and I had my usual dilemma with Grant. He could be detailed and precise—even eloquent—in his despatches from the field, and shut-mouthed in my presence. I asked him what would happen if Lee and Jeff Davis took a gamble, gave up Richmond, and fled deeper into the South. At first he didn't answer, but I didn't have to pull the grit out from under his gray eyes. He was on Cincinnati, his favored mount, and I was on Egypt, his other bay.

We rode for half an hour in treacherous islands of mud, where

Egypt would sink up to his shoulders and slog through terrain thick as tar. And suddenly Egypt sank deeper still, and I had a reservoir of mud around my eyes. Egypt snorted and most of him disappeared in that morass, with the bells on his bridle. I was certain I would drown, certain I'd never see Mary and Bob and Tad again, that the war would *ravel* out of control until North and South were one great swamp of misery where nothing could reside. It was Grant who lifted me off my saddle with one hand, and held me there, until Egypt's finicky ears and black mane rose out of the mud, and my horse moved onto much higher ground. But Grant hadn't uttered a word. And while he steered his horse and mine like a river pilot, he said out of the blue, "Mr. President, each morning I awake from my sleep with the worry that Lee has gone, and that nothing is left but a picket line. I fear he will run off with his men and his ordinance. He can move much more lightly than I can, and if he gets the start, he'll leave me behind, and I'll have the same army to fight again farther south and the war could be prolonged another year."

I was startled some, since he could have been reading out one of his despatches right from his saddle. And I panicked that Petersburg might not be the final chapter.

"General, where would he go?"

Grant scratched his scrub of beard. "He could sweep down the coast of Florida, capture the Dry Tortugas, and squat there for the duration."

He saw my hollow cheeks and the *unholies* that were coming on, and it was the first time I could remember Grant with a smile.

"It will never happen. The stakes are too high. But the longer they sit in their so-called capital, the stronger we get. They'll have to evacuate, and when they do, the whole South will crumble. Richmond is their pet rattlesnake, their last vital sign, and Lee knows it."

THE CAVALCADE BEGAN with Mrs. General Ord at my side, her red hair under a plumed hat, her riding boots without a single crack, as she sat high in the saddle on her bay horse, while I was half hidden on Egypt's back.

"Mr. Lincoln, I am vexed."

The sun lit up her red hair, and I'd never known a vexation that sweet.

"What's the matter, Mrs. Ord?"

"My husband's men are saluting us, as if I were your bride."

"Well, we won't *unlearn* them," I said, enjoying myself at this cavalcade, with Bob right behind me, looking more and more genuine with Grant, and not a toy solder in a captain's cape.

Ord's men were delighted—until we all could hear that infernal *crack* as Mary's ambulance lumbered over the logs like some license of doom, and she appeared with mud all over her satin gown, her bonnet askew, her face all red, her temples beating with an ungovernable rhythm. No one had to learn me what had happened on that corduroy road, where a crooked *ladder* of logs had to cover a quagmire of soggy ground. Mary had bumped her head as the ambulance careened off the logs with a wilder and wilder bounce, and she near broke her neck. She insisted that the ambulance halt in the woods, so that she could arrive faster at Ord's encampment on foot. As Mary floundered in the mud, Julia said with a look of bemused pity, "Madame President, this wagon is our only ark of refuge."

Three officers had to extricate her, tugging with all their might, until they returned her to the ambulance, while Mary bristled—and that's how she arrived at the cavalcade, deep puckers in her forehead, as Mrs. General Ord leaned in her saddle with an elegance and a grace Mary couldn't have missed. My wife ran across the mud with her tiny feet, while Mrs. General Ord tried to welcome her. But Mary couldn't be stopped. She looked satanic with her veil over one eye. I could sense the pain that welled up in her after that catastrophic ride. City Point had become a series of humiliations in her mind, and now she had to deal with a much younger woman on a magnificent bay.

"Hussy," she said, "making eyes at my husband. Do you think I haven't noticed?" And Mother had a perfect audience—soldiers on parade. "What does this woman mean by riding at the side of the President? People might mistake her for a duchess. We don't have duchesses here, at least not in the swamps around Malvern Hill."

There was no mercy in Mother's eyes, no chance of conciliation, and Mrs. General Ord galloped off the field in tears. I watched Bob, whose face swelled with some of Mary's rage. He would have kidnapped his own mother, carried her off the field, if we hadn't still been on parade.

Mary continued to rip. Next she attacked Julia Grant. She wasn't completely mad. She knew I couldn't have been reelected without Ulysses, that I needed my own *general* to outmaneuver McClellan, so she had to dethrone Julia, whittle away at her because she couldn't whittle Grant.

"I suppose you think you'll get to the White House yourself, don't you?"

I could see how difficult it was for Julia, with her homely looks and horseface; she couldn't even fasten onto her walleye. So she stared at the ground. "I'm quite satisfied where I am, Mrs. President."

And Mary smiled like the Hell-Cat Billy Herndon and my secretaries believed she was. She fought with everyone who'd had the littlest sway over me. She'd fought with her own sisters and cousins, fought with Senators' wives who'd curtsied to me at some shindig. And why shouldn't she fight with Julia Grant and Mrs. General Ord when she didn't have a solitary female friend in the capital, without her couturière?

"Oh," she said to Julia, in her most practiced lilt, "you had better take it if you can get it—it's very, very nice, my darling Mrs. Grant. And next time, don't you dare seat yourself in a carriage, until I invite you!"

I could sense Julia's anguish. She couldn't flaunt herself, play the Hell-Cat, since she was the general's wife. But Mother shut her eyes like a weary child, and one of Grant's aides drove her back to the *River Queen*.

I returned around midnight. The river had a perfect black sheen, without a ripple. We could have been on the Nile. Mary sat in the upper saloon, knitting a sweater for Tad. And there wasn't a mark of madness on her face.

"Mr. Lincoln, you mustn't bother about me. I had a fit—but it's over now. I banged my head while we were on that awful wooden road. And that Todd temper does run in our family—it's like living with a ghost. I have written a *lavish* note to Mrs. Grant. I know, I know. I should be shot at dawn. But will you forgive your child-wife, just this once?"

I knew she was crafting something in her skull. She wanted to make amends, have a dinner for my generals *without* their wives. Mary was clear on that particular subject. And her dinner would be aboard the *River Queen*, where she could be the hostess, since this tub was a portion of the President's House—while we were on the premises.

I had to lend a little of myself, or keep her locked up in the lower saloon . . .

She didn't have Mrs. Keckly to groom her, but she had some of Keckly's wiles—she wore a white lace gown with garlands in her hair. I couldn't recognize my own wife. All the vacant looks were suddenly gone, that sense of exile at City Point. Her old luxuriance had come back, the plump arms and shoulders, the jiggle of her breasts under the gown. And then, with one delicate touch, she put on a black veil below the garlands.

"Mary, it's not a funeral. It's a dinner party. Why a black veil?"

"To fight mosquitoes," she said.

There was no epidemic of mosquitoes in March, but I wouldn't argue with my wife. Grant arrived with General Ord and some of his young captains, including Bob. No one dared mention the veil. She flirted with the generals in her own childlike fashion, lit their cigars.

Her voice wasn't shrill. We all chomped on our salads. She didn't meddle in military affairs. But she told Grant that my little stay at City Point did wonders for my dark complexion. And Ulysses was under the spell of Mother's soft lilt. He shut his eyes and sat there with his fingers crossed, like a soldier sleeping in his saddle.

"Well, Madame President, once we chase the Rebels down into hell, you can have the manor house."

"Gracious," Mary said, with girlish charm, her bosoms *breathing* under that buttress of lace and silk, while every captain watched. "We wouldn't dream of disowning you. Where would you stay?"

"In my cabin, ma'am. I'm quite content."

She giggled, but I heard a note of hysteria, as if her *music* now had a ragged edge, and her little plan of seduction had gone awry. Did she want to bewitch Ulysses and all the young captains—including Bob—like some Salome of the Seven Veils? And it seemed as if her signals were stuck somewhere between her rôle of enchantress and Lady President, and she was lost in her own bewildered world, where generals and captains and Presidents were all replaceable figures in a frozen field—except for Bob. She watched him with one blazing eye in the midst of her performance and scowled at the cook, who was also our butler on board the *River Queen*. She picked up Grant's fork, squinted at it, and said, "Josiah, that fork is filthy. Would you want

General Grant to die of some gastric disorder? Then you must wash and *re*wash every fork on the table."

"Damn if I won't eat with my hands," one of the captains muttered under his breath.

But Mary had too much ammunition under her veil. She sidled down next to Grant, with the perfume of her bosoms right under his beard, stroked his hand and said, "I am piqued by one of your generals, sir."

Grant was still jovial; her perfume might have intoxicated him a little, but he couldn't comprehend the *waft* of her ferocious will.

"And why is that, Madame President?"

She continued to stroke his hand, even while she stung him between the eyes. "You must remove General Ord *immediately*. He has harmed my husband beyond repair, sent his little wife to distract and confound the President with her wiles. He's unfit for service, and so is Mrs. General Ord. She's a hussy—and a witch. She has her own horse in a diabolical trance."

My fault. I should have run into the privy rather than ride with Mrs. General Ord.

"Mary," I said, but she was already beyond my reach.

General Ord stood up in a bewildered rage; he stroked his silver mustache out of nervousness, I imagine. He bowed to Mary, saluted Grant, and begged his permission to leave, while Mary snorted under her veil.

"Coward, what would you do if I were not Mr. Lincoln's wife?"

He was Grant's most trusted general. Ord hadn't busted up Atlanta, like Wild Bill, but he'd been wounded twice in the heel, and commanded his own corps during the current siege.

"Madame," Ord said, bowing again. "I am not in the habit of insulting ladies."

Ord was beside himself. But Mary continued to goad him.

"Tell me—tell me what you would do."

"I would find a way to end your silliness—without insulting Mr. Lincoln or Mr. Grant."

He looked like a ghost in that silver mustache of his. And he rushed out the saloon in several short strides. I'd never seen Grant so shaken. His ash gray eyes seemed to disappear inside his skull. Mother's tirade had jolted Grant out of his own private shell and filled him with confusion and some kind of fatigue. How could he have known that living with Mary was like a constant barrage of fire?

"Mr. President, my men are tired. We will have to conclude this meal."

"But it is forbidden," Mary said. "You cannot interrupt a dinner on the *River Queen* without the President's approval—even if *you* are General Grant."

"Mother," I said, in a voice that was near a whisper. "He has my approval."

"But he does not have mine," Mary said. "He's your best battler, well, let him battle with me."

Now Robert stood up. The most junior of junior officers had to protect Ulysses Grant.

"*Mother*, shut—your—mouth, or I will drag you to the river and drown you, help me God."

Mary hadn't expected her own boy to bark at her like that. The veil fell off and floated onto the table. She wasn't much of a menace without that veil. Her cheeks were bloated. Her eyes had the vacant stare of a sleepwalker. She seemed helpless—alone—on the *River Queen*. Bob took her in his arms, petted her hair, like he'd pet his own Puss, and accompanied her out the saloon, as if she were some wayward little sister of his who had lost all sense. They had their own language of little caresses and secret looks . . .

We fell into total silence, Ulysses Grant and I. This was one scrape he wouldn't have to describe in a despatch. He left with his young captains, except for Bob. I sat there, mesmerized by that black butterfly, the silken veil. The mind played its own muscular tricks.

Bob returned to the saloon. I saw both our fatigued faces in the mirror. He was his mother's child—had her aristocratic mien and a soft, sullen glow around the eyes.

"Father, she's asleep, and she'll stay like that—in her own trance. There's nothing you can do when she's that way. I witnessed the fights she had with the butcher, haggling over pennies. She always won. I watched her donnybrooks with the Irish maids, saw it all when I was a little boy. There was that *itch* just under the surface, that need for a reckoning. She made war on Billy Herndon and your other allies. And if you had been around more often, she would have declared war on you."

"But I never . . ."

"You were on the circuit, Father, somewhere with your saddlebags . . . when she wakes up, she won't remember much. She'll write the most charming letter in the world to General Ord. She'll have flowers sent from the White House to Mrs. Mary and Mrs. Julia. And the rancor will build up again. She'll seethe at some new offense. And she'll blame it on her *monthlies*, or blame it on you, that you slighted her in front of the general, or that you wasted a lot of time kissing Mrs. Julia's hand. But you must promise me one thing."

I felt enfeebled in front of my own boy, as if I could juggle battlegrounds in my head, but couldn't cure the wildness in my own wife.

"Son, I'll do what I can."

And Bob's dark eyes grew infinitely sad. "It's not about Mother. You must rescue me. I cannot go on as my general's pet, bundled up in captivity, away from the war. I will not stay here and liaison with Senators' wives. I will not dance with local debutantes while our siege guns travel closer to the enemy's line. I will pick my own bride, without Mother or Mrs. Grant—I want to go with my general to the front. I insist."

"And have your mother go completely mad? She'll ride with you in the same troop train, and I'll have to join you both on one of Grant's war horses."

Oh, I could whistle with my boy about rebellion—I was in my stride. Mary wasn't the culprit in this piece. My own fears had periled me. I could risk *other* sons, could see their ragged remains on the battlefield, but didn't want Bob's bones to arrive in a metal box. All my proclamations were like bugle calls on a narrow hill—full of thunder and tin. And Bob was sick of my White House reveilles.

"Father, should I play Hotspur, and have you be my Hal? Or whack you with a wooden sword—"

I was astonished when Bob shoved me with the flat of his hand. He was just as astonished by his own fury. His shoulders shivered as I toppled over and landed on my rump, in the upper saloon. I shouldn't have gone *overboard* with one simple shove. I was a head taller than Bob.

"Father," he said, standing there forlorn, in all the finery of his polished buckles and straps. "It was unforgivable. I . . ."

I scrambled to my feet and couldn't bear to watch him crumple up, as if he wanted to leave the country and vanish from my sight. I took him in my arms, but his body stiffened against my touch, and I had to let go.

"Son, I needed that spill—it kind of cleared my head."

I scribbled a note to General Grant. Bob folded it into his pocket, pecked me on the forehead, and raced the hell out of there—like a disheartened boy who'd gotten a little bit of enchantment back. I didn't wander into the stateroom, fearful I might wake Mary from her own charmed sleep; I sat there with her silk veil in my hand, soft as night, and worrying that I'd never see an end to this war, that Grant would falter somehow, that the Rebels would remain in Richmond through time and eternity, and that Bob wouldn't survive the next onslaught, that he would lie down in an unrecorded grave, and no one would ever find him again.

50.

The Lone Rider

I'D SEEN BOB go off on the battle train, in the very car with Grant, our own prince of darkness in a rumpled coat. This wasn't like McClellan's forays, with his lackeys looking at him in awe, while he preened himself. Grant had no ornaments. His eyes were already screwed inward, into some landscape where no one else could follow, not my Bob nor the President of the United States. Then I heard that thump, thump of hooves and a neighing as furious as the Rebel yell. Cincinnati was beside his general, his flanks glistening, as the train lurched with a groan. And I went back down the hill to the *River Queen* and had to deal with my wife.

It was all a ruse—to stop the chatter, I suppose, like a feint of war, to mask her epic battles with *two* generals and their wives. She did not want to be remembered as Mr. Lincoln's mad lady. So I acquiesced to her little scheme. She would pretend to be my sergeant, my sentinel. I watched her eyes flutter as she memorized her lines, like an actress on a riverboat. "I'll say, Mr. Lincoln had a dream when downriver at City Point . . . that the White House was in ruin. Sent me up the river to see."

She was diminished, shrunken, when I accompanied her to the wharf. Bob wasn't there to say goodbye, so half the drama was gone. She couldn't make her grand exit without Bob, couldn't make an exit at all, couldn't tolerate the idea that he'd gone to the front while she was still asleep. He'd left her the shortest of notes.

Mother, I'm with my General.

Love, Robert

Her mind had taken flight to some far sea. Her blue eyes were no longer with me and Tad. Then she wrapped a white lace shawl around her, and her blue eyes came back from that far flight—with a *hint* of madness.

I should not have given Bob to those barbarians, she said, meaning Grant and his charger, Cincinnati, whom she considered a war monster that could belch fire and whiskey, like Grant, and foul the air with his stinking breath. She would never forgive me if Bob lost so much as a finger at the front. And she cursed the two Mrs. Generals for mocking her and belittling her station in front of the troops.

In her moment of folly she did not even say goodbye to Tad— she'd removed herself from City Point, since she couldn't reign at some army camp where a President was just another privileged guest. Luckily I had wired Elizabeth to come and fetch my wife. She'd arrived from Sixth Street that same morning on a revenue cutter, and stepped onto the wharf wearing a simple black gown. It didn't take Mrs. Keckly more than a single glance to estimate all the damage. But Tad was bewildered. He couldn't understand why Yib was here. He wondered whether she was a war bride, who'd traveled up the James to be with a *soljer* boy.

Yib started to cry. She must have sensed that Tad was caught between the Titan in the tall hat and a First Lady in disrepair. And she was startled by the *abruptness* of City Point, how deserted the camp was without its generals. Even the sutlers had scattered, and the embalmers, and the array of concubines, as if the generals and their battle horses were never coming back. Their stables loomed above Grant's cabin like a ghost town on a hill. But we did have our own chorus—the generals' wives had come down to bid the Lady President adieu. Julia Grant and Mrs. General Ord were there on the wharf, with a kind of inexorable charm; they didn't want to slight Mary, knowing she was unwell. But her eyes sailed right over their heads. She wouldn't acknowledge them, and I couldn't heal the rift, that war among the wives.

I let Mother have the *River Queen*, so she could hold on to her stateroom and all the little condiments of the Presidential steamer. Her luggage had been carried aboard, every one of her hatboxes and valises, with the extra curtains and footstools, but she dallied on the wharf, couldn't seem to climb onto the *Queen*. And suddenly she was aware of all the faces around her, and that arctic face of hers unfroze. She waved her fist at Julia Grant, and I couldn't tell if it was out of defiance. But she curtsied to all the generals' wives, thanked them for their graciousness.

"*Mesdames*," she said, clutching at the lace around her throat, "I'm so, so sorry I have to part, but duty beckons. There's been talk about some blatant damage at the White House. Charges have been leveled. And my husband is sending me upriver to deal with the ruckus."

Then she tousled Tad's hair with such warmth, I thought she'd had a spontaneous eruption of joy.

"Don't you trouble your *Pa*," she said. "And I'll bring you a charlotte russe from Gautier's on my next trip."

Her eyes had a remarkable sheen in the morning sun, like a kitten without claws. She was the same coquette I'd first encountered at a Springfield ball, with that plumpness I adored.

"Father," she whispered, "don't forget me, hear?"

She nuzzled me with her nose in front of the mechanics, pilots, porters, and generals' wives. And she climbed aboard the *River Queen* with Mrs. Keckly clutching her long, black train. She stood at the edge of the gangplank for a moment, waved to us with her fat little fingers, and sang, "*Au revoir, Mesdames et Messieurs.*" I was mightily confused, as if some bullet was bouncing in my brain, and I could no longer tell the mad from the unmad, the generals from the carpenters, the Rebels from our own boys. And then I caught a last glimpse of my wife, with that fork of distemper in her forehead, as she disappeared with her long black train under the dark mantle of the deck.

※

MOST TIMES I WAS at the telegraph office, waiting for some news from Grant. "I intend to close the war right here—at Petersburg," he'd told me, as he mounted his car to the front, with troopers snaking along the tracks for much of a mile, their cheeks smeared with gunpowder to guard them against the sun; they didn't have that *brilliant* look of McClellan's boys, when every soldier in the Union was under his command; these boys had grubby hands and rag-tail uniforms; several even wore Rebel caps as their own private insignias. And then there were the engineers, rugged boys in dirty red neckerchiefs, who had to carry lumber on their backs and build corduroy roads every foot of the way while the general's brigades advanced, or we wouldn't have had a piece of artillery at the front—that's as much of the spring offensive as I ever saw. There were reports of our men mounting the parapets and hurling themselves inside the enemy's line, reports that the Rebels broke and ran, and still other reports that our own boys had been repulsed. So I didn't know what to believe and which despatches to trust. In the thick of this hurly-

burly, the machine clattered on the second of April, and I had word
from Grant.

> *We are now up and have a continuous line of troops, and in a few
> hours will be entrenched from the Appomattox below Petersburg to the
> river above. . . . The whole captures since the army started out gunning
> will amount to not less than twelve thousand men, and probably fifty
> pieces of artillery. . . . I think you might come out and pay us a visit
> tomorrow.*

That was the whole drama of Grant—not that Petersburg had
been taken after a siege of nine months, but that I could come tomorrow and catch a few of the sights. Then the machine clattered again,
and I prayed that the war news hadn't swirled around and that Grant
had to leap back over the parapets with all his twelve thousand
captures. But the news wasn't from Grant. Word from Mary came
through the wires.

> *Miss Taddie & yourself very much—Perhaps, may return with a little
> party on Wednesday—give me all the news.*

And I wondered if that voyage upriver had healed her, a little.
Safely ensconced at the White House, she was plotting her return
to Soldier Land, and all the perils it entailed. But her telegram had
nothing to do with City Point. It was all about *Bob—Bob—Bob*. She'd
have sailed above the parapets in a silk balloon, tethered to the *River
Queen*, if that could have brought her closer to Bob.

I ducked outside the telegraph office, where a little band of pickets
were already celebrating the end of the siege—they must have had
their own despatch rider or some *internal* telegraph. They whooped
and hawed and played Axe-on-the-Handle with an old rusty axe,

but none of them could raise that axe up high with one hand. They stopped their whooping when they saw me.

"Mr. President," they said, "is it true that the general had a game of checkers with Bobbie Lee while they were on the parapets, and that Bobbie won, but he still had to run to Richmond on a corduroy road?"

There were no corduroy roads to Richmond, but I didn't want to dampen their tale. I hefted the axe and raised it up with my right arm until it was even with the horizon—and held it there without a single quiver. I took a certain pride in holding that axe, as if I were the main feature at a monster show.

Suddenly all the pickets close to the telegraph office wanted to compete with their President—they were burly boys, but none of them could hold on to that rusty axe; it dropped to the ground, and never once rose above their knees.

I didn't revel. Pa had me handle an axe before I was six. One of the boys offered me whiskey from his canteen. But he scampered with the other pickets when he noticed an officer come charging up the hill on a big bay. I recognized the horse—Egypt—but not the rider, who sat low in the saddle and chased after the pickets with his riding crop. "I've never seen such rascality," he shouted. "You were supposed to guard the perimeter, not carouse on a hill with an axe." His voice had a *falsetto* that was suddenly familiar. And the officer had a wild look about him; with his cap over one eye, he could have been deranged—it was Bob.

His shoulder straps had been ripped off; his sleeves were ragged; his tunic was torn. He scrambled down from his horse like some Cossack, not my son Bob.

"Father, my general sent me here—I didn't want to come back."

I was dumfounded and so dizzy I had to drop the axe.

"Son, did you bring a despatch from Ulysses?"

"Sir, I'm not his messenger boy—not yet."

He tossed his cap into the air—his left eye was swollen shut; he had a patch of blood on his cheek, like some mysterious sign.

"Bobbie," I said, "the blood . . ."

"I was in a skirmish," he said. "Two Johnny boys broke through our perimeter, wearing National uniforms—they crept close to head-quarters and would have murdered *Lucifer* if they'd had half a chance."

Bob could sense my dismay and confusion.

"That's what some of us call Mr. Grant—*Lucifer*. . . . There was a scrape right outside his tent. Grant never blinked. He smoked his cigar and watched it like the-*ay*-ter, as you might say. But you mustn't worry. *Lucifer's* bodyguards were with me during the entire skirmish. Your precious Prince Hal only suffered a scratch as we scuffled with the invaders. It wasn't pretty, Father. Those two Johnny boys were cut down in their tracks. They ended up as bags of blood and shit. And we sent them back across the lines with a little doggerel that I crafted myself."

There once were a pair of bitches who belonged to Bobbie Lee . . .

I got more about my General-in-Chief in a few minutes with Bob than I ever got in my encounters with other commanders, or with Grant himself. *Lucifer*, it seems, would sit on the ground writing a despatch while the trees shattered over his head—nothing could disrupt his concentration. He stood on the parapets outside Petersburg and directed our battle lines, strumming his fingers through the air, like a magician with multiple wands, and taking as little notice of Rebel sharpshooters as he would a bunch of bothersome bees. And when he found a sutler whipping his horses in brutal fashion, he had the wretch tied to a tree for six hours—and confiscated the horses.

"And did you enter Petersburg with *Lucifer*?" I asked Bob, who had suddenly become my chief scout.

"Yes, I did. The Rebels were running like rabbits. And when he saw them all packed up on the streets near the little bridge at the Appomattox bottom, he told me that he didn't have the heart to turn his artillery on such a mass of defeated and dispirited men, but he planned to capture them as soon as possible, and capture them he will. The Rebels can't hold on to Richmond—they'll have to run."

Bob mounted his horse in a cavalryman's high stride and clucked at Egypt like a coyote. He wasn't some poor prince surrounded by Grant's bodyguards; he'd grown into a warrior in less than a week.

"I have to get back to *Lucifer*. I wouldn't want my general to race ahead and run me right out of the war. . . . Oh, and how is Mother? Did you say goodbye to her and Tad for me?"

"Mother may be back with her own little peace mission come Wednesday."

He paused for a moment and grabbed one of Egypt's ears with his fist.

"Father, you must disallow all her attempts to return to the base. She has sown havoc here. I had to apologize on my knees to Mrs. General Ord."

The boy wasn't wrong. But I couldn't corral Mother like that, imprison her in one of her own hatboxes.

"It's *jest* a fancy, Bob—I doubt she'll come."

"Father, that's not good enough," he said. "She is her own portable insane asylum. And when she walks a very narrow perimeter at the White House, all is well. She can cuff the maids and gardeners to her heart's content, and bribe them with a couple of coins. Who will ever notice? She can reign in her ballet slippers, but she cannot meddle with matters at an Army camp, interrupt a parade, flaunt her bosoms like a high-strung schoolgirl, and insult my general—Father, if you will not tell her, I will. Goodbye."

Bob crouched in his saddle like a Comanche, thumped Egypt's

flanks with the crushed bill of his cap, and galloped back down the hill, past the wharves, past the crooked railroad tracks, with that special right of passage held by one of the general's staff, as hospital orderlies and pickets flew from his path, and lesser officers waved to him with their own crushed bills, and I realized that Bob didn't belong to Mary or his Pa, perhaps not even to Grant, that he was a lone rider, returning to the front.

51.

Richmond

N O O N E C O U L D say where the first fires started, or who had started them, but our generals surmised that the retreating Rebels wanted Richmond's tobacco warehouses burned, so they could deprive us of their stores. Still, their soldiers didn't set half the business section ablaze, from the south side of Franklin Street to the river. I was told by a secret source that the Female Orphan Asylum on Leigh Street was where the immolation began—that it had nothing to do with tobacco and cotton or grog. Another witness claimed that the Quartermaster's men wanted to burn Richmond to the ground before the mayor had a chance to surrender the city. Hence, these men skulked across the Hebrew Burying Ground at midnight, when they wouldn't be trifled with, and carried their torches into the inner wall of the Powder Magazine, and they themselves were trapped in the explosion that roared above Richmond like a pernicious ball of fire and blood—with flying shards of glass and brick. And whatever else happened, a mob of angry, drunken men intervened; some were stragglers from the retreating Rebel garrison, and others were escaped prisoners from the penitentiary; they stole whatever cotton and tobacco they could, and while martial music was heard in the distance, they set fire to the warehouses, the City Jail, the First African Church, the County Courthouse, and a dozen hotels. So our Federal troops entered Richmond as firefighters rather than conquistadors, but the mob had destroyed all the fire engines. We couldn't feed the starving population with our own stores—and the last Rebel rations—until some of the smoke cleared and we corralled the half-crazed horses that leapt across the burning husks of buildings.

I wouldn't be daunted by fire and smoke. It was Tad's twelfth birthday—the fourth of April—and I couldn't wait all morning for a wire from my wife. My Secretary of War was worried about sharp-shooters in a town the Rebels had forsaken and set on fire—that fire was still raging, and they'd left a team of snipers behind. Jeff Davis had run to Danville, skedaddled a hundred and fifty miles with all his records and all his clerks, Stanton barked with ferocious glee. "The Rebels are beyond repair, Mr. President. They have *nothing* in their bag of tricks but a desperate assault upon your life." He wanted me to enter Richmond with a whole armada, like some admiral-king who would overwhelm every landing on the James. But I wasn't going to wait around for a gallery of gunboats. So we left City Point at seven in the morning on the *Malvern*, a tub that couldn't even accommodate my legs. That was my birthday present to Tad—a ride to Richmond.

Turns out Tad's nurse, Mr. Crook, came along. He was a corpulent man who'd been my bodyguard once upon a time, but was better suited as a nurse, even with the pistols tucked in his vest. We had sharpshooters of our own—half a dozen marines in blue coats and round blue caps were on board, equipped with carbines. And as we steamed up the James, they watched both shores with their Indian eyes, but there were no bushwhackers lying about, at least none that my sailors could see. Tad was transfixed by their tiny rifles.

"*Paw*," he said, "it's my birthday, *Paw*."

I had the marines learn him how to fire that sailors' gun. Tad squeezed the trigger once, with his eyes shut; the carbine kicked against his shoulder and could have knocked him flat, if a pair of marines hadn't formed a buttress right behind Tad; the carbine had a crystalline sound that reverberated from here to Richmond, and into the tympans of my skull.

I should have rejoiced, barked my pleasure, like Mr. Stanton, or scarified the Rebels, at least, grimaced like a donkey and yowled my own version of the Rebel yell. But I wouldn't even have frightened my own boy. No, I was like a man rising up out of a nightmare, and realizing that the nightmare had shifted ground, and skirted along a river road. I reckon I wouldn't find much release in Richmond—just smoke and blood in a war that was like a family feud. So I was starting to fear that ride to Richmond.

The Rebels had mined the river; torpedoes floated right past us with their humped backs bobbing out of the water; there were dead horses along the route, their bellies all bloated, their yellow eyes fixed on some horizon that had nothing to do with our struggles; there were broken pieces of ordnance and broken boats, put there by some devil's design.

The rapids were fierce, and I was befuddled. I thought for a moment we were on the Sangamon, and I'd have to rise out of the river, declare myself to a town of dusty men, but it was no more than a disillusion of light on the James. I was a Pa now, and Commander-in-Chief, and I didn't have to collect the gear of a land surveyor, or fight Injuns you could never find, though I'd rather have pursued Black Hawk's invisible braves than ride past torpedoes with humped backs that could give a body the chills.

We heard strange noises, as if the spirits of the dead were crying out to us with their own muted lamentations. And I could have been with Mother at a séance on the sea, because for one flat second I pictured the dead, and they weren't wearing butternut or blue but long white hospital gowns. They were right on our tail, in a little boat that was like a funeral barge, packed with guidons and regimental banners. The noises didn't grow slack even after the cortège had passed, with the banners and the hospital gowns. I covered Tad's ears with my hands, but we were all enfeebled by that incessant hum. One of the sailors looked as if he was going mad. We had to restrain him, or he would have jumped off the *Malvern* and been swallowed up by the currents.

Then, as suddenly as it started, the humming stopped. The *Malvern* had gone aground, and we had to remove ourselves to a rowboat. A sunken wheelhouse sat in the middle of the James, like a grim reminder that we'd come to Rebel country at our own peril; we passed fort after fort on both riverbanks that could have knocked us out of the water with a couple of *cannonades*; but there wasn't a soul in sight, except for a single creature in a Federal cap who ran along the shoreline with gigantic shears and cut the electrical cords that could have tripped one of the *iron turtles* some ordnance captain had left us as a little surprise. The main ambition of their chief engineer, according to Stanton, was to fill the waters as full of torpedoes as there were catfish in the James.

Tad's favorite marine steered around all those *iron turtles* with his own élan; it was like having Prospero on board, in a round blue cap. But my courage shriveled up after my first glimpse of the capital; I saw a city of black smoke on a clutter of hills, with burning embers that bumped along, like an army of locusts on some relentless trail; and behind that *curtain* I could catch the outline of corroded walls on hill after hill.

That army of locusts seemed to lift as we moved closer and closer, but not all the Rebels had abandoned Richmond; there must have been a few demolition demons around the river. A railroad bridge fired up in front of our eyes, shook like a palsied metal snake, and dropped into the water with a soft, angelic crump, as we arrived at Rocketts Landing—in Richmond—but couldn't dock there. I looked at all the smoldering stumps, the disused sheds, the sunken warships, and broken torpedoes, like a land and sea surveyor. Rocketts had been a thorn in our side—the Rebel Navy Yard—where Mr. Jeff's ironclads were made; it sprawled on both banks of the James like a series of carbuncles that populated the harbor with a monstrosity of sheds and machine shops—until the Rebels dismantled their own yards and set fire to their ships.

Rocketts wasn't a landing at all; its wharves had buckled in the fire, and there was hardly a landing slip left. I had to carry Tad ashore. The general and white officers of the all-black 25th Corps should have been at Rocketts to lead the way into Richmond, but I couldn't find one solitary soldier at the wharves. And without a general to guide us, the war had *devolved* upon me and my 3rd Lieutenant, and Mr. Crook, and our six marines, who had to serve as a welcoming committee for the United States in Mr. Jeff's conquered capital.

I stood on the burnt edge of Rocketts and stared into the hills of Richmond, with entire blocks where nothing but chimneys remained, like tall tombstones, surrounded by rubble, with ashes swirling in the wind. The smoke hadn't quite settled, and tiny scraps of fire still flared up along the river, where some oil must have spilled. The *Confederates* had gone to Danville with all their ghosts and left us a town of ashes and dust. Dixie had become the heart of hell. Even a wild Injun like Tad could lose his soul in a place like this. I had to dig hard to recall what Prospero's own sprite had whispered to his master. *Hell is empty, and all the devils are here.*

And then I saw them, not devils—no, no, but colored families on a barge in the canal, with their spinning wheels and cradles, bundles of clothes and sticks of furniture—bureaus and tables and mirrors scattered everywhere on the barge, like landlocked items after a tornado, with children pretending they could rock along the water in wooden saddles, and old men in punctured bowler hats peering over the sides like cashiered pirates; they must have all been free or bonded blacks who worked in the tobacco warehouses and the shipyards and had lost their homes and their livelihood in the fire.

They were stunned to see a party of white men *walk* out of a burning river, and they whispered among themselves and leapt out of the barge and onto the wharves. They stood in that welter of ashes and dust, and they fondled my black coat with an aura of disbelief, as if I were a river god, and went down on their knees—men, women, and little girls.

"It's the tall Messiah," they said. "Glory, Hallelujah! Mr. Lincoln has come to town."

I was struck by the unfairness of it, that such blacks should have been sent flying out of their homes by some mad *kindlings* of the Quartermaster's men and had to scrounge on a barge with their spinning wheels.

"You mustn't kneel. You mustn't. I'm not the Messiah. I'm *jest* a man, come to help if I can," I had to protest.

My words were straw in the wind. They'd still be on that barge into next season. The young men stood up like winsome giants—some were sappers who had dug the trenches around Richmond, and built the parapets of Petersburg; others had labored at the shipyards, and the Rebels had abandoned them all to the fire. They bowed to Tad and entertained him with a little *fandango* on those buckled wharves.

Then some black women in butternut appeared out of the same ashes and dust—I was astonished to see such ladies in Rebel cords, with boots and caps, and a couple even had sabers at their sides. They didn't dance with the sappers and stevedores, but they clapped their hands. They were "Mollies," bonded servants and slaves who followed the Rebel soldiers into battle as cooks and washerwomen, and became the mascots of some regiment or another.

Cooks and concubines.

That would have been the rôle of mascots and regimental wives among our own men, but we didn't have colored mascots, only white *vivandières* who followed their sweethearts to war. And it was pretty damn peculiar to watch these ladies in their yellow bandannas and butternut caps.

"Bless the Lord! Uncle Abraham has come with his little boy."

"Ladies," I said, in my best Southern drawl, "I'm mighty glad to meet ye, but shouldn't you get out of that Rebel attire? Richmond is a Federal city now, and if we ever find some general, he might decide to arrest you on sight."

"Then we'd be *nek-kid.* We lost most of our apparel in the fire."

I shut my mouth and we walked up Church Hill together, with its grogshops and groceries, its warehouses and mechanic shops, and we crossed the piss-colored waters of Bloody Run Creek, with my six marines clutching their carbines, and my escort of Rebel lady scouts. We arrived on Main Street, with its vista of rubble and burnt façades as far as the eye could tell, as if some ogre of an army had belched fire all along the route. We passed Libby Prison, a brick warehouse on Tobacco Row, where Union officers had been held in damp, dark rooms—until their own keepers fled; the walls were charred; a portion of the roof had caved in. We were always wheedling, throughout the war, to get our officer prisoners removed from those caves, where tobacco had once been cured. But I had been the culprit. Nothing was done on account of me. I couldn't afford to swap prisoners with the Rebels and refurbish their supply of men. So *their* officers remained in Old Capitol, and ours were stuck here, in this sink near the wharves.

I wanted to have a look at Libby before our little peace parade

went into the depths of Richmond. So we walked back down the hill
to Cary Street and stood in front of that brick and mortar mountain
with its cobblestone path. A sentry stumbled out of a huge hole in the
wall where the main door must have been. He was the first Union
soldier I'd seen in Richmond, and he snarled at my Rebel ladies and
poked at us with a bayonet that twitched like an errant tongue in the
blinding sun off the river.

"You have no business here. This is Federal property. It belongs to
the Army of the James."

He must have recognized Tad and then me in my tall hat. He
saluted and kept peering at the ladies, but he didn't keep us from
walking through the hole in the wall and entering that big barn with
its metal shutters and banks of barred windows. Libby had been
gutted by the Rebels; there were flights of stairs that didn't lead to
any landings, a cesspool the fire had sucked dry, howitzers with their
own embrasures in the walls that an artillery captain must have put
there as part of some fictitious last stand. It was a monstrous place,
with its perfect pyramid of cannonballs, its dry latrine, its floors
coated with blood like *impossible* shellac or the hardened gelatin of a
slaughterhouse.

We were about to step back into the ghostly calm of Main Street
when an odd murmur pricked my ears, like the fatalistic moan of
dying cattle. But these were men hunched up in a far corner of the
old warehouse, who'd been silent until now. They were Libby's new
prisoners of war, stragglers and deserters from the Rebel garrison in
clownish clothes—hats and pantaloons that were far too big or far
too small, and cummerbunds that some Oriental grocer might have
worn. They were guarded by one of our irregulars, a boy of fifteen
who must have been a graduate of the bugle corps. He didn't have a
rifle or a bayonet, but they still cowered. And they kneeled in front
of our little cavalcade, while they looked at my Rebel lady scouts

with anger and lust in their little pink eyes. All the saloons had been raided, they said, and the streets ran with rum and brandy right down to the river; they had lost time licking that rum off the stones like a pack of wild dogs, and that's how the Union cavalry had captured them. "Black devils out of nowhere," they said.

"They're liars," the bugler-sentry insisted. "My colonel found them lying in a ditch and asked me to hold them here."

"At the Hotel Libby," rasped one of the louts. "Without vittles or a place to pee. And no one could have captured us excepting that colored cavalry . . . say, ain't you Mr. Jeff's brother-in-law, honest Abe Lincoln?"

The bugler-sentry told him to shut up and shoved his stash of prisoners deeper into their corner. I had little interest in these louts, who'd robbed and plundered and made merry while Richmond burned, so we lit out of there.

We still hadn't met *one* white inhabitant of the city, though we did see some faces staring at us behind the half-shuttered, broken windows of a mansion that remained in the ruins—women in bombazine mantillas, like Spanish maidens in mourning, with blue eyes and the pinched nostrils of Richmond aristocrats.

Mr. Crook thought he could see a sniper on one of the ripped roofs. There was a metallic flash from a dormer window. Crook floated in front of us like a dolphin in the middle of a ballet and put his own corpulence between that window and Tad—and me. Still, I wouldn't halt our march because of some damn feller with a gun. He waved it at us, with the Rebel Stars and Bars twisted around the barrel.

I tipped my hat like some political genius at this first white citizen who had condescended to notice us, notice us with a gun. Then we ran into a company of black soldiers in bedraggled uniforms, with chalk on their hands and faces, who were among the first to enter this fire pit of a town. But their captain had obliged them to bivouac across the river, because he didn't want to create civil unrest and frighten half the population of Richmond.

I asked them the way to the Rebel White House; and they fell into line, acted as our escort. A few white folks joined us—stragglers, I suppose, who'd come to jeer and then changed their minds. Others left their mansion-caves out of curiosity perhaps, to catch the Lincoln Show. A young lieutenant limped toward us in a butternut tunic, clutching a pair of canes; he'd become an invalid, he said, after his *second* horse was shot out from under him at Antietam and crushed both his legs.

"Master Lincoln," he said, with a lot of salt, "have you come to Richmond to be our King?"

He was still gallant in his torn tunic, but I pitied him and his twisted legs.

"Son, I'm here on furlough—to see the sights."

He let out a bitter laugh. "Well, you're a little too late. The sights are all gone. Our soldiers set fire to the tobacco warehouses, and the fire never stopped. They drank all our liquor and looted all the shops. They blew up the Powder Magazine, and it was like Vesuvius— buildings crumbled and every pauper in the Alms House was killed. Richmond sat in a sea of fire. We thought the Yankees would murder us in our beds, but they're the ones who put out the fire—don't fool with me now. You're the incoming King."

I didn't argue with a lieutenant who had to grimace with each jerky motion of his mangled legs. He hadn't lied about Richmond. We passed the looted shops on Main Street, with their twisted signboards and hollow interiors, like dark little dungeons where all the windows had been smashed. I saw wind-up dolls with their mechanical eyes ripped out; I saw a dead dog; rats scurried here and there, round as beavers. The Rebels had burnt every bridge, according to my young lieutenant. They'd blown up every ironside in the canal; and that's how come we had to arrive in a rowboat—Rocketts Landing was littered with debris.

The fire had leveled the landscape, scouring markets and churches and warehouses in its wake, so I could see clear to the river, with the blackened stumps of Mayo Bridge, like monumental gaps in a giant's mouth, and deeper into the harbor, with its canals and basins looking like broken hinges, there was Belle Isle, a little desert of stunted trees in that haze of cinders. It had once been a Rebel camp for our captured recruits; I'd read the surgeons' reports on Belle Isle—prisoners had to live in the wild, without warm clothes, and suffered from scurvy, frostbite, and the runs; they had lice in their eyes and ears, and a good number fell into a constant state of melancholy and mindlessness, couldn't even recollect their names, or why and where they had been captured; and so I was troubled and aroused as I walked Richmond's streets and recognized the sites: the forlorn façade of the Custom House, with its crumpled roof; the grim remains of the Exchange Bank—a pair of bruised marble pillars, standing in a mound of rubble.

We passed a fire-scarred hotel with craters in the front wall like sinister eyeholes. We passed a little park with scorched grass. I would have lifted Tad high on my shoulders, but I had a lingering fear that some fool sniper—abandoned by his comrades—would have taken his revenge on my little boy. My stovepipe hat, I knew, was target enough. I didn't want to die here, yet somehow I felt my journey was near complete. Richmond was no Jerusalem, but it was holy ground for the Rebels, where they had enshrined themselves, and I had to break through the wall of their reverie and hold their convulsive heart in the flat of my hand.

Finally we strode past the *reach* of the fire, and I saw women and girls who sat on the ground with all the furnishings they could salvage from their homes—mirrors, mantles, and enameled trunks that could have contained some pirate's treasure. Among them were the war widows, women in black veils who'd lost brothers, husbands, and sons. They slapped at the burnt embers around them. And when a particular widow's veil caught fire, I *smothered* her in my own black coat until I licked whatever fire was left.

Mother in her mourner's gown. Alone, alone in another capital, half crazed without Bob.

"Ma'am," I asked, forlorn in this capital of burnt embers and black smoke, "I'm a newcomer here, but can I be of some assistance?"

"My," she said, in front of the other widow ladies, "you have a lot of sauce, *manhandling* me like that. If we had a Provost worth his salt, he would slap you silly and put you in one of the colored cribs, and you could eat corn the rest of your life. . . . Why did God make you so tall? You're the Emancipator, aren't you?"

She commenced to sob and clutched at the weeds of a much younger widow. "Angelina, he's brown as an ape, and twice as ugly. Our three boys suffered and died on account of Lincoln's War. We don't even have a picture of them in their battle shirts—Jeb and Farley and Jim, lying somewhere among Yankees on Yankee soil."

"Mama," said the younger widow, who peeked out from under her veil, "he can't be much worse than our own President, who tucked in his tails and took the last train to Danville."

"But Mr. Jeff didn't bring in no colored riders to unlock the cribs and scare us *mortally* out of our minds . . . and turn this sweet capital into a nigger barrack."

I wrote down the names of the three dead boys like some clerk from the Sanitary Commission. But I knew that our commissioners wouldn't have torn up battlefields for the right to register Rebel graves, while the *Secesh* never had a Sanitary Commission. So I couldn't help these widows find the buckles and bones of their dead boys. I felt like a huckster who hadn't arrived with any bonuses or bargains.

Richmond had become a city of white "contrabands," who had to congregate on the streets with their precious mirrors and bundles of fine clothes; they *rent* a ragged line longer than a mile; and I wasn't sure what our own battle corps could do about these contrabands. Then I turned the corner and stumbled upon a slave crib with its iron fence torn apart and ribbons of blood on its narrow wooden walkway. I couldn't pretend to blush at all its *crime*. I wasn't much of a neophyte. I'd seen a hundred cribs in Orleans and Louisville and in the District, too, when I was with the Congress, and Washington had the largest crib in the country, with cage upon cage, like some impossible tower that leaned into the wind, and where the cries of men and women could *clot* the air . . .

But it was *this* crib, between the Post Office and the City Jail, that troubled me most. It was some kind of open-air veranda with cages on both sides; the cages had metal grilles where no woman could hide her modesty. I walked on the wooden planks, saw the slave catcher's own little cabin, with its cot and leather chairs, and polished stand for his saddle—and I stood there, forgetful of where I was and who I am.

The cages rattled then; dust and cinders flew; little sparks of fire swirled around my head. A bugle sounded once, like a lamb's bleat rather than a complicated mouth of tin. I leapt through the crib's wall, while they rode out of the cinders in their yellow stripes, first black buglers who sat three on a horse, with cymbals in their saddlebags, then a wagon that must have carried their supplies, though I saw none, and finally the colored cavalryman; six I counted with sabers and yellow stripes on their trousers and coats, their eyes peering *inward* at some magical point, while I gripped Tad, who might have been crushed by the cavalrymen, but couldn't bear not to watch the rhythmic rise and fall of their saddles. They must have had field glasses in their rumps, since they paused in midstride to slash off the buttons and insignias of my Rebel lady scouts without drawing a drop of blood, and then the last cavalryman twisted slightly in his saddle and said, "Welcome to Richmond, Mr. President. We've been patrolling this damn sink for twenty hours."

And they disappeared into their own dust storm, perfunctory and supernatural at the same time. I wanted to stick within their spell, to remain with these riders, whoever they were. But I didn't have their sabers or their sass—I hadn't rounded up stragglers and dumped them into a corner of Libby Hotel, hadn't cleared all the slave pens, hadn't charged up and down the hills of this hellhole like avenging angels, with three buglers riding the same horse. I was just a flimflam-mer from the North, with one boy at my side and another boy with Grant—husband, father, and President, worried about my wife.

We passed the smoking walls of the First African Church, with its charred pews lying like a scatter of coffins behind the church gate, and arrived at the pristine colonnades of the Rebel White House—its walls and little garden hadn't been touched; the Rebels could have blown it up, but they left it there, like some religious shrine. The Rebel White House had gray stucco walls. It sat on a hill. I'd heard a hundred tales and rumored reports about its prized inhabitant, and reveled in every one. Jeff Davis had a frozen nerve in his face—he twitched half the time; his old war wounds had never healed; he was blind in his left eye; and he suffered from insomnia. He would prowl the Mansion every night in a ragged shirt, pace his office on the second floor. He seldom left the White House. My Cabinet mocked him night and day. General Sherman had called him an old wife. Others said he had the skills and the temperament of a grocery clerk and couldn't have led a little band of firemen, let alone a gang of rebellious States.

But I was closer to Mr. Jeff than to my Cabinet and my generals, in some perverse way. Both of us were besotted by every horse trader and office seeker under the sun, both of us had to wield a nation out of some lyrical belief that we alone held, both of us were pigheaded, and seldom sought advice, both of us had to brood over the battle dead while we rushed more and more boys to die, like some beast of blood.

Jeff Davis had scattered with his government. The Stars and Stripes hung over the colonnades—that stucco Mansion was now Union headquarters. Its stairs and portico were swollen with officers and politicians and sutlers who had come to Richmond to barter in the *bidness* of war. They'd suck the town dry, sign monumental deals, sell the Rebel White House to the highest bidder, turn it into a museum with wax dolls of Mr. and Mrs. Jeff. I shunned them all, wouldn't even tip my hat, as they tried to grab my coattails and seek some damn favor. I'd never been as rude in all my life.

"Gentlemen," I muttered, "a man worked here, Mr. Davis, and I'd be much obliged if you didn't befoul his nest. Do your *bidness* and go on out of this place."

I skirted around them and entered the White House with Tad. The pickets were startled by the proportions of my peace parade.

"Mr. President, where did all those colored soldiers come from?"

"They're my bodyguard," I said. I chatted with the general who was in charge of Richmond, a burly man in a pale blue coat covered in plaster and soot. He was quite flustered by the enormity of his task. He'd spent a whole day putting out fires and procuring rations for *Richmonders* who wouldn't bother to greet him. He couldn't earn the respect of a town where the men were mostly phantoms and the women were widows in black who regarded him as a barbarian inside the burnt walls of their own little Troy.

"Mr. President, I cannot deal with endless bamboozlement, sir. What should we do with all the prisoners? And people won't come out of their homes, if they have a home left. We can't count them, or check them, or see if they're harboring spies. I'll have to arrest the whole lot."

"General," I said, "if I were in your place, I'd let 'em up easy. They'll have to live a long time with their wounds. And whatever spies they're harboring won't carry much weight in a feral town. We're not philosophers and churchmen. We can bring vittles, not provide for their souls. They'll come around. They have nowhere else to go. I'd like you to find shelter for all the citizens who are stuck out on the street."

"But that's the gist of it, sir. They'll never think of us as liberators."

"General, they can hate us or love us, but I don't want to stand on this hill and see a town of wanderers and vagabonds."

Then I climbed the stairs with Tad and several marines, and some of the stevedores and black soldiers I had met on Main Street. We went into the nursery, which was next door to Mr. Jeff's office—it must have delighted him to hear the chatter of his children while he was at his desk. Our own spies had captured a letter from Jeff Davis back in '62, when Varina and the children had gone to Raleigh, in the Carolinas. "I go into the nursery as a bird may go to the robbed nest." For a little while one of the cooks at the Rebel White House belonged to McClellan's secret service, and Allan Pinkerton had talked of kidnapping Varina and the children to break Mr. Jeff's heart, but I wouldn't hear of it, and neither would McClellan.

The nursery was as grand as the Crimson Room at our own Mansion; the cribs all had mosquito curtains, and the cloth on the walls was patterned after pink and white roses; there were miniature rockers with a doll on every seat, miniature cast-iron cannons, and a horse coated with shellac was attached to a wooden stand by a metal pike; I was startled to see how close this *mock horse* resembled Cincinnati—some Richmond toy maker had installed a replica of Grant's big bay right in the middle of Varina's nursery. The horse was near life-size, and I wondered who were its riders.

I discovered a child's silhouette of George Washington over one of the cribs, a portrait in pigtails. His left eye was shaped like a perfect almond. His nostrils flared out, his jaw was supple, with a teasing smile on his mouth. That portrait had no ominous intent. It wasn't on any currency. It was for a child's amusement, a child's fancy. It was the first portrait of Washington I'd seen in this somber, smoking town. And I pitied Mr. Jeff, just a little. I couldn't find a hint of politics in this nursery.

There were relics on the wall of Little Joe Davis, who was five when he plummeted from the portico last April and never woke up: a tinted photograph, with Joe looking as severe as one of his father's colonels; a white glove embalmed in glass; a miniature officer's cap on a metal peg. I was curious how Mother might have behaved in this room. She would have caressed every doll and every chair, cried for Varina and Little Joe, but these mementos would have summoned up Willie's death.

Perhaps I saw Mother's reaction in Tad, who was tentative about these toys, and didn't even try to mount that mock horse, even though it had its own ladder; the place must have saddened him, as it saddened his *Paw*. We strode through the nursery's rear door and into Mr. Jeff's office—our own boys had raided it for souvenirs; most of it was picked clean. I didn't mind. They hadn't ripped the amber wallpaper yet. They'd gone off with whole sections of the carpet, but there were still a few red diamonds left in the design. And Davis still had his rosewood desk, even if every drawer had been removed.

I allowed myself to sit in Mr. Jeff's plush chair, sank into the pink cushions, when a bunch of Provost Marshal's boys arrived with black powder on their faces and little red tails tied to their caps. They were shoving along a woman with an even dirtier face than theirs. She was dressed up in a cartridge belt and tattered grays, like some poor soul who'd just survived a barrage of cannon fire.

"We caught her, Excellency," they sang, jumping up and down like agitated bullfrogs. "She's Colonel Kate—had her own squad of Rebel rangers. We'd like your permission, Excellency, to *enfilade* her against the rear wall of the Rebel White House."

Something about their little colonel rubbed at me. That gal should have been petrified. She was about to face the lick of a firing squad. Then I noticed her pockmarks under all the gunpowder and that soft, subversive smile of the lady Pinkerton who had rescued my hide in Baltimore.

"Friends," I said to the Provost boys, "you can leave the little colonel with me. I'll arrange for her enfilade."

I had to borrow some biscuits for the lady Pinkerton, who was famished.

"What in tarnation are you doing in Richmond, Mrs. Small?"

She had quit Allan Pinkerton for a while, attached herself to Stanton's own secret service, but my Secretary of War had never bothered to mention a word. She went into the heart of Dixie Land, formed her own company of Rebel rangers as the fictitious Colonel Kate, and led these men into one suicide mission after the other.

"Mr. President, I must have had a couple hundred boys *kilt*. And I'm not too proud of that. . . . I wanted to meet up with you at Rocketts, but I had a chore to do."

Seems a clever little band of female agents, posing as flower girls, had decided to assassinate me and Tad once we got to Richmond, and the lady Pinkerton had to deflect the flower girls.

"What happened, *Paw?*" Tad asked.

"They're pretty much defunct," she said.

And I talked to her about the Provost boys. "They weren't smart enough to capture you, were they, Mrs. Small?"

"No," she said with a smile that revealed the gaps in her mouth. "I had to *capture* them. I knew they couldn't resist bringing a prize packet like Colonel Kate to the Commander-in-Chief."

There was a certain disquietude—a despair even—under all that bravado. Her hands were trembling. She'd become the Union's own *benevolent* monstrosity of war.

"You could remain here with my party, Mrs. Small."

"Oh, I couldn't do that," she said. "I'm going to Danville. I might steal some of President Davis' despatches."

I scrutinized that pockmarked face. "The war might be over by then."

She looked right into the dark well of my gray eyes. "It will never be over, sir. There will always be more Rebels to catch. The woe has just begun."

She chomped into a cracker, shook Tad's hand, and was gone in her tattered grays. I guess she had a Pinkerton's point of view, that war was some kind of continuous stripe, a battleground for spies. Her misfortunes—her own early life as a pickpocket, her *bondage* to Allan Pinkerton—had made her into a curious sibyl. She could pierce that curtain of the unknown and predict every sort of *desolation*. And while I pondered all that, a porter appeared. His clothes were much cleaner than mine.

He saluted me. "General, Mrs. President Davis said I was to keep the house in good condition for the Yankees."

"That was mighty kind of Mrs. Davis."

He brought everyone in the room some bourbon—and water for me and Tad. A courier arrived with a telegram from Mary at the *other* White House, a telegram for Tad; but he couldn't even mouth a word. Still, I had him take a stab at it. A 3rd Lieutenant had to read his own telegram.

Tad-d-die—I—am—des-s-s-o-late—not—to—be— with—you—and—Fah-thuh—on—your—b-b-birth-day. I—love—you—more—and—more—and—more

I was feeling kind of strange—in the *President's* chair, as if I were Mr. Jeff, presiding over some great ruin, with a bullet on my desk that must have served as a paperweight, and a few scattered documents no one seemed to want. Before I had a chance to blink, General Grant's own courier arrived with a bundle wrapped in butcher paper. His field glass was inside—in a silver casing—and a note scribbled on the back of an envelope.

The telescope is for Lieutenant Tad.
Captain Bob is fine. He's at the front with all the generals.
He worries about you and Tad in the old Rebel capital.
It would dishearten him, he says, if you caught Confederate fever. I told
him he could always come and rescue the Commander-in-Chief.

Tad was filled with wonderment. He'd never had a general's glass before. He kept poking out the window with it plugged to his eye.

"What do you see, Son?"

"Angels, *Paw.*"

The marines in the room smiled while they polished their carbines with their own spit. I didn't smile at all.

"And what are the angels doing, Taddie?"

"They're flyin' on top of the smoke. But their wings are all filthy from the fire."

"And are they laughing—or crying?"

"Both, *Paw.* Have a peek."

I shuddered at the sound of my own boy, at the innocence—and the certainty—of his invite. But I wouldn't allow Grant's glass to scarify me. I screwed it into my lazy left eye. Richmond didn't smolder or burn from the President's rear window. I saw a rose garden. It must have bloomed like black blood during the fire, nourished by all the ashes and a wild wind. The roses weren't dusty; they had a bountiful black sheen. But the general's glass was playing tricks. Because at the edge of the garden I discovered Mr. Jeff—he hadn't gone to Danville with all his record books.

Then I realized it wasn't him, but a Rebel scout wearing the President's fine frock coat. Perhaps he had been stationed there like a scarecrow, to distract us while Mr. Jeff was riding the cars on the Richmond and Danville line. A woman was with this scout, in ballet slippers and a blue silk dress; his female accomplice, I suppose, some facsimile of Varina Davis—or my wife, since she had Puss's reddish brown hair. It was no trick of the glass, meant to *unfrock* me and gnaw at my heart. But it did gnaw, as my mind played its own tricks, and I imagined Molly as a Kentucky gal, dancing in her ballet shoes. And then a great roar from the river knocked me out of my reverie. The whole house shook—some phantom Rebel ironclad must have exploded in the harbor.

The woe has just begun, as the lady Pinkerton had predicted, but I didn't unscrew my eye from the glass. I was tired, I told myself. Perhaps Mrs. Jeff's servant had fed me a cup of rotten water—but all we had was a rose garden that slanted down into an isolated apple orchard—beyond that was the James, with smoke swirling above the river, like the random plumes of time. It was as if my damn life had been a trajectory to this very moment, from my near drowning in the Sangamon to the *ravelment* of war that entangled all our lives— President and plumber, pilot and *vivandière*, contraband and Copper- head. And I'd come to Richmond like some pilot out of the sea, with the dead riding in their own barge, not as ghosts, but as companions who might instruct a President. And I sorely needed instruction.

Tad tugged at my elbow. "*Paw*, do ye see the angels, *Paw*, with filth on their wings? I'm dyin' to know."

My lazy eye was still screwed into the glass, but now I could see all the soot. People were scurrying in and out of the swath the fire had left, like a sickly gray river of ash; not even all the ash in Richmond could undermine that monstrous movement of people with their bundles and carts, like a relentless surge, almost supernatural. No flag or musket we had ever brought to Dixie could deflect the path of that melodic sway. And from the distance, high on a President's hill, I would have sworn that people were floating through the ash.

"*Paw*," said Tad, "what do you see with my glass?"

"Angels laughing and crying."

And I held him as close I could.

I never liked Lincoln. It took me a month to memorize the Gettysburg Address for my fifth-grade class. But my first encounter with Honest Abe wasn't at public school. It was at a Bronx movie house that couldn't afford first-run features and had to play half-discarded films. And so I risked eighteen cents—the price of a ticket in 1947—to watch my favorite actor, Henry Fonda, wear a false nose in John Ford's *Young Mr. Lincoln*. I'd adored Fonda as Wyatt Earp in *My Darling Clementine*, also directed by Ford, but here he looked like a tall yokel in a tattered top hat. And when he rode into Springfield on some little nag, with his knees near the ground, he was so far removed from Wyatt Earp's quiet menace and masculine charm, that the real Abraham Lincoln fell from my mind for fifty years.

Then several winters ago, I happened upon a book about Lincoln's lifelong depression—or *hypos*, as nineteenth-century metaphysicians described acute melancholia, and suddenly that image of the backwoods saint vanished, and now I had a new entry point into Lincoln's life and language—my own crippling bouts of depression, where I would plunge into the same damp, drizzly November of the soul that Melville describes in *Moby-Dick*. But I was no Ishmael. I couldn't take my *hypos* with me aboard some whaler. I had to lie abed for a month until my psyche began to knit and mend, while some hired gunslinger of a novelist taught my classes in creative writing at the City College.

Henry Fonda's false nose and long frock coat began to fade the further I read into Lincoln's life. He suffered from two severe bouts of melancholy, the first in 1835, after Ann Rutledge died, and he couldn't bear the thought of rain pounding on her grave; and the second after "that fatal first of January," 1841, when he broke his engagement to Mary Todd, went around Springfield like a disheveled loon, and claimed he was the most miserable man alive. He would endure other bouts of the *hypos*, until a permanent sadness settled onto his sallow face. Billy Herndon, his law partner and most lively chronicler, described him this way: "He was lean in flesh and ungainly in figure. Aside from the sad, pained look due to habitual melancholy, his face had no characteristic or fixed expression."

This ungainly man soon percolated in my own melancholic imagination. And I realized I had been unjust to Lincoln all these years. He had his own quiet menace and a poetic voice that Wyatt Earp never had. According to Edmund Wilson, in *Patriotic Gore*, Lincoln's poetry wasn't revealed only in his letters and speeches and the tall tales he loved to tell. "He created himself as a poetic figure, and he thus imposed himself upon the nation."

Yet he was molded by Mary Lincoln, might not have become President without her. Billy Herndon believed that Lincoln never loved his wife. But Herndon isn't always reliable about Mary; they never got along. She was, in her own way, much more complex than either of them. Better schooled than most of the men around her, she wasn't permitted to practice any profession, or disclose her own penchant for politics: she could become a schoolmarm, a nurse, a wife, or an old maid. As Adrienne Rich wrote in "Vesuvius at Home" of another nineteenth-century sufferer, Emily Dickinson: "I have come to imagine her as too strong for her environment, a figure of powerful will"—too strong and too intelligent, like Mrs. Lincoln. And Mary had to endure the deaths of two children.

How are we to measure her grief or that desperate desire to become part of her husband's band of rivals? She used whatever powers she had as Lady President, intrigued with Manhattan politicos and other unscrupulous men. She would buy a hundred hassocks and three hundred pairs of gloves out of some insatiable need to own and possess, just as she clung to her eldest boy, Robert, wouldn't let him go off to war, protected him in a way she couldn't protect the President, and finally went half mad, because she could protect no one, not even herself. She was part Medea, avenging betrayals that never took place, and part Ophelia, Lincoln's child-wife.

I hope that the Robert Lincoln I reveal will rip through some of his enigmas, the aloofness that one finds in photographs of him—that essential sadness around the eyes, and sense of displacement, as if he longed for his own invisibility, and like his mother, was mourning a President who was still alive.

I'm no biographer. I've written a work of fiction, not a historical tract, and have invented where I had to invent. I've held to the chronicle of Lincoln's life, haven't violated any important dates, though I have tinkered with certain of Lincoln's letters and speeches when I had to create my own sense of continuity. And I had to embroider the history of others a little. Henry Ward Beecher didn't deliver a sermon on John Brown when Lincoln visited Plymouth Church in 1860, but the drama of that sermon seemed essential to the book, and I borrowed it for this occasion. And the pulpit I consigned to Beecher was like the gondola of a hot-air balloon, because I liked to imagine him as an aeronaut in his own church; such a gondola presaged the war itself, where generals of both sides had a fanciful notion about the utility of reconnaissance balloons.

Most of the characters in the novel, including Mrs. Elizabeth Keckly, were pulled from Lincoln's life. A former slave, she worked for Mrs. Jefferson Davis before she went to the White House to become Mary Lincoln's confidante and couturière. Her closeness to the Lady President would give her a certain prestige, but something else must have compelled her. Was she seduced by Mary's terrifying isolation in a capital that called her the *Traitoress*, since so many of Mrs. Lincoln's Kentucky relations fought on the Confederate side? Mrs. Keckly had her own workshop, could have grown rich as a mantua-maker for the wives of merchant princes. Yet she moves her workshop into the White House in my novel. She would have fights with Mary, who paid her a pittance and often flew into rages. The Lincolns were dependent on her nonetheless. Tad, their youngest child, who had a speech impediment, called her *Yib*, a "corruption" of Elizabeth, and Yib had a powerful presence in the White House.

I've invented very few characters—an odd soldier here and there, some African American farmers, a delinquent coachman who sets the White House stables on fire in a feud with Mary. But one invented character does have an important rôle in the novel: a lady Pinkerton named Mrs. Small. She's no anomaly. Allan Pinkerton did use female agents during the Civil War, and I have *my* Pinkerton help foil a plot on Lincoln's life in Baltimore.

I Am Abraham is a family chronicle, where the fury of war and politics rumble in the background, while Lincoln does a macabre dance with his generals, feuds with his eldest boy, and tries to contain the furies of his wife. The novel is told entirely in Lincoln's voice, that strange mix of the vernacular and the formal tones of a man who only had a few months of learning at a "blab school" and essentially had to teach himself. And so we have reverberations of the Bible in

his letters and speeches and spoken voice, echoes of Blackstone and
Æsop, and the yarns Lincoln heard as a boy (his Pa was reputed to
have been a gifted storyteller). I also thought of Mark Twain, as I
imagined Lincoln inhabiting the voice Huck Finn might have had
as an adult. Twain modeled Huck on his own boyhood companion
Tom Blankenship, who became a frontier marshal in Montana. And
Lincoln himself was like a marshal in the "badlands" of wartime
Washington, suspending habeas corpus and bending whatever laws
had to be bent.

In a gorgeously crafted introduction to *The Adventures of Huck-
leberry Finn*, Lionel Trilling writes about the music of Huck's voice,
which revels in the dread and deep truth of the Mississippi, but
also has another kind of power—"the truth of moral passion [that]
deals directly with the virtue and depravity of man's heart." Lincoln
embodied much of the same moral passion. We deify him now. Yet
his own Party wanted to get rid of him in 1864 and nominate Grant.
Lincoln prevailed, wearing his green shawl in the White House, and
gripped with melancholy, his feet constantly cold, he preserved a
nation that had begun to unravel, often holding it together with
nothing more than the flat of his hand and his unfaltering sense
of human worth—a frontier marshal with a sense of poetry and a
profound sadness in his soul.

It was while wandering through the nursery at the Confederate White House in Richmond that I re-imagined the ending of
this novel. I would like to thank Dean Knight of the Museum of the
Confederacy for taking me on a wondrous two-hour trip through the
halls and rooms of Jefferson Davis' White House and sharing some of
his wisdom and lore about Lincoln's voyage to Richmond.

I would never have discovered the enormous cloth checkerboard that Lincoln employed to play with Tad—and "whup" him some-times—if I hadn't visited Lincoln's Cottage at the Soldiers' Home in Washington, DC. And I would like to thank John Davidson and Callie Hawkins of Lincoln's Cottage for allowing me to inspect every mysterious corner of the Lincolns' summer retreat.

I would also like to thank National Park Service Ranger Clyde Bell, Civil War enthusiast Michael Plunkett, and novelist Fred Leebron for their many kindnesses on my own pilgrimage to Gettysburg.

I might not have written this novel if I hadn't had lunch one after-noon several years ago with literary critic and social historian Brenda Wineapple, and talked about Lincoln as a prose poet rather than a politician.

I couldn't have navigated the James River without the help of environmentalist Kurt Riegel, since that damn river always seemed to be going up when it was really going down.

I would also like to thank Georges Borchardt for his percep-tive reading of the novel, Samantha Shea and Phil Marino for their particular insights, and Michael Gorman for his miraculous map of wartime Richmond. Most of all, I would like to thank Robert Weil for taking me to the furthest point on the voyage of *I Am Abraham*.

Illustration Credits

Frontispiece	Lincoln Family at Home
p. xii	Lee on Traveller (Corbis Collection)
p. 1	Lincoln wrestling Jack Armstrong (Abraham Lincoln Presidential Library & Museum)
p. 69	Lincoln's law office, Springfield, Illinois (Corbis Collection)
p. 115	Mary Lincoln, c. 1846 (Courtesy of Paul McWhorter)
p. 167	General George McClellan riding Dan Webster (Courtesy of Paul McWhorter)
p. 235	Willie Lincoln (Courtesy of Paul McWhorter)
p. 273	Lincoln and Tad (From the Lincoln Financial Foundation Collection, courtesy of the Indiana State Museum and Allen County Public Library)
p. 299	Gettysburg, 1863 (Courtesy of Paul McWhorter)
p. 357	Negro soldiers of the North (Courtesy of Paul McWhorter)
p. 397	Lincoln and Tad enter Richmond (Courtesy of Paul McWhorter)

About the Author

JEROME CHARYN has received the Rosenthal Award in Fiction from the American Academy of Arts and Letters and was a finalist for the PEN/Faulkner Award. He was named a Commander of Arts and Letters by the French Minister of Culture in 2002. His stories have appeared in *The Atlantic, The Paris Review, Narrative, The American Scholar, StoryQuarterly,* and other magazines. His most recent novel was *The Secret Life of Emily Dickinson,* published by Norton. He lives in New York and Paris.

Large stain back cover page noted Jan 2011 R Cir

FEB -- 2014